A FAMILY AFFAIR

Janet Tanner

Century · London

Published by Century in 1999

1 3 5 7 9 10 8 6 4 2

First published in the United Kingdom in 1999 by Century
Random House UK Limited
20 Vauxhall Bridge Road, London SW1V 2SA

Random House Australia (Pty) Limited
20 Alfred Street, Milsons Point, Sydney,
New South Wales 2061, Australia

Random House New Zealand Limited
18 Poland Road, Glenfield
Auckland 10, New Zealand

Random House South Africa (Pty) Limited
Endulini, 5a Jubilee Road, Parktown 2193, South Africa

Random House UK Limited Reg. No. 954009

A CIP catalogue record for this book is available from the British Library

Papers used by Random House UK Limited are natural,
recyclable products made from wood grown in sustainable forests.
The manufacturing processes conform to the environmental
regulations of the country of origin

ISBN 0 7126 7993 6

Typeset by SX Composing DTP, Rayleigh, Essex
Printed and bound in Great Britain by Mackays

For the light of my life,
my granddaughter,
Tabitha Jane.

A special thank-you to Dr Margaret Randell, who fascinated me with her account of qualifying as a doctor in the days when it was still very much a male-dominated profession. I am very grateful for her help, and if I have made any errors, they are entirely my fault.

BOOK ONE

1951–1954

Chapter One

She was late.

The van bearing the logo 'SCC – School Meals Service' – was already parked on the mud-crusted gravel outside the prefabricated hut that served as kitchen and dining hall for the Hillsbridge Church School. Carrie Simmons half-ran towards it, her worn fur-lined bootees squelching in the puddles because she did not have time to pick her way along the grass verge which separated the path from the wire-netted physical training yard.

She was late – and Ivy Burden, the meals' supervisor, would at best give her the length of her tongue and at worst threaten her with the loss of her job. Not that Ivy could actually dismiss her – she didn't have that much power, though to hear the way she talked to her staff you'd never guess it, Carrie thought aggrievedly. But she could have a word with Bill Denning, the headmaster, and he in turn could recommend to the governors that changes should be made. Carrie couldn't afford to lose her job and even if it didn't come to that, she could do without the hassle. Heaven only knew, she was getting enough of that at home without getting it from Ivy and Bill Denning as well.

Hassle at home was the reason Carrie was late now, and her face burned with indignation as well as from running almost the entire half-mile to the school as fury and resentment bubbled up inside her again.

She and Joe's mother were always falling out these days and Carrie asked herself for the hundredth time how it was that such a seemingly pleasant woman could be so darned unreasonable. But she knew why, when she wasn't so cross that she couldn't think straight. 'Two women in one kitchen will never hitch it,' her own mother had said

3

when Carrie had told her that she and the children were leaving their home in Bristol and moving out to Hillsbridge to live with Joe's mother and father. 'It won't work, our Carrie. Mark my words, it'll end in tears.' But at the time it had seemed there was no choice. The war had been on, Bristol was being bombed, and Joe was away serving in the Royal Navy.

There had been other reasons, too, reasons Carrie didn't care to think about any more. A desperate situation had called for desperate measures, and she, Heather, David and Jenny, who was just a baby then, had packed up their belongings and left war-torn Bristol for the comparative peace of Hillsbridge.

It was just as well they had. Only a few weeks later their street – their house – had been bombed, so that all that remained of it was one exposed wall, still half-covered with peeling paper that she herself had hung and a window frame at which shreds of torn curtain flapped in the breeze. The next-door neighbours – sharp-tongued Lil Phelen and her husband, Harry, who had never done anyone any harm in his entire life – had been killed, buried in their beds beneath a mountain of bricks and roof timbers. Homeless, Carrie and her children had been left with no choice. Like it or not, they had to remain with Joe's parents in Hillsbridge.

Even when the war was over there had been nowhere to go. They couldn't have afforded to buy a place of their own, and rented accommodation was scarce and expensive. Joe had been torpedoed by a German U-boat while his ship was escorting the conveys in the Mediterranean and after spending forty-eight hours in the water he was fit for nothing but light – and badly paid – work. He was an electrician's mate now at the Royal Naval Stores at Copenacre in Wiltshire, making the hour-long journey there and back each day by working men's coach, which stopped to pick him up and drop him outside the house in Westbury Hill. And as the months turned into years, there they stayed. Prisoners, Carrie thought grimly. Squatters without a home of their own.

Wally Targett, who delivered the school meals from the

4

central kitchen at South Compton, four miles away, was staggering up the concrete path towards the dining hall with a pile of aluminium trays. The aroma of boiled beef and cabbage wafted towards Carrie and she put on a fresh spurt, breath coming so fast that her chest felt tight and the flush burned hotter in her cheeks. She pushed open the door which had slammed shut behind Wally and burst into the kitchen where the other dinner ladies were already helping to unload the containers, unbuttoning her gaberdine raincoat as she went.

'Sorry . . . sorry . . .'

Ivy Burden glanced meaningfully at the bland-faced clock above the row of sinks.

'What happened to you, then?'

'I'm sorry,' Carrie repeated.

She didn't want to say there'd been trouble again with her mother-in-law, didn't want to have to talk about the row, though every angry word spoken was going round and round in her head together with all the things she could have said if only she'd thought of them at the time.

Such a stupid row, Carrie thought, stuffing her arms into the sleeves of her overall and buttoning it around a body that a forties-style corselet turned into a plump tube shape. A row that had started over next to nothing, as they always seemed to, and escalated with sharp words and unspoken resentments.

This morning it had been the scorched airing that had provided the spark to light the fuse. Not as petty as some of the catalysts, it was true – relatively serious, really, since some of the underwear that had been drying in front of the fire was almost new, bought at the Co-op drapery store only a few weeks before when winter had begun to set in.

It had rained almost incessantly for a week now and the only way to be sure the washing was properly dried and aired was by putting it on the clothes' horse in front of the living-room fire. This morning, when they had cleared away the breakfast dishes, Carrie had draped the still-damp vests, knickers and underpants and Jenny's fleecy liberty bodice over the rails and propped the clothes' horse

5

up against the brass fender. It had been perfectly safe – as long as the coal didn't start spitting – and she had gone to make the beds and dust down the stairs without giving it a second thought.

Halfway down the stairs Carrie had smelled burning. It took a moment for it to register, then she propelled herself off her knees and ran along the hall, duster in hand.

The clothes' horse had toppled over, saved only from falling into the flames because one corner had wedged against the maroon-coloured tiles that surrounded the fireplace beneath the broad dark wood mantelpiece. Carrie made a dive for it, jerking it upright so violently that a vest fell off into the coal box which, when the top was down, formed a little fireside seat. It was open now. When she had triggered up the clothes' horse it had been closed.

Carrie swore, not very seriously – she didn't use what she called strong language – but loudly and with feeling, and Glad Simmons, Joe's mother, appeared in the doorway leading to the kitchen.

'Whatever is going on?'

'The washing's in the fire. Couldn't you smell it?'

'I've been out in the lav. With the door shut.'

'Just look at it!' Carrie held out the scorched liberty bodice for her to see. 'It's ruined! Did you touch the clothes' horse? Before you went to the lav?'

'Of course I didn't!' Gladys was a big woman in her early sixties who had once been handsome. Now her concertina of chins trembled with indignation. 'You couldn't have left it safe.'

'It was perfectly safe when I left it,' Carrie stormed. 'But you've been putting coal on the fire, haven't you? I know you have because you left the box open. You must have touched the airer and knocked it over then.'

'I put a bit of coal on the fire, yes, but I didn't touch your washing.'

Carrie looked at the liberty bodice again, and at Joe's vest, almost new, which now had a great dark banana-shaped scorch right down the front, and wanted to weep with frustration.

6

He'd worn his old vest until it was threadbare under the arms and still said it was all right, that Jenny needed new shoes more than he needed a new vest. When Carrie had insisted he must have one – what if he was knocked down by a bus – she knew he'd gone without his Woodbines and the pint of beer he liked to have of an evening in the Working Men's Club to pay for it. Now it was ruined. Even if he wore it like this it would go in a hole next time she washed it.

'What did you want to put coal on the fire for anyway?' she asked crossly. 'There was no need.'

Glad's chins wobbled even more aggressively and she folded her arms across the wrap-around overall she wore to cover her working dress.

'I'll put coal on the fire if I want to! It's come to something if I can't put coal on the fire in my own house!'

That was the crux of it, of course. 'My own house.' The all-too-familiar feeling of being trapped began to bubble up inside Carrie, worse even than the frustration of the scorched clothes. The clothes could eventually be replaced – at a price. There would be no more Woodbines or beer for Joe for a bit, no new stockings for herself, and certainly not the jumper she'd seen in Hooper's window and hoped to save up for.

What wouldn't change was the situation. Unless they could get one of the new council houses that were being put up. They'd had their name down on the list for years, and Carrie lived in hope that it would come to the top when the new development at Westbury Hill got underway. Work had started on it, she knew. She and Joe had walked up and looked at the foundations, great concrete scars on what had once been fields and farmland. But they weren't the only ones on the list by a long chalk, and a lot of other families were worse off than they were, living in rat-infested houses that had been condemned, where the walls ran with water and there were no indoor toilet facilities. In moments of depression like this one Carrie couldn't imagine how they could ever be lucky enough to be allocated one of the new houses. At least Glad's house had four bedrooms, even if two of them were

7

very small. With their family grown up, she and Walt, Joe's father, would rattle around like peas on a rump of beef, and Carrie couldn't see how they could be treated as a special case. The council wouldn't care that she and Joe had their three-quarter-size bed squashed into the little front bedroom that had only ever been meant to take a single, or that Jenny had to share with Heather, who was now twenty-three and ought to have a room of her own. They certainly weren't going to take into account the fact that Carrie spent most of her life feeling like a lodger or a skivvy or both, with no real rights, a daughter-in-law taken on sufferance, supposed to be grateful to Joe's mother and father for putting a roof over their heads.

'I know it's your home,' she said now. 'I know that. There's no need to rub it in.'

'Yes. Well.' Glad was blustering now, still annoyed at being blamed for the catastrophe but wishing she hadn't defended herself in quite those terms. 'Let's have a look, see what the damage is.' She pulled the remaining clothes off the horse, examining them. 'Oh, it's not so bad. It could have been worse.'

Glad's apparent belittling of the damage infuriated Carrie again.

'It needn't have happened at all!' she snapped. 'We can't afford to lose stuff like this. We're not made of money, even if you are. You ought to have been more careful.'

'Don't you speak to me like that!' Glad retaliated. 'And don't you tell me what to do, either. I'm old enough to be your mother, just you remember that, and treat me with a bit more respect.'

And so it had gone on, both of them saying things that would have been better left unsaid and which neither of them really meant.

If we didn't have to be under one another's feet we'd get on all right, Carrie thought now, jamming the thick wedge of greying curly hair under her white uniform cap.

In the beginning, when she'd first met Joe, a handsome rating, and he had brought her home to Hillsbridge to introduce her to Gladys and Walt, she had thought how lucky he was to have such nice parents. Her own mother could be a bit of a shrew and she had never known her father, who had run off with a younger and prettier woman when Carrie was just a baby. By contrast, Glad had seemed warm and welcoming, a plump and comfortable woman who quickly put the nervous Carrie at her ease, and Walt was everything she might have hoped her own father would be. He was an engine driver by profession, a quiet, serene man who liked his pipe and his *News Chronicle*, voted Liberal rather than Labour as most people in Hillsbridge did, and hated rows, drunken behaviour and having to leave his home for any reason whatever – even refusing to join Glad and his children on holiday at Weston-super-Mare or Seaton. From the moment she met him, Carrie adored Walt.

The house, too, which now seemed so claustrophobic, had seemed spacious to the point of luxury. The kitchen was large and square with a huge stone sink, electric light and an old gas mantle, and it looked out on to a small sunny yard from which a flight of steps led up to a strip of garden almost a hundred yards long. There was a living room and also a front room with a piano which Walt had bought when he and Glad were married and which he still played sometimes on a Sunday evening whilst the others gathered round to sing Sankey hymns. A long hall, overseen by a large oak-framed print of a pencil portrait of John Bunyan led to a walk-in pantry. Most impressive of all, there was an indoor bathroom beyond the kitchen. It didn't boast a washbasin or running hot water. That had to be heated in the huge copper boiler and bailed out by means of saucepans or the dipper. But it did have a white enamel bath on legs and a flush lavatory and proper Izal toilet paper – though Walt still liked to keep a wad of torn-up pages from the *News Chronicle* tied on to a length of string on a nail in the wall for his own use. Altogether the house, the end one of a terrace of four, with its own roofed-over side passage and wedges of snow-on-the-mountain hanging pendulously over the wall that enclosed the back yard had seemed the height of luxury to Carrie.

Even when she had married Joe and they had moved into their own little rented terraced house in Bristol,

Carrie had still liked visiting the house in Hillsbridge, where life always seemed more leisured, more sunny. Joe had left the Navy and taken a job in the docks and she had been kept busy bringing up their children. Then, when Heather was fourteen and David eight, the war had come and everything had changed. Joe had rejoined the Navy and she had been left with the children and the bombing. She had come to Hillsbridge as a refuge, but now it had become a prison. And her relationship with Glad had gradually deteriorated into a war zone of its own.

'I'll make a start laying the tables, Ivy,' Carrie said.

She grabbed a tray of cutlery, went through the hatch into the main hall and began setting out knives, forks and spoons. The sharp rattle they made as she banged them down on to the long Formica-topped tables reflected all the frustration and despair she was feeling.

In the big square room in the main school building used by Junior Four, the last lesson before dinner was almost over. At the front of the class, Ron Heal perched his short plump frame on the edge of his table, removed his spectacles and jabbed them in the general direction of the thirty-odd pupils who sat in rows at the double desks facing him.

'All right – who can describe a chair for me? Jimmy Tudgay.'

Jimmy, a well-built boy with a reputation for fighting, brushed a lick of hair out of his eyes and made an effort to look as if he had been listening, rather than flicking rolled-up scraps of paper at the other pupils whenever Mr Heal's back was turned.

'Sorry, sir.'

'A chair, Jimmy. How would you describe a chair to me if I'd never seen one?'

'Uh – what d'you mean, sir?'

Ron Heal repeated his question with a little more asperity and Jimmy rocked his chair on to its back legs, considering.

'Don't do that, Jimmy. You'll break the legs.'

'Four legs,' Jimmy said, inspired.

'And?'

10

'A seat. And a back. Sir.'

'A good start. Anything else?' Silence. 'Anyone?'

'Struts. To join the legs together.' That was Christopher Jenkins, the class cleverclogs.

'Very good. Anything else?'

A longer silence. Thirty-odd faces contorted in concentration. Only Tessa Smith, known for being a little simple, stared vacantly into space. This was the first year that Tessa's knickers had not regularly festooned the guard around the evil-smelling coke-stove almost every day, a constant reminder of her continuing incontinence. Tessa was ridiculed and reviled and generally ignored, but she hardly seemed to notice.

'Come along – come along.' Ron Heal jabbed his glasses encouragingly into the air again. 'Let me give you a clue. How does a chair differ from, say, a settee?'

Jenny's hand shot into the air.

'Yes, Jenny?'

'A chair is for a single person, Mr Heal.'

Ron Heal smiled indulgently.

'A single person, Jennifer? You mean married people can't use them?'

The titters began. First from Valerie Scott, the most popular, self-assured girl in Junior Four, then spreading into a ripple. Jenny felt the hot colour flood into her cheeks. She so desperately wanted to do well. How was it she always seemed to manage to end up as the butt of the others' laughter?

'I meant . . .'

'Mr Heal! Sir!'

'Yes, Christopher?'

'A chair is for just one person to sit on.'

'Very good, Christopher. You see how important it is to choose exactly the right word for what you want to say? In your exam this will be very important.'

The Exam. The dreaded eleven-plus which they would all be taking after Christmas; the eleven-plus that would either allow them the glory of going to the Grammar School at South Compton or consign them to the Secondary Modern – thirty-odd children who had spent

11

every term-time day together since they were five years old divided suddenly into those who succeeded and those who failed. Most of them pretended they didn't care, but they did, and their parents cared even more. It was more than an educational divide. It was seen as a social one too. Only the no-hopers, like Tessa Smith, were indifferent, knowing that nothing short of a miracle would ever transport them out of the realms of 'the duds'.

Of all the children in Junior Four, no-one wanted to pass The Exam more desperately than Jenny. She was capable of it, she knew. Mr Heal had told her often enough. So had Heather, her older sister. Heather had failed her own eleven-plus. 'By the skin of her teeth,' Granny Simmons said. And her schooling had been disrupted by the war. When they had moved to Hillsbridge, Heather had gone to 'The Board School' on Conygre Hill for a year before leaving to start a job at the glove factory, but she was forever urging Jenny on with her studies.

'You don't want to end up working on a machine all day like me,' Heather would say. 'You can do better than that.'

'You're all right,' Jenny would say loyally. She worshipped the sister who had already been a teenager when she was born and she hated to hear her put herself down.

'I wasted my chances.' Heather's blue eyes, so like Jenny's own, would cloud with regret. 'Don't you do the same.'

'I'll try, honestly I will. But I'm really scared I'll mess up.' The thought of sitting The Exam – the all important paper that would determine her future face down on the desk in front of her; Mr Heal's voice: 'You can turn your papers over'; the clock on the wall, its black hands moving relentlessly but imperceptibly whilst the pendulum beneath it ticked away the minutes – all started a feeling of panic in Jenny's stomach.

'Of course you can do it!' Heather said fiercely. 'You've got a brain, Jenny. You're a lot more clever than I ever was!'

Jenny didn't believe that. She was pretty certain Heather had a brain too. She could have done it if she'd

12

tried. Only for some reason she hadn't tried.

'Boys were always our Heather's downfall,' she had heard her mother say once, and she thought it might be true. As well as her lovely blue eyes, Heather had thick brown curly hair, a pretty tip-tilted nose and a wide, smiling mouth. She also had a lovely figure that had developed early, a small waist and curvy hips, shown off to perfection by the shirt-waist blouses and pencil-slim skirts she wore, and long slender legs. Boys flocked round her like wasps around a jam jar, and though none of her boyfriends seemed to last more than a few months at most, there was always a new one to bring her home from the Palais de Danse on his motorbike, the pencil-slim skirt stretched round her shapely bottom and rucked up over her slender thighs.

I don't know about the brains, but I certainly wish I *looked* more like she does! Jenny often thought.

In some ways, there *was* a likeness. 'You can see they're sisters,' people would say, but Jenny thought they were just being kind. She and Heather had the same blue eyes, but until a year ago Jenny's had been hidden behind National Health spectacles because measles had damaged them in some inexplicable way. 'The pupils are egg-shaped instead of round,' the specialist had said. 'They'll sort themselves out in time.' And so they had. But not before Jenny had endured agonies of embarrassment over the horrid glasses.

Then there was her hair, not curly but almost straight, with an annoying wave across the front that often looked as if her mother had put a metal curling clip in it. She hadn't, of course, but she did insist on parting it on one side, which Jenny felt sure made her round face look even rounder and plainer than it already was, and tying a bow of ribbon in it. *White* ribbon. If it had been red or green or yellow or even sky-blue-pink, whatever that was, Jenny thought she could have borne it – but *white*! It made her feel babyish, just as the hand-knitted jumpers and pleated kilts and white knee socks made her feel babyish. Most of the others wore grey or fawn socks and red or even navy-blue hair ribbons. No wonder they laughed at her!

13

As for the shape of her – well, she was fat, there was no other word for it. As the youngest of the family she had always been indulged, the others saving their sweet rations and their butter rations and their sugar rations for her, and she still drank milk with her meals instead of tea like the others.

'You've got all the rest of your life to drink tea,' her mother would say. 'Milk will do you a lot more good while you're still growing.'

The indulgences showed. Jenny's legs might have been a similar shape to Heather's, but they were also plump, so plump that in cold weather she got chaps between her thighs where they rubbed together. Being plump meant she couldn't run as fast as the others or play games or do physical training as well, and being good at games and physical training was one of the things that really counted in the popularity stakes. But Jenny had come to accept that was the shape she was and there was nothing she could do about it.

'We're all made different,' her mother would say. 'You're all right as you are.'

And of course, if the truth were told, her mother was plump too.

It was only when it came to school work that Jenny felt truly confident. She was good at English – sometimes the lessons came to her so easily it was almost boring and she couldn't understand the difficulty the others had in grasping it; she was disappointed if she failed to get less than ten out of ten for spelling tests, and she had read voraciously since she was six. Her grasp of English stood her in good stead for all the other lessons except arithmetic, which she struggled with, but still managed to do better than many of the others. The teachers would pick her out to answer questions when the inspector came, though she never felt they liked her as much as some of the less able, even naughtier children – perhaps because she tried so hard to be good! But the rector seemed to like her. He always beamed at her when he came in to take the weekly RE class – something which she suspected did not endear her to her classmates.

No – she *could* pass The Exam. She was expected to. And it was that which terrified her most of all. If she failed she would be letting them all down – Mr Heal, the rector, her mother, Heather. But most of all she would be letting herself down. It was her chance to shine, to really do well, to make a better future for herself than a job at the glove factory. If she failed she didn't think she could bear it.

The school bell pealed suddenly, bringing the morning's lessons to a close. The children began scraping their chairs, chattering, until Mr Heal called them to order, making them line up neatly before he opened the door to release them. They thronged out through the classroom beyond – the Infants' Room – and down the stone steps to the cloakroom, the walls of which ran with water at this time of year when the weather was wet.

Mr Heal stood on the top step, supervising, as they took their coats from the pegstands and put them on, rosy faces peeping from the hoods of gaberdine mackintoshes or eager beneath bonnets and caps. Then he marshalled them into a crocodile, two by two, for the walk across the playground and through the churchyard to the dining hall.

As usual, Jenny found herself at the back. It always took her longer than the others to get herself organised, though she could never work out why this should be. Only Tessa Smith was inevitably slower. Jenny managed to work her way further up the line to avoid having to walk with her. The move put her immediately behind Valerie Scott. Jenny smiled at her hopefully but Valerie turned away with a toss of her shoulder-length bunches, not smiling back but linking her arm through that of Margaret Hodges, her best friend of the moment, and whispering. Margaret giggled and Jenny flushed, unexpected tears pricking her eyes. Valerie had said something about her, she was sure, and they were laughing at her. If only I could be like them! Jenny thought. If only I could be like Heather! If only I could be like *anybody* except me!

Through the churchyard they went, under the dripping trees, down the little flight of steps and into the lane.

'Watch out for the puddles!' Mr Heal called, but Jenny had already squelched into one, and now there were mud

15

splashes on her clean white knee socks.

The warmth and the smell of food greeted them as they went through the door of the prefabricated hut and hung their coats on yet another set of pegstands.

As Jenny joined the queue she caught sight of Carrie, standing behind the row of containers, and her heart lifted. Her mum always made her feel safe and wanted. Her mum was always there for her, putting things right when they went wrong, giving her little treats Jenny knew she could ill afford.

At almost the same moment Carrie saw Jenny and smiled, a wide smile that lit up her square, rather worn-looking face. Jenny smiled back, waving before she could stop herself.

'Jenny's Mum, the Dinner Bum,' Valerie said to Margaret in a whisper loud enough for Jenny to hear. And then again, in a sing-song chant, with which Margaret joined in: 'Jenny's Mum, the Dinner Bum!'

'Don't say that!' Jenny protested. The flush was beginning again.

They turned to stare at her, eyes wide and innocent, barely concealing laughter.

'Why not?'

'Bum's a rude word,' Jenny said.

Valerie tossed her bunches again, challenging, taunting.

'Jenny's Mum, the Dinner Bum!' she repeated, emphasising each word. Then she and Margaret turned their backs on her, helpless with giggles.

The tears pricked behind Jenny's eyes again. She couldn't understand why they were so horrible to her. Even the pleasure of seeing her mother had been spoiled.

'I'll show them,' Jenny thought, fighting back the tears. 'One day I really will show them!'

The two sittings of dinner were over, the children gone back to their afternoon classes. Carrie was elbow-deep in greasy water at one of the sinks. The feeling of trapped helplessness remained but she had stopped being angry with Glad now, and even felt a little guilty for having been so sharp with her. Perhaps she'd make a detour to the Co-op bakery on her way home and buy some jam tarts for tea by way of a peace offering.

'Your Jennifer didn't look very happy,' Ivy Burden said, taking a pile of washed plates and stacking them in one of the overhead cupboards. 'She's a funny little soul, isn't she? So serious.'

'She's a good girl,' Carrie said, sensing an unspoken criticism and springing to Jenny's defence. 'She's never any trouble.'

'That's what I mean,' Ivy said. 'I mean – most of them are full of it at that age. I know our Brenda was.'

'And our Billy,' Joyce Edgell chimed in. 'Still is, come to that.'

Carrie's lips tightened. Everyone knew Billy Edgell had been up before the Juvenile Court for stealing sweets and even a handful of cash from the till in Morris's shop when Ev Morris's back was turned. And Joyce was 'no better than she should be'.

'Takes after his mother, if you ask me,' Mary Packer joked, and Carrie smiled to herself, though she said nothing. Her sentiments exactly!

Joyce laughed, taking no offence.

'His father, more like! I've told him he'll have to pull his socks up when we move to Alder Road. I don't want him upsetting the neighbours there and getting us off on the wrong foot.'

Carrie froze.

'You're moving into the new estate?' Mary asked, a tone of awe in her voice.

'We shall be, yes. We had the letter this morning. Number 14, Alder Road.'

'You're a dark horse!' Ivy said. 'I should've thought you'd have told us as soon as you came in.'

'We were busy, weren't we? Three of us doing the work of four.'

Carrie was so staggered at hearing that Joyce Edgell had one of the new houses that she failed to rise to the taunt. The letters had started going out then, and just as she had feared, she hadn't had one. Unless of course it had

17

come by second post.

'You won't know yourself up there, Joyce,' Ivy said. 'They say those houses are going to be lovely. You've been lucky there.'

'Luck doesn't come into it!' Mary snorted. 'We've all got a pretty good idea how Joyce managed to get to the top of the list, haven't we? It isn't what you know, it's *who* you know that counts.'

'Mary! Watch what you're saying!' Ivy admonished her, and suddenly Carrie was burning with outrage as it all came clear. George Parsons, Clerk to the Council – of course! Joyce and George Parsons!

Some days Joyce was in a hurry to leave. She was off along the lane before them, not stopping to chat, and one afternoon when Carrie had left early herself, before any of them, for an appointment at the dentist's, she had seen George Parsons' car parked under the trees on the corner where the lane joined the main road. She'd put two and two together and made four and she guessed now that the others had seen something to make them suspicious too.

For all her dubious background, Joyce was an attractive woman, tall and boldly handsome, with thick lustrous black hair, dark skin and eyes that had something of a Mediterranean look about them, though her mother and father were both Hillsbridge people, as solidly Somerset as they came. No, it didn't take a great stretch of the imagination to guess what was going on, but nothing had ever been said. Until now.

Mary had hit the nail on the head without a doubt. The atmosphere in the steamy kitchen had become charged suddenly, the comradely banter had become a minefield.

'You've got a cheek, Mary Packer!' If Joyce's dark skin had been capable of flushing, she would have flushed now. As it was her eyes blazed out of a face that had the unmistakable look of guilt surprised.

'Well, it's true, isn't it?' Mary said, but a little defensively, as if she knew she'd overstepped an invisible boundary.

'I'll thank you to mind your own business!' Joyce blazed.

'Sorry, I'm sure.'

18

'And so you should be, making accusations like that!'

'All right, all right, keep your hair on.'

'Yes. Well. If ever I hear you say that again, I'll have you up for libel!' She reached for her overall. 'I'm going. I was here early, unlike some.'

She grabbed her coat and hurried out buttoning it as she went, more hot and bothered than Carrie had ever seen her.

'I bet he's up there waiting for her now,' Mary said, chastened but still defiant.

'Mary!'

'I bet he is. That's why she's in such a hurry, to make sure they're well out of the way before we get along there. You know as well as I do what's going on there, and has been for years.'

'Perhaps, but I've got more sense than to say so.'

'There was no need for her to fly off the handle like that.'

'Well, I can't say I blame her. Goodness only knows what would happen if something like that got out.'

'I can't see as it would make a lot of difference,' Mary said defensively. 'George Parsons isn't the first she's been with and I don't suppose he'll be the last. And that husband of hers is no better. Funny sort of marriage, if you ask me.'

'Like she said, that's her business,' Ivy retorted. 'In any case, it wasn't her I was thinking of. It's George Parsons. He'd lose his job if it got out.'

'And so he should if he's trading favours with Joyce Edgell or anybody else for that matter.'

'We've got to work with her, Mary,' Ivy said sternly. 'When you work with somebody every day you get to know things, but you've got to keep quiet about it. What sort of atmosphere would it be if you go causing trouble?'

'She should get the push.'

'*You're* the one that'll get the push if you don't watch your p's and q's. I mean it, Mary. You're the one causing trouble. Joyce isn't doing anybody any harm.'

Throughout the exchange, Carrie had said nothing. But the outrage was swelling inside her, swelling and swelling

19

until she felt she would burst with it.

It was so unfair – so grossly unfair – that one of the coveted new houses should be given away to someone as a reward for being no better than she should be. And goodness only knew what state the place would be in before you could say Jack Robinson. That tribe would turn it into a junkyard, whereas if she had one of the houses she'd keep it like a new pin. In moments when she allowed herself to dream, Carrie had imagined her own kitchen, with her own modern bits and pieces that she'd accumulated over the years and the other things she'd buy if she had the money. She'd pictured an airing cupboard with an immersion heater instead of the clothes' horse in front of the fire. She'd pictured herself working in the front garden, mowing the lawn and planting grape hyacinths for the spring and marigolds for the summer. And best of all she'd pictured the privacy. She and Joe able to argue and plan and make love without fear of being overheard. Her own home. Not a lodger in somebody else's.

But she wasn't like Joyce Edgell. She kept herself decent. And because of that, Joyce was getting one of the new houses and she wasn't.

Unless of course the letter had come second post. Suddenly Carrie couldn't wait to get home and find out. When they locked up she hurried on, not waiting for Ivy and Mary. Up the hill she went, forcing herself to keep going though her legs ached and she could feel the sweat breaking out under her armpits.

But there was no letter propped up on the table against the yellow glass vase and bowl that made a centrepiece when the cloth wasn't laid for a meal. Nothing but the sense of claustrophobia that descended on the room when the doors and windows had to be kept shut for winter and the windows steamed up against the damp air outside. There was still the faint odour of scorched clothes in the air too, reminding her of this morning's catastrophe.

'Anything come second post?' she asked Glad, without much hope.

'Not that I've seen,' Glad replied.

20

And Carrie's heart sank until it felt as if it had relocated in the very bottom of her fur-lined zip-up boots. She'd missed out, this time anyway. And for the moment she didn't know what she could do about it.

The idea came to her as she and Glad were getting the tea. Carrie was putting a plate of liver and vegetables liberally covered with gravy to warm over a saucepan of hot water so that it would be ready for Joe when the coach dropped him off outside the door at six thirty, Glad was buttering bread for the rest of them, cutting slices which always managed to be wafer-thin at one end and doorstep wedges at the other because she insisted on holding the loaf against her chest instead of resting it on the bread board. Everyone but Joe had eaten their main meal in the middle of the day – Carrie and Jenny at school, the others at home. Heather and David, who worked in the carpentry shop at Starvault Pit, had an hour for dinner, and Walt, who had retired from the footplate now and did lighter work in the railway sheds, finished for the day at one.

Some of the atmosphere left over from this morning's row still hung in the air and was discernable in the slightly clipped tones the two women used to one another, though they were now being carefully polite, treading round one another's feelings as if on broken glass. Even Jenny had noticed it, Carrie thought. She was curled up in the chair beside the fire – 'Grampy's chair' that she loved to sit in when he wasn't – reading as usual.

She should have a room of her own, Carrie thought, somewhere she could go to be quiet when she wanted, in summer at least. At this time of year it was far too cold to be anywhere but beside the fire. But it wasn't right, her having to share a room with Heather now that she was getting older. Heather's clothes took up most of the wardrobe, the floor was always littered with her shoes, and there was scarcely an inch of spare space on the dressing table for all her pots of make-up and cleansing cream and the Vitapointe she used on her hair. And besides . . . there were other reasons Carrie didn't like them in together. It just wasn't right.

21

Not, of course, that they were likely to get a four-bedroomed house now if they got one at all. Carrie had heard that the four-bedroomed ones had been put up first because of the greater needs of the larger families, and if the numbers up to fourteen had already been allocated it was likely they'd all have gone. She'd put in for a four-bedroom; now there probably wouldn't be any more until the next phase was started, heaven knew when. But a three-bedroom would be better than nothing. At least it would get them out from under Glad's feet. Perhaps she should go and see somebody from the Housing Department, tell them they'd be happy to accept a three-bedroomed house, if they were lucky enough to get one. Perhaps tomorrow she'd get on a bus and go over to the Council Offices at South Compton before she went to work. Yes, that's what she would do.

And then the idea occurred to her, starting a small pulse of excitement deep inside her and yet frightening her a bit at the same time because of its audacity. George Parsons had secured one of the new houses for Joyce – not a doubt of it. And if he could swing it for Joyce, then what was to stop him swinging it for her too? Not that she'd use Joyce's tactics, of course. But there were more ways than one of skinning a cat.

'We want another jar of jam down, Carrie,' Glad said, piling the last slice of bread and butter on the bread plate. 'Will you get it? That shelf's too high for me.'

Carrie went to the pantry, stood on the low wooden stool and looked to see what there was to choose from amongst the pots of home-made jam stacked alongside the big Kilner jars of bottled fruit.

'Plum or blackcurrant?' she called.

'Oh – let's have the plum. I like a bit of nice plum jam.'

Carrie got it down, took off the cover, and scraped away the top layer which had some mould growing on it. And all the time she could hear Ivy's voice in her head, repeating and repeating what she had said to Mary. 'George Parsons would lose his job if it got out.' Well, maybe he wouldn't actually lose his job, but it would certainly make things very awkward for him. And I wouldn't mind betting he

22

wouldn't want that stuck-up wife of his to find out what's going on either, Carrie thought.

Without realising it, the women she worked with had handed her just the weapon she needed. And though the prospect set butterflies fluttering in her stomach, Carrie knew that nothing was going to stop her using it.

'I'm going down to change my library book,' Carrie said.

Joe, who had just finished his tea and was sitting back with a Woodbine and the *Daily Mirror*, half smiled at her and nodded. But Glad, in her big chair with her feet up on a footstool, gave her a sharp look.

'Aren't you going to wash up first?'

'It's all done,' Carrie said. 'All washed and on the draining board. I'll put it away when I get back.'

'I don't know when you get time to read,' Glad said. 'I'm sure *I* don't.'

Carrie bit her tongue. Truth to tell she *hadn't* finished her library book. Sometimes she read a bit in bed, but this week it had been too cold to keep her arms out over the covers and she'd been dog tired anyway, hardly able to keep her eyes open. But this was Tuesday and the little library in a room in the Victoria Hall opened for an hour between seven and eight on a Tuesday. She wanted to get out of the house without telling anyone where she was going, and the library provided just the excuse she needed.

'I won't be long,' she said, putting on her coat.

'Well, if you're going, see if they've got anything by Ethel M Dell for me,' Glad said, making a nonsense of her previous statement.

Carrie could have sworn. She had to pass the library on her way to George Parsons' house, but they'd be suspicious if she was gone too long. She'd intended to do what she had to do first and only call in to the library if she had time.

With the darkness, fog had come down, not thick, but enough to hang in clouds around the street lamps and shroud the valley so that the lights of the houses on the other side hung suspended in it like will o' the wisps. The black mounds of the batches – the mountainous coal waste tips – had merged into the darkness and the sound of a train steaming its way along one of the two railway lines which bisected the town was nothing but a muffled throb. Carrie pulled her scarf higher under the neck of her coat, tucking it snugly around her throat, and hurried down the pavement side of the road, where allotments fell steeply down towards the mill, the river and the yard that was the headquarters of Amy Porter's haulage business. Past the bombsite that had once been the Methodist chapel she went, over the lines which snaked out of Starvault Pit and allowed a team of horses to tow wagons of coal waste to the batches, crossing the road again when she reached the Planning Offices and descending into the tunnel beneath the railway lines that was known as The Subway.

When she emerged again she saw that a light was burning in the window of the small corner room of the Victoria Hall which housed the library and wondered if she should change her plans and go there first in case her visit to George Parsons took her past the time when it would be closed. But she decided against it. She was too strung up, all the things she was going to say to George Parsons going round and round in her head. Get that over first. If she missed the library, she missed it.

George Parsons lived in Withies Lane, which angled away from the main road just past the church. On one side it was lined with a rank of miners' cottages, on the other were newer, smarter houses and bungalows, detached and semi-detached. George Parsons owned the second one in, a square bungalow with bay windows and a large garden, hidden from the road by hedges and shrubs. The light was on in what she supposed must be the living room and also one outside the porch, which sent a tunnel of hazy light down the path.

Carrie opened the gate and went towards it. Her heart had begun to thud uncomfortably and her mouth was dry with nervousness, but she pressed the bell without hesitating, afraid that if she delayed the moment she might lose her nerve. She heard the faint chime echoing in the house and swallowed hard, clutching her library book tightly to her chest with her gloved hand.

After a moment a light came on in the hall, shining out

through the coloured glass panels in the door and illuminating the bird of paradise centre piece. The door opened. It was Alice Parsons, George's wife. She was wearing a thick tweed skirt that looked as if it had come from one of the posh shops in Bath, and a heavy-knit cardigan.

'Good evening.' Her voice sounded faintly surprised as well as 'potty'. 'Alice Parsons puts on the pot,' people said, scathing, because 'putting on the pot' was a sign that some folk considered themselves a cut above everyone else.

'Good evening,' Carrie said. 'Is your husband in? I'd like a word with him.'

'We're just having dinner,' Alice said severely.

'I won't keep him long.'

Alice Parsons stood her ground, her considerable bulk almost filling the doorway.

'What do you want to see him for?'

'I'd rather tell him that, if you don't mind.'

'If it's to do with his work, you should go to the Council Offices and make an appointment. He's not an elected councillor, you know, on call to all and sundry.'

George Parsons appeared in the hall behind his wife. He was a dapper man with a small military-style moustache and jet-black hair that looked suspiciously as if it had come out of a bottle. For work he always wore a smart pinstriped suit with a flower in the button-hole, but now, like his wife, he was clad in a cardigan.

'Who is it?' he enquired.

'It's Mrs Simmons. She wants to see you.'

'You'd better ask her to come in then, hadn't you?'

Alice stood aside reluctantly and Carrie went into the hall.

'Mrs Simmons – what can I do for you?'

He had more charm than his wife – she'd give him that.

'I'd like a word with you – privately,' Carrie added, glancing at Alice who was showing no signs of leaving.

'Very well. Come into my study.' He turned to Alice. 'You finish your dinner, my dear.'

Her face showed her displeasure.

'I'll put yours in the oven to keep warm.'

25

'It's all right, I'd finished anyway.' He gestured to Carrie to follow him along the hall, and threw open a door. 'My study – that's what Alice calls it, anyway. I like to think of it as my den.'

It was a small room, dominated by a desk and leather-backed chair, the walls lined by more books than even the library boasted, Carrie thought, a little overawed. George turned on both bars of the electric fire and rubbed his hands together.

'Not very warm in here, I'm afraid. It hasn't been used all day. But I presume this won't take long. Now – what did you want to see me about?'

'The new houses,' Carrie said. 'The estate that's going up at Midlington.'

'Yes?'

'We've had our names down on the list ever since the end of the war, and we really need one. There's five of us living with Joe's mother and father, and it's not fair on them or us. I know the first lot of the letters have gone out, but we haven't had one,' Carrie said, all of a rush, then added: 'One of the three-bedroom ones would do if the four-bedroom ones have all gone already.'

George Parsons gesticulated helplessly, then thrust his hands into the pockets of his cardigan.

'I sympathise, Mrs Simmons, I really do, but I'm afraid the allocation of the houses is outside my jurisdiction. When your name comes to the top of the list, I'm sure your case will be considered on its merits, along with all the others. Until then . . . I'm afraid there's nothing I can do to help.'

Carrie took a deep breath. This was it then, the moment to play her trump card. Inside she felt like a bowl of melting jelly, but neither her face nor her voice betrayed this as she said into the momentary silence: 'You got one for Joyce Edgell.'

'I *beg* your pardon?'

For just a moment the shock and disbelief was plain to see. Then it was gone, hidden by his usual smooth manner and a small dismissive smile.

'I'm sorry, Mrs Simmons, but I think you are making a

mistake. If Mrs Edgell has been allocated one of the new houses it has nothing to do with me.'

'I think it does,' Carrie persisted. 'I know for a fact she hasn't had her name down on the list as long as we have because I work with her in the Church School kitchens and we talk about these things. And that isn't all I know either.'

She saw the colour drain from his face and then come back in a scarlet flood and knew she'd drawn the right conclusions. Well, that was a relief anyway! Until that moment a little nagging voice of doubt that could not quite be silenced by the outrage and furious determination had been nagging at her that she might be building her case on a foundation of quick sand.

'There's all sorts I know,' she went on, 'like why she hurries off when we've finished for the day and who's waiting for her under the trees at the end of the lane. And all I can say when she gets a house ahead of the rest of us who keep ourselves to ourselves is that it stinks!'

Her voice was rising; he glanced towards the door with something like panic in his eyes.

'Mrs Simmons – keep your voice down – please!'

'Oh, I'll shout a lot louder than this, Mr Parsons, if I don't get one of those houses. I'll shout so loud they'll hear me all the way over to the Council Offices in South Compton!'

He was patting the air now in a conciliatory motion.

'All right – all right – I'll do what I can. But I can't promise anything.'

'I can, Mr Parsons – I already have. If you don't want everybody else to know what I know, you'll do more than just try to fob me off like that.'

'Mrs Simmons . . .'

'I won't keep you any longer, Mr Parsons. I've said what I came to say. There's no point you trying to tell me I'm wrong, because I happen to know I'm right.' She paused. He was very pale now, the scarlet colour concentrated in two high spots in his cheeks. She felt almost sorry for him and shocked that she could have reduced the pompous Clerk to the Council to this so easily.

'I'm a discreet woman, Mr Parsons. I don't go round gossiping like some do. If I get a letter in the next couple of weeks, this will be just between ourselves. Nobody will hear a word of it from me, not even my own husband. They don't know I'm here, and I shan't tell them. But if I don't get a letter, well, then it will be a very different story.'

He opened his mouth to say something but she cut him off by moving decisively toward the door. He opened it for her, pausing with his hand on the knob and nodding at her almost imperceptibly. She held his gaze for just a moment, then went through into the hall.

'Good night, Mr Parsons. Thank you.'

'Good night, Mrs Simmons.'

'I'm sorry for spoiling your dinner.'

'Don't worry about that.'

They both knew the exchange was for the benefit of Alice, who could, for all they knew, be listening on the other side of the living-room door.

She went out into the night, into the cold and the mist, and her face began to burn, whether from the cold or from the release of tension and relief that it was over she did not know and could not be bothered to wonder. She walked fast, adrenalin driving her along, incapable of coherent thought.

The light was still on in the library room, the outside door ajar. She went in, asked Miss Phillips to renew her book while she looked on the romance shelves for something by Ethel M Dell. Only when she picked one out did she realise her hands were shaking.

'I think Glad's had this one,' Miss Phillips said. 'I think so.'

'Oh well, never mind, she'll have to have it again.'

'How is she? All right? This weather . . .'

'She's fine,' Carrie said. 'I'm sorry, Miss Phillips, I can't stop to talk.'

'No, I shall be closing in a minute anyway. Remember me to Glad, will you?'

Carrie went back under The Subway, back up the hill, still unable to organise her racing thoughts. The first nervous elation was beginning to subside; she didn't know

28

what Mr Parsons would do when he'd had a chance to recover himself, and she didn't know what she'd do if he failed to respond to her threats. She wouldn't carry them out, of course. She wasn't the sort to make trouble for the sake of it – and what would be the point? Revenge – but that wouldn't get a house for them, only ensure that her name went to the very bottom of the list. Suppose *he* knew that – George Parsons – and called her bluff? Suppose *he* took revenge and moved her name to the bottom of the list anyway? She hadn't thought of that before.

Oh well, what was done was done. Now all she could do was wait and hope that it worked!

'You bloody bitch!' Joyce Edgell hissed.

She had cornered Carrie in the serving area; Ivy and Mary were both out in the main hall, setting tables.

'You bloody bitch!' She stabbed Carrie with her forefinger.

'I don't know what you're on about,' Carrie said, pretending indignation.

'You do! You know very well! I'll get you for this!'

'Oh grow up, Joyce, for goodness sake!' Carrie elbowed her out of the corner. 'You sound like one of the kids.'

She saw Ivy heading back towards the serving hatch and called out to her.

'Looks like it's going to rain again.'

'It is a bit dark, yes,' Ivy called back, and the moment passed.

Carrie wondered what George had said to Joyce, whether he'd finished their affair or just told her they'd have to be more careful. Either way, she'd made an enemy. Not one enemy but two. It didn't worry her what George thought of her. But Joyce was a different matter. She had to work with her every day and if things turned out as she hoped, have her for a neighbour too. But it couldn't be helped. At least she wouldn't have to *live* with her. At least she'd have her own four walls around her and a home to call her own when she shut the front door at night.

Carrie set her chin, high hopes racing, and went on with her work.

*

The letter came the following Wednesday.

When she saw the franking on the envelope, Carrie was almost afraid to open it. It wasn't addressed to her, of course. It was addressed to Joe. But Carrie had never been one to let a little thing like that stop her.

She took it into the bathroom – always the best place for a bit of privacy, sometimes the *only* place – and tore it open. Then, as she read it, she felt a great surge of excitement that made her want to whoop with joy and burst into tears, both at the same time.

She'd done it! The council was offering them one of the new houses. A three-bedroomed semi-detached. Number 27, Alder Road. It should be ready for occupation soon after Christmas.

Carrie flung open the bathroom door, ran into the living room where Glad was having her usual breakfast of All Bran and toast.

'Glad! What do you think! We've got one of the new houses! We've got one of the new houses!'

Chapter Two

Above the crowded dance floor of the local Palais de Danse
a net of balloons swung precariously beneath the myriad-
faceted globe which bathed the hall in twinkling light; on
stage the best dance band in the district – Jack Tucker and
his Swinging Strings – were playing 'Charmaine'. Heather
Simmons sat on one of the chairs which lined three of the
walls, the apricot taffeta of her full, ballerina-length skirt
spread around her like a blown rose, her chin resting on
her knuckles as she leaned forward to watch the dancers.

The Annual Carnival Queen Selection Ball was in full
swing, but Heather was not really enjoying it. There had
been a stream of young men asking her to dance as there
always was and she had accepted some of them, twirling
under that twinkling globe on her three-inch heels,
smiling, laughing sometimes, sparkling as if she had not a
care in the world. But beneath the façade the uncomfortably familiar feeling of emptiness, of not quite
belonging was always there as it had been for more years
than she cared to remember and she thought, as she so
often did, of another dance, not nearly as glamorous as
this one but a thousand times more meaningful. It was the
tune that had set her off, she knew, the sweet haunting
strains: 'I wonder why you keep me waiting; Charmaine,
my Charmaine . . .' Such a long time ago, and yet still so
fresh in her memory that every one of her senses recalled
it, right down to the scent of her mother's Evening in Paris
perfume that she had dabbed behind her ears. Such a long
time ago and yet still a part of her, her past, her present,
her future, all rolled into one.

The music slowed, came to a climatic end. The dance
floor emptied as the waltzers returned to their seats and
Heather saw Julia Chivers making her way back towards

her. The two girls worked together at the glove factory and they were close friends, although Julia was almost five years younger than Heather. 'The Glovlie Twins' the men in the factory jokingly called them, though in fact they did not look like twins at all – Heather with her shoulder-length brown hair and wholesome, girl-next-door appearance and dark yet fragile Julia who looked more like a china doll who would break if she wasn't treated with tender care. Tonight she was wearing apple-green chiffon, which floated around her legs in a pale green cloud, and pinned to the bodice was a single white rose. Heather thought she had seen Julia in colours which suited her better, but the dress had been loaned to her by one of the local traders, and the rose denoted that she was one of the contestants for Carnival Queen.

'It can't be long now before they do the choosing, can it?' Julia said, lowering herself into the chair next to Heather's, then jumping up again and looking around to see if the officials had yet made an appearance.

'For goodness sake sit down!' Heather said, smiling. 'You're like a cat on hot bricks! You're making *me* nervous!'

'I can't help it! It's such a responsibility, being Miss Hillsbridge.'

There were sixteen other girls besides Julia wearing white roses; sixteen other girls who had been chosen to represent their village – a Miss South Compton, a Miss Withydown, a Miss Purldown and so on. All would get the chance to ride in the Queen's Coach in the torchlight carnival procession but fourteen of them would be banked on one side, moving backwards along the route, whilst the Queen and her two attendants had the honour of facing the way they were going and the crowds would see them first. All the girls wanted to win for their village as much as for themselves, but Heather knew that on the night of the carnival they would all feel nothing but incredible excitement. She had been Miss Hillsbridge twice – five years ago she had failed to win a place in the top three, much to the amazement and disgust of her supporters, and the following year when she had been crowned Queen. The thrill of following the town band through the main streets of South Compton, whilst Boy Scouts with flaming torches marched alongside, had given her such a glow that she had not even noticed the cold; her arms beneath the velvet cloak of office had been bare to the frosty November night and she hadn't thought twice about it, though Carrie had been convinced she would end up with pneumonia. This year, however, it was Julia who wore the coveted Miss Hillsbridge sash.

'Julia, stop worrying! You look absolutely terrific. If they don't choose you they should all get a free pair of glasses,' Heather said.

'But why can't they have the choosing and get it over with? At least then I'll be able to enjoy the rest of the evening.'

'Even if you *don't* win?'

'Yeah. At least I'll be able to have a drink. A *real* drink, not cordial! I daren't yet or I might trip over in the parade and make a complete fool of myself.'

'There you are!' Heather said. 'They're coming out now!'

A small group had emerged from the manager's office, which was being used as the committee room – three men immaculate in dinner jackets and black 'dicky-bow' ties and two women in long floaty chiffon, their hair set rigidly into elaborate coifs. Heather recognised Harry Hall, their MP and a local boy – Harry had been the Miners' Agent in Hillsbridge before he had been elected to parliament. Tonight he was to be one of the judges, and they had heard that Margaret, his wife, had been asked to be a judge too, but had declined. Set hairdos and floaty chiffon dresses weren't Margaret's thing, and she was uncomfortable with being in the limelight, although, as the wife of the sitting member, there were times when it was unavoidable.

Basil Thatcher, owner of the Palais de Danse, who was acting as MC, went up on to the stage, took the microphone and called for the village representatives to come forward.

Julia stood rooted to the spot, and Heather gave her a little push.

'Go on! This is what you've been waiting for! If you don't

33

look out you'll miss it!'

'Oh – I can't! I can't! All those people.'

'Go on!'

Julia went, nervously, joining the other girls who, in the interests of a fair contest, would not be identified until after the selection. That was a farce, really, of course – even without their sashes it was obvious to everyone which village they came from by the cheers of their supporters.

The minute the spotlight fell on her, Julia's nervousness seemed to disappear. In Heather's opinion there was no contest – Julia outshone the others by a mile. But she knew anything could happen, and her heart began to pound as it had when it was she herself up there parading before the judges.

As the girls lined up to loud cheers and whistles, Heather edged her way to the front of the crowd.

'Hello, gorgeous, trying to get in on the act?' one man quipped.

Heather ignored him. She had recognised him as a miner from Purldown – Brian Jacobs – and knew his reputation as something of a troublemaker. He was one of those who squatted on the pavement outside Starvault Colliery waiting for the coach to take him to the pithead baths and when he was on the morning shift he always seemed to be there when Heather was going back to the glove factory after her dinner break, catcalling, whistling and making suggestive remarks as she passed. Tonight he was with a gang of others who had come along to support Miss Purldown – and ogle the other girls.

'Oh – too snooty to speak to us!' he said now. 'Not good enough for you, are we, darling?'

His voice was slurred – he had obviously had too much to drink already, and it was still early.

Heather refused to so much as glance in his direction. She kept her eyes fixed firmly on Julia, willing her to do well.

One by one the girls paraded across the floor in front of the judges, twirled, sashayed back again, teetering on their high heels.

The Purldown group sent up a loud cheer as their

representative made her walk, hoping, no doubt, to sway the judges, but Heather thought she didn't stand a chance. Compared to Julia she was downright plain.

The girls retired to the side of the hall, marshalled by Basil Thatcher. The judges put their heads together, conferring, then asked them to do it all again. It must be a close run thing, Heather thought, her heart in her mouth.

Basil Thatcher had the microphone in his hand again. He was clearly enjoying himself.

'Ladies and gentlemen, the judges will now retire to consider their decision. Whilst they do so, would you please take your partners for a waltz.'

The band picked up their instruments, the floor began to clear. A finger jabbed Heather hard between the shoulder blades and she turned to see Brian Jacobs grinning at her.

'Come on then, gorgeous.'

'No thank you.'

'Aw – don't be a spoilsport! Come on!'

She could smell the odour of sweat and carbolic soap mingled with beer. It revolted her.

'I said no thanks.'

She turned away, trying to sidestep him, but he grabbed her around the waist, pulling her back towards him and pushing his hips against hers. She wriggled, not wanting to be forced to dance with him but not wanting to make a scene either.

'Look . . .'

'The lady said no.' A hand as big as a small ham came down on Brian's shoulder; surprised, Heather looked up into a square-jawed face and deep violet eyes.

'Get off, Steve!'

'No. You get off.' His voice was deep, soft yet surprisingly firm, with the trace of an accent she did not recognise.

For a few moments the two men stared each other out, the one still holding Heather by the waist and wrist, the other equally intransigent, standing his ground, and Heather's heart came into her mouth. There was going to be a fight, one of those horrible brawls that started all too

35

often in dance halls – or outside them, afterwards, and ended with whole gangs of youths and men being locked in the police cells for the night. Then, to her surprise, the miner released her as suddenly as he had grabbed her, muttering something she could not catch because it was drowned by the swelling dance music, and waving his fist threateningly in Steve's face. Steve stood motionless, not flinching, and Brian stumbled off, bumping into a twirling couple as he went and looking as if he might threaten to hit them too.

'I apologise for him,' the man called Steve said. 'He's had too much to drink.'

'Friend of yours, is he?' Heather asked, recovering herself.

He shrugged his massive shoulders. 'I suppose so.'

'Then you ought to keep him under control!' Heather said tartly.

'I try.'

He turned and walked away between the dancers, the light from the twirling globe making his hair gleam like spun gold.

'Well!' Heather said. She was still shaking a bit. 'Well.'

She made her way back to her seat, carefully avoiding anyone else who looked as if they might be about to ask her to dance. But almost without realising it she was scanning the crowded room, trying to catch a glimpse of her rescuer.

'You should have won,' Heather said to Julia.

'Well I didn't.' Julia was trying to look as if she didn't care. 'I'm second attendant anyway. I shall get a dress – and get to ride on the best side of the coach.'

'You should have won!' Heather said again. 'I can't understand it. You were the obvious choice. They were playing politics, I expect. Spreading it round the villages.'

'They aren't supposed to know which one we represent.'

'But they do, don't they? I suppose they think they daren't give it to Hillsbridge *again*. Especially with Harry Hall being one of the judges, and him born and bred in Hillsbridge.'

'Maybe. It doesn't matter.'

36

'It matters to me. I wanted *you* to win.'

The girls were waiting in the queue to get their coats. It was just after one a.m. but they were both too hyped up to be tired. As they went down the stairs one of a gang of boys managed to get alongside Julia, only falling back to join his friends when they reached the street.

'I just walked down the steps with a beauty queen!' he boasted

It was a fine night and much warmer than of late. The stars were shining and a full moon bathed the street in a soft light and reflected in the slowly moving water of the river which ran its full length, disappearing only briefly beneath the little bridges which had been constructed to join the walkway on the Palais side to the road beyond. The girls walked towards the town centre and stopped outside Wiltons, a big grocery store which occupied the entire corner at the junction with the main road. They had ordered a taxi to pick them up here. Though they had known they would have plenty of offers of lifts home they had decided that both the lateness of the hour and the elaborate nature of their dresses would make it a more suitable option.

There was no sign of the taxi. It should have been here and waiting, but it wasn't. Heather and Julia stood back in the shop doorway, watching the other revellers drift past and looking up and down the street hopefully.

'It's not like Jim Fisher to be late,' Heather said. 'You did remember to book him, didn't you?'

'Of course I did! He'll be here in a minute.'

But he wasn't. The stream of passers-by thinned to a trickle.

'I don't think he's coming,' Heather said.

'It is peculiar,' Julia agreed.

'What are we going to do? We can't walk all the way home in *these* shoes!'

'If he doesn't turn up we won't have any choice.'

'We could ring and find out what's happened to him.' There was a phone box on the corner. 'Have you got any money?'

They both turned out their purses, but they had used

37

the last of their change to pay the cloakroom dues. The pound and ten-shilling notes they had saved for the taxi fare would be no use in a phone box.

It was twenty past one now and the streets were almost deserted.

'He's not coming,' Heather said. 'Let's go back and see if anybody is still at the dance hall who could give us a lift.'

'They'll all be gone by now.'

'The organisers might still be there.'

They started back up the street. Heather's feet were already beginning to hurt in her high-heeled sandals and the thought of having to walk the three miles back to Hillsbridge was not a pleasant one.

The doors of the Palais were still open. Light spilled out on to the pavement – and with it shouts and the sounds of a scuffle.

'Oh no – there's a fight!' Julia said.

She backed swiftly away from the doorway, just in time. Two young men came tumbling out. They were back on their feet again almost as soon as they hit the ground, rushing at one another, punching and grabbing. Behind them the stairway was full of fighting youths. Frightened, Heather and Julia retreated into the doorway of the nearby Drill Hall. The two lads who had fallen out of the doorway were now struggling against the rails that guarded the river, others were spilling out around them.

'Oh my lord!' Julia said. 'We don't want to get mixed up in this!'

Heather had recognised several of the lads – Brian Jacobs amongst them.

'It's the Purldown boys after the ones from South Compton. They're mad their girl didn't win.'

'Stupid fools!'

'You'd better not let them see you. After all, you came third. Their girl didn't come anywhere.'

A lone policeman on a bicycle came into their line of vision – PC Dark, stationed at South Compton. He waded into the mêlée but the lads were in no mood to have their fun spoiled. As Heather and Julia watched in horror one of the lads grabbed the bicycle and threw it into the river, then, as PC Dark turned on him furiously, several more grabbed him and threw him in after it. One minute he was bent backwards over the rails, arms and legs flailing, the next there was a great splash and a cheer from the watching crowd. Apart from a few scuffles on the outskirts the fighting had stopped, and as the policeman's head appeared over the river bank the immediate crowd began to disperse, making a run for it before they could be recognised. PC Dark clambered out of the river – which fortunately was less than a foot deep despite the recent rain, water dripping from his heavy cape in a steady stream. He gave chase up the High Street and the girls crept out of the doorway, unable to resist the temptation to see what happened.

At that precise moment a car they recognised as Jim Fisher's taxi cruised down the High Street on the opposite side of the river.

'There he is! Come on!'

They began to run away from the scene of the fight, towards the corner by Wiltons' grocery store where they had arranged to be picked up, but in their high heels and flowing skirts it was like trying to run in a bad dream. The taxi had stopped outside Wiltons, but they were still thirty yards from it when it began to pull away again.

'No! No – wait!' Heather was running and waving wildly at the same time, but it was no use. With no sign of his fares waiting where they should be and gangs of rampaging youths the length of the High Street, Jim Fisher had no intention of hanging about and becoming involved in the trouble. As Heather reached the broad part of the pavement where the river ran under the road, the taxi accelerated away and disappeared around the corner.

Breathless, almost sobbing, Heather stood looking helplessly after it. Some way behind her Julia was hobbling to catch up. In the mad dash she had broken the heel of her shoe.

'He's gone without us! Why did he go without us?'

'I expect you told him half past one, not one o'clock,' Heather said, despair making her angry.

'I didn't!'

'Well, he's gone, anyway. He thought we weren't here, and he's gone.'

'What are we going to do?' Julia, too, was close to tears.

'I don't know. We can't go back up the High Street with all those louts fighting.'

'They pushed the policeman in the river! Did you see . . .?'

'Perhaps we ought to dial 999 and tell somebody. Then maybe *they'd* give us a lift home.'

There was somebody in the telephone box. Incredibly they hadn't noticed before, intent as they had been on trying to catch their taxi. Now, as he opened the kiosk door, Heather recognised the young man who had rescued her from the unwelcome attentions of Brian earlier. He recognised her too. He let the door slam to behind him and stood staring.

Julia caught Heather's arm in panic.

'It's one of them! Come on!'

'No – he's all right,' Heather said. She went up to him. 'There's a fight. They threw the policeman in the river. We want to dial 999.'

'Don't worry – I already have.'

'Oh!'

'Why are you still here?' he asked. The unfamiliar accent sounded even thicker now than it had in the Palais.

'We missed our taxi. We're stranded.'

'You should not be here. At this time of night, on your own.'

'You don't have to tell us that!' Julia wailed.

'We don't know how we're going to get home,' Heather said.

He only hesitated a moment. 'OK – I'll take you.'

'You've got a car?' Heather asked.

'An old one, yes. But it goes. Come on.'

Julia grabbed Heather's arm again. 'Heather! We don't know him!'

'He's all right, I tell you.' She turned back to the tall young man. 'Where's your car then?'

'Over there. In the Island.' He nodded towards a square, surrounded by shops, on the other side of the road.

40

Yells and the sound of running feet from the direction of the High Street announced that some of the rampaging gangs were heading back towards the town centre.

'Come on!' he said sharply. 'You don't want to get mixed up in that.' He began to cross the road and this time Julia did not argue.

The car – an Austin Seven – was the only one still parked in the Island. He unlocked the doors and Julia tumbled into the back seat whilst Heather got into the front. Looking over her shoulder she saw that the fight had started up again in the very spot where they had been standing minutes before.

'You'd better tell me where you live,' he said, starting the engine.

'Hillsbridge,' Heather said, and sank back against the battered leather seat shivering with relief – and something else. Though she didn't have the time or the inclination to analyse it yet, it felt rather like excitement.

She couldn't stop thinking about him. She couldn't remember when she had last felt this way – well, actually yes, she could remember, but it was so long ago it seemed as if it had happened to a different person, not to her at all. To wake in the mornings with a sense of anticipation bubbling inside, to go to sleep at night picturing his face, hearing that heavily accented voice speaking in her head, and feeling a glow that began in the area around her heart and spread little shivers of warmth into her veins.

She knew his name now – Steven Okonski – and she knew that he was Polish. That much she had learned from David by questioning him discreetly. But that was all she knew. Since Steven was a miner and David worked in the carpenters' shop there was no real point of contact. Each day after lunch she set off eagerly down the hill, hoping to see him there squatting under the wall opposite the colliery waiting for his coach, and each day she was disappointed. He must be on a different shift, she supposed. And what good would it do her if he *was* there? He was hardly likely to say anything to her in front of the other men. She just wanted to see him. For the moment,

41

with the thrill of attraction new and exciting, that would have been enough.

On the night of the dance he had dropped off first Julia and then her. He had been pleasant and polite but that had been the end of it. In the slight pause when she got out of the car – he had come around and opened the door for her – she had thought – hoped! – he might ask to see her again. But he hadn't.

That, perhaps, was part of the attraction. Used as she was to being chased and propositioned, the fact that he showed no sign of interest posed a challenge. And yet she had the unmistakable feeling that, contrary to the evidence, he *was* interested. There was a spark in the air between them, a frisson that she was sure wasn't all one-sided.

Well, there was nothing she could do about it except perhaps try to be in the places where he might be too. But she didn't think he was much of a one for the social whirl of the young and unattached in Hillsbridge and the surrounding villages. She couldn't remember ever having seen him at the weekly dance at the Palais – and if he'd been there she felt sure she would have noticed him. No, he was definitely different, and the difference and the slight air of mystery that surrounded him helped to make him a romantic figure, the stuff that dreams were made of.

After a week or so of savouring her new-found emotions, impatience and a nagging feeling of helpless impotence began to set in. If it had been summer she would have gone for walks in the general direction of Purldown, but it wasn't summer. It was November, and no-one in their right mind would be going for walks in the cold and the dark unless they had a good reason. Heather didn't want to be so obvious and, in any case, the chances of bumping into Steven in those circumstances were practically nil.

By the night of the carnival she was close to despair. She was going with a crowd of others, a big loose group who 'got around together' as Carrie called it. Some of them met up in the centre of Hillsbridge, on the corner outside the Rectory, and gathered up several more as they walked towards South Compton.

The road was thronging with people all with one objective in mind, and the carnival spirit was already evident even before they reached the outskirts of the town and the first of the booths selling candyfloss and hot dogs.

Heather and her friends made their way back along the route the carnival would take. They wanted to get an early view of Julia riding in the Queen's Coach and later, when the procession had passed, they could slip through a short cut to the town centre, catching the tail end of it again and being in the right place to enjoy all the attractions of the street fair and the squibbing – the ritual setting off of firecrackers – which would follow.

They found a vantage point on a wall and before long the collectors who always circuited the route were rattling their buckets on the pavement beneath them. Heather dug into the pocket of her coat which she had filled with loose change and tossed some in. The proceeds from the carnival always went to local charities. By the time the procession was over her pocket would be empty and so would the pockets of all her friends.

At seven thirty on the dot a rocket soared up into the night sky, signifying that the procession had begun and a hum of anticipation ran through the crowds now lining the route three-deep. Someone in front of Heather had lifted a child on to his shoulders to give her a good view; Heather offered to hoist her up on to the wall beside them and they all squashed up to make room and put their arms around the small girl, smiling at her eager face. That was all part of the spirit of carnival. And besides – they didn't want their own view obstructed.

The procession came into view, one of the local fire engines leading the way to clear the route, then the town band, playing their hearts out, and then the Queen's Coach. All the girls looked beautiful in their ball gowns, velvet fur-trimmed capes and small sparkling tiaras, but Heather still thought Julia was far and away the most attractive. As the coach moved slowly past, flanked by the Boy Scouts with their flaming torches, she cheered until she was hoarse.

Behind the coach came decorated collecting vehicles,

43

groups of comic masqueraders and more bands, all interspersed between the floats – or carts as the carnival club members called them – which were the highlight of the procession. And what floats! Most had taken months, if not the whole year, to build, the carpenters, electricians and artists working late into the night whilst their womenfolk stitched costumes and planned make-up. Some of the enthusiasts even took their two weeks' annual holiday to enable them to compete at every single carnival on the North Somerset circuit.

The most famous of all these torchlight carnivals was, without doubt, Bridgwater. But the villages and towns such as South Compton who were on the circuit saw almost as impressive a spectacular. There were features where gaily-dressed characters danced choreographed routines to the popular tunes that blared through loud-speakers, and comedy floats that squirted water and bounced fake sausages on long strings of elastic at the watching crowds. But best of all Heather loved the tableaux. How on earth could anyone manage to stay so still on a jolting cart for the entire length of the procession? she always wondered. Each and every character looked like a waxwork figure at Madame Tussaud's. Of course, those who had to stand slipped their feet into shoes that were bolted to the floor and there were certain places on the route known as rest areas where they could relax for a few minutes and coax their numb and aching muscles back to life, but their achievement was still little short of miraculous and Heather thought that every one of them deserved to win one of the coveted trophies. Tonight she clapped wildly as they passed by: The Beheading of Anne Boleyn, the cart depicting the Court of Henry VIII, Anne kneeling meekly with her head on the block; an Egyptian scene, complete with Pharaoh and handmaidens; a Victorian tableau that might have come straight out of *A Christmas Carol*.

All too soon it was over and Heather and her friends joined the scramble to run down the alley to the High Street so they could see the end of the procession pass by again.

The High Street was even more crowded than the spot from where they had watched the procession and the nearer one got to the town centre the more frenetic it became. Here the street fair was already in full swing, with dodgems and a switchback known as the Noah's Ark in the Island and a big wheel on the wide pavement outside Wiltons' grocery store. There were booths and sideshows too and as they passed a shooting gallery Heather spotted David taking aim at the tin ducks that sailed across a make-believe river. She stopped to watch as he picked them off one by one and squealed with delight as the stall holder handed him his prize – a huge pink teddy bear.

'David – you fool!'

He turned, pleased with his performance but embarrassed by his prize, and saw her.

'Hey – you can have this!'

'It's yours! You won it!'

'Not bloody likely!' He thrust the teddy bear into her arms, moving on, laughing with his mates.

Heather looked around for her own friends but they had disappeared into the milling crowd. She began making her way towards the rides, looking for them. They couldn't have gone far. But in the wake of the procession the Island had become a mayhem, a cacophony of the whirr of the generators and the music blaring from the Noah's Ark, the crashes and flying sparks from the dodgems and the general gaiety which had escalated a notch too far into frenetic merrymaking. An unsolicited squib scattered the crowd, carving a zigzag path through the revellers, then hopping in a totally new direction, heading straight for her.

Heather made a dive for safety as the squib followed her like a guided missile homing in on its target – or so it seemed to her. Once when she had been a little girl a Bonfire Night rocket had gone off course, zooming horizontally across the garden and catching Heather on the shoulder as she stood watching. Her thick woollen coat had saved her from injury, but she had fallen off her stool in terror and been too upset to watch the rest of the fireworks. Ever since then they had reawakened echoes of that terror; now, for a moment, she became a child again, faced with a danger over which she had no control.

She screamed, trying to get out of the way, but the crowd was thick and she cannoned into a solid body. Then, without warning, as the squib changed direction yet again, popping its way across the street, she turned to apologise to the person she had bumped into.

'I'm sorry . . .' Her voice trailed away, her heart pounding suddenly not from fear but something quite different.

It was Steven.

He smiled at her, that slow, almost lazy smile that she had been seeing every night in her dreams.

'Hello. Having trouble again?'

'Well . . . yes . . . it does seem like that, doesn't it? I don't know why . . . I'm not usually like this . . .'

'Perhaps it is me. I cause chaos for you.'

'Oh no! I'm sure that's not true . . .'

They were shouting to make themselves heard over the noise of the generators and the blaring music, but to Heather they might have been in a world of their own.

Steve spotted the teddy bear.

'You win that?'

'This?' She looked down, almost surprised to see she was still clutching it. 'Oh on – not me. David did. He gave it to me.' She saw his face go closed-in and realised what he was thinking. 'David is my brother. Don't you know him? He works at Starvault Pit. David Simmons.'

'Oh – yes.' But she got the impression he didn't really know him. 'Are you on your own? Your friend was in the procession, wasn't she?'

'Yes. She looked smashing, didn't she? I came with a whole gang from Hillsbridge. I seem to have lost them though . . .'

'So – would you like to come on the Big Wheel with me?'

Heather smiled, and the reflection of the bright lights made her eyes sparkle.

'Why not?'

They joined the queue, waiting their turn to climb into one of the little gondolas and Heather was very aware of

46

Steven's solid presence beside her. Once in the car she caught at his hand, pretending to be scared as they jolted upwards, one station at a time whilst the other cars were loaded, and he put his arm around her, so that they were squashed together, the teddy bear cuddled into her lap. From the top of the wheel the whole of the town centre was spread out beneath them, an ever-moving sea of people speckled red and blue and green by the twinkling lights. Heather spotted some of her friends standing on the deck of the Noah's Ark and wondered if they were looking for her, wondering what had become of her. She hoped they wouldn't see her and come rushing over to spoil things.

They didn't. If they had seen her they had the good sense to realise she wanted to be left alone. After the Big Wheel, Steven took her on the dodgems and then they walked up the street where the sickly-sweet smell of candyfloss mingled with the pungent aroma of onions frying on the hot-dog stalls and hot petrol, to another small square where the Wall of Death had been erected. Here it was the roar of motorcycle engines that was the predominant sound and a voice distorted by a megaphone attracting customers. They went up the steps to the viewing gallery, marvelling at the skill of the riders as they roared up the sheer side of the drum.

It was getting late now. They'd missed the squibbing and Heather was glad. She had had enough of fireworks for one night, even if it had meant she'd met Steven because of one.

'I cannot offer to drive you home tonight . . .' he said and her heart sank like a stone.

'Oh no . . . of course not . . . that's all right . . .'

'. . . because I did not bring my car. The roads are all closed for the procession. But I will walk with you if you would like. Unless of course you want to meet your friends.'

'No – no,' Heather said, breathless suddenly. 'I don't know where they are. They could have gone already, and if they haven't, I'll never find them in this crush.'

'We walk together then?'

'Yes. Thank you.'

47

He wasn't a great talker. Heather chattered endlessly to fill the silence when they left the fair behind, but she didn't mind that. She felt wonderfully happy, intoxicated almost, and at the same time utterly at ease, as if she was with an old friend she had known all her life.

The night was clear, the stars shining, but there was a deep pool of shadow on the pavement beneath the wall that retained their elevated garden. The road was deserted and the wall hid the pavement from the house. There was no-one to see when he kissed her good night, but if there had been she didn't think she could have cared less.

'Can I see you again?' he asked, a little diffidently, very politely.

'I'd like that.'

'On Saturday?'

'Yes – why not?'

'I'll pick you up then. About seven thirty? We could go to the pictures, perhaps.'

'That would be lovely.'

She climbed the steps, happiness bubbling, and stood for a moment listening to the sound of his footsteps going back down the hill and hugging the teddy bear as it were him. Then she let herself into the sleeping house and crept up the stairs to bed.

'I saw you with that Polish chap last night, didn't I?' David said as they ate breakfast next morning.

'Did you?' Heather pushed away her plate of half-eaten toast. She was feeling decidedly bleary this morning – on top of the late night, excitement had kept her from sleeping.

'What Polish chap is that?' Carrie asked, bustling in from the kitchen with a fresh pot of tea. Her tone was sharp – she didn't miss a thing, Heather thought.

'Steven,' she said.

'Steven who?'

'I don't know. It's a funny name. I can't remember.'

'Steve Okonski,' David supplied. 'He works at our pit.'

'A miner,' Carrie said, faint disapproval in her tone.

'What's wrong with that?'

'And a foreigner.'

'A Pole,' Heather said. 'They were on our side in the war, remember?'

'Maybe so, but you still don't know where you are with foreigners.'

'Oh, Mum . . .'

'You can't be too careful,' Carrie went on, refilling the teacups. 'He could have a wife and half a dozen children at home for all you know.'

'In Purldown?'

'In Poland. And there's no need to be sarcastic, Heather. You know very well what I meant.'

It might almost be funny, Heather thought, if she didn't know the reason for her mother's overcautious interfering.

'I'll find out, Mum. I'm seeing him on Saturday.'

'Bit soon, isn't it?'

'What do you mean?'

'To be seeing him again. You don't want to appear too keen, you know.'

Heather ignored this.

'I'll find out what I can, Mum, if that will satisfy you.'

'It's not *me* that needs to be satisfied. It's you.'

'And I will be,' Heather said wearily. 'I'll find out all about him, I promise you.'

But that was more easily said than done. Steven, quiet on most subjects, was almost totally uncommunicative when it came to talking to himself. Heather didn't think it meant he had anything to hide, simply that he was what the paper novelettes she liked to read called 'the strong silent type'. She didn't mind that. In fact she rather liked it. And it had its advantages. He never questioned her either, never probed for more information than she was willing to offer. Because she had become so emotionally close to him so quickly, there were times when the things she had left unsaid felt like a leaden weight inside her, a burden on her heart. She couldn't yet bring herself to share it, and the fact that he did not seem to think the past important for either of them was comforting. So she chattered in the open sunny way that was her outer nature, her protective shell, and what silences there were were comfortable ones.

She couldn't help being curious about him, though, wanting to know all about him, but as she prised certain nuggets out of him she began to suspect that perhaps there *were* things – not things he wanted to hide, as in a wife and children, but things he didn't want to think of, much less talk about.

She didn't press him. All in good time he would tell her the secrets of his past and she would tell him the secrets of hers. In the meantime she would simply enjoy his company and enjoy falling in love.

'Heather, I want a word with you,' Carrie said.

It was a Sunday afternoon, quite pleasant for November. Whilst Joe had retired to bed for a 'snooge' – his usual treat after Sunday dinner, and well earned too, Carrie thought, considering he was up at five in the morning every weekday and rarely in bed before eleven – she had gone for a walk to the site of the new houses. She was anxious to see how they were progressing and eager to find out where exactly Number 27 Alder Road would be.

The four-bedroomed houses were almost finished, she discovered, even to the point of doors and windows being fitted, and when she clambered on to a plank that straddled the expanse of red mud outside the kitchen window of one and peered through, she had been impressed to see that a sink had been fitted, cupboards hung and electric wiring completed to the point where the bare wires hung in loops from the walls. She had walked on around the already made-up road, counting as best she could, though one long rank of eight houses almost threw her, until she reached Number 27.

It was – or would be – almost opposite the last of the rank of eight, for the road was shaped like a ship's decanter – a narrow neck ballooning out to a sweeping curve around an area of grass that would come to be known as the Green. As yet the house had barely progressed past the foundations' stage, and what would one day be the garden was a sea of red clay on which piles of building materials had been deposited. Carrie had stepped gingerly over the low breeze-block walls into what she imagined would be the living room when the house was completed, treading out the rooms and trying to picture what they would be like. The imagining excited her but also produced a little niggle of disappointment. It wasn't going to be as big as she had hoped, and again she thought of the problem with the bedrooms. Heather and Jenny would be no better off than they were now – in fact, things might be worse for them, since the room they would have to share would probably be smaller than the one they had already.

The idea had come to her as she walked back down the steep lane to the main road. When she got home, she sounded out Glad, and then waited her chance to speak to Heather. It had come just before teatime. Heather had gone up to her room to get ready to go out with Steve and Carrie had followed her up.

'Heather, I want a word with you.'

Heather was at her underwear drawer sorting out a clean pair of stockings. She looked round, surprised. Something in Carrie's tone told her this was no chat.

'It's about the new house.' Carrie sat down on the edge of Jenny's bed. 'I've been thinking. There's not that much room in it really and I just wondered, when we move in, if you wouldn't rather stay here.'

Heather was silent. The clean stockings dangled from her hands.

'Well – you're grown up now. You ought to have a bit more independence. And Jenny is getting to an age where she needs her privacy too.'

A shadow passed across Heather's face; for a moment she looked on the point of tears. Then she said in her usual bright voice: 'Trying to get rid of me, are you?'

'Of course not! How can you say such a thing? It's just that I thought . . .'

'Oh, Mum, I know very well what you thought. You don't have to tie yourself in knots trying to explain.'

Carrie bristled.

'I wish you wouldn't speak to me like that, Heather. I'm only trying to do what's best for all concerned. And that includes your gran and grampy. They're not getting any younger, and it's going to be a big miss for them, suddenly left on their own.'

'I thought Gran was looking forward to having the place to herself,' Heather said.

'Well, she is, of course. But it's a very different kettle of fish just having you and not the rest of us under her feet all the time. I've had a word with her and . . .'

'It's all settled then, is it?' Heather asked tonelessly.

'I wouldn't say that. Not unless you're in agreement. But I do think it would be ideal. After all, you'll still come here for your dinner, won't you? And you'll have this room to yourself when we go.'

'You didn't think of asking David to stay here instead of me, I suppose?' Heather said. The tears were suddenly bright in her eyes again. 'No – I thought not.'

'Oh, Heather – now you're just being silly.'

'Am I?' She smiled slightly, a small bitter smile. 'Oh, it's all right, Mum. Yes, I'll stay here if that's what you want.'

'Heather, I don't want you to think . . .'

'I said I'll stay. I know you'd be more comfortable if I . . .' She broke off. She had been about to say 'if I wasn't around'. But she didn't want to open old wounds, didn't want to make things unpleasant. 'It will be quite nice to have a room to myself,' she conceded.

'Only if you're sure it's what you want,' Carrie said. Now she had her battle won she could afford to be magnanimous.

Heather shrugged her shoulders, not trusting herself to answer, and turned back to her underwear drawer. She wasn't at all sure it was what she wanted, but then, what she wanted never seemed to come into it where Carrie was concerned.

Carrie was the sort of person who liked to be in control. She did it with the very best of intentions, it was true, but for all that, her certainty that she knew best made her ruthless. It seemed to Heather that Carrie never for one moment entertained the slightest doubt but that her way was the right one, her decision provided the best possible outcome for any problematic situation. Once upon a time, Heather had seen her mother as a rock and safe haven, some kind of paragon and champion and protector all rolled into one. Now, she was no longer so sure that Carrie knew best. But Carrie was still a force to be reckoned with!

Her mother was just a human being, after all, and as fallible as anyone else. Her total belief in herself was in itself a weakness. Carrie riding into battle with determination as a sword and self-righteousness for a breastplate could be terrifying, even if her intention was to fight on your side. Especially, perhaps, when her intention was to fight on your side.

And whatever her motive, you argued with Carrie at your peril.

Chapter Three

In years to come, when she looked back on the spring and summer of 1952, it seemed to Jenny that scarcely a day passed without some momentous event taking place. It was an illusion, of course, but the fact that more life-altering things happened that year in the short space of six months or so than had happened in the whole of her life so far meant that even the quiet days, the ordinary days, were imbued with a sense of purpose and excitement and change.

Some of the things didn't affect Jenny personally, of course, but the memory of them would always remain with her. One such thing happened on a grey February day, when Mr Denning, the headmaster, came into their classroom just before the bell rang for the end of morning lessons. He looked very serious, very sombre, and a hush fell over the room as he spoke quietly to Mr Heal and then turned to address them.

'Those of you who go home at dinner time may hear some very sad news, and I would like you all to hear it at the same time.' The hush grew even deeper; they stared at him, round-eyed, and he went on: 'I have to tell you that it has been announced on the wireless that the King has died.'

A murmur ran around the class; Jenny felt it whisper over her skin like a shiver. She had never encountered death, never lost anyone dear to her, but in that moment King George *felt* close, his passing a bereavement in which they all shared. It wasn't just the shock of hearing of the death of a much-loved monarch whose face was so familiar from newspaper photographs that it could be summoned up with no effort at all, it was also the realisation that even being a king was no protection against the grim reaper.

'Princess Elizabeth is flying home from Kenya. She is now our Queen,' Mr Denning went on, but Jenny scarcely heard him. Her brain was whirling with the enormity of it. The King dead. For the rest of her life she would always be able to recall the way she felt at that moment.

Neither would she ever forget sitting The Exam – the dreaded eleven-plus – leaving home with the good wishes of the family and their exhortations to 'Do your best now!' ringing in her ears; feeling sick with nerves as she took her place in the examination room; feeling relief when she read through the paper; feeling anxiety that she must be missing something – it couldn't be that easy! And afterwards, the days and weeks of waiting until the letter dropped through the door inviting her to the local grammar school for interview – and a short interview at that – just ten minutes, whereas some of the others had to go for the whole morning, to do more written papers.

Heather grabbed her the moment Carrie read out the news, swinging her round, dancing round and round the table, laughing and crying. 'You did it! You did it! I knew you could!', whilst David beat a tattoo on the fender with the fire-irons and Glad beamed.

'I don't know where the money's coming from for your uniform,' Carrie said, but Jenny knew from her tone just how pleased she was too.

In spite of the fact that she had a short interview and was therefore considered certain to be offered a place, Jenny was still terrified she might say or do something utterly stupid and ruin her chances, and she found the interview even more nerve-racking than the exam had been. At least then she'd been able to sit and write the answers, something she felt comfortable with; at an interview she would have to make a good impression by saying the right things. She fretted about it endlessly and on the day of the interview, when Mr Heal accompanied the successful half-dozen pupils to the Grammar School, travelling by bus, she looked enviously at Valerie Scott in her smart grey flannel costume with its fitted jacket and pleated skirt and wished she had something like that to wear instead of her hand-knitted Fair Isle jumper – OXO the pattern around her chest read, the others teased her – and the skirt, which, although pleated, had been made for her by Carrie on her Singer sewing machine.

The interview must have gone well, however, for a few weeks later the letter offering her a place at the Grammar School arrived and Carrie began worrying all over again about how she was going to afford all the things on the list – blazer, tie, beret, navy-blue skirt, cream Viyella blouses, all to be purchased from The Don, a very grand shop in Bath that specialised in school uniforms, not to mention a satchel, hockey stick and gym kit.

The whole family chipped in to help get it together, even David, and Jenny knew that Heather had gone without the new dress she had wanted, and probably a good few other things besides in order to ensure Jenny had all she needed. She felt humble, and weighed down by responsibility knowing they had sacrificed so much because they were so proud of her.

One of the really memorable events in that memorable year, of course, was taking possession of the new house.

They moved in on a Saturday in May when the patchy washed-out blue of the sky looked like being overwhelmed by heavy black clouds that were moving in over the hills from the direction of Bristol – never a good sign – and Carrie was panicking that their furniture might take a soaking in the back of the open lorry they had hired from Herby Haines. Herby tried to calm her fears, saying he had a tarpaulin for use in just such an emergency but Carrie didn't care for the idea of such a dirty sheet, which had covered everything from coal to chicken coops getting anywhere near her bed or three-piece suite.

In the event they managed two loads up the hill to Alder Road before the rain began and the things that were left – Joe's garden tools, the coal shovel, David's bicycle – would come to no harm. By four o'clock they were in and relatively straight though Carrie was still rushing around, sweating profusely and snapping at anyone who failed to respond to her orders with equal alacrity, and Jenny retreated to her new room to unpack her things from the cardboard boxes Carrie had begged from the Co-op grocery store.

The room was at the back of the house, quite a large room – David had opted for the smallest bedroom for some reason Jenny could not understand, perhaps because he had been put off large dormitories by his army National Service, she thought. It housed a built-in airing cupboard and was quite bare apart from her bed, a dressing table, a wardrobe and bookcase Carrie had picked up at a house clearance sale and a bright rag rug which Glad had begun making for her as soon as they'd got the news about the house. Jenny paused at the landing window, looking out at some boys playing football on the Green – she recognised Billy Edgell among them – then went along the landing, peeping into the bathroom with its smart blue suite, and into her own room.

Her own room. The words had a wonderful ring. 'My own room,' she said out loud, savouring them. She unpacked her clothes from a battered suitcase, layering them neatly in the drawers, and arranged a few bits and pieces on the top of the dressing table – a little pottery vase containing a bunch of lucky purple heather, a pair of old glass candlesticks, a china rabbit and a jewellery box she'd had for Christmas last year and which now contained plastic brooches, a bead necklace and an ARP badge of uncertain origin. She was just stacking her books in the bookcase, taking great care to put the titles in some sort of order, when she heard someone clattering up the as-yet uncarpeted stairs.

It was Heather, who had been helping with the move.

'I'm going now, Jen.' She looked around the room. 'Gosh, you've been busy!'

'It looks nice, doesn't it?' Jenny said with pride.

'Pretty good, yeah.'

'My own room,' Jenny said, trying out the magic words yet again.

Heather nodded. 'You're really growing up, Jenny.' Her voice cracked momentarily. 'I'm going to miss you, kid.'

'I'm going to miss you too,' Jenny said, catching the mood.

Heather gave a forced little laugh. 'No you won't! And you certainly won't miss all my clutter!'

'I will!' Jenny said loyally. 'I will miss it, Heather.' She ran to her sister, hugging her. 'Do you remember when I was little and I had bad dreams? You'd let me get in bed with you and you'd sing me to sleep.'

Heather didn't answer, just hugged her back.

'I'll miss that too,' Jenny said, overwhelmed suddenly by nostalgia.

'You don't get bad dreams any more,' Heather said.

'I do!'

'Not bad enough to have to come in bed with me. Not for ages. It's like I said, Jenny, you're growing up.'

'I'm not sure I want to grow up,' Jenny said.

For a few moments longer they stood there, hugging one another, then Heather moved away almost abruptly.

'I've got to go, kid. And you've got to finish your unpacking.'

She kissed the top of Jenny's head and clattered off back down the stairs calling her goodbyes to her mother and father. Jenny stood at the landing window to watch her go.

The boys on the green had given up playing football now and were fighting instead, a heap of thrashing bodies and a circle of cheering onlookers, but Jenny, who would normally have been fascinated by such unruly behaviour, scarcely spared them a glance.

Her eyes were on Heather, clacking down the path between the clay-red mud patches that would one day be lawn on the high heels she wore almost all the time, even with slacks, which she was wearing today. As Heather turned out of the gateway, Jenny tapped on the window. Heather waved, then started off along the pavement.

Suddenly Jenny was overwhelmed by unbearable sadness, the thrill of the new house receding to be swallowed up by an enormous aching. She couldn't really understand why she should feel this way – after all, Heather would still be living less than a mile away and she would see her every day, almost as much as she did now. But knowing that did nothing to lift the sadness.

To Jenny, it felt like the end of an era.

And in a way it was, for that momentous year had not yet

finished with them. At the beginning of September, Heather told them she was going to be married.

She arrived unexpectedly in Alder Road around seven o'clock one evening. Jenny, who was in her room struggling to learn her very first Latin homework – 'amo, amas, amat . . .' – heard her voice and rushed downstairs to greet her still clutching the almost brand-new exercise book in which she had written the conjugation of the verb 'to love'.

'Heather!'

'Hello, Jenny. How are you doing?'

She looked, and sounded, a little strained and tired, Jenny thought.

'All right.'

'At school, I mean.'

'Yes, I know. It's all right.' Actually it wasn't, not completely. A week into her first term and Jenny still felt completely lost in the rambling red-brick building. Everything was so strange – teachers wearing flowing black gowns, timetables she could scarcely make head or tail of, a terrifying gymnasium with wall bars and ropes and vaulting horses, the strictest of rules and regulations, and she a very small fish adrift in a very large pond where everyone was bigger or older or more important or more self-confident than she was.

'What are you doing here, Heather?' Carrie asked. Not a very nice question, Jenny thought, since Carrie was Heather's mother too, and her home, therefore, should also be Heather's home.

And then Heather dropped her bombshell.

'I came to tell you that Steve and me are going to get married.'

Carrie's jaw dropped. 'You *what*?'

'We're getting married.'

'Yes, I heard you the first time,' Carrie said. 'I just couldn't believe my ears, that's all. You've only known him five minutes.'

'It's nearly a year now,' Heather protested.

'All the same – it's not as if he's – well – like us, is it?'

'Of course he is,' Heather said. 'He's Polish, that's all.'

'That's what I mean. He's a foreigner. If it hadn't been for the Poles, we wouldn't have had the last war, would we?'

'Oh, Mum, that's rubbish and you know it.'

'Well, he's still a foreigner. Their ways are different to ours . . .'

'I think it's lovely, Heather!' Jenny said, daring for once to interrupt her mother, disagree with her even. 'I think Steven is lovely. Can I be a bridesmaid? I've always wanted to be a bridesmaid . . .' Her voice tailed away as she saw Heather become vaguely uncomfortable.

'I'm . . . not sure, Jen.'

'Why not!'

'Because . . . well . . . it might not be that sort of wedding.'

'Heather!' Carrie said, her voice like thunder. 'You're not . . .?'

'We'd have got married anyway,' Heather said defensively.

'Oh, Heather! I should have thought you'd have had more sense! After . . .'

'What are you talking about?' Jenny asked, puzzled. 'Why are you so cross, Mum?'

'I think you'd better tell her, Heather, don't you?' Carrie had stuck her hands in the pockets of her overall and her chin had come up as it did when she was angry, jutting and pugnacious.

'Mum, please . . .' Heather said, distressed now.

'Well, I'm not going to!' Carrie said. 'If you will get yourself into these . . . situations . . . you're the one who's going to have to do the explaining.'

The first niggle of suspicion worried at Jenny. She pushed it away. She couldn't believe it, wouldn't believe it, wouldn't even think it.

'Oh, Jenny,' Heather said. And to Carrie: 'You're really not being fair to me, Mum.'

Carrie spluttered, an explosion of scorn. 'Go on. Tell her.'

Heather turned to Jenny. She looked close to tears.

'Jenny . . . I don't want you to make the same mistake

60

Mum's making. I want you to understand – Steve and me are going to get married because we love one another.'

'Of course you are!' Jenny said.

'But there's a reason why it's going to be sooner rather than later. A reason why it might be . . . well, a quiet wedding . . . I'm going to have a baby. I know we should have waited until we were married, but really, in the long run it doesn't make any difference. We'd have got married anyway. It's just that – well, we really have to get on with it.'

Jenny felt sick. Heather – going to have a baby – Heather, who wasn't married. How could she?

'How could you?' she said aloud.

Heather recoiled as if Jenny had struck her.

'How could you? How could you *do* that?'

'You see?' Carrie said. Her tone was not angry any more but bitter, which somehow made it worse. 'I don't know, Heather. I should have thought you'd have learned your lesson, but it seems you haven't. You're no better than the girls from Batch Row! Having to get married! The shame of it!'

'I haven't *got* to get married,' Heather said.

'What else do you call it then?'

'I already said – we'd have got married anyway.'

'How do you know that? How does anybody know? You know what people will say.'

'I don't care what people will say!'

'Well I do!'

'I know that! You've always cared about *that*. It's the only thing that matters to you, Mum – what people will say.'

'Because I care about being decent!'

'Yes. More than you care about us. Any of us. You measure us by what people will say. I can't stand it, Mum. I can't bear it any more. Jenny . . .'

But Jenny had fled. If there was one thing she hated it was people shouting at one another. Particularly when those people were the two most important in her world. She ran back upstairs to her room twisting the exercise book between her hands.

'Amo . . . amas . . . amat . . .'

But the words meant nothing. They weren't going in at all. Jenny threw herself down on her bed and burst into tears.

As she walked away down Alder Road, Heather felt the tears pressing so hard at the back of her eyes she knew she could no longer control them. She could hear her mother's angry voice, see the hurt in her father's eyes when he had been called in from the garden where he was bedding out late cabbage plants, feel Jenny's shock and disgust, and suddenly it was all too much to bear.

The boys were playing football on the Green, and she held herself in a grip of steel until she was past them, past the long rank of four-bedroomed houses and the units – a row of strangely modern-looking semis that was still being built – and into the lane that ran steeply down to the main road. Then the tears came, first a hiccupping gulp, a hot welling in her eyes, then a flood that she could not stop.

Terrified someone might drive up the lane and see her crying, knowing she was certainly not ready to walk down the main road and into Glad's house, she ran to a gateway overlooking the fields which sloped gently down to one of Hillsbridge's valleys, leaned on the gate and covered her face with her hands while her body shook with sobs.

Why did her mother have to be like that – so cold, so unforgiving? The same woman who could almost suffocate you with her warmth and loving and caring? But she knew, of course. She'd let them down. Negated all Carrie had done for her. Brought shame on a family to whom respectability meant so much. Everything she had said was true. She loved Steven and he loved her. He would have married her anyway . . . wouldn't he? The first seed of doubt entered her mind and started a fresh wave of tears.

Why had she done it? Why had she let him? She knew that too and it was more than just simply because she loved him, more than the desire he quickened in her until the wanting was almost unbearable. She could have withstood the temptation if it had been just that. She had made up her mind that never again would she do anything

62

that would place her in such a position of vulnerability and she would have stuck to it if . . . if . . .

If, at a time when she was feeling so low, so totally bereft, so much in need of comfort, she hadn't learned his secrets – the secrets she had known from the very beginning he kept – discovered that his need for comfort and reassurance and love was as great as her own. Perhaps greater.

She thought now of the night it had happened, the night when, she was almost sure, she had conceived the child she was carrying. There had been other times since then, of course there had – once the rubicon had been crossed there could be no going back. But on those other occasions they had been more careful, more aware of where their actions could lead them. That first time it hadn't been so. They had given themselves to one another without restraint and the only thought in her mind had been washing him clean of his memories, giving him respite from the demons that tortured him.

He had been more silent than usual that night, she remembered, more morose than she had ever seen him. She had been talking about her own sadness, her hurt at being left behind when the rest of the family had moved to the new house, the fact that although her head told her it was the most sensible arrangement, that she and they would be more comfortable, that her grandparents needed her there and she needed her freedom – her heart had not been able to accept it.

'They just don't want me around Jenny,' she said. 'I'm a bad influence.'

'Don't be silly. I am sure that is not true.' He smiled at her, that slow smile she loved so much.

'It is true.'

'Oh, Heather . . . Heather . . .' He pulled her close so that her head was against his chest, her face buried in the soap-scented sweater he was wearing because the weather – particularly in the evenings – was still cold for the time of year.

'I know I'm being pathetic,' she said after a moment. 'It's just . . . well, it's not very nice, knowing your family . . .' She broke off again, unable to finish, and into the silence he said:

'At least you still have your family.'

She looked up at him.

'What do you mean? Because your family are still in Poland?'

'I have no family,' he said. 'Not any more.'

And then he told her. He told her in a long monologue, his voice breaking, of what had happened to them when Hitler had invaded. He told her of the killing and the looting and the burning, of his village in flames and his mother and sister dead in the wreckage of their home. He told her of his father and brother, killed in the last cavalry charge, and of how he had escaped and continued to fight until the end of the war with the Polish Free Army, when he had come to Hillsbridge, as a miner, to try to make a new life.

He told her all this, all the things he had never been able to bring himself to speak about before, and once he began, he was unable to stop until he had relived it all, purged himself of the horror of his memories and the loneliness and grief which had followed. When he finished he was crying, strong Steven, Steven the rock, who never showed any emotion beyond a tenderness that was surprising in such a big, masculine man. The tears rolled down his face and she kissed them away, ashamed that she could have been so selfishly concerned with her own troubles which seemed petty now in the face of what he had been through. And his anguish was a sharp chord within her, a desperate need to somehow make amends, help him to overcome the darkness in his soul.

She held him and kissed him and stroked his hair as if he were a child, and after a while, when the loving and the giving and receiving of comfort became passion, there was no way – no way at all – for holding back.

And I'm not sorry! She thought fiercely now as her own tears dried on her face. I'm sorry I've upset Mum and Dad and Jenny, but I'm not sorry I gave myself to Steven and I'm not sorry I'm carrying his child.

A warm evening breeze blew across the valley, bringing

on it the scent of grasses and baled hay, of mud where the cows had trampled and evacuated, of a couch fire somewhere in the distance; warm, evocative, natural smells that had been part of her life for as long as she could remember and always would be. Smells that had been the same for generations of people living their little lives, procreating and dying, and the sense of continuity was comforting, a world that would be here long after she was gone and her problems and heartaches nothing but dust in the wind.

She placed her hands on her belly, imagining the life beginning there which would link her for ever to those days yet to come, and felt humble and overawed. Then she set off once more down the lane, leaving her past behind, striding purposefully towards her future.

The wedding took place three weeks later, and Jenny was a bridesmaid as she had wanted to be. She wore a dress of stiff organdie with three rows of frills around the hemline that Carrie had made for her, sitting up late at night over her Singer sewing machine, and a matching coronet of pink silky stuff in her hair instead of the usual ribbon bow, and a pair of silver sandals. She stood behind Heather in the Catholic church, feeling immensely proud in spite of the fact that Heather was wearing a frock with a loose-fitting coat over instead of the ivory dress Jenny had always imagined she would wear and holding Heather's trailing bouquet of roses, stephanotis and maidenhair fern while she and Steven made their vows.

Outside the church the whole family posed for photographs. The menfolk were in their Sunday suits with white carnations in the buttonholes – Jenny thought how handsome David looked and was proud all over again that he was her brother. Glad looked more suitably dressed for a funeral than a wedding in her black silk coat, black button shoes and stockings and her best black straw hat trimmed with a big rosette of silk flowers, but in order to enter into the spirit of an occasion of celebration she had a corsage of pink carnations pinned to her shoulder. Carrie, too, wore a corsage, and a costume in what she called Marina blue – after the Duchess of Kent, she explained to anyone who asked. Though she was tightly corseted, the skirt pulled a little across her stomach and she thought ruefully that for all that she never seemed to stop running about she had still managed to put on weight since she last wore it.

No-one looking at her would have guessed she was anything but delighted that her elder daughter had become Steven's wife and, indeed, she had mellowed towards the idea in the three weeks since Heather's shock announcement. She still wished Steven wasn't foreign, she still wished Heather had gone to the altar under different circumstances, but at least she was safely married now, she would have no more worries on that score. Steven hadn't left her in the lurch as some might do, he had stood by her and although there might be a certain amount of counting of months when the baby was born it would soon be forgotten – a nine days' wonder. She wouldn't have to endure the shame of this grandchild being born out of wedlock. Now all she had to do was make sure Jenny didn't get herself into trouble and she could hold her head up high and know the respectability that was so important to her had been preserved. And it would be a long time yet, hopefully, before she had to start worrying about that. Jenny was young for her age and as yet, thank goodness, had not shown the slightest interest in boys.

Carrie stole a proud sideways glance at her, at her round smiling face and plump body encased in pink organdie. Could she detect the first hint of development beneath the tightly fitting bodice? She rather thought she could. But Jenny didn't look like Heather in any respect, except for her eyes, and Carrie was glad. She couldn't have gone through all that again, the boys standing in line, the fearful realisation of the temptations she would face, the constant watchfulness combined ultimately with the knowledge that in the last resort she couldn't be there all the time, couldn't know what her children were up to every minute of the day. And Jenny wasn't like Heather in her ways, either. She had none of Heather's wilfulness. She was a good girl. Carrie only hoped she would stay that way.

When the photographs had been taken it was into the church hall for the reception – a glass of sherry, a sit-down meal of ham salad followed by trifle and the two-tier cake, topped by a miniature bride and groom, which had been baked by the Co-op. Afterwards there were the speeches and the usual jokes about the stork, which made Heather blush and caused Carrie's mouth to set in a tight line for a few moments – the first and only time during the whole day.

Heather and Steven were going to Paignton for a week's honeymoon – since Heather intended to travel in the same outfit she had been married in there was no need to go home and change and the family showered them in confetti as they waved them off in Steven's car with tin cans tied to the rear bumper.

Carrie had ordered a taxi to take them home afterwards, dropping Glad and Walt off on the way, though David was going on for a drink at the Working Men's Club with his friends. When she had packed Jenny off to bed – not easy, since although Jenny was tired, she was also overexcited and reluctant to take off her bridesmaid's dress – she went to the sideboard and got out the quarter-bottle of brandy she always kept there for medicinal purposes.

'I don't know about you, Joe, but I could do with a drink!'

'That would be very nice, m'dear.'

His preferred tipple was whisky – 'a nice drop of Teachers' – but brandy was better than nothing, even if it did recall childhood days of bilious attacks when his mother had poured him a little to settle his stomach.

'It all went off very well, didn't it?' Joe said.

'Yes. Considering.'

'She'll be all right with Steven,' Joe said. 'He's a nice chap. I felt very proud taking her up that aisle today.'

'I'd rather circumstances had been different.'

Carrie sat down in one of the fireside chairs they'd bought especially for the new house, feeling her skirt strain around her stomach as she did so.

'She's not the only one by a long chalk,' Joe said philosophically, getting out a packet of Players and lighting one. 'It's just nice to see her settled.'

'I suppose so.'

'You worry too much,' Joe said.

And you don't worry enough, Carrie thought, but did not say. This was the Joe she had married, quiet, easy-going, taking the rough with the smooth stoically, good-naturedly. It occurred to her that in many ways Steven was very like him. Perhaps our Heather hasn't done so bad for herself after all, she thought.

'Well, if they're as happy as us after twenty-five years, I dare say they'll be all right,' she said, smiling at him.

'I hear your Heather *had* to get married,' Joyce Edgell said.

Carrie banged the lid down on to a container of cottage pie and swung round. 'What do you mean by that?'

'Come off it, Carrie, you know very well what I mean. She's in the club.' There was a smirk on her face.

'You don't miss a chance, do you, Joyce?' Carrie said bitterly.

It was true. Ever since the episode when Carrie had blackmailed George Parsons into giving them a house she and Joyce had been at loggerheads and things had been made even worse by Jenny passing The Exam. None of Joyce's brood had made it to the Grammar School, nor were likely to, Carrie thought.

'At least she didn't get married in white, like some I could name,' Joyce went on. 'I expect you'd have liked her to, though.'

'All I want for our Heather is for her to be happy.'

Joyce ignored this. 'Oh well, she's been lucky so far, from what I hear.'

That did it. Carrie rounded on her furiously.

'Now look here, Joyce Edgell, just because you behave like an alley cat doesn't mean everybody else does, and certainly not our Heather. So you can just keep your dirty mouth to yourself, or I swear I'll swing for you.'

'OK, OK, keep your hair on!' Joyce smirked, knowing she'd touched a raw nerve. 'All I'm saying is . . .'

'I know what you're saying. And you can just shut up. Talking about our Heather like that . . .'

'Brought you down a peg or two though, didn't it?' Joyce sneered.

It was all Carrie could do not to hit her.

'I had that Joyce Edgell on at me today about you,' Carrie said to Heather.

Heather and Steven, who were living with Glad and Walt, had walked up to Alder Road as they often did for a cup of Bournvita and a chat. Steven had gone to the outhouse, where Joe was trying to sort out his tools and the garden implements that needed cleaning and oiling for the winter, to lend him a hand and the two women were toasting their knees in front of the open fire.

'She's heard from somewhere that the wedding was a rush job and she was determined to let me know she knew it.'

'I hope you told her it was none of her business,' Heather said.

'I did. In no uncertain terms. But all the same, I wish . . .' She broke off, looking at Heather's bulge, now fairly obvious under her jumper and skirt.

'Don't start that again, Mum, please,' Heather begged.

'No. Well. All I can say is it's a pity it arose at all.' Carrie was aware she was taking her humiliation out on Heather, but she couldn't stop herself. It had been burning away inside her all day like a dose of bad indigestion. 'It's a pity you never learned self-control. I should have thought after what happened before . . . well, I should have thought you'd learned your lesson.'

Heather was on her feet, hurt and anger in her heart, tears in her eyes.

'How could I ever forget? How could I ever forget what you and Dad made me do?'

'Not your dad. Don't blame him.'

'No. Not Dad. You. What *you* made me do. Do you think I can forget it for a single day? A single moment? Do you think I'll ever forgive you?'

'Heather . . .' Carrie was frightened suddenly, without quite knowing why. Only that she had never seen her daughter quite like this before. Heather was usually merry-hearted, if wilful. A smile to hide the pain, like her father. Now the look in her eyes was close to hatred and it chilled Carrie to the core.

'Heather . . .' she said again.

'I'm sorry, Mum, I'm going.' Heather was reaching for her coat, hung over the back of a chair. 'I don't want to stay here and listen to this.'

'All right – go!' Carrie snapped, aware even as the words passed her lips that she didn't mean them. But on the defensive she always attacked – within the family, anyway. 'I just wish you'd realise what we did was for your own good.'

'I'm sure you thought so,' Heather said. 'I'm sure you still do. That's what is so terrifying about you, Mum. You think you can do anything – *anything* – and as long as it's for *our good* then it's all right. Only sometimes it isn't. Keeping up appearances is what it's about. And that isn't always the same thing as *our good* whatever you might think.'

Joe and Steven appeared in the doorway.

'Hey – hey – hey – what's going on here?' Joe asked, mildly concerned.

'Heather?' Steven said.

'Come on, Steve, we're going,' Heather said.

She went through into the hall to the front door, deliberately avoiding the kitchen, the heart of the house, her mother's domain.

Jenny was on the stairs. She had been in her room, with the Aladdin oil stove to take the chill off the air, doing her homework, rushing at it in an effort to finish so that she could go down and spend some time with Heather and Steven – whom she already hero-worshipped – when she had heard the raised voices. Heather looked up and saw her, looked away again, opened the front door.

'Heather!' Jenny called.

But for once Heather ignored her. Not waiting for Steven, not waiting for anything, she went out into the night.

70

Chapter Four

Jenny was not enjoying school. It was just the same as it had been in the Juniors – the lessons were fine – well, most of them – physics and geometry made her mind boggle, but she could cope with everything else, even Latin, which she rather enjoyed. But when it came to her social standing, Jenny still felt like an outsider. On the whole the other pupils in her class seemed quite nice, but they already had their own groups, tight little knots of girls who had been together since infant school, which were self-sufficient and impenetrable – except by outgoing, confident girls like Valerie, who had quickly formed an alliance with a pretty but precocious girl from one of the neighbouring villages who was known, for some unfathomable reason, as 'Baba'. The boys, of course, might as well have been aliens from another planet. As yet, they were a race apart; they took no notice of the girls and the girls, with the possible exception of Valerie and Baba, took no notice of them.

Just as before, Jenny found herself paired off or left with the other outcasts no-one wanted to be associated with. The trouble was, she didn't want to be associated with them either. At least they weren't stupid, of course, not like poor Tessa Smith. They'd never have passed The Exam if they had been. But in spite of her problems, Jenny still saw herself as vastly superior to the wimpish Diane Witcombe and the gangling Penny Presley with her bandy legs and mouthful of teeth. Yet invariably she found herself forced into their company, left, with them, on the sidelines. Particularly when it came to games.

To Jenny, games and physical education – as PT was now called – were the lesson periods she most dreaded. To begin with, her slowness at changing into aertex shirt and

71

shorts meant she was always the last to leave the cloakroom, scooting hot and breathless after the others as they made their merry way down the road to the playing fields or along the corridor to the gym. And once there the nightmare began in earnest.

Jenny hated the gym, hated having to line up and take her turn at balance hangs and gate vaults on the horizontal bars which descended from the ceiling by means of pulleys, hated rolling about on the mats and struggling to get a foothold to climb the ropes. But all these tortures were as nothing compared to the ultimate torture of the vaulting horses.

Each time Miss Foster, the rosy-cheeked, mannish PE mistress, ordered them to pull out the bucks and horses and beating boards, Jenny's heart sank and she felt sick with dread. She couldn't do it. She simply couldn't do it. She would stand in line, watching the others running purposefully on to the beating board and sailing effortlessly over the horse, and make up her mind that this time she too would clear the horrible obstacle even if it killed her. She would make her run, trembling inside but determined, but the moment her feet hit the beating board her nerve would fail her. She would jump on it too cautiously to gain any momentum and either crash into the vaulting horse or flop like a beached whale, landing ignominiously on top of it. Then she would have to climb down and slink to the back of the queue whilst Valerie or Baba or one of the others sailed over as if they had wings and her face would be scarlet both from the effort and from knowing that she'd made a fool of herself yet again.

It wasn't that she was physically incapable, she knew, but that she was afraid. Afraid, deep down, in a part of her psyche she could not reach with any amount of logic. Afraid because when she had tried to climb or jump or be wild in any way at all when she was little, Carrie had drummed into her: 'Don't do that, Jenny, you'll fall. Don't do it, Jenny, you'll hurt yourself.' The message had gone home and stuck at a time when Jenny had not doubted for a moment that her mother knew everything there was to know.

72

She might have been quite good at hockey, Jenny thought, if only she was given the chance. It was something she could really put her heart and soul into and she longed to be part of a team. But she didn't yet have her own hockey stick – Heather had promised her one for Christmas – and she had to use one of the school's supply. Because she was always last changing, the best ones had invariably gone, and she was left with some battered relic with the binding coming unwound. Besides this, because she was so dreadfully useless in the gym, Miss Foster assumed she would be equally useless on the hockey field, and when she picked her two teams of eleven girls to play on the main pitch, Jenny would find herself left out yet again, banished to the second pitch, which didn't have any proper goals, struggling to play some sort of ordered game with Diane and Penny and a few other rag, tag and bobtails who had also been excluded. Just occasionally Miss Foster, who was nurturing future stars for the school team, sent the best players off to practice on their own and Jenny got a chance in the match proper. But when she did she was so unpractised and overeager that she was liable to race all over the field for impossible balls and let go the ones she should have safely passed.

She was a failure, Jenny thought, a total failure, and she hated it. Most of all she wanted to succeed. No – most of all she wanted to be popular! But popularity too seemed a goal too far. After all, being good at sport was the best passport to popularity if you didn't happen to be witty or pretty. And Jenny was none of these.

Another miserable time was the period devoted to cookery. Again, Jenny's slowness with any physical activity meant she was always the last to finish rubbing in her pastry and oiling her tins, so the most favourable parts of the ovens were already in use before she tried to fit her effort in, and it ended up either burned or under-cooked. And her corner in the DS room was always the last to be cleared up, so she earned the dislike of Miss Weymouth, the cookery teacher, as well as the scorn of Miss Foster.

One day, however, Jenny did manage to produce some very edible-looking biscuits, and she was pleased and

73

proud as she loaded them into the tin and packed it away in her basket beneath a red-checked tea towel.

'If they're nice, we can have them for tea,' Carrie had said, after complaining as usual about the expense of the ingredients she had had to provide.

Jenny boarded the coach that would take her home and which picked up at the Secondary Modern school en route, and sat down, nursing her basket and trying to hang on to the strap of her satchel at the same time. The other children – particularly the older ones, who at the ripe old age of thirteen or fourteen should have known better – had been known to snatch her satchel if she didn't hold on to it, take out her ruler and pencil case and exercise books and play catch with them. Today, however, someone spotted that Jenny had been baking.

'What you got there?'

'Biscuits,' Jenny said.

'Let's have one!'

'No,' Jenny said. 'I've got to take them home.'

'Go on – spoilsport!'

'No!'

'Well, just let's have a look. Bet they're rubbish. All burned or something.'

'They're not!' Jenny said indignantly.

'Let's see, then.'

And Jenny was tempted by the chance to show that she wasn't a complete ninny, as they seemed to think. She wriggled the tin out of the basket and took off the lid.

It was the biggest mistake she could have made. In a flash Wendy Pearce, who was an older version of Valerie, had snatched the tin and helped herself to a biscuit.

'You can't have them! They're for our tea!' Jenny protested.

Some of the others mimicked her.

'Not bad!' Wendy said, munching first one biscuit, then another, and passing the tin around, always just out of Jenny's reach. Before the coach reached Jenny's stop half the biscuits had been eaten, the children were helpless with laughter, and Jenny was hot, flustered and close to tears.

When she got home there was nothing for it but to explain to Carrie what had happened. Carrie was furious.

'I'll go up to the school and complain. Little toads! How dare they!'

'No – you can't go to school!' Jenny pleaded. 'You can't!'

'If they think they can get away with this, they've got another think coming!'

'No – please, Mum!' Jenny said. 'You'll only make things worse.'

'We'll see about that!'

Jenny felt sick with anxiety. For the first time in her life she positively did not want her mother to come out fighting her corner. To have a parent turning up at school complaining about the behaviour of other pupils would be appallingly humiliating. She'd never live it down. With a flash of insight Jenny realised her mother couldn't be there all the time and the other children would find other, subtler ways of making her life a misery. Even the teachers, whilst ostensibly taking the side of law and order, would feel nothing but scorn for her, put her down as a no-hoper, an overgrown baby fledgling unable to survive outside the nest.

Argument with Carrie was, she knew, useless. Carrie's mind was made up, and Carrie knew best. In the old days, Jenny might have sought Heather's help, but not only did Heather no longer live under the same roof, but she and Carrie were barely on speaking terms. Since the night she had walked out, taking Steven with her, there had been no more weekly visits, and Carrie got a face on, as Jenny called it, whenever Heather's name was mentioned. It was a thoroughly upsetting development and one which Jenny was at a loss to understand, though from the little she had overheard she had a dark half-formed suspicion, something she shrank from thinking about and certainly would not have dreamed of raising with Carrie.

No, Heather couldn't help her this time, and David as an ally never entered her head. David had a girlfriend now, Linda Parfitt from South Compton, about whom he was very secretive and evasive, and he spent less time at home than ever. No, there was only one person she could turn to – her father – though she rather doubted that even he would have much influence on a Carrie with her mind made up. Certainly if the subject were raised in front of her, she would not so much defend her plan of action as simply assert it – this was what she was going to do, and that was that. Joe would probably back her up without even listening to Jenny's point of view. Even if she put it to him on his own there was always the possibility that he would simply say: 'It's no use arguing with your mother. She'll do as she thinks best.' He tended to take the line of least resistance, Jenny knew, because he hated discord of any kind, and his watchword seemed to be: 'Anything for the sake of peace.' The thought that she might put him in an awkward position also worried Jenny, as everything seemed to worry her these days, but this was too important to her not to at least try to do something about it.

Her chance came later on in the evening. She had gone to bed, taking with her the map of South America whose states, mountains and capital cities she was supposed to memorise for homework, but which had refused to go in because concentration was beyond her, and was lying sleepless when she heard her father come upstairs. She knew it was him because she could smell the comforting aroma of his cigarette – for all her life Jenny would associate the smell of cigarette smoke and petrol lighters with safety and comfort. She heard him go into the bathroom – having 'a swill', no doubt, before going down to the Working Men's Club for an hour – and when he came out again she called to him.

'Dad! Daddy!'

The door opened a crack and light from the landing spilled in.

'What's the matter?'

'Can I talk to you?'

He didn't say, as many fathers would, that he was just going out, and couldn't it wait. The door opened wider and she saw him silhouetted against the light, a wiry, slightly built man.

'I'm really worried, Dad,' she said, and she told him

76

what had happened, ashamed to admit to him that she had been the subject of teasing, because she thought it would belittle her in his eyes and it was incredibly important to her that, of all the people in the world, her dad should think well of her, but needing to share it all, unload some of her anxiety.

'They'll think I'm a terrible baby,' she finished. 'If Mum goes to school they'll know I've been telling tales. I'll never live it down.'

'All right, m'dear, I'll have a word with her,' he said.

'Will she take any notice of you, though?'

'Don't worry about it any more,' Joe said. 'She doesn't always think, your mother.'

Jenny was beginning to feel relief, but she was also rather shocked. It was the first time anyone had ever uttered a word against Carrie to her. Even Glad had her arguments with her up front, never seeking to involve the children. And for Dad to say 'She doesn't always think', mild as it was, was still an admission that Carrie was not all-wise and omnipotent after all. But the four little words were somehow far more than simply a gentle criticism of Carrie, more than the simple comfort to Jenny he no doubt intended them to be. In that moment a bridge was suddenly built between father and daughter, a bridge of shared confidence, a feeling that he was no longer talking to her as a child but as a young adult, who could take on board the failings and imperfections of those she had always believed to be infallible.

'She won't go up to the school,' he said. 'I promise you.'

When he had left her, pulling the door to after him, Jenny lay nervously listening to the rise and fall of their voices in the living room which was immediately below her bedroom, aware that, on Carrie's part at least, the discussion was a little heated and realising that it would now probably be too late for Dad to go out for his drink tonight. She wondered what they were saying, but she was beginning to feel drowsy, and hopeful too. If anyone could get around Mum it was Dad.

Her confidence was rewarded. Nothing more was ever said about the biscuits. Carrie did not go to the school to complain. And Jenny knew she had forged a very special bond with her father.

As if the incident with the biscuits had somehow constituted a watershed, things gradually began to improve. The Grammar School no longer seemed such a vast and frightening place, the pupils on the coach home began to lose interest in teasing her, and she even made friends with Ann, Rowena and Kathy, three girls from South Compton who had seemed an inseparable trio but who had accepted her into what had become a foursome. She still disliked gym, physics and cookery – the Christmas cake she had made had been an absolute disaster, soggy in the middle, with garish green icing which hadn't turned out at all the way she'd intended it – but she was doing well at practically everything else, and beginning to enjoy herself.

The house in Alder Road was beginning to feel like home now, with lawn sprouting and new little plants poking bravely out of the bright red soil which became a quagmire of heavy mud in wet weather and a cracked desert in summer drought, and each of the rooms had taken on a character of their own. Jenny particularly liked the row of outhouses, joined by a roofed-over passage to the main house and consisting of an outside lav, a coal house and a store room in which her newest and most treasured possession was stored – her bicycle.

As they had promised, Carrie and Joe had given her the bicycle as her Christmas present, and she still got a tickle of excitement in her tummy each time she remembered coming downstairs on Christmas morning to see it leaning against the wall in the hall covered with a blanket and swathed in tinsel.

She had to learn to ride it, of course, never having been on two wheels before, and Joe and David took turns to go along the lane with her, holding on to the saddle and running behind, steadying her, until she got the hang of it and sailed off, wobbling, on her own. By the time spring came she was quite proficient, and on fine days, when she did not have cookery paraphernalia to carry, she was able to cycle the three and a half miles to school, her satchel

78

propped in an old-fashioned bicycle basket which attached to the handlebars.

But the really big event of that year was the birth of Heather's baby.

It came on a Saturday in February when spring seemed just around the corner. Jenny had gone into Hillsbridge, to do the Saturday morning shop for Carrie, with Heather, who was doing her own shopping. Jenny was acutely conscious of the stares of other customers as they queued for bacon and cheese at the Co-op – Heather was now very close to her time, and embarrassingly enormous. She was also behaving oddly this morning, shifting about impatiently while they waited their turn, not really listening to anything Jenny said to her.

'Oh for goodness sake!' she snapped when the little wooden cup carrying the money and paper check got stuck halfway along the wire which carried it to the cubicle in the corner of the shop where the cashier sat in solitary splendour. 'Blooming thing!'

Jenny glanced at her anxiously. She liked the change machine and when she was little had longed to pull the cord to send the wooden cup on its way high above the heads of the customers as the shop assistants did.

'Are you all right?' she asked.

'Of course I'm all right! I just wish we could get on and get home!'

But for all that she seemed to be buying more than she usually did – as if she were stocking up for Christmas or a Bank Holiday, Jenny thought, as the assistant weighed out biscuits, sugar and tea at the grocery counter.

'Thank goodness for that!' Heather said as they eventually emerged from the shop. 'We'll just call at the bakery for a loaf of bread, and that's it.'

'I've got to get Dad's cockles,' Jenny said.

'Oh – do you have to?'

'You know I do.'

For as long as they could remember Joe had had a quarter of cockles, swimming in vinegar, for his Saturday tea, eating them whilst listening to the football results. It was a ritual, and could not be broken.

'Go on then, but be as quick as you can. I'll wait for you down outside the chemist's.'

Jenny went to the Co-op wet fish shop and queued for the cockles and some kippers Carrie had asked her to get. When she came out of the shop, Heather was nowhere to be seen. Jenny walked down the hill to the chemist's, looking round anxiously. One of the assistants appeared in the doorway.

'Jenny! Your sister's in here. She's not well. She had to sit down.'

Jenny rushed into the shop. Heather was sitting on a chair just inside the door, with Mr Mackenzie, the pharmacist, and another assistant hovering solicitously.

'Let me see if I can get hold of the doctor,' Mr Mackenzie was saying, but Heather was shaking her head.

'No – no . . .' She saw Jenny and got up with an effort. 'I've got to get home, Mr Mackenzie.'

'Well, at least let me call you a taxi.'

'I'll be all right.'

'I've got my car round by the Hall,' a man who Jenny vaguely recognised as someone who lived at the top of Westbury Hill said. 'I'm going home myself now, and I pass right by the door.'

Jenny's concern was at last outranking her embarrassment. The car was fetched to the door of the shop, Heather installed in the front seat, Jenny and all the shopping in the back. When they were dropped off outside the house, she struggled to manhandle all of it by herself whilst Heather, with a very peculiar gait, hauled herself up the steps.

'I think I've started, Jenny,' she said.

She opened the door and went in, calling out for Steven and Glad, only to be met by comfortless silence. Only Walt was in the kitchen, peeling potatoes for dinner. When he was not at work, Walt enjoyed cooking and was actually rather better at it, Jenny thought, than Glad, who tended to be slapdash, and certainly better than Carrie, who never cooked at all if she could help it – probably put off by all the food she served up at the school canteen day after day.

80

'Where is everybody?' Jenny asked him.

'Young Steven's took your gran to get some flowers. It's her turn to do the altar at church this week.' He looked at her, registering her panic-stricken face. 'What's wrong, my old Dutch?'

'It's Heather. She's . . .' She couldn't bring herself to say the words. Not to Grampy.

'You'd better go and find them,' Walt said, not looking unduly concerned. Joe got his stoic nature from his father. 'I expect they'm down the market. Or they could've gone over to the nursery, I suppose.'

The nursery they used was at South Compton. Jenny's heart sank.

'That's no good then . . .' She broke off, trying to think logically. If Heather was in labour the doctor should be told, or the midwife, or both. But she honestly didn't know what to do first, and she knew she could not expect any help from Walt. Having babies and all it entailed was totally outside his field of experience – something women saw to. He would simply go on peeling his potatoes while the world turned upside down around him, and afterwards he would risk a cursory glance into the cot, mutter: 'Well, well, well,' and go back to his old routine.

No, she couldn't rely on Walt for assistance. In fact, there was only one person she wanted in this emergency – one person above all others who would know what to do. That person was Carrie.

Carrie was doing the bedrooms when she heard the front door slam and Jenny's voice calling her name. She went to the top of the stairs.

'I'm up here . . .'

Jenny was in the hall, breathless, her face scarlet from running the half-mile up hill.

'What in the world . . .?'

'It's Heather. She's having the baby. Oh, Mum, come quick!'

'Where is she?' Carrie asked.

'At Gran's. There's nobody there but Grampy. They're all out . . .'

'All right. You stay here.'

'No . . . I'm coming with you . . .'

Carrie was pulling on a coat over her checked nylon overall, calling to Joe to tell him where she was going. Then they were hurrying back down the hill, Jenny's face still on fire, trying to explain breathlessly to her mother what had happened. There was a pain in her own stomach, a dull ache running from the very pit to her hips and back again; she assumed it was from running up hill – or perhaps she was empathising with her sister, feeling something of what Heather was feeling.

They turned into Glad's house; to Jenny's enormous relief, Glad was there.

'Steven's gone to ring the doctor,' she said.

Bunches of chrysanthemum wrapped in paper still lay on the table where she had put them down when she and Steven had arrived home to the crisis; Heather had been despatched upstairs. Jenny went to follow Carrie up; sharply, Carrie told her to stay where she was. Jenny was quite glad to do so; she could hear Heather moaning, a frightening sound that reminded her, grotesquely, of the awful lowing cows made when the farmer took their calves away from them.

Soon the house was in uproar. Steven arrived back, out of breath and looking more worried than Jenny had ever seen him, Glad was rushing to and fro boiling kettles and tearing up old bed linen, there was a ring at the front door followed by Dr Stephens' voice in the hall and footsteps on the stairs, a banging at the back and the midwife, aptly named Nurse Stork, bustled through carrying her bag and some sort of apparatus that looked like an oxygen cylinder. Steven paced; of Carrie there was no sign. Only Walt seemed unmoved by the chaos which had engulfed the house, appearing in the kitchen doorway still wearing his serge apron over an old pair of railway trousers and enquiring mildly what he should do about dinner.

'The potatoes are spoiling . . .'

'Go and dish up yours and Jenny's,' Glad said. 'And Steven's. You might as well get a good meal inside you, Steven. It could be hours yet.'

Steven said he didn't feel like eating, so Jenny sat at the oilcloth-covered table in the kitchen with her grandfather, eating bacon and potatoes and cabbage swimming in the fat from the pan. Then, when they had washed up and Glad was sitting down to eat hers, Jenny went into the front room, turned on a bar of the electric fire, and played Chopsticks on Walt's piano in an attempt to drown out the sounds coming from upstairs. She wished she could go home, to Joe and David and normality, but she couldn't tear herself away.

Soon after four o'clock she heard a baby's cry and suddenly all her fear and anxiety dropped away and she was filled with wonder. She went out into the hall and after a little while Dr Stephens came down on his way to the bathroom to wash his hands and told her she had a little niece. Then, a bit later, Carrie came down and asked her if she would like to go up to see the baby.

Heather was propped up against the pillows looking dishevelled and tired but very happy and Steven sat on the edge of the bed with his arms around her so that they somehow both encompassed the little bundle she was holding. Jenny could just see a little face peeping out of the tight swathing, a little wizened red face topped with wisps of fair hair that reminded her oddly of a miniature version of Walt.

'What do you think then, Jenny?' Heather asked.

She unwrapped a tiny hand, pink and wrinkled and perfect with tiny oyster-shell nails.

'She's lovely,' Jenny said, shy suddenly.

'Vanessa,' Heather said. 'We're going to call her Vanessa, aren't we, Steve?'

She smiled at him, holding the baby close against the frills and ruches of her new nightie and quite unexpectedly Jenny's awe was overshadowed by a wave of emotion she couldn't put a name to, but which felt oddly like jealousy.

She and Heather had always been so close; now, suddenly, she felt excluded. Heather and Steven and Vanessa were a unit, a family in which she had no place, and the sense of loss, of bereavement almost, was overwhelming. She wanted to join them on the bed, knew that if she did Heather would not push her away, but would put an arm around her, draw her into the group. But it would be a charade. She wasn't part of their family and never would be again. With her innate honesty, Jenny could have none of it.

'You timed that very well, Heather,' Glad said, coming in with a tray of tea in the best bone-china cups – in honour of the occasion – and a plate of biscuits. 'You missed your dinner, but you weren't going to miss tea as well, were you?'

Suddenly Jenny remembered the cockles she had bought for Joe's tea.

'Dad's cockles!' she said. 'I'll have to run home with them!'

They all laughed.

'And you can tell him he's now officially a grandfather,' Heather said.

'Oh my lord, and I'm a great-grandmother!' Glad said, and they all laughed again.

Jenny put on her coat and left them to it, hurrying up the hill with both the news and the cockles. The ache was back in the pit of her stomach, dull and dragging, and there was a wetness that she thought must be sweat between her legs.

When she had told her father and David what had happened, she went to the lavatory – the upstairs one, because it was too cold for comfort in the outside one at this time of year – and that was when she discovered that what she had thought was sweat was, in fact, blood.

Her face flamed even though she was alone. She'd started her periods! Oh no! She had hoped fervently that wouldn't happen for a long time yet and wished now, even more fervently, that Carrie was here, not still with Heather. But they'd already discussed it and there was a packet of sanitary towels stored in the bottom of Jenny's wardrobe against just such an eventuality.

Jenny fetched them, feeling oddly grown up and terribly vulnerable both at the same time. Somehow the feeling related to the way she'd felt when she'd looked at Heather

84

and Steven and the baby; for many years they were inextricably linked in Jenny's subconscious.

'It must be really funny to have a baby.'

David shifted slightly, squinting down at his girlfriend, Linda Parfitt, who was sitting beside him on the sofa in her parents' front room with her head on his shoulder.

'What?'

'Well – not really *funny*. Scary.'

David ignored this. The fact that he had become an uncle had left him totally underwhelmed; he was much more interested in snogging Linda. He had been seeing her for more than three months now, something of a record for him, and so far he had not experienced any of the usual warning signs that he was getting tired of her. This worried him slightly. Three months was getting serious and David had no intention of getting serious about anyone for a good while yet. He'd lost two precious years of his youth to National Service and he had a lot of catching up to do before he was ready to settle down. But he did like Linda a lot, even if she did annoy him sometimes by trying to have these deep and meaningful conversations when all he wanted to do was kiss and cuddle her – and more, if she gave him the chance.

Sometimes the chance came when they were alone in her parents' front room, where they spent a lot of their time. Although it was only a small terraced house it had a front room with a comfortable sofa – and a wind-up gramophone in a tall wooden cabinet with a good selection of records in the storage space. If Jim and Doreen, Linda's father and mother, were at home, David and Linda used the gramophone as an excuse for some privacy and since he had been going out with Linda, David had contributed quite a few records to her collection – they had no gramophone at home.

Tonight they were alone in the house. Jim was a prime mover in the social club at the nearby printing works where he was a foreman and most weekends he and Doreen went there for the evening. But David and Linda had had a record session anyway until they grew tired of having to get up every two or three minutes to change the record or put it on again if it was a particular favourite, and now they were listening to the radio.

'Fancy you being an uncle!' Linda said, teasing. 'Uncle David. Fancy!'

'Yes – fancy.' He slipped his hand under her jumper; she removed it.

'It was very quick though, wasn't it?' she said.

'What do you mean?'

'Well, for a first baby. Usually with a first it goes on for hours – my cousin Jane was in labour for two whole days! But your Heather fitted it in between dinner and teatime.'

'*I* don't know,' David said.

'You do know! You told me!'

'Did I?' David was getting uncomfortable with this conversation. 'Shall we have some more records? This programme's a bit boring.'

'It's all right!' She wasn't listening to it anyway and she knew he wasn't either. 'Leave it.' She paused, musing. 'Yes, very quick for a first baby. *I* wouldn't mind having a baby if I thought it was going to be as quick as that.'

She said it teasingly; he knew, with his conscious mind that it was a prelude, an invitation to play the usual games, when he tried it on and she rebuffed him, the 'so far and no further' and: 'David! Behave yourself! What do you think I am? I'm not that sort of girl!' The games were pleasant, if frustrating, and he lived in hopes that one day he might be able to breech her defences.

Tonight, however, he only heard warning bells coming from all directions. For one thing he was very afraid he might have said too much, all unwittingly, about Heather. And for another, he didn't care for the way Linda had said, 'I wouldn't mind a baby'. It reminded him of the downside of getting his wicked way – thinking of friends, more than one, who had fallen into the tender trap and found themselves on the way to the altar with a shotgun at their back. One day he'd settle down to being a husband and father and the way he felt about her at the moment, it might even be with Linda. But not yet. Not for a long time yet.

'I'm hungry,' he said suddenly. 'Let's go out and get some fish and chips.'

'Da-vid!'

But she went with him anyway, and for that evening at least talk about babies – Heather's, or anyone else's, for that matter – was forgotten.

Something of a kerfuffle was going on in Alder Road, and Billy Edgell was at the centre of it.

When she had finally returned after making sure Heather was comfortable and set up for the night, Carrie had found him creeping about in her back garden.

'What do you think you're doing?' she demanded.

'Lookin' for me ball, that's all.'

'In the dark? I wasn't born yesterday, Billy Edgell.'

'Honest!'

'And how did the ball get in my back garden, I'd like to know?' The back garden of Number 27 was accessible only from the gardens of the neighbouring houses or through the covered passageway between the kitchen door and the outhouses and it was enclosed at the far end by a fence which marked a steep drop to what had once been a quarry but now housed a rank of cottages.

'I've been playing with the Clarks next door to you.'

'You never have, Billy Edgell. Ivy Clark would never have you in her garden. Not a ragamuffin like you. We'll go and ask her, shall we?'

She went to grab his collar and he dodged away. 'Went past me like greased lightning,' she told Joe later. 'Up the path and through our side passage before you could say Jack Robinson!' Carrie shouted after him but by the time she reached the front of the house Billy was nowhere to be seen.

Ten minutes later, however, when she had put the kettle on to make herself a much-needed cup of tea and gone upstairs to change out of the overall she had been wearing all day and which now felt sticky and uncomfortable, she saw him again. As she went to pull the bedroom curtains before putting the light on she spotted him standing on the pavement immediately beyond her low

87

boundary wall and in the orange glow of the street lights there was no doubt whatever as to what he was doing.

Outraged, Carrie threw open the bedroom window.

'Billy Edgell! How dare you wee in my garden!'

He looked up, clearly shaken at having been caught in the act, but still cheeky, still defiant.

'I'm coming over to have a word with your mother about you!' She slammed the window shut and pulled the curtains. All thoughts of changing forgotten, she stamped downstairs and pulled on her coat.

Closing the front door behind her, she set off across the Green, her boots squelching in the wet grass. Lights were blazing from every window of the Edgell house – how in the world they paid their electricity bills, Carrie couldn't imagine. She strode up the path and rapped loudly on the door.

It was opened by one of the Edgell tribe – Marilyn – at thirteen, small and skinny with hair that flopped untidily round her shoulders.

'Is your mother in?' Carrie demanded.

'Mum!' Marilyn hollered without moving from the doorway.

After a minute or so Joyce appeared, a cigarette dangling from her mouth and wearing a shrunken-looking cardigan and shabby slippers. If George Parsons could see you now! Carrie thought in disgust.

'Oh – it's you!' Joyce said rudely.

Relations between the two women had never recovered; if Carrie could have given up her job and still been able to afford to pay the bills she would have done so rather than continue working with her. But she couldn't afford to and couldn't see why she should be the one to suffer.

'I've come about your Billy,' she said. 'He was round my back when I came home just now – up to no good, I expect. And now I've just seen him relieving himself over my front garden wall.'

Joyce glared at her.

'What are you on about?'

'I don't think I could make it much clearer. He was using my garden for a public convenience.'

88

'Our Billy wouldn't do that!'

'Well, I'm sorry, but he did. He didn't know I was at the window – I didn't have the light on – and I caught him nicely. You want to bring your children up to know how to behave themselves, Joyce.'

'And you want to mind your own business.'

'When your Billy relieves himself in my garden it is my business!' Carrie returned tartly. 'You'll have a word with him if you know what's good for you.'

'What's that supposed to mean?'

'It means I shall have the bobbies on him if he does it again,' Carrie returned tartly. 'You'll have a word with him if you know what's good for you.'

'What's that supposed to mean?'

'It means I shall have the bobbies on him if he does it again,' Carrie said. 'Indecent behaviour, that's what it is.'

'Oh, get bloody lost!' Joyce snarled, prodding Carrie in the chest. 'Go on – get off my bloody doorstep, or I'll call the bloody police myself.'

'Don't you threaten me, Joyce! And don't you touch me neither!' But Carrie had retreated a step or two. Angry as she was, her sense of propriety was still strong – getting into a brawl in public just showed you up for what you were – common. And no-one was going to think *her* common if she could help it!

She had been home for about half an hour when she heard the tinkle of breaking glass, and on investigation, discovered someone had put a stone through the glass porthole window in the outside lavatory. There was no sign of anyone outside, but it didn't take much to work out who was responsible, or who had put him up to it, Carrie thought, fuming with helpless anger.

Battle lines had been drawn between her and Joyce. And things could only get worse.

BOOK TWO

1955–1956

Chapter Five

Helen Hall drove her Morris Minor along the narrow lane
that swept through the valley parallel to the river, past the
mill pond where her aunt Grace had once tried to drown
herself, past the farmland and the yard that housed the
headquarters of the Roberts Transport business, turning
up a steep little hill that branched off opposite Ralph
Porter's timber yard and into the drive of Valley View
House.

She got out of the car and stood for a moment looking
back down the valley. Hillsbridge. Her family's home for
generations. Now to be her home too.

A small thrill tickled at her, the thrill of knowing that at
last – at last! – she had achieved her lifelong ambition to
work as a general medical practitioner, and also a warmth
that felt oddly like nostalgia satisfied. It couldn't be
nostalgia, of course. She had been born and brought up in
Minehead, where her father Jack was headmaster at the
local school, and she only knew Hillsbridge from the
briefest visits – a few days at Christmas or Easter, a week
during the summer holidays when she had stayed either
with Charlotte and James Hall, Jack's parents, in their
terraced home, or with her grandmother and grandfather
on her mother's side, in the vast house that had gone with
Grandfather O'Halloran's job as General Manager for the
Spindler family who had owned the collieries before
nationalisation. The two ends of the social spectrum and
she knew them both intimately, and loved them equally,
though truth to tell she had always had a special place in
her heart for courageous, warm-hearted Charlotte and the
house in Greenslade Terrace where her father had grown
up. Perhaps it was because there she was able to
experience so many things that were completely alien to

her middle-class upbringing, Helen sometimes thought. It had been a novelty to look at the *Jane* cartoon strip in the *Daily Mirror* – at home they took the *Telegraph* – and she had been totally fascinated by the *News of the World*, which she seldom got a chance to look at because it was stuffed under a cushion out of sight whenever she was around. But deep down she knew it was the earthy honesty that drew her like a magnet. The same earthy honesty which ran in her own veins. No wonder she felt so at home, here in the shadow of the black batches.

The O'Hallorans had gone now, and the big house was empty and falling into disrepair. Hal and his wife were both dead, as was Grandpa Hall, and Charlotte had moved out of the house in Greenslade Terrace to live with her eldest daughter Dolly and her husband Victor when her health – and her legs – had begun to fail her. It saddened Helen to think that if only she had been a little older and the opportunity of a position here had arisen a few years earlier she could have moved in with Charlotte and saved her from having to leave the house she had lived in all her married life. But there it was, it hadn't been meant to be, and at least she would be able to visit often and build on the bond that she felt drew her and Charlotte together.

Charlotte had been the first of the family to hear Helen's news. Helen had driven out from Bristol, where she worked as a houseman at the city hospital for her interview with Dr Hobbs, senior partner in the Hillsbridge practice now that Dr Vezey had finally retired. The practice needed an assistant to take his place and as soon as she had left Dr Hobbs' house with his offer of the job ringing in her ears and her fingers half numb from his enthusiastic handshake to seal the agreement, she had called to see Charlotte and share her excitement.

'This is a surprise and no mistake!' Charlotte said, beaming, when Dolly took Helen into the front room where Charlotte had been having an afternoon nap on the sofa. 'Fancy you coming all the way from Bristol to see me!'

'You know I always love to see you, Gran.' Helen put a box of Terry's All Gold chocolates down on to the arm of Charlotte's chair. 'But I have to admit you're not the only reason I'm in Hillsbridge this time!'

'Oh?' Charlotte might be older, perhaps she couldn't see as well as she'd used to be able to, but there was no mistaking the flush of excitement on Helen's fair skin. 'A young man, is it?'

Helen laughed. 'No. It's a job. I didn't mention anything about it before in case I didn't get it. It seemed like tempting fate.'

'A job?' Charlotte frowned, her almost unlined face creasing into small furrows across the bridge of her nose. 'But I thought . . .'

Helen told her all about it, and Charlotte listened intently, shaking her head from time to time and looking at Helen wonderingly.

'Well I never! You a doctor!'

'I've been a doctor for a long time now, Gran,' Helen said, smiling.

'I know that! But a doctor *here*, in Hillsbridge!'

It was the most respectable job Charlotte could imagine – everyone still stood in awe of the doctor, who held the strings of life and death in his hands and was treated as a god. And as for a *lady* doctor . . . the very thought made her swell with pride.

'You'll be buying a house here then, I suppose,' Charlotte said, easing her swollen ankles into a more comfortable position.

'Eventually. When I find my feet and get some money saved up. I'm hoping that I might be able to stay with Auntie Amy and Uncle Ralph for the moment,' Helen said.

'Well, they've certainly got bags of room. Have you asked yet?'

'No. I wanted you to be the first to know.' Helen had hugged her grandmother. 'I'm going to see them now, see what they say. I expect I'll find Amy at the yard, won't I?'

'I expect so,' Charlotte said tartly. 'She's never anywhere else. I don't know why she goes on working. There's no need. She and Ralph aren't short of a penny or two.'

'She works because she enjoys it, Gran,' Helen said. 'I can't say I'd want to give up and sit at home at her age.'

'Hmm!' Charlotte snorted, a snort which in a way signified her agreement. Nobody sat around at home from choice, especially when they'd always kept busy – especially when they didn't have their own home to sit around in.

'Oh, Gran!' Helen said, reading her mind. 'I'm sorry . . .'

'Old age doesn't come on its own, that's the trouble,' Charlotte said ruefully. 'You make the most of your youth whilst you've still got it, Helen.'

'I intend to.'

'Well, we shall be seeing a bit more of you soon then,' Charlotte said. 'You don't know what a treat that will be.'

'For me too. I mustn't stay too long today, though. Not if I'm to see Auntie Amy and still get back to Bristol tonight.'

'That's all right, my love. But you can tell our Amy from me I wouldn't mind seeing *her* when she can spare the time.'

Helen didn't. She didn't want to upset Amy – she knew sparks often flew between mother and daughter – and hopefully there would be other opportunities to put it more tactfully when she was staying with Amy – *if* she was staying with Amy.

As she had expected, however, Amy was only too delighted.

'Of course you can stay with us – as long as you like,' she had said at once. 'Ralph and I rattle around in that great house like two peas in a colander.'

'That's super of you, Amy,' Helen said. 'I'll pay my way, of course.'

'You'll do nothing of the sort! You'll need every penny you earn if you're going to buy into the practice and think about getting a home of your own.'

'Well, we'll see about that,' Helen said. 'I'd never have asked if I'd thought you wouldn't let me contribute something.'

'It's a bad job if I can't help my niece out,' Amy replied tartly and Ralph, who had been listening from the sidelines intervened.

'We can sort out all that later. But rest assured, we shall be very happy to have you, Helen.'

Helen found herself remembering the conversation now as she stood outside Valley View House, looking back towards Hillsbridge. She hoped Amy wasn't going to prove stubborn on the point. It would be embarrassing to feel she was taking advantage of their hospitality, although it was perfectly true that she was hardly flush with money. The long training had meant she had reached her middle twenties without a penny to her name, and the hospital post in Bristol, where she had worked since qualifying, had not been well-enough paid for her to be able to put anything by.

At least the advent of the National Health Service had widened her horizons. The days when a doctor had had to practise where there was a living to be made and find a large sum of money to buy into an established firm whilst paying off a sizeable loan from the Education Authority at the same time were thankfully over and Helen felt the change had come at just the right time for her. It was almost as if she had been born as a doctor along with it.

For as long as she could remember, Helen had wanted to do nothing else. As a little girl at home in Minehead she had spent many happy hours lining up her dolls on the sofa to wait their turn for an operation – conducted on the dining-room table under an old cot sheet, or to have arms and legs bandaged or fixed with a pipe cleaner splint. During her growing-up years she had read every medical fiction she could get her hands on – whilst her sisters enthused over *Ballet Shoes* and *Jane Leaves The Wells* – Sadlers Wells, of course – she had been buried in the Sue Barton books and, later, *The Citadel* and *Dr Finlay's Casebook*.

She had specialised in sciences and gone on to read organic chemistry, physics and botany at university, sharing most of the course subjects with the engineering students. Then it was medical school for three years – one of only five women in a year's intake of thirty – after which she had emerged fully qualified to be let loose on an unsuspecting world, as Jack, her father, had proudly put it.

97

And he wasn't so far out, Helen sometimes thought. Though for the first six months in her hospital post the senior medical staff had been there to keep an eye on her, nominally at least, the pressures had been such that she had been expected to do anything and everything from casualty to anaesthetics, from delivering babies to performing operations. 'The Appendicitis Queen' they had called her, so many angry appendixes had she whipped out. It had been a baptism of fire. She had worked twenty-four-hour duties, snatching an hour's sleep when she could. There had been no antibiotics to speak of – though M & Bs had become available towards the end of the war, the new wonder drug penicillin was extremely scarce and was to be used only in very special cases, usually serving soldiers or pilots. And all this for the princely sum of ten shillings a week for which she knew she must be grateful – housemen in London were not paid at all for the first six months, their board and lodging their only reward.

Five years she had worked at the city hospital, two years longer than she had intended. Her carefully mapped out career plan – three years university, three years medical school, three years hospital experience and then a move to general practice had gone awry for reasons she had never explained to her parents, Jack and Grace, when they teased her about it, and even pointed her in the direction of vacancies for assistants that arose from time to time in the villages of South Somerset.

'There's a lovely little post going over in Dulverton,' Grace had said to her once. 'I'm sure you'd stand a good chance of it, being a local girl.'

But Helen had fobbed her off. She was going to stay in Bristol for a while longer. For the time being she was happy there, she told her mother. The real reason she kept to herself.

Now, however, she had finally decided the time had come to make a move. And Hillsbridge was ideal. An area she knew and loved, but not quite the backward step she felt going home would be. Far enough from Bristol to put some distance between her and Guy, close enough to have some contact with him if circumstances altered.

But circumstances weren't going to alter, Helen thought, and tried to close her mind to the regrets that nagged like an aching tooth. Only she could change the pattern of her life and the best way she could do that was to make a clean break, return to her original career plan and look for a position in general practice. The Hillsbridge vacancy had come up at just the right moment – almost as if it had been meant to be. A fresh start.

As she stood on Amy and Ralph's drive looking across the valley that had given the house its name, Helen's heart lifted again. A fresh start. In every sense of the phrase, that was what she intended it to be.

Next morning Helen drove over to the big house on South Hill where Dr Hobbs lived and from which he ran his practice. Though she was not due to start work until the following week, she was anxious to begin familiarising herself with her new surroundings and moving in the bits and pieces she had brought with her.

She parked her Morris Minor on the gravel turnaround at the top of the steep drive and went round to the side door Dr Hobbs had shown her when she had come for her interview. The passageway beyond it had been converted into a waiting room and Helen was surprised to see that it was already quite full. Surgery didn't begin until nine, and as yet it was barely a quarter to. Presumably these people had all come early with a view to being first in the queue and someone had taken pity on them waiting outside in the chill October air and opened the door for them to come in.

Eight or ten pairs of eyes trained curiously on her and Helen felt a rosy glow of embarrassment.

'Good morning,' she said to no-one in particular.

In the moment's awkward silence as she picked her way between the two rows of chairs which faced one another across the passageway, her embarrassment grew. Then someone muttered: 'Morning,' and she turned her head gratefully to see a wizened little man with a red face and rheumy blue eyes, wearing a tweed sports coat and muffler. She smiled briefly but there was no answering smile, just those rheumy eyes appraising her, summing her up. She turned away again, disconcerted, and hurried to the end of the corridor as fast as she safely could without tripping over feet or shopping bags.

The two consulting rooms were at the end of the corridor, the small one, which was to be hers, to the left, and the larger one where Dr Hobbs received his patients, straight ahead. Dr Hobbs had shown her the room when she had attended for her interview; at the time it had still been the domain of Dr Stephens, and cluttered to the ceiling with his things. Presumably he would have moved them by now to the new surgery in Tiledown.

Until his retirement Dr Vezey had run the Tiledown surgery in tandem with the Hillsbridge one, seeing patients in a room in his house there four mornings a week. But with his departure, changes had been made. The practice had taken the lease on a former small shop and converted it into a surgery for which Dr Stephens was to be responsible, leaving the vacancy for an assistant at the Hillsbridge end. The Tiledown surgery would in future be open for five mornings instead of four, with an hour on Saturdays for emergency cases. At her interview, Dr Hobbs had explained the new set-up and the thinking behind it – with a sprawling new estate of council houses going up in Tiledown, there was plenty of opportunity for expanding the practice and Dr Stephens was just the man to do it.

Helen was less sure on that score. Dr Vezey had been popular with the villagers, a bluff doctor of the old school and very much a local man who could converse with patients in their own language. His accent was unmistakably local and when he talked to the old miners and their families it thickened into a dialect that was practically unintelligible to anyone not born in the valley.

Paul Stephens, on the other hand, was a Tynesider, quite young and, from what she had seen of him, dour and uncommunicative. Throughout their introductory meeting he had said scarcely two words and she had wondered anxiously if he had his reservations about taking her on. It might be, of course, that he was silent by nature, but if she had found his manner slightly off-putting, then so might his patients. Almost certainly he wouldn't be the sort to suffer fools – or malingerers – gladly.

That wasn't her problem, though. Along with Reuben Hobbs, Paul Stephens was a partner, and as such, her employer. He and Dr Hobbs would make the decisions as to the way the practice was run and all she had to do was go along with them. At least Paul Stephens hadn't vetoed Reuben Hobbs' decision to take her on, which, given the continuing discrimination against women as medical practitioners, coupled with a north-countryman's inbred attitude to women in general, he might well have done!

The door to Dr Hobbs' room was ajar; Helen knocked on it and looked in.

'Good morning.'

'Helen! I wasn't expecting to see you!' He looked up from sorting the post, a dapper man in his middle fifties with a neat pepper-and-salt beard and a pair of gold-rimmed half-moon glasses perched on the end of his nose.

'I'm in Hillsbridge now, so I thought I could at least begin sorting myself out.' Helen still felt vaguely uncomfortable, an intruder in this brand-new world.

'Good idea. I can't spare any time myself at the moment. Why don't you go through and have a cup of coffee with Brenda?'

'Oh no – I don't want to make a nuisance of myself.' Brenda was Reuben Hobbs' wife, and from what Helen could make out, a very busy lady, not only serving on every imaginable committee but also a magistrate on the local bench. 'If I could just get my surgery in some sort of order, at least I'd feel I'd made a bit of headway.'

He looked faintly surprised. 'Well, yes, by all means. You know where it is, don't you?'

She nodded, feeling more like a fish out of water with every passing second and he looked at her over the top of his spectacles.

'Sorry not to be able to spend more time with you, but I've got a busy day ahead. It'll be good to have you on board, I can tell you. Since Paul's taken over Purldown I've been rushed off m'feet.'

'I could help out if you like.' Helen offered tentatively.

'No – no. You're not due in harness 'til next week.' *On board – in harness –* Reuben was obviously a man who mixed his metaphors! 'We'll break you in soon enough.'

'But if you're having to cope with Paul's patients as well as your own.'

'It's all right. I've coped before and I'll cope again. There's life in the old dog yet!' There was something a little smug in the way he said it and for the first time it occurred to Helen to wonder if Reuben Hobbs might be just a little too fond of himself.

'Right – I'll be in my room if you need me.'

She left him and went next door to what had been Paul Stephens' surgery.

It was a small room, perhaps only half the size of the surgery she had just left, and uncompromisingly drab. A typical man's room, Helen decided, with its coarse brown hessian carpet and mustard-coloured walls. Like the carpet, the paintwork was also brown, and the windows were hung with a heavy, striped brocade in a shade of gold which clashed oddly with the mustard walls. The desk was huge and heavy, stained with ink and decorated with white circles where coffee cups had stood year after year, the circles overlapping and entwining to make a haphazard pattern; the small sink, spotlessly clean but streaked beneath the taps with greenish rivulets; above it, a brown-painted cupboard clung to the wall. A tall metal filing cabinet blocked out a good deal of light; Helen decided it would have to be moved. She had a thing about light; dimness depressed her, inhibited her thought patterns. There must be a better place for it, surely!

For half an hour she pushed and pulled the pieces of furniture around the little room looking for the optimum solution. At last she was satisfied with the result; her desk at right angles to the window to catch the light whilst also allowing her a view across a corner of lawn to a lilac tree which hopefully would erupt into bloom next spring, the patients' chair to one side so that she could swivel to talk to them without the vast expanse of desk between, and the offending filing cabinet tucked into a corner. She peeked

102

out of the door; the hallway was still full of patients. She could hardly weave her way between them to her car and back again laden with her own bits and pieces. Instead she decided to take a look through the files of patients' records and familiarise herself with the names of at least some of those she would be treating.

The medical records were stored in sturdy brown manilla envelopes, covered with an almost illegible scribble of dates and headings and stuffed with wads of notes. Some of the names leaped out at her as familiar and characteristically local – Latcham, Clements, Brixey, Button – others were strange, exotic even – Polish, she thought. She had heard there had been an influx of Poles into the coal mines when the war had ended; here was proof of it. She pulled one out at random – Okonski, H J – and was surprised to find it belonged not to a miner but a woman who had previously been called Heather Jean Simmons. Well, of course, it was only to be expected that some of these men would marry local girls.

She dipped into the records – quite thin by most standards. Heather Okonski was obviously one of the healthier of her new patients. Heather had given birth to a child in February of the previous year, but before that there were no records of any visits, apart from a bout of bronchitis and some treatment for a verruca. And nothing whatever about her childhood, nothing earlier than 1943, when she had apparently been treated for anaemia with doses of iron. Strange. Her curiosity aroused, Helen looked to see if any other members of the Simmons family were registered with her. They were. Gladys and Walter, Caroline and Joseph, David and Jennifer – obviously three generations of the same family. But there was a clue there; Caroline, Joseph, David and Jennifer had a previous address in Bristol – they had moved to Hillsbridge in the war, to escape the bombing, in all likelihood. And the chances were that Heather's records had been lost in the move, maybe even destroyed by one of the bombing raids. Oh well, it scarcely seemed to matter, since Heather did not appear to suffer much from anything in particular.

For another half-hour or so Helen browsed through the

files. Twice Dr Hobbs popped in to take a pack of notes, not stopping to explain who the patients were or why he was seeing them, and Helen felt vaguely affronted. He might at least have asked her to sit in! The third time it happened she suggested it and after a moment's perplexed hesitation, Reuben Hobbs agreed.

Helen followed him into his consulting room – so large and sunny by comparison with her own. An elderly woman, rather overweight, wearing a tweed coat and headscarf, was sitting in the patients' chair, which was stacked around with shopping.

'Mrs Uphill, may I introduce Dr Hall?' Dr Hobbs smiled at her graciously. 'Dr Hall will be working with us from next Monday, replacing Dr Stephens here in Hillsbridge. She'll be looking after you in future – with your permission, of course.'

'Oh!' Mrs Uphill's expression was both startled and suspicious.

'So perhaps you wouldn't mind if she sat in on our consultation today?'

'No – no . . .' Mrs Uphill sounded thoroughly disconcerted.

'So – what can we do for you?'

'It's me bunions, Doctor. They're giving me gyp.'

'Let's have a look, shall we?'

Mrs Uphill somehow managed to remove her stockings without exposing so much as an inch of bare flesh above the knee and stretched out her feet for inspection. Her toes were swollen and deformed, the big toes almost at right angles to her feet.

'This is going to mean an operation,' Dr Hobbs told her.

She looked at him in horror.

'An operation? You mean go into hospital?'

'It's the only thing that will give you any lasting relief.'

'Oh – I don't want to go into hospital! I hate the places . . .'

'Worth it, though, surely, if you can walk about without being in pain? I'll get a letter off today, see when they can fit you in.'

'If you think it's really necessary, Doctor.'

'I do.'

'There's one other thing, Doctor.' She glanced furtively at Helen, looked away again quickly. 'What you said about me having to change doctors. If Dr Stephens isn't going to be here any more, I'd rather come on your list.'

For a moment Helen was too stunned to feel the pain of rejection.

'I thought you said I could choose,' Mrs Uphill said, a little belligerently.

'Well, yes – but . . .'

'Then I'd rather come with you, Doctor. And I'm sure my Frank would say the same. If it's all the same with you. I mean, you can't be too careful when it's your health you're talking about.' She glanced at Helen again, and all her doubts were there in her face. A new doctor. A young doctor. A young *woman* doctor.

'My list is very full, Mrs Uphill,' Dr Hobbs said warningly. 'And Dr Hall is very experienced, up to date with all the latest developments.'

'Just the same, Doctor. If it's all the same with you.'

'I'm sorry, Helen,' Reuben Hobbs said as Mrs Uphill left the surgery. 'I did my best.'

'Yes, of course. It's understandable, I suppose.' But she didn't understand. She felt inordinately hurt. In the hospital no-one had given a second thought to her age or sex. They'd simply been grateful that someone was there, treating them.

'I only hope the rest of Paul's patients don't feel the same way or there won't be a great deal of point having you here!' Reuben Hobbs gave a small tired shake of his head. 'People round here can be so old-fashioned in their thinking.'

'I hope so too!' Helen said emphatically. But as she returned to her new surgery she felt totally crushed. Supposing no-one was prepared to give her a chance? What then?

She flicked through a few more files but her heart was no longer in it. She sat down in the swivel chair, swinging it from side to side, then standing purposefully. Patients waiting in the hall or not, she was going to bring in some of her things. They'd have to get used to the idea she was a part of the practice sooner or later – it might as well be sooner.

Her hand was practically on the door knob when it opened. Take by surprise she took a step backwards and collided with the newly arranged patients' chair.

'Oh, sorry – I didn't know there was anyone here!'

Paul Stephens. He came into the surgery, a tall, well-built man in his middle thirties with hair that was already receding at the temples and a square-jawed face. His eyes flipped past her, taking in the changes she had made to the surgery and frowning slightly.

'What in the world . . .?'

'I moved things around,' Helen said.

'I can see that. What for?' He looked genuinely puzzled; Helen, already feeling hurt and vulnerable, bristled.

'I thought it was an improvement.'

'Hmm.' He didn't say what he was obviously thinking – that there had been nothing wrong with the layout of the surgery before – but his disapproval communicated itself to her anyway.

'I have to do things my way,' she said defensively. 'After all, I'm the one who's going to be working here.'

'Yes, but not until next week.'

'I'm sorry,' she said sharply. 'Have I inconvenienced you?'

'Actually – yes. I only had a few patients at Tiledown this morning and I've come back to help Reuben out with the surgery here. From the crowds still out there, it looks as if he could do with some assistance.'

Her face flamed.

'I did offer to help out myself, but he said he could manage.'

He ignored this and she realised what he was waiting for her to say that she would make herself scarce and leave the consulting room to him. She felt mutinous suddenly, as well as rejected by all and sundry before she had even begun, but she was painfully aware she didn't actually have a leg to stand on. She wasn't supposed to be starting work until next week, but it seemed ridiculous to be so pedantic about it. She'd arrived full of enthusiasm – her only fault as far as she could see – and they seemed not to want her there. Could it be that they had heard similar reactions to her appointment as the one she had witnessed from Mrs Uphill earlier on, and were beginning to regret choosing her to fill the vacancy? In that moment it seemed to Helen to be the only possible explanation.

'I take it you'd like me to go,' she said.

His face changed; he was clearly taken aback.

'Look – I didn't mean . . .'

'Don't worry about it.' Her tone was still brittle. 'I can always come back later. Or leave it until next week.'

'If I could just have the use of my surgery for half an hour.'

'Of course.' She felt hurt and oddly disappointed. In the big impersonal hospital she had so looked forward to having her own surgery. Now here was Paul Stephens still referring to it as his, and obviously resentful about the changes she had made. 'So long as you don't mind using it the way it is,' she added wickedly.

'Helen . . .'

Some sort of disturbance in the passage outside, followed by a knock at the half-open door interrupted him. He turned and opened the door wide. A gangling youth wearing a butcher's apron stood there, red-faced, out of breath and agitated.

'Clive?' Paul said. 'What's wrong?'

'There's been an accident down the street. Can you come, Doctor?'

'What sort of accident?'

'A woman's got knocked down. She's in the road by our shop. Mr Evans told me to come for you.'

'I'll go,' Helen said.

'Helen . . .'

'Let me, please. My bag's in the car.'

'But . . .'

'I am a doctor too,' she said with asperity. 'And I've spent the last five years doing my share of A & E. What's more, I'll be out from under your feet.'

'Well – if you insist . . .'

'I do.'

She pushed past him. The people still waiting in the corridor moved their feet for her to go through, gazing in open curiosity, excited by this unexpected diversion, getting ready to speculate as to what had happened and who had been hurt the moment the door closed after her.

Helen collected her medical bag from the car, already wondering about the wisdom of her hasty decision. It was possible she might have upset Paul Stephens by taking it out of his hands, but she'd had just about enough today of being treated like a raw student straight out of medical school and if she didn't start as she meant to go on, it might very well continue that way.

She went down the hill, Clive the butcher's boy hurrying along beside her. A group of people had gathered on the pavement outside the shop where he worked, and to her surprise she saw one of the green baize-covered wagons that delivered parcels from the railway station pulled up in the road, the great horse that drew it standing patiently between the shafts. For all her casualty experience, Helen's heart came into her mouth. If the woman had gone under the wheels of the wagon or been trampled by the horse, it could be very nasty indeed.

She crossed the street towards the small crowd.

'Could you all move back please? I'm a GP.' They moved respectfully, but not so far as to spoil their view of the drama. 'Please! Let's give her some air.'

She went down on her haunches beside the woman – thin, elderly, sprawled awkwardly with her skirt rucked up to reveal long-legged Directoire knickers. Gently Helen pulled her skirt down enough to preserve the woman's dignity.

'Hello. Can you tell me your name?'

'It's Maud Perkins,' one of the onlookers volunteered. 'She was just crossing the road and a boy on a bike went straight into her!'

For the first time Helen noticed a lad standing a little apart, looking worried and holding a bloodstained handkerchief over his knee. So it hadn't been anything to do with the delivery wagon. And there was no sign of any obvious injury either.

108

'Can you tell me where you think you're hurt, Mrs Perkins?' she said to the woman.

'My shoulder . . . my arm . . . oh!' She winced and cried out as Helen investigated.

'Your back doesn't hurt too much? Can you move your legs?'

Mrs Perkins did so. Helen investigated further.

'I don't think you've done any serious damage, Mrs Perkins. But your shoulder is dislocated. I'm going to try and put it back in for you. It'll be very painful, but only for a moment. Hold tight now.'

'Come on – stand aside!' The voice was authoritarian, bullying almost. Still holding Mrs Perkins' wrist Helen looked up, startled, to see a heavily built man towering over her. 'Stand aside!' he ordered again. 'I'll deal with this.'

Helen frowned. 'I beg your pardon?'

'Out of the way, Miss, please. Leave the lady to me.'

'Who are you?' Helen asked, annoyed by his overbearing attitude and the way he appeared to be on the point of physically manhandling her out of the way.

'I'm a trained first aider, that's who.'

'Really?' Helen said coldly. 'Well, I'm a doctor and I'd be very grateful if you would let me get on with treating my patient.' She turned back to Mrs Perkins, completely missing his flabbergasted reaction. 'OK – let's get this shoulder back in.'

As the shoulder blade snapped back into place, Mrs Perkins screamed.

'What do you think you're doing?' The man's voice was at a fever pitch of outrage now. Helen ignored him.

'I'd like to take you over to the Cottage Hospital for a few X-rays, just to make quite sure there isn't any other damage,' she said to the woman who, although still white and shaken, was obviously now more comfortable. 'My car is up at the surgery. If someone could give you a seat while you're waiting, I'll fetch it.'

'She can sit down in my shop.' That was Percy Evans, the butcher.

'Fine.' Helen helped Mrs Perkins to her feet, and Percy armed her inside the shop.

'You shouldn't have done that!' The first aider was following Helen along the pavement, belligerent once again. 'She shouldn't have been moved!'

Helen stopped and turned to face him.

'You are Mr . . .?'

'Gilson. *Superintendent* Gilson, actually. Of the local St John's Ambulance Brigade. And we advocate . . .'

'I'm sure you do an excellent job, Mr Gilson, but I'd be grateful if you would take account of the fact that as a GP with five years' experience, I am probably better qualified than you. Now, if you want something to do I suggest you have a go at that boy's knee and elbow.' She indicated the lad who had crashed into Mrs Perkins. 'It looks as if he's grazed them quite badly.'

Leaving him almost apoplectic with rage and humiliation she hurried back up the hill.

The queue in the waiting room had reduced to a handful and Paul Stephens was in the doorway of their shared surgery on his way to call the next patient.

'Can I have a quick word?'

'Yes, surely.'

She went in, closing the door behind her, and explained to Paul what had happened and what she proposed doing.

'Is Mrs Perkins one of our patients?' she asked when she finished.

'She is, yes. One of the "heartsinks", I have to say. You know – the ones who make your heart sink when they appear round the surgery door? But you've clocked up some brownie points today, no doubt – especially by taking her to hospital in your own car. If there's one thing Maud Perkins likes, it's having a fuss made of her.'

'She had that all right!' Helen smiled grimly. 'A man who said he's the superintendent of the local St John's practically had a tug o' war with me over her.'

'Albert Gilson. Thinks he's God Almighty. You have to handle him with great care, though. The St John's can be very useful.'

'I didn't do that, I'm afraid. Tact isn't my strong point in that sort of situation.'

'Don't say you upset him!'

110

''Fraid so.' Although the memory of his belligerence could still make her blood boil she was beginning to regret the way she'd spoken to him. 'Anyway, I'd better get back down to Mrs Perkins. Having her sitting in the shop looking like the knell of doom is probably putting off all the butcher's other customers.'

'Nonsense. I expect he's doing a roaring trade with everybody going in to find out what they can about what's happened, if I know anything about Hillsbridge!'

Helen smiled. 'You're probably right – human nature being what it is.'

Perhaps, she thought, Paul Stephens wasn't so bad after all.

'So – how did your first day go?' Amy asked.

They were having dinner – an excellent meal of lamb chops and onion sauce prepared by Mrs Milsom, Ralph and Amy's housekeeper. Mrs Milsom was quite old now, and should have retired long ago, but she maintained retirement would be the death of her and certainly Valley View House would not have been the same without her.

'It was swings and roundabouts, really,' Helen said. 'I managed to upset one of the big cheeses of the local St John's.'

'Oh him!' Amy interrupted. 'You don't want to take any notice of *him*!'

'But I think I won over one of the ladies on my list – a Mrs Perkins from Butter Buildings. With any luck she won't be one of those asking to transfer to Dr Hobbs.'

Amy frowned.

'Why should anyone want to do that?'

'Search me. They think I'm too young and inexperienced, I suppose. And a woman to boot.'

'Surely that's an advantage?' Amy said. 'There must be loads of women who would rather see a lady doctor when it comes to . . . well . . . female problems. I know I would.'

'*You*, Amy?' Ralph threw her a mischievous glance as he helped himself to more runner beans. 'I thought you had a penchant for doctors of the young male variety.'

'For heaven's sake, Ralph!' Amy said sharply. 'I don't know what you're talking about.'

'Oliver Scott?' Ralph teased. 'Now don't try to tell me you didn't have a thing for Oliver Scott.'

'That was years and years ago,' Amy said impatiently. 'I'm older and wiser now. And if I had a personal problem I'd far rather take it to Helen than to some man.'

'I expect she'll be very popular with all the male patients too,' Ralph said. 'Particularly the older ones. They'll take the view that a pretty face will do far more for the good of their health than a bottle of AOT.'

'AOT?' Amy repeated, mystified. 'What's that?'

'Tell her, Helen,' Ralph said.

'What is it, Helen?'

'I think Ralph is referring to the name we give in the trade to a bottle of coloured water. AOT. Any old thing.'

'I'm shocked!' Amy said. But she was laughing.

The telephone began to ring.

'I'll get it,' Ralph said.

A few moments later he was back.

'For you, Helen.'

'Me? Who is it? Mum?'

'No. It's a man.'

Already halfway to the door, Helen froze, a torrent of conflicting emotions welling within her.

'Did he say . . .?'

'No. Just asked for you.'

'Are you all right, Helen?' Amy asked, looking anxious.

'Yes – of course.'

But she wasn't. Her heart was beating a tattoo, her stomach churning.

She went into the hall; picked up the phone.

'Hello?'

'Helen . . . it's me.'

The voice that could still churn her inside out with love, desire, despair.

'I had to talk to you, Helen.'

'I thought we'd agreed,' she said. Her voice was hard, hiding the tumult within. 'I thought we'd agreed, Guy. A clean break.'

112

'Helen . . .'

'No, Guy. There's no point going over it all again. I've stuck to my side of the bargain. You stick to yours.'

Without waiting for a reply, afraid that if she did she might yet weaken, Helen slammed the phone down and went back to join Amy and Ralph.

Chapter Six

'What on earth have you got on your face, my girl?' Carrie demanded.

'It's only a bit of lipstick,' Jenny said.

'It is not only a bit of lipstick. You've got blue muck on your eyelids as well. Don't try to tell me you haven't. I'm not blind, and I'm not stupid.'

'But Mum – all the others wear it.'

'That doesn't mean you have to follow like a sheep. And I thought I'd said before, you're not old enough to wear earrings, either. Where did you get them?'

'They're Rowena's. She lent them to me.'

'Well, you can just give them right back to her. Earrings! At your age! I never heard anything like it!'

'But Mum . . .'

'You're not going out looking like that, Jennifer. Either you wash that muck off your face and take off those earrings, or you can stay home.'

Jenny wanted to weep with frustration. She'd spent ages applying the eyeshadow and lipstick. It hadn't been as easy as she'd thought it would be and she'd had to wipe it off several times and try again before she was satisfied. She knew how Carrie was about make-up, calling it cheap and common, but she'd hoped she'd done it subtly enough so that Carrie wouldn't notice – or wouldn't mind if she did. But she'd reckoned without Carrie's eagle eye and strong views on the subject.

'Dad . . .' Jenny appealed, without much hope, to Joe, who was sitting in the easy chair reading the paper.

'You look very nice, m'dear.' He hadn't really been listening.

'It makes her look far too old,' Carrie said. 'I've had my say, Jenny. I've agreed to let you go to this youth club – so long as you behave yourself – but I'm not having you go like that. It's asking for trouble. Go and wash it off now, and we'll say no more about it.'

Argument was useless, Jenny knew. Miserably she went up to the bathroom, looking at herself one more time in the mirror. The make-up had worked such wonders! But then, almost imperceptively, nature had been working wonders too. The face that looked back at her was somehow, miraculously, no longer plain. The small even features which once had seemed bland and insignificant had matured, childish chubbiness had become rounded prettiness and the fringe she had grown had altered the shape of her face, drawing attention to her eyes – always her best feature – and the heart shape her jaw had become. Jenny, who had spent most of her life so far hating the way she looked, was almost in awe of the change, half afraid to take pride in it because she felt it was somehow fragile, ephemeral, a product of her wishful thinking which would disappear overnight, leaving her once again the old plain Jenny.

It wasn't only her face that had changed, either, but also her body. She was, it was true, still a little on the plump side, but as the curves had developed she had also grown taller without putting on weight so that the stodginess had become rounded womanliness. The changes had generated a dawning of confidence in her, still fragile, still easily shattered, but a major step forward nonetheless. The attitude of others towards her was different too, she was no longer the butt of their jokes, but looked upon with something close to admiration, and Jenny grew within its warmth, blossoming almost daily, gradually leaving her awkward old self behind like a butterfly emerging from a chrysalis.

Had she but known it, of course, it was this emergence which made her mother so hard on her. Carrie looked at Jenny, saw what was happening to her, and was afraid.

She looked up now as Jenny came back downstairs, peering closely at the newly scrubbed face for the slightest remaining trace of the forbidden make-up. It had gone, as had the earrings.

'That's better,' she said, still a little huffy. 'Now, you're to be home by half past nine. You know that, don't you? Don't be late.'

'I won't.'

'And stay away from the boys.'

'Oh, Mum!'

'You're not old enough to be getting off with boys.'

'I know. I won't.'

'You shouldn't keep on to her,' Joe protested mildly when the front door had closed behind Jenny.

'You can't be too careful. After what happened to our Heather I should have thought even you would realise that.'

'She's only a child.'

Carrie turned away, raising her eyes heavenward. Pointless to argue with Joe. He never saw danger, not even when it was staring him in the face. What would it take to make him alter that infuriatingly easy-going attitude? An earthquake, probably, and as the ground shook and parted beneath him he'd still be saying: 'It's nothing to worry about, m'dear.'

Carrie shook her head, feeling suddenly old and powerless, and went back to her ironing.

The youth club was in the centre of town in the building that had housed the Working Men's Club before it had moved to its new premises in the Street. Downstairs, what had once been the public bar had been turned into a coffee bar, with chairs both easy and upright and small tables. The upper floor was the recreation area, usually set out with a table-tennis table. Tonight, though, this had been dismantled and stacked away, and the record player which provided entertainment in the coffee bar area brought up and balanced on a card table. It was the night of the weekly 'Hop' and as Jenny pushed open the door, the husky voice of Ruby Murray rolled down the stairs to greet her.

The coffee bar area was crowded and Jenny's fragile new-found confidence all but deserted her. They all looked so grown up! – girls in pencil-slim skirts and kitten heels, their hair tied in ponytails or waving to their shoulders,

116

boys who looked more like men, except that their hair was longer than a man would ever wear it, smoking, chatting, some sprawled in chairs with their feet on the tables. She hesitated for a moment, wondering if she dared go into this grown-up world. Then she spotted Rowena on the stairs, waving to her, and stepped into the smoky, noisy womb.

It was the first time Jenny had been to the youth club and it had taken all her powers of persuasion to talk Carrie into letting her come tonight.

'I've heard things about that club,' Carrie had said darkly.

'Rowena goes! Her mum doesn't mind.'

'That's all very well . . .'

'Rowena's a very nice girl,' Joe had said.

'I'll think about it.'

She had thought, long and hard. Rowena *was* a nice girl, and she was also what Carrie called 'a cut above', by which she meant middle class. Rowena's mother, whom Carrie had met at school functions, was a highly respectable widow with a quiet demeanour and an accent that was almost cut-glass. Like Carrie herself, she was older than most of the mothers and had once been 'in service' – a lady's maid to the gentry in London. It was good for Jenny to have a friend like Rowena, Carrie decided. After much deliberation she had decided to let Jenny go to the youth club.

'Our crowd's all upstairs,' Rowena said. 'We'll get a drink first though. What would you like – orange squash? It's a bit hot up there for coffee.'

'How much it is?' Jenny asked. She only had two shillings – two weeks' pocket money.

'Don't worry – I'll get it. I'll have to, anyway, because you're not a member yet.'

'I'll pay you back,' Jenny promised.

'No you won't. I got five pounds for my birthday.'

Five pounds! Untold wealth! Rowena never seemed to be short of money.

They got their drinks and Rowena led the way upstairs. The record player was belting out 'Cherry Pink and Apple

Blossom White' and the floor vibrated as couples jived. Jenny spotted Valerie Scott sitting on a small sofa with a much older boy. He had his arm round her and they were kissing. Jenny looked away, shocked. Ann and Kathy were bopping with two boys who also looked several years older and Jenny felt a qualm of misgiving.

'Who are *they*?'

'Tim and Dave. I'm feeling a bit fed up really,' Rowena shouted over the music.

'Why?'

'I think they're getting off with them. I know Ann likes Tim and I think he might like her too. I quite fancy Dave myself, but it looks like I've missed the boat.'

'I'll dance with you if you like,' Jenny offered. The two of them often practised steps around Rowena's front room.

'Maybe. Later,' Rowena said without enthusiasm. And then: 'You know, I can't imagine ever going out with anyone. I mean – how does it actually *happen*? It always seems that if you like somebody, they don't like you, and if they like you, you don't like them. It's hopeless, really.'

They'd had this conversation before, when one of them developed a crush, or one of the other girls from their class was asked out on a date.

'I think we're going to finish up on the shelf,' Rowena said.

'You won't,' Jenny said. 'I probably will.'

'No – you're really pretty! Haven't you seen the way the boys look at you?'

'Not really,' Jenny said.

'See – look – Barry Price is looking at you now!'

Jenny turned and saw a tall good-looking boy in a red sweater. He was indeed looking at her. Their eyes met and he wasn't the one to look away. Jenny felt her cheeks go hot.

'Who is he, anyway?'

'Barry Price – I told you. He's seventeen. And he's got the most incredible green drop-handlebar bike you ever saw in your life.'

'Oh!' Jenny felt quite pleased with herself.

'I bet you could get him to ask you out.'

'I couldn't,' Jenny said. 'Anyway, I wouldn't be allowed.'

This was all part of the turmoil she felt when she thought about boys. Hoping someone gorgeous would ask her out, yet at the same time afraid they might because then she really would have a problem. Carrie would never let her go in a million years and she'd have to say no and look a complete fool.

'Mum says I'm not allowed to go out with boys until I'm sixteen.'

'Sixteen! That's *years* away!'

'I know.'

'She wouldn't stop you,' Rowena said. 'Not if you had a really nice date.'

'She would. She'd go into a foul mood and never come out.'

'Your mum – in a foul mood? I can't imagine that!'

'She would. She does.'

'I can't believe it. She's really good fun, your mum.'

'Anyway,' Jenny said, 'it's not going to happen, so there's no point talking about it.'

'Don't be so sure – look! No – don't look! Barry Price is coming over. Half a crown says he's going to ask you for a dance. Oh! If he asks you to dance I'll kill myself, I really will!'

'Don't worry, I'll say no,' Jenny said, and she meant it. A feeling of utter panic was flooding between her ribs.

'Don't be so silly – you'll do no such thing!'

'Hi, Rowena,' said the boy in the red sweater. And to Jenny, 'Hi.'

'Hi,' Jenny said weakly.

'Haven't seen you here before, have I?'

'No, this is my first time.'

'Jenny's my friend at school,' Rowena said, attempting to get back into the conversation. 'I told her this is where the action is.'

'Yeah.' But he was still looking at Jenny. 'Do you want to dance?'

Jenny hesitated. The panic was really building up now, suffocating her. One part of her wanted to run away, back down the stairs – home! But at the same time another part

119

desperately wanted to be part of this noisy, fun, grown-up scene.

Rowena gave her a small push.

'Go on!'

'All right.' Jenny smiled nervously, self-consciously. She was horribly sure she'd make a complete fool of herself, be unable to manage to dance a single step, fall over his feet, her feet, simply fall over full stop! But after the first few self-conscious twirls she fell into the rhythm and began to enjoy herself. It was just like dancing with Rowena, only easier, because he was taller than Rowena, she didn't have to duck to get under his arm, and her feet moved more easily on the bare wood floor than on the carpet in Rowena's front room.

She danced until she was breathless, her eyes shining, exertion making her cheeks glow. Then the music changed. They had put on a slow record – 'Red Sails in the Sunset'.

'Do you creep?' Barry asked her.

'I don't know . . .'

'It's easy.' He put his arms around her waist. Nervously, Jenny put her hands on his arms, which seemed a great deal more intimate than the position they adopted for the waltz and quickstep in dancing lessons at school but infinitely preferable to putting her arms around his neck as she could see most of the other girls were doing with their partners. It wasn't that she didn't like him – she did – but this was all happening much too fast for her.

His arms felt nice beneath her fingers, very – well – *strong* – and his jumper was soft and smelled of soap. She slid her hands up a bit further so they were resting almost on his shoulders and her feet moved effortlessly as he guided her backwards. He was right – it was easy!

When he pulled her closer, though, the panic began again. Someone had dimmed the lights. Supposing he tried to kiss her? Kissing was something she really didn't know how to do and anyway . . . she thought of Valerie, snogging on the sofa, and the disgust she had felt, and thought: *No! No! I'm not ready for this!*

He didn't try to kiss her, just laid his cheek against hers, but the panic wouldn't go away. When the record ended she looked round for Rowena, but couldn't see her anywhere.

'She's all right.'

'No – I must find her! Thanks for the dance . . .' She fled, like Cinderella on the stroke of midnight.

Rowena was in the coffee bar area downstairs with a group of other young people.

'Oh *there* you are!' Jenny said, relieved. 'I thought you'd gone!'

'I thought *you* had. *A* dance! That's a laugh! You must have had at least half a dozen!'

'I couldn't get away.'

'I could see that! I thought he'd forgotten to have his supper and was going to eat you instead!'

'Oh, Rowena – it wasn't like that . . .' She hesitated. 'Shall we go back up?'

'No, I'm down here now,' Rowena said. She turned away from Jenny, back to the crowd she had been talking to. They obviously all knew one another but Rowena made no attempt to introduce Jenny and Jenny experienced a feeling of déjà vu – this was how she had used to feel. An outsider, looking in, afraid to join in the conversation in case they thought she was gate-crashing, afraid anyway that she'd say the wrong thing.

She watched the stairs surreptitiously, hoping that Barry might come down looking for her and at the same time afraid of what would happen if he did. But when he did come down it was with another boy and he didn't so much as glance in her direction, just bought a drink then disappeared back upstairs again.

Rowena must have noticed. She took pity on Jenny, linked arms with her and included her in the conversation.

Some time later Jenny glanced at the clock and was amazed and horrified to see it was almost half past nine.

'I'm going to have to go home,' she said to Rowena.

'Already?'

'Right this minute! I'm supposed to be in . . .'

'My mum's coming for me,' Rowena said. 'She'll give you a lift if you wait.'

'I can't – honestly! I'll be in dead trouble!'

She ran all the way home. Carrie was looking out of the front-room window.

'What time do you call this, young lady?'

'I'm not very late, am I?'

'When I say half past nine, I mean half past nine, not quarter to ten.'

'I'm sorry,' Jenny said. 'We were talking. I didn't notice the time.'

'She's here now,' Joe said. 'Did you enjoy yourself, Jenny?'

'Yes. It was super.'

'Well, we'll say no more about it this time,' Carrie said. 'But if you want to go again, you'll remember to keep an eye on the clock.'

'I will. I promise.'

She'd got away with it this time. Jenny sighed inwardly with relief. She went up to bed but she was much too excited to sleep. A whole new world was opening up. Jenny couldn't wait to be part of it.

When she went to school on Monday, Rowena was waiting for her in the cloakroom.

'Have I got something to tell you!'

'You've got a date,' Jenny said, feeling hollow inside suddenly. She and Rowena had often commiserated that they must be the only girls of their age in the whole world who had never been on a date – now the only one would be her.

'Yes.' Rowena smiled smugly. 'But I'm not the only one. So have you.'

'Me? What are you talking about?'

'Listen and I'll tell you! After you'd gone, Trevor Wallis asked me to dance. And then he asked me out. Trevor Wallis – you know? Anyway, he's friends with Barry Price. So *I* said I'd only go if it was a foursome. And *he* said Barry Price wanted to go out with you anyway. So there you are! I've said we'll go for a bike ride with them on Thursday.'

Jenny's heart had begun to hammer a tattoo.

'Thursday! This Thursday?'

'Yes. What do you think? I couldn't wait to tell you! Isn't it smashing?'

'I don't know!' Jenny said. 'I won't be allowed. I know I won't. Not with a boy.'

'Don't say you're with a boy then. Just say you're with me.' The bell rang, summoning them to class. 'We can't miss a chance like this,' Rowena said.

Throughout the morning's lessons Jenny found concentration impossible. She kept turning the options over in her mind: (1) Tell Rowena she didn't want to go; (2) Ask Carrie's permission which would almost certainly be refused; or (3) Go along with Rowena's suggestion. She didn't like the thought of deceiving Carrie but she wouldn't actually be telling a lie. She would be with Rowena and it was pretty unlikely Carrie would ever learn they hadn't been alone. If by some remote chance they were spotted she could always plead innocence – say they'd just happened to run into the boys by chance.

'All right,' she said to Rowena at lunchtime. 'I'll come.'

'I should think so too!'

'Where are we supposed to meet them?'

'They're coming to my house at seven o'clock.'

Jenny felt a stab of envy. Lucky Rowena, having such an understanding mother!

'Could I come to tea at yours?'

'If you like.'

That was the answer, without doubt. If she had to cycle from home to keep her date, Jenny was sure Carrie would spot her guilt a mile off, and in any case, being with Rowena would ensure she didn't lose her nerve!

It was almost frighteningly easy.

'Rowena's asked me to tea on Thursday,' she said. 'We can do our homework and then go for a bike ride or something.'

Close to the truth as it was, she still kept her fingers tightly crossed in her blazer pocket as a sort of insurance.

'As long as you do *do* your homework and not waste time chattering,' Carrie said. 'And as long as you're home before it gets dark. I don't trust that battery in your bicycle lamp.'

123

'I will be,' Jenny promised.

It was May now; the evenings were getting longer and lighter all the time. Her only worry was that it might be raining on Thursday and Carrie wouldn't let her ride her bike to school at all.

She need not have worried. Thursday dawned a perfect day. Jenny packed a cotton skirt and a blouse into a bag and draped it over the handlebars of her bicycle. Rowena's mother would let her iron them if they came out creased.

All day she was in a state of nervous excitement and by the time school was out panic had set in.

'Oh, I don't want to do this!' she wailed. 'I won't know what to say! I'll look a complete nana.'

'Jenny! Ooh, I'm beginning to wish I hadn't fixed this up for you! Did you really want to be the only girl in the year not to have been on a date?'

'Diane hasn't. I'm sure she hasn't!'

'Well, if you want to be classed with Diana.'

'I don't!'

'Well then – buck your ideas up!'

They had tea – ham and salad, followed by gooseberry fool. Jenny was so worked up by now she could scarcely swallow. Afterwards, they went upstairs to get changed and Jenny risked borrowing some of Rowena's lipstick. It was quite pale really and she could always wipe it off before she went home!

Just before seven o'clock, Jenny and Rowena looked out of Rowena's bedroom window and saw the boys sitting astride their bicycles against the wall on the opposite side of the road. The nervousness was physical now.

'I feel sick,' she said.

'No you don't.'

'I do! I can't go, Ro!'

'It's too late to back out now,' Rowena said.

They collected their bicycles and the boys rode over to meet them, acting very casual. They cycled down the road in a loose group, then turned into the lanes, exchanging banter as they went. Jenny still felt sick and she was very conscious of the wind getting under her skirt and blowing it up to expose her legs. She rode with one hand on the handlebars whilst trying to hold her skirt down with the other.

After a while they stopped in a gateway and the boys suggested they should split up. Jenny wasn't at all sure she liked the idea but didn't want to look like a spoilsport by saying so. They agreed to meet back at the gateway in an hour and Rowena and Trevor cycled off.

'We don't have to ride if you don't want to,' Barry said. 'We could leave our bikes here and walk if you like.'

He must have noticed the trouble she was having with her skirt, Jenny thought.

Barry lifted the bicycles over the gate and they hid them in the hedge. The field sloped in a series of hummocks to the valley beyond. Barry put his arm around her, quite lightly, and she was surprised how nice it felt.

'I didn't think you'd want to go out with me,' he said.

'Why did you think that?' Jenny asked.

'You going to Grammar School and that. I mean . . . it's a bit posh compared to where I went, isn't it?'

'I wouldn't call it *posh*,' Jenny said.

'You know what I mean. You learn Latin and all that stuff, don't you?'

'Well . . . yes . . . but . . . it's just a school.'

He pulled a face that said it was much more than that.

'Anyway, when you dashed off the other night I thought that was it.'

'I told you – I had to find Rowena. And then I had to go home. My mum's very strict. If I'm not in when I'm supposed to be, she goes mad.'

'I expect that's because she worries about you,' he said.

Jenny looked at him, surprised. It was how Carrie explained her rules and regulations certainly, but she hadn't expected to hear it coming from an extremely dishy seventeen-year-old boy.

'Rowena's mum's not like that,' she protested.

'You should be glad,' he said. 'You should be glad she cares so much about you.' There was something in the way he said it that was almost wistful. Jenny found herself wondering what his home was like, and his parents.

125

'What do you do?' she asked.

'Me? I'm an apprentice mechanic.'

'Oh.' She knew nothing about cars and engineering and didn't want to show her ignorance. She pulled a long blade of grass, waving it between her fingers, watching the seeds fly.

'Next year,' she said, 'those seeds will be more grass.' She didn't stop to think as once she would have done what a very banal and naive thing that was to say. At that moment she felt as if she was uncovering some deep universal truth, savouring it for the first time.

And then he kissed her.

Afterwards, she wasn't at all sure how it had come about, only that both his arms were around her instead of just one and his mouth was on hers, quite gentle yet also firm, and his lips were moving against her lips. It happened so naturally there was no awkwardness at all, none of the nose-bumping she and Rowena had worried about, none of the yuckiness she had imagined. There was a moment when she wondered what she should do with her arms but they slid around him comfortably enough and before she knew it she was kissing him back.

'You aren't going to slap my face and run away then?' he said, squinting at her.

'No.'

'Can I do it again?'

She nodded. She couldn't speak but her heart was shouting, singing: Oh yes! Yes please! Yes, yes, yes.

He kissed her at least half a dozen times – she began by counting so that she could relay a full account to Rowena, but she was enjoying it so much she lost count. He smelled nice – of soap and grass and sun-warmed skin; he tasted nice – indefinable but totally delicious. And his arms around her felt good and his hard muscular back beneath her hands and the soft wool of his jumper beneath her cheek. Joy and entrancement rose in her, a heady wave, and in the space of half an hour, Jenny fell in love.

Trevor and Rowena were already waiting in the gateway when they made their way back across the field. They were standing apart, Trevor sullen, Rowena flushed and aloof.

They all cycled back along the lane together but when they reached Rowena's house, Trevor waited a bit further along the road while Barry said goodnight to Jenny, and Rowena went into the shed to put her bicycle away.

'Can I see you again?' Barry asked. 'Say Saturday?'

'Yes, all right,' Jenny said.

'Shall I come to your house?'

'No!' Jenny said quickly. 'I'll meet you here.'

When he had gone she ran to find Rowena.

'Oh, he's super! Super! I'm seeing him again on Saturday. Are you seeing Trevor?'

'No,' Rowena said. 'I'm not.'

'Why not?' Jenny asked, dismayed.

'I don't like him. He's not very nice.'

'I thought he was. I thought . . . Why don't you like him?'

'If you must know he *tried it on*,' Rowena said. She sounded highly affronted. Jenny didn't like to press her. Did she just mean he's tried to kiss her the way she and Barry had kissed? Jenny felt herself flush at the thought and with it came the guilty feeling that perhaps she had been too forward. Or did Rowena mean he really had TRIED IT ON – put his hand inside her dress or something? Either way, she could see she had a big problem on her hands if Rowena wasn't going to be going out with Trevor again. Meeting Barry was going to be very tricky. But somehow she'd find a way. Nothing in the world was going to keep her from seeing him again.

For the first time in her life, Jenny became deceitful.

'You're seeing a lot of Rowena these days,' Carrie said when she got her bicycle out for the third time in a week and prepared to ride off yet again.

The warm May weather had lasted into a perfect June and Jenny lived on a knife's edge between blissful happiness and guilty terror. All she and Barry ever did was go for bicycle rides and walks, though they did once risk a visit to the pictures. Afterwards, Jenny had very little idea of what film they had seen – or been supposed to see since they had spent the entire time kissing and cuddling in one of the double seats in the back row of the balcony, so it was really rather a waste of money. They could do that just as well for free under the clear blue sky!

'You really like kissing, don't you?' Barry said one day. They were lying in the long grass, their bicycles hidden in the hedge covered with tall white cow parsley.

'Mmm.' It was heaven, the sweet-scented grass tickling her neck, the evening sun warm on her face, the heady feel of him close to her. Even the feel of his hand lying carelessly on her bare leg was good. Then, as it began stealthily to creep up her thigh, she tensed.

'Come on,' he urged teasingly, his mouth tickling her ear. 'Don't be a spoilsport!'

'Stop it, Barry!' There was a tight knot of panic inside her.

He stopped and she pulled him down to kiss her again, not wanting him to think she was really angry with him. But there was a distance between them now and suddenly she *was* angry, with herself as much as with him, because between them they'd managed to spoil all that perfection.

'Don't you like me any more?' she asked, a trifle petulantly.

'Of course I do.' But he still sounded cross. 'Come on, it's time we went.'

He got up and she followed suit reluctantly. She hadn't had nearly enough kisses yet; she was still hungry for more and she couldn't understand why he wasn't too.

'When will I see you again?' she asked as they pedalled back along the lane.

'Umm . . . Sunday afternoon. I'll meet you at the crossroads up the lane from your house.'

'OK.' She should have felt happy again but somehow she didn't. The shadow was still there. It felt like a nameless foreboding. She pushed it away. 'See you Sunday then.'

'Yeah.' And he was gone, pedalling away, bent double over the handlebars of his green racing-style bicycle.

We can't go on like this, Jenny thought. He's cross because I haven't told Mum I'm going out with him. Rowena was beginning to be cross about it too, fed up with constantly providing alibis. She had been quite snappy with Jenny the last time they'd talked about it.

'It's ridiculous,' Rowena had said. 'You really should own up.'

'I can't!'

'Well, I'm not going to tell lies for you, Jenny. I keep having this horrible nightmare that your mum is going to turn up at our house one evening and want to know where you are. And if she does I am not going to lie to her.'

'She won't! She wouldn't do that!' Jenny said, but she had to admit it was a nightmare that troubled her too. If Carrie suspected and followed her – if someone was taken ill – died even! – and they wanted to get hold of her in a hurry – if someone saw her with Barry (she always tried to hide her face if a car passed them in the lanes) – the terror of being discovered was growing stronger all the time. So far she'd been lucky – but how much longer could her luck hold? Sooner or later we're going to be caught out, and it really would be better if I owned up first, Jenny thought.

Owning up might even have its advantages; she'd be able to enjoy her time with Barry without the guilt, even do the things that other couples who were going out properly, without secrecy, did – although quite honestly there was nothing she really wanted to do one quarter as much as simply kiss and cuddle. I'll have to own up, Jenny thought, but still she couldn't bring herself to do it and she felt herself becoming silent and moody.

'Jenny,' Carrie said on the Saturday evening. 'Is there something worrying you?'

'No,' Jenny said, but it sounded unconvincing even to her own ears.

'I think there is,' Carrie said. 'You're not at all yourself. Is it something at school?'

'No!'

'Well, I have to tell you, Jennifer, that when I went to school for the parents' evening your teacher mentioned it too. You're in a dream half the time. And I want to know the reason.'

Jenny had begun to tremble violently as all the guilt and anxiety she had experienced these past weeks came to boiling point, a foaming froth of emotion.

129

'Jenny?' Carrie said, sharply, perceptively.

Jenny said nothing but everything she was feeling was there in her eyes.

'Jenny . . . whatever it is, you can tell me,' Carrie said.

Jenny shook her head, the longing to make a clean breast of it all vying with the fear of her mother's reaction, and between them making her incapable of speech.

'Come on, my love . . .'

'I can't,' Jenny said. 'You'll be angry with me.'

'I won't. Tell me.'

Jenny swallowed hard and at last her trembling lips framed the words.

'I've . . . Mum . . . I've got a boyfriend.'

She saw the dark shadow cross Carrie's face, then lift slightly.

'Who is it? Someone at school?'

'No. I met him at the youth club. He's a mechanic at Compton Motors. Well – he's doing his apprenticeship anyway.'

Carrie frowned. 'And how old is this . . . boy?'

'Seventeen. He's . . .'

'Seventeen!' Carrie repeated, horrified.

'Yes.'

'When have you been seeing him?' Carrie's voice was low, controlled.

'We go for rides on our bicycles . . .'

'When you're supposed to be with Rowena, I suppose! I *knew* there was something funny going on! I *said* you were seeing a lot of her all of a sudden! Where do you go?'

'Oh – just around . . . Anywhere, really, where we can go for a walk, and . . .'

'And what?'

'Nothing, just talk and . . .' But her cheeks were flaming.

'I can't believe this,' Carrie said. 'I thought I knew you, Jennifer. How long has this been going on?'

'About three weeks . . .'

'Three weeks. For three weeks you've been telling me a pack of lies so you could get off with this *boy*.' She spat the word as if it were an obscenity. 'What have you been doing with him?'

'Nothing!'

'Well, I hope not! Oh, Jennifer, Jennifer . . .'

'You see? I told you you'd be cross,' Jenny said wretchedly.

'I'm not just cross. I'm disappointed. I never expected this. Not from you.'

'I'm sorry,' Jenny said. 'I'm really sorry, Mum. I would have told you – I wanted to – but I thought you wouldn't let me go.'

'Well, you thought right there!' Carrie said. 'Seventeen! I never heard anything like it! Boys of that age . . .' She broke off, her own thoughts choking her.

'He's ever so nice . . . If I brought him home, Mum . . . if you met him . . .'

'You're not seeing him again,' Carrie said.

'Oh, Mum – please, don't say that!'

'I am saying it. You'll put a stop to it before it goes any further. Seventeen! He's much too old for you.'

'Mum . . . I *love* him!'

Carrie laughed, a harsh explosion utterly without mirth.

'Love? Jennifer, you don't know the meaning of the word! And nor should you, at your age.'

'That's not fair.'

'Life isn't fair, my girl. You'll learn that – but not too soon I hope. At the moment you should be concentrating on your school work and doing nice things.'

'He *is* nice!' Jenny was close to tears now. 'You can't stop me seeing him, Mum – you can't! Rowena's mother didn't mind her going out with Trevor . . .'

'Oh! Rowena's mother knows about this, does she?'

The idea that there was a conspiracy against her was the last straw for Carrie.

'Mum . . . please . . .!'

'You are not going out with him again, Jennifer, and that is final. In fact, you're not going out of my sight for the foreseeable future.'

'I'm supposed to be seeing him on Sunday,' Jenny said. 'I'll have to go, if only to tell him.'

'You are not seeing him again.'

'But he'll be waiting! I can't just let him down.'

'Where are you supposed to meet him?'

Jenny told her.

'All right,' Carrie said, *'I'll* go. I'll tell him you're much too young for any of this and I am not allowing it.'

'Mum – you can't!' Jenny was appalled.

'I certainly can. And I shall give him a piece of my mind at the same time. Tell him to find a girl his own age.'

'Oh, Mum – please!' Jenny was sobbing now.

'Don't be so silly,' Carrie said scornfully.

'I knew you'd be like this, I knew it . . .'

'Then why,' Carrie demanded, 'were you stupid enough to go behind my back? You must have known you'd be found out in the end. I'm very disappointed in you, Jennifer.'

And that was that.

She hardly spoke to Jenny for the rest of the day; next morning at breakfast she was still cold and disapproving, boiling with barely contained fury underneath. Jenny was utterly wretched, deeply ashamed, unable to meet her father's troubled blue eyes, anguished by the realisation that never again would she lie with Barry in the long grass, never again feel his lips on hers, his arms around her, tormented by the humiliating prospect of Carrie keeping her date for her, terrified at what she would say to him. Right up until the last moment she harboured the vain desperate hope that Carrie would change her mind, let her go this one last time, but that too disappeared when, after washing up the dinner things in stony silence, she took off her overall and went upstairs to change into a decent frock.

Jenny followed her up, trembling, tearful.

'Mum . . . please . . .'

'I've said my last word on the subject, Jennifer. Now, tell me again, where is it you're meeting him? By Bluebell Woods, was it?' Jenny nodded mutely, knowing that further argument would only make things worse. 'Right. I won't be long.'

It was said finally, brooking no further argument.

As the door slammed after her, Jenny went to her room, lay down on her bed and cried until the tears ran dry.

Half an hour later Carrie was back.

'Are you sure you told me the truth, Jennifer?'

'What do you mean?'

'About where you were supposed to meet this boy?'

'Of course!' Jenny looked at her mother with fear-filled eyes. 'What happened? What did he say?'

'Nothing.' Carrie stood in the doorway, arms folded across her chest, an avenging angel in a floral frock. 'He wasn't there.'

'What do you mean – he wasn't there?'

'He never came. I waited ten minutes and more. He never came.'

'I don't understand . . .' Jenny said.

'Did you get a message to him somehow?'

'No!'

'You'd better be telling me the truth, young lady.'

'I am telling the truth.'

'Well,' Carrie said, 'I expect that's the last we'll hear of him, but if he should get in touch with you, you know what to tell him. Don't you?'

Jenny nodded. She was puzzled now as well as upset. She couldn't understand why Barry hadn't turned up. Had something happened to him? An accident, perhaps? Oh – he could be injured – dead even – and she wouldn't know. The tears flowed again. In an agony of wretchedness, Jenny wished that she, too, was dead.

The mystery was solved a week later.

'Barry's going out with a girl at the youth club,' Rowena told her.

'He can't be!' Jenny was devastated. 'Who is it?'

'One of the older girls. You know – the one with the bleached blonde hair – June Farthing.'

'I don't believe it!' Jenny said. But of course it would explain why he hadn't turned up that Sunday afternoon. He had someone else and, rather than telling her, he'd simply stood her up. It made no real difference, of course.

133

It would have been over anyway. But the extra turn of the screw made it even more painful, if such a thing were possible.

For the first time in her life, Jenny discovered what it felt like to have her heart broken.

Chapter Seven

'Look – I'm really sorry, Mr Button, but you're going to have to stop driving for a while,' Helen said.

Cliff Button stared at her almost uncomprehendingly. Then he chuckled, a small dry sound.

'You'm having me on, doctor.'

'No, Mr Button, I'm not.' Heather riffled the papers on her desk so that the report on Cliff's tests were directly in front of her. She already knew word for word what they said, but being able to actually refer to them somehow gave a weight of authority to her words, she felt, and at the same time absolved her of some of the responsibility of what was going to be a devastating blow for Cliff. 'I'm afraid these tests confirm what I suspected. The turns you've been having are caused by epilepsy.'

'Fits, you mean,' Cliff said.

'Well – if you want to call them that . . . yes.'

'What else can you call them?' Cliff was hiding his dismay with a show of impatience. 'Fits.' He shook his head in disgust. 'I never thought I'd come to this.'

'It's not the end of the world, honestly,' Helen said. 'New treatments are being discovered all the time. We have to find the right one for you, that's all. Once we get you stabilised the chances of it happening again reduce dramatically.'

'And until then I can't drive, you say.'

'I think that speaks for itself, don't you? You'd be a danger to yourself and others if you were taken ill when you were behind the wheel.'

'It's my job though, Doctor. I've been the taxi man in Hillsbridge since before you were so much as a twinkle in your father's eye.'

'I know.' Helen remembered as a little girl being

fascinated by the big black cab that was often parked near the Market Place. Long before that, Cliff had owned one of the very first motor cars ever seen in Hillsbridge, and Helen had heard Charlotte, her grandmother, relate how during the Great War she had hired Cliff to drive her and the boys – Jack, Helen's father, included – to Salisbury Plain to see their brother Fred, who was in training there. Charlotte had never forgotten the excitement of riding in the open-top car with the wind tearing her hair down from its combs, and though the memory was tinged with sadness – for Fred had died in France – the story was still worth the telling. 'Believe me, Mr Button, I do know that. But really I'm afraid it's all the more reason why you mustn't take any risks. Your passengers have a right to safety, don't you think?'

'I s'pose so.' Cliff sounded unconvinced. 'I'd know, though, wouldn't I, if I was g'waine to be bad? I'd pull over straight away. I bain't daft.'

'No-one's suggesting you are, but you must not drive,' Helen said firmly. 'It's not just me saying that – it's the law. All right?'

Cliff stared into space for a moment, pulling on his moustache, grey, now, and bushy on a face that had become all planes and hollows.

'What be I s'posed to do? That's what I'd like you to tell I.'

'Why don't you retire?' Helen suggested.

'Retire!' He sounded shocked.

'Why not? You're well past retirement age.'

'Don't go reminding me!'

'So why don't you take things a bit easier? Most men of your age would be only too glad of the excuse to put their feet up.'

'Not me,' Cliff said stubbornly. 'Start putting your feet up and next thing you know you'm pushing up the daisies!'

Helen hid a smile.

'Why me, that's what I'd like you to tell I,' Cliff went on. 'I've always had the best of health, unlike most of 'em round here. Always out in the fresh air, not breathing in that filthy muck like them as do work down the pit, don't

136

drink much – well, only in moderation – never smoked, always ate good fresh vegetables out of me own garden. I just don't understand it.'

'I can't give you an explanation, Mr Button. Sometimes these things just happen. What I can do, though, is try to find a treatment that will suit you. Let's talk about that.'

But Cliff still looked horribly morose and as he left the surgery she noticed the defeated slope to the shoulders that had previously been of almost military bearing and a grizzled look to the back of his head and neck that had not been apparent to her before. He seemed to have aged ten years in as many minutes, and though she might have smiled inwardly at his reference to pushing up the daisies, in reality there was nothing even remotely amusing about it. Helen had seen it happen in too many cases – men and women who were remarkably good for their age suddenly entering a downward spiral when the cornerstone of their life was abruptly shaken. She hoped fervently that wouldn't happen to Cliff.

This was the downside of general practice, as opposed to working in a large city hospital of course; the doctor/patient relationship was so much more personal. You worked hard at building up trust, you got to know the patient and their family and often in the process they came to feel like friends. The sense of responsibility for their welfare was overwhelming too; on more than one occasion Helen had lain awake at night worrying about a diagnosis or treatment, afraid she might have missed something that would have been glaringly obvious to a more experienced eye. If she was really in doubt, of course, she could always talk to Reuben Hobbs, and on occasion she had done so, but it was always a question of justifying the necessity of that to herself. She didn't want to run to him unnecessarily, undermining his confidence in her, and her confidence in herself.

Not that her judgement was in doubt in this case. As soon as Cliff Button had walked through the door she'd suspected epilepsy and the tests had proved her right. This time it was just the inability to put things right for him that niggled, the unpleasant feeling that with a few well-chosen words she had destroyed his life.

Helen packed Cliff's notes back into their brown envelope, reminding herself that she must avoid becoming emotionally involved. That way led to disaster. But she *was* emotionally involved, whether she liked it or not, not least because Cliff had been one of the first patients to give her a chance.

It was strange, Helen thought, that in the middle of the twentieth century people could still be so prejudiced against a woman doctor. Only two of the five women she had qualified with were now practising – one of them in London, where perhaps attitudes were a little more liberal. But here in Hillsbridge the old prejudices remained. Women made excellent nurses, but doctors – doctors should be men, and preferably older men.

'Don't worry about it – I had just the same sort of problems when I first came here,' Paul Stephens had said to her when they had adjourned to the best room at the George for a much needed drink after a practice meeting.

'You?' Helen had said, surprised. 'You are very obviously not a woman!'

'You noticed.'

'Uh-huh.'

'I may not be a woman, but when I joined the practice I was what the old folk round here called "a young whippersnapper". They were used to Dr Vezey, who was damned near in his dotage even then – and of course Reuben had been here donkey's years. They didn't trust me. Particularly the mothers of nubile young girls.'

Helen was shocked. 'That is appalling!'

'Understandable, I suppose. We've all heard of doctors who want to do a full examination for a sore throat.'

'All the same . . .'

'They got over it eventually. A few successes and the word got around. And of course, time was my greatest ally. If you wait long enough, there's nothing surer than young men become old ones.'

'That won't be much help to me! Ten years from now I'll still be a woman.' She sipped her rum and black, looking at him over the rim of her glass. 'In any case – you're not old!'

'Older than I was. Which I suppose helps compensate for the fact that I'm still unmarried. That, I'm afraid, is the other cardinal sin. Young and single must equal Lust, with a capital L, for every unclothed female body within a ten-mile radius.'

'Oh, Paul, you're impossible!' Helen said, laughing.

She had revised her opinion of him considerably since that first rather awkward morning. Though on occasions he could be short to the point of rudeness, he could also be very good company with his dry sense of humour, and she knew now she had been wrong to suspect he had not wanted her as the assistant GP. Reuben Hobbs had admitted to her that initially he had been the one to have doubts and Paul who had talked him round, pointing out the advantages of a lady doctor in the practice once the patients got over the first shock and accepted her. When Reuben had said it, Helen had been incredulous, yet now it seemed to fit with the Paul she was getting to know.

Occasionally she wondered, just as his patients did, why, in his middle thirties, Paul was still unmarried. He was good-looking in a rather rugged way, with a reasonable income and the status that went with being a GP – every matchmaking mother in the district should have had her sights set on him as a prospective son-in-law. But so far it hadn't happened.

'Because I've never yet met a woman I wanted to give up my freedom for,' Paul said once, and Helen thought that was it in a nutshell. Paul was the sort of man who probably valued his freedom too much to give it up for any woman.

Helen stacked Cliff Button's notes on the pile at the back corner of her desk and went to see if there were any other patients waiting. She rather thought Cliff had been the last – for her, at any rate – and soon after she had called him in she had heard Dorothea Hillman, who came in three mornings a week to type up the correspondence and deal with the accounts, stalk along the corridor and lock the door against any latecomers.

As she had thought, the only patient still waiting was a woman with a small child – a long-term patient of Reuben Hobbs. But someone else was in the corridor too, not

139

sitting patiently on one of the hardbacked chairs, but pacing in the far corner where the passage broadened out into a small lobby, and glancing, at that moment, at the posters and bits and pieces of information that were pinned on to the baize noticeboard. His back was towards her, but she recognised him anyway. She knew every line of those narrow shoulders beneath the natural linen jacket and the thick dark hair speckled through with premature silver only too intimately.

Shock ran in a hot tide through her veins.

'Guy,' she said.

He turned and their eyes met for the first time in more than six months. Dark eyes, flecked with gold, just as his hair was flecked with silver. Eyes that had the power to melt her inside, turn her heart over, make her ache with longing.

But now the quick flash of disbelieving pleasure was shot through with anger. What was he doing here? What right had he to materialise this way as suddenly as an unwelcome apparition in the safe haven of her new world?

'You'd better come through,' she said. Her voice was very cool, very controlled, masking all those churning emotions.

'See your patients first,' he said. His voice was cool too – but wasn't it always? That cool, cool voice that matched his cool, cool hands and could instil confidence in the most nervous patient, calm the panic of an accident victim, restore equilibrium on the most chaotic ward. 'I don't mind waiting.'

Helen turned to the young woman with the child, forcing a faint smile.

'I expect you want to see Dr Hobbs, don't you?'

'I might as well, yes. He knows all about our Celia.'

Helen nodded. The corridor felt overpoweringly hot suddenly; hot, airless and claustrophobic. She wondered how patients could bear to wait here, sometimes for hours on end. She must speak to Reuben about it, see if they could get some kind of fan installed.

'It's all right,' she said to Guy. 'Come through.'

He followed her along the passage. She could smell his

aftershave hanging in that hot, still air. It excited another treacherous wave of longing, a stirring of nostalgic memories. Delights she had worked so hard at forgetting.

She went into her consulting room and he followed, closing the door after him and looking around, appraising, critical.

'So this is where you spend your days now.'

'Well, part of them – yes.'

'Somewhat different to what you've been used to.'

He meant the paucity of it, she imagined, the lack of all the up-to-the-minute paraphernalia of a busy modern hospital.

'I like it,' she said defensively.

'Good. You never were a town mouse.'

'I was never a mouse – town or otherwise.'

He smiled briefly, that slow smile that lit his eyes and was gone.

'I miss you, Helen.'

She chuckled, a mite bitterly.

'I thought that was the general idea. Why are you here, Guy?'

'I just said. I miss you.'

'Oh, Guy!' She turned away, not wanting to look at him, pressing her fingers to her lips. 'You can't do this to me. It's not fair.'

'Life isn't fair though, is it?' he said. 'It's not fair that you and I can't be together.'

She swung round then, eyes blazing.

'We could have been, Guy. If you'd been prepared to leave Marian. But you wouldn't. You wanted it both ways.'

'I wanted *you*.'

'But you wouldn't leave *her*. Five years I waited, Guy. Five bloody years. All wasted.'

'Well, if you think they were wasted . . .'

'All right. Not wasted the way you mean, but where did they get me? I'm thirty-one years old and I'm on my own. If I'd known in the beginning how things would turn out . . . I never set out with the intention of being the eternal mistress, Guy. In the beginning . . .'

'We fell in love.'

'All right – we fell in love. Or *I* fell in love. I'm not sure about you.'

'How can you say that?' he demanded, interrupting. 'I'm here, aren't I?'

Her anger died again, quite suddenly, leaving her feeling tired and defeated.

'Yes. You're here, all right. My point is that if you'd felt the way I did you wouldn't have let anything stop us being together. I'd have crossed oceans for you, Guy. Literally. And I certainly couldn't have continued to live in a sham of a marriage.'

'Oh, for heaven's sake, Helen, do we have to go over all that old ground again? The children . . .'

'Yes,' she said. 'We do have to. Unless something has changed. Has it, Guy? Has anything changed?' He was silent and she sighed. 'I thought not. You'll never leave her. I know that now. And all this business about the children is just an excuse and you know it.'

'It is not an excuse, Helen. They are ten and eleven years old. I can't leave them. I'd destroy their world. When they're older . . .'

'You think? When they're older, Guy, there'll be another reason – perfectly good, perfectly sound, perfectly . . . plausible . . . a very comfortable life with the daughter of a top surgeon for a wife and all the goodies that spring from the cornucopia of Daddy's generosity. If you left Marian for me you'd have to leave the house – that grand monstrosity with an address in Bristol 8 – and you'd have to forego the sort of lifestyle that goes with it. All the consultants' jollies, all the port-soaked dinners, all the little white-aproned catering staff who come in and fluff around when you entertain. You wouldn't even *be* entertaining, Guy. Not if you were with me. There'd be a chorus of outrage and disapproval in all the circles that count with you. It would probably even affect your career. Have you thought of that? Oh yes, I bet you have!'

His head was bowed; he raised it to look up at her.

'Have you quite finished?'

'Oh, Guy . . .' Suddenly she wanted to cry. 'Why the hell did you have to come here? Why start it off all over again?'

He shook his head, splayed one hand helplessly.

'I suppose I hoped . . .'

'That I might have changed my mind? Gone soft?'

'If you put it like that.'

'Well, I haven't. Five years, I gave you, Guy. Surely to God you can't expect me to give you more, without anything in return?'

'Nothing in return. What about this?'

His hand shot out, grasping her wrist and taking her completely unawares. With a forcefulness she remembered only too well he held her pinioned like a butterfly against the solid frame of her desk, bending his head to hers. Powerless to resist, emotionally if not physically, she let him kiss her and for all their anger, all their conflicting needs, it was a kiss they both enjoyed, briefly at any rate. It had always been this way, from the very beginning, the chemistry between them could make a nonsense of reason. Had it not been so, the relationship would have ended many times during those five years.

'You see?' he said, drawing back. 'You still want me, Helen.'

'I never said I'd stopped wanting you.'

'Why then? Why does it have to be like this? Let me come and see you. I'll take you to dinner.'

She could feel the temptation eating away at her defences.

'To dinner.'

'Yes. It would be safe out here. We wouldn't be likely to bump into anyone I know.'

And with those few words he undid all the progress of the last moments.

'You see? That, Guy, is what I can't take! That's it in a nutshell. Being your guilty secret. I want more! I'm *worth more*, for God's sake!'

'I know that, Helen. Don't be like this, please! I love you. I can't live without you . . .'

'Guy – don't. You shouldn't have come and I'd like you to leave. Please go.' Her voice was rising.

'Helen . . .'

'Go!' She was shouting now.

The door opened without so much as a warning knock. Paul stood there, looking like nothing so much as a scrum half in a rugby team – hair rumpled, jacket rumpled, eyes narrow with suspicion. The contrast between him and the smoothly elegant Guy might, under other circumstances, have been almost laughable. But as things were, no-one was laughing.

'Is everything all right here?' His thick Tyneside accent lent something close to menace to his voice.

Helen smoothed her hair. She could feel her face flaming scarlet.

'It's all right thank you, Paul. I'm fine.'

Paul stood his ground, looking at Guy suspiciously.

Guy took the initiative.

'Guy Holden.' He extended his hand in Paul's direction. 'Helen and I are old friends. We used to work together.'

Paul ignored the outstretched hand.

'And you are?' Guy asked.

'Paul Stephens. A partner in this practice. If you don't mind, Mr Holden . . . I think it might be best if you were to pursue this conversation outside surgery hours.'

'He was just going,' Helen said. 'We've said all we have to say to one another, haven't we, Guy?'

For an uncomfortable moment she thought he was going to argue. Then: 'You know where to find me if you change your mind, Helen.' And he was gone.

'What the hell is going on?' Paul demanded.

'Just don't ask.' Helen felt on the verge of tears, partly as a result of her churning emotions, partly with a wretched, and particularly perverse, longing for Guy. All very well to tell him to get out of her life. That was her head talking. But loving him still made it an incredibly difficult decision to stick with. Pain washed over her and she swallowed at the tight knot in her throat. 'I apologise for my private life impinging on the professional. That was a totally unexpected visit.'

'So I gathered.'

'I hope it won't happen again.'

'Helen . . .' He touched the sleeve of her jacket. 'Are you sure you're all right?'

'Mmm.'

'You don't look it. Put the kettle on, why don't you, if you've finished your surgery, and we'll have a cup of tea.'

'No – thanks all the same. I've got a big round to do. I really ought to be getting on.'

To be honest, all she wanted was to get out, to feel the fresh air cooling her hot face, blowing the cobwebs of confused emotions out of her brain. His obvious concern was only making her feel worse. She was embarrassed, too, that he should have overheard at least part of what had been said.

'What about afterwards?' he said.

'Afterwards?'

'When we've both finished work for the day.'

'You mean I come back here and make a cup of tea for us?' she said, trying to lighten the mood and regain some of her equilibrium.

'Not quite. By that time I shall want something a bit stronger than a cup of tea. I was thinking more on the lines of a beverage of the alcoholic variety. Something to eat, too, if you like.'

She might have laughed if she hadn't been so close to crying. Two invitations to dinner within the space of a quarter of an hour. For an old spinster like her – unbelievable!

'Purely in the interests of getting to know one another better, of course,' he added quickly. 'With me at Tiledown and you here we don't ever really get the chance.'

'All right,' she said. 'If you put it like that, how can I refuse?'

That, of course, was it – in a nutshell. The last thing she felt like doing was socialising, but it was a good idea to get to know Paul better. They could very well be partners one day – her greatest ambition now was to be offered a partnership – and for that she would need the support of both Reuben and Paul.

And besides . . . There was something pleasantly solid and undemanding about him. In his own way he'd been a good friend this morning, coming to her aid when he'd thought she needed it. This much she owed him.

'I'll pick you up then, shall I? Say – what? – half-seven?'

'OK.'

The cobwebs had lifted a little, the heat in her cheeks burning less fiercely. But Helen still felt sick at heart as she went out to make a start on her home visits.

Why the hell was she still in love with such a selfish bastard? Why couldn't she simply tell herself she was well rid and leave it at that? But there is no accounting for the vagaries of the heart. Helen knew that if only – if only! – Guy would meet her halfway she would gladly run to him, and to hell with the consequences.

David couldn't understand what was wrong with Linda. For the past couple of weeks now she hadn't been herself at all and the change in her left him puzzled and frustrated. She had always been such a fun-loving girl, warm and affectionate with a sense of humour and bound-less energy. She could dance the night away and still be quite prepared to sit with him in his old Zephyr Zodiac for hours saying good night as they euphemistically called it. She had always been ready for a party or a visit to the pictures or an afternoon drive to the country or the coast.

But something had changed. She was evasive now when he suggested some outing or other, pleading tiredness as an excuse. She had no appetite, pushing her ham salad round her plate when she came to tea on a Sunday after-noon and causing Carrie to complain under her breath about the waste of good food as she was forced to scrape it into the kitchen bin. And perhaps most disturbing of all, she didn't seem to want to snog any more.

This of all things was most unlike her. Though David had never been able to persuade her to go as far as he would have liked, she had always been fond of kissing and cuddling, even petting a little. No longer. And David, who had previously felt that Linda was erring towards taking their relationship more seriously than he was comfortable with, simply couldn't understand it.

The first thought that occurred to him was that she was playing hard to get in an effort to push things along. That would fit in with the impression he'd got a while ago that

146

she wanted a ring on her finger, something he had wanted to avoid for as long as possible. If it was that, she'd discover soon enough that those tactics were useless where he was concerned. He didn't like games, and he didn't like to feel he was being manipulated either.

But somehow he didn't think Linda was that sort of girl. She'd accepted his invitation out for a date in the first place without hesitation and her open sunny nature just didn't lend itself to artifice. That only left one other possible explanation. She was going off him. David was surprised at how much he minded that this might be the case.

Tonight, a Saturday, they were at Linda's, and, as they so often did, they had the house to themselves. They had adjourned to the front room and played some records in which Linda seemed totally disinterested, and when he pulled her down on to the sofa, she squirmed away.

'Don't, please.'

He frowned. 'What's wrong?'

'I just don't feel like it, that's all.'

'You never feel like it these days.'

'I do! We're always snogging.'

'I thought you liked snogging.'

'I do – but not all the time.'

He gave her a puzzled look, then got up and stared out of the window, hands in pockets, shoulders slumping, while the question burned itself on his lips. Should he ask it – or not? If he got the answer he was dreading, then that would be it. All over, bar the shouting. No, not even shouting. Just a few awkward goodbyes.

Quite suddenly David made up his mind. One way or the other, he had to know. He turned round. Linda was half lying on the sofa, her head tucked into the curve between back and arm. Her eyes were closed. He felt a quick wave of tenderness before the resentment flooded in. Did he bore her so much that he sent her to sleep? If so, he didn't intend hanging around so that she could moan to her friends about him as girls seemed to do in their whispered confidential huddles.

'Is it that you don't fancy me any more?' he asked.

147

Her eyes flew open in an almost startled expression. 'What?'

'I'm beginning to think you're trying to tell me something. Like you don't want to go out with me any more.'

'Oh, David!' She levered herself up so that she was sitting on her feet. 'How could you think that? Oh – I'm sorry. Come here!'

He hesitated, looking at her, fully realising for the first time just how much she meant to him. He still wasn't satisfied with her reply – an impression of such an enormous change in her couldn't be negated so easily, and the thinking part of him wanted to pursue the subject now he had raised it, and try to find out exactly what was wrong. But his body had other ideas.

He went to her, holding and kissing her. She felt fluid and fragile in his arms, her mouth moving beneath his with sweet acceptance, her body moulding to his with a sort of passive compliance that was even more erotic than her usual frenzied approach.

She was wearing a little jersey cardigan. He eased it from her shoulders and ran his fingers down her arms. They felt almost childlike, tiny bird bones barely covered with baby-soft flesh. A little shocked, he glanced down at them and was even more shocked to see a dark bruise staining her upper arm just above the elbow.

'How did you do that?' he asked.

'I don't know.' She sounded almost irritable.

'What do you mean – you don't know? You must know!'

'Well, I don't.' She pressed her lips against his chin. 'I thought you wanted . . .'

But he found he had forgotten what he wanted; his aching desire of a moment ago was lost in the sudden churning of his thoughts. Was this the reason behind the change in her? He levered himself up, looking down at her.

'Has somebody been hitting you about?'

'Of course not! David . . .'

'Are you sure? It's not your dad, is it?'

'Oh, don't be so silly! My *dad*! That's an awful thing to say!'

'Well, you got it from somewhere.'

'Obviously,' Linda said. 'I expect I bumped myself. I just don't remember. And if you don't mind, I'd like to put my cardigan back on. I'm not very warm.'

David stared at her, his mouth dropping. It had been a perfect summer day and the residue of the sun's heat had been trapped in the small room. This sounded like another rejection to him. Another excuse.

'How can you not be warm? It's like an oven in here.'

'You might be warm. I'm not.'

She pulled the cardigan back over her shoulders, but not before he had touched her bare arm again. It was true. She didn't feel warm. Her flesh felt a little clammy to his touch. His puzzled irritation became edged with concern, not for their relationship, not for himself, fobbed off again, but for her.

'Are you all right, Linda?' he asked anxiously.

'What do you mean?'

'You're not ill, are you?'

'No. I just don't feel *well*, that's all.'

'Perhaps you're sickening for something.'

Her face crumpled suddenly, her thick lashes dropping on to her pale cheeks like dark butterfly wings.

'Well, if I am, it's a long time coming. I've felt like this for weeks now.'

'Like what?'

'Oh – I don't know – tired, cold, everything's just too much effort. I'm sorry, David, it's not you, honestly. I've been a pain, I know. I just don't feel very well.'

And she began to cry.

He was alarmed now. Really alarmed. He held her, mopped her tears with his handkerchief, because she made no attempt to wipe them herself, just let them roll down her crumpled face. She wasn't even *crying* hard, he realised. She seemed to lack the energy even for that. She simply whimpered weakly. His anxiety became anger, mainly directed at himself for taking such a self-centred view of the change in her, but also, just a little, at her, for not telling him before now how she felt.

'Why didn't you say?' he asked. 'Why didn't you tell me you weren't well?'

She took the handkerchief from him, summoning the energy to blow her nose.

'I didn't want to sound like a wet blanket.'

'Don't be so silly! You can't help it if you're not very well.'

She sniffed, trying to smile.

'I thought you'd think I was a moaning Minnie. You don't want a girlfriend who's complaining all the time.'

'Linda! Am I such a monster?'

'Of course you're not. But I'm terribly afraid of losing you, David. I always think . . . well, I'm scared you'll get tired of me – that you don't really want me at all.'

'How long have we been going out together, Linda?'

'Nearly two years.'

'Well, there you are! Do you think I'd have gone out with you for two years if I didn't want you?'

'But you never say! And if ever I mention anything to do with . . . well . . . love . . . I can feel you shut off. You *do*, David. You can't change the subject fast enough. And you go funny on me.'

She was right, of course, and he knew it. Had this been a normal evening he would most likely be 'going funny' as she put it now. But it wasn't a normal evening. This conversation, coming on top of his anxiety that he might be losing her had shown him just how deeply he cared for her.

'I think we've had our wires crossed, Linda,' he said. 'You're right in one way, though. I know I can be a bit weird at times. I just didn't want to get tied down, that's all.'

'I don't want to tie you down, David. Well – perhaps if I'm honest, I do. But what I mean is, I'd never force you. I'd rather have you the way we are than not at all. I couldn't bear it if I didn't have you at all.' She began to cry again weakly.

'Linda! Don't start that again! Please!'

'You see?' she sobbed. 'You want me to be jolly. Good fun. Good old Linda. But I can't always be Good old Linda.'

'I know that,' he said. 'Of course I like it when you're your usual bouncy self. But nobody can be like that all the time. And the truth is ... well, I want you, Linda, whatever sort of mood you're in. I just want you, full stop.'

'Really?' She was smiling at him tremulously through her tears. Tenderness swamped him.

'Yes,' he said roughly. 'Really, Linda.' He hesitated briefly. 'What would you say if I asked you to marry me?'

Her expression was momentarily so startled he thought that in spite of what she'd just said, she was going to refuse. He suddenly felt an utter fool, but more than that, he minded terribly. Suddenly, though he had totally taken himself by surprise by his proposal, he knew it was what he wanted more than anything in the world.

Then: 'Oh, David – yes!' she said. 'If you're asking me – and I think you are – then of course the answer is yes!'

'Good,' he said, quite bluntly, typically understating all the relief he was feeling. 'That's settled then. We'll go to Bath and get an engagement ring and we'll get married ... what ... next spring?'

She was laughing now, very gently.

'If you like. Anything you like. Only there's one thing ...'

'What?'

'You still haven't said you love me.'

He looked at her, at her pale, tear-wet face and her tousled hair and her red-rimmed eyes. He looked at her with all the seriousness that he would bring to their marriage vows. To speak these words, the words he had never spoken to anyone before in his life, was every bit as important to him, and a great deal more difficult to say.

'I love you, Linda.'

'And I love you.'

Some time later he cradled her in his arms, stroking her hair and remembering the bruise, the coldness, the fact that she felt tired and ill.

'Promise me something.'

'Mmm.'

'Promise me that if you're not feeling better by Monday, you'll go to the doctor.'

'OK.'

'Promise now. I want you fit and well again.' *If you're*

151

going to be my wife, he was going to add, but didn't. This expressing emotion was too new to him. Heaven alone knew, the emotion itself was still too new!

'I promise,' she said solemnly.

And David thought he could never remember feeling happier or more content.

Chapter Eight

Jenny was still feeling utterly wretched. She couldn't –
simply couldn't get Barry out of her head. Though she
knew it was true he was going out with June Farthing –
she'd seen them together, and Barry had totally ignored
her, though he'd gone a violent brick-red colour – she
wanted nothing more than to go out with him again. She
tortured herself by reliving over and over the way it had
felt when he had kissed her, smelling again with the senses
of memory the sweet scent of crushed grass and sun-
warmed skin, feeling the texture of his jumper against her
cheek. She puzzled over it too, wondering when it had all
gone wrong. What had she done – what had she said – why
– why – why? She went over and over it, finding endless
ways to blame herself and always, reluctantly, coming
back to the same thing. He'd gone off her because she
wouldn't let him touch her. June Farthing, she felt sure,
would have no such qualms.

Just to make matters worse, Carrie was watching her
like a hawk. At least she'd got over her silent mood and
was being quite nice – she'd even suggested they might get
a puppy – something Jenny had always longed for. A family
who lived in the newly completed units – the semi-
detached houses further down the road – had a bitch in
whelp and Carrie said she was thinking of giving one of the
pups a home. But not even this could cheer Jenny. Her
heart had been broken, she was obsessed with Barry, and
that was all there was to it.

On that Monday morning in June, however, Jenny was
feeling even more wretched. Today it wasn't only her heart
that was aching; it was her ear as well.

Jenny had always suffered with her ears. As a toddler
she'd had a mastoid scare and after that it seemed she had

153

a weakness. The little bottle of olive oil warmed in front of the fire before being dribbled into the offending ear, the piece of hot flannel Carrie instructed her to hold over it, the excruciating pain worse, far worse even than tooth-ache (she thought) – all had been an integral part of her childhood.

It didn't happen often nowadays, but when it did all the miserable memories came flooding back, and that morning the pain was so severe it even drove thoughts of Barry from her mind, though the misery of losing him remained, a dark weight around her heart.

'Are you sure you're all right to go to school?' Carrie asked.

'Yes, I'll be all right,' Jenny said. That afternoon her form were due to go to the local cinema to see the film of *The Pickwick Papers* which they were studying in English Literature.

By mid-morning, however, the pain in her ear was much worse. She felt drowsy and hot and she laid her head on the desk.

'Jennifer Simmons!' The voice of the French mistress, Miss Vokes, roused her. 'What are you doing going to sleep in my lesson? Didn't you go to bed last night?'

Jenny raised her head with an effort.

'I'm sorry, Miss Vokes. I've got an earache. It's really bad.'

Miss Vokes studied her. She did look pale, and it was unlike Jenny not to be attentive in lessons, although French, admittedly, was not one of her best subjects.

'The county doctor is in today, examining the first years,' she said. 'I'll see if he can see you. The rest of you – get on with doing Exercise XII.'

A few minutes later she was back.

'Go and wait outside the headmistress's study, Jennifer. The doctor will see you when he can.'

Jenny made her way along the corridor and sat down on one of the hardbacked chairs outside the headmistress's office. The wait seemed interminable. First-year pupils came and went and she was still there, trying hard not to cry from the pain. Eventually the doctor emerged – a square tweedy man with a brusque voice.

'All right. You can come in now. You've got earache, I understand.'

Jenny nodded wretchedly.

'Let's take a look.'

He shone his otoscope in Jenny's ear, leaning over her so that she could smell pipe tobacco in the tweed of his jacket, but it did not comfort her as the smell of her father's cigarettes did, and when he moved the otoscope around to get a better look she squealed with the sharp stab of pain it produced.

'I can't see anything wrong,' he said at last, straightening up and screwing the top back on the otoscope. 'You've been in a draught, I expect. Take a couple of aspirin and it will probably be all right by tomorrow. For now, I can see no reason why you shouldn't go back to class.'

Jenny felt relieved, but at the same time defensive. She suspected he thought she was a malingerer. She took the aspirins he offered her to the cloakroom and swallowed them with a mouthful of water from the drinking fountain, then went back to the classroom. The French lesson was just finishing; next period was Geography. Somehow Jenny sat through it but the aspirin seemed to be doing little to dull the pain.

When the bell went to end the lesson she followed the others into dinners, wishing Carrie worked in the kitchens here instead of the Junior School so that she could tell her how dreadful she felt. She collected her plate of stew and dumplings and took it to her place at one of the long trestle tables. The vegetable today was a green salad – geared to the first choice of cheese and onion flan, which had all gone by the time Jenny's table had filed through the kitchen to collect their food. As she looked at the lettuce leaves floating in the plate of stew, Jenny realised she actually felt sick, and the first mouthful confirmed it. She put down her knife and fork, gazing at the glass-panelled swing doors at the end of the hall and willing her nausea to subside.

'Jennifer!' Miss Vokes' voice penetrated the gathering

sense of isolation – Miss Vokes was also the mistress in charge of her dinner table.

Jenny swivelled her eyes and Miss Vokes, from her seat at the head of the table, gesticulated towards Jenny's plate. Obedient to the last, Jenny tried to force down another mouthful. It stuck in her throat. She put down her knife and fork again, covering her aching ear with her hand.

'Jennifer!' Miss Vokes called again, more sharply.

Wordlessly, Jenny shook her head. Miss Vokes rose and squeezed between the rows of chairs to stand behind Jenny, holding her gown wrapped around her so that she looked like a skinny black crow.

'Eat your dinner, Jennifer.'

'I can't,' Jenny said. 'I don't want it.'

'You can't waste good food. If you don't eat your dinner, you'll have no pudding.'

'I don't want any pudding,' Jenny said. 'I feel sick and my ear hurts.'

'The doctor said there is nothing wrong with your ear,' Miss Vokes said. 'Well, if you don't eat it, you'll have no pudding tomorrow either. Or for the rest of the week!'

Jenny said nothing. At that moment she did not care if she never had pudding again, but she knew better than to say so. One was cheeky to teachers at one's peril. Miss Vokes returned to her place tight-lipped with fury at what she saw as Jenny's wilful disobedience.

After what seemed like a lifetime the table finished eating and were allowed to dismiss. Jenny sat in the cloakroom on one of the long forms trying not to cry with the pain and wishing Rowena was here. But Rowena and her other best friends were away at the annual school camp. Jenny had begged Carrie to let her go too, but Carrie didn't agree with camping.

'You'd catch your death, sleeping in those damp tents!' she had said, and Jenny hadn't liked to argue because she suspected Carrie couldn't really afford for her to go. Money was tight, she knew – as it always had been.

When the bell rang it was time for those who were going to see *The Pickwick Papers* to line up ready to walk the three-quarters of a mile to the cinema. Jenny put on her blazer and went to join them. They started out in a crocodile down the steep winding hill, but before they had gone very far Jenny realised she felt very sick again – worse – she was going to *be* sick and there was nothing she could do to stop it. She went to the pavement edge and threw up into the gutter what dinner she had managed to force down.

Nobody took much notice. Some of the children looked and looked quickly away, and Mr Peters, the English teacher who was accompanying the party, asked her if she was all right. Jenny nodded weakly and assured him she was. She was so embarrassed she wanted to fade into the background and in any case she was tired of complaining about an earache nobody would believe she had. Only one person seemed concerned, and ill as she felt, Jenny still managed to be surprised at who it was. Jimmy Tudgay.

Since the days they'd been at Junior School together, Jimmy had changed very little. He was still big for his age, a bruiser of a boy with hair that flopped into his eyes and a reputation for getting into all kinds of mischief. He had grown out of playground fights now, but he could still handle himself, and the sports master had persuaded him to take up boxing. At this and every other sport Jimmy excelled and this had given him a certain self-confidence he might otherwise have lacked. Everyone had been faintly surprised when he had passed The Exam to go to the Grammar School, not least Jimmy himself. Now he stopped beside Jenny looking at her anxiously.

'You shouldn't be going to the pictures, Jen. You should be going home.'

'I'm all right,' she said. 'I feel better now I've been sick.'

'Does your ear still ache?'

She nodded. The pain was continuous now, not coming in bouts as it had done before, and oddly that made it more bearable. The brief periods of relief had only seemed to make the returning pain seem worse as it built slowly to its awful throbbing crescendo. Now that it was constant it seemed to have become a part of her.

'Why don't you tell them you want to go home?'

'No.' She shook her head. She'd done enough drawing

157

attention to herself for one day. 'I'll be all right.'

'Stay with me then,' Jimmy said. 'I'll look after you.'

She stayed with him. They reached the cinema and filed in. Jimmy sat next to her.

'Do you want to take your blazer off?'

'No, I'm not very warm.'

The lights dimmed and the film started, black and white images that flickered larger than life until they seemed to bound her world. She tried to concentrate but her eyes felt heavy and she couldn't bear to look at those huge flickering images any longer. She closed her eyes, letting her chin rest on her chest. The harsh soundtrack became a distant background buzz and as Pickwick and his cronies strutted and rolled across the screen, Jenny fell asleep.

The next thing she knew, Jimmy was shaking her gently.

'Jen! Jenny!'

She opened her eyes. The lights were on again in the cinema.

'You've been asleep,' he said. 'You've slept right through the picture.'

'Have I?'

She moved her head gingerly. Her glands felt stiff but her ear didn't seem to be hurting so much. Then she became aware of something tickling her neck. She put up her hand to touch it and felt a stream of something wet and sticky. She felt a moment's panic. Was it blood? Then her fingers encountered the collar of her blouse and found it stiff. Moist and stiff.

'What's on my collar?' she asked Jimmy.

'I don't know. It's all yellow.' He sounded frightened. 'It's all down your blazer too. And on your tie.'

Suddenly Jenny wanted only one thing in the world.

'I want to go home,' she said.

'You go on the coach, don't you?' Jimmy said.

'Yes, but not tonight. I won't be back at school in time for it. I was going to catch the bus.'

'Come on then,' Jimmy said.

He lived in Purldown, which was on the same route.

He walked with her to the bus stop, sat beside her on the

bus when it came and watched when she got off in Hillsbridge. As the bus passed her she saw his square, tough-guy face looking at her from the window with a worried expression. She felt a frisson of surprise. She couldn't ever remember seeing Jimmy look worried before, and who would have thought that of all of them it would be him who had taken the trouble to be concerned about her. Hardly knowing how to put one foot in front of the other, horribly conscious of the stiff yellow matter staining not only her blouse but her very expensive blazer too, Jenny struggled up the hill.

When she got in, Carrie gazed at her in horror.

'Whatever has happened to you?'

'Oh, Mum – I've had the most awful day,' Jenny said. And finally burst into tears.

The doctor was sent for next morning. Though medical treatment was now free on the NHS, Carrie could not get out of the habit of trying to avoid unnecessary bills, such as out-of-hours visits, and since Jenny's ear was no longer aching she thought perhaps she would be well enough to go to the surgery. But Jenny was still rather ill, couldn't even manage a piece of toast, and so in the end Carrie went out to phone.

'You realise it will be Dr Hall, don't you?' Dorothea Hillman, who answered the phone, said. There was a note of acidic triumph in her voice. Dorothea, who did not approve of lady doctors and had been personally affronted that one had been appointed to the practice she liked to think of as her own, always enjoyed imparting this information and enjoyed even more the dismay with which the news was sometimes received.

This morning, however, she was to be disappointed.

'Yes, she's seen our Heather's Vanessa a couple of times, and very good she was too,' Carrie said.

'As long as you're aware,' Dorothea said sniffily.

And added the call to Helen's list.

Helen arrived in Alder Road shortly after midday. As she parked her car outside Number 27, a group of boys playing

159

football on the green with heaps of discarded jumpers for goalposts stopped their game to stare, and a few curtains in the surrounding houses twitched.

'I'm sorry to have to get you out, Doctor,' Carrie said when she opened the door. 'But I really didn't think our Jenny was fit to bring to the surgery.'

Helen found Jenny propped up against the pillows, a copy of *Little Women* open and face down on her knees. But her eyes were bleary and Helen guessed she had been asleep when the doorbell had wakened her.

'You're not very well I hear, Jenny,' she said. 'Would you like to tell me about it?'

'It's my ear,' Jenny said. 'It's a lot better today though.'

'You should see the stuff that come out of it!' Carrie interrupted. 'And they kept her at that school all day! I'm furious, I can tell you. Some doctor from the county looked at her and said there was nothing wrong. Nothing wrong! A blind man could have seen how bad she was. I'm going up there and have my say, I can tell you!'

'Mum, you can't!' Jenny pleaded.

'I can and I will!'

'Shall I have a look then, Jenny?'

Jenny winced as Helen slipped the otoscope into her ear. A few moments later, Helen straightened up.

'You have a perforated eardrum, Jenny.'

Carrie was practically jumping up and down.

'You mean the county doctor missed a perforated ear drum?'

'It wouldn't have been perforated then,' Helen said.

'He must have caused it when he put that thing in her ear!' Carrie said furiously. 'Jenny said he hurt her. I'll have him up in court for this!'

'He wouldn't have caused the eardrum to rupture,' Helen said. 'That will have happened because of a build-up of pressure. She had an abscess, I expect, and when it swelled and burst there was nowhere for the fluid to go. Have you had a cold recently, Jenny?'

'A bit of a one,' Jenny said. 'I hate colds in the summer.'

'And you've been stuffed up, I expect.'

Jenny nodded.

160

'OK. Well, I'm going to give you some penicillin to clear up any infection. Have you had penicillin before?'

'No, she hasn't,' Carrie said, speaking for her.

'No, well, as you know, it's only recently become available for general use, but I think in your case, Jenny, it will be very useful. It may make you a bit weepy and depressed and if you have any other problems, let me know at once. And I think you should stay in bed for a day or two, just until you're feeling better.'

'I'll miss the end of term things at school,' Jenny said. 'I don't want to miss them! It's always such fun . . .'

'You'll do as the doctor says, my lady. And I'm going up there tomorrow to complain about that other one – the county man.'

'Mum – please!' Jenny looked totally desperate.

'He needs to be told!'

'There's no need for you to trouble, Mrs Simmons,' Helen said, taking pity on Jenny. 'I'll have a word myself.'

'With the county?' Carrie sounded awestruck.

'Yes, I'll speak to the doctor concerned myself.'

Helen thought it unwise to add that Jenny's ear problem had probably been obscured by wax. The suggestion that Carrie might have been in some way negligent about Jenny's personal hygiene and so indirectly the reason why the abscess hadn't been diagnosed would not, Helen felt, go down well. Plenty of time to mention that later.

'Well, all right, thank you, Doctor. I'll leave it to you. Say thank you to the doctor, Jennifer.'

Helen's sympathy for Jenny increased. Not only had she had a very painful twenty-four hours, on top of that she had a mother who treated her like a baby.

'I see you're reading *Little Women*, Jenny,' she said.

Jenny smiled. 'For about the third time.'

'She's always loved reading,' Carrie said.

Helen ignored her.

'I love *Little Women* too. Have you read *Good Wives*?'

'Some of it. I couldn't finish. I got really upset when Jo married that awful old German professor. I wanted her to marry Laurie.'

For the first time, Carrie did not interrupt. Helen

161

guessed she was out of her depth and she was right. Carrie had never read *Little Women*.

'You cared about Jo, then.'

'She's my favourite.'

'Mine too,' Helen said. 'I know what you mean about her marrying the professor. I didn't much like that either. It seemed jolly unfair.'

'She loved Laurie so much,' Jenny said.

Carrie could not resist a snort at this.

'Love!'

'At least you'll have a nice lot of time for reading over the next few days,' Helen said, ignoring her again. 'Have you got plenty of books?'

'Oh yes,' Jenny said, brightening. 'I've got all my old favourites – and the Home Readers from school too. I'm halfway through *The Old Curiosity Shop*, but I just felt like reading *Little Women* today.'

'That's it – you indulge yourself,' Helen said.

'Well, thank you, Doctor,' Carrie said when she saw her downstairs. 'And you won't forget to do something about that school doctor, will you?'

'I won't.'

'It'll come better from you than me.'

Helen wasn't so sure. And she wasn't sure either whom she should be angrier with – the school doctor or Carrie. Between them they'd caused Jenny a lot of pain. There was nothing she could do about Carrie – the way she treated her daughter was her business – but she could at least tell the school doctor, whoever he was, what she thought about him.

'I'll see Jenny again in a couple of days,' she said.

The next call for Helen was a farm cottage further along the lane on which Alder Road had been built – an old miner who suffered from silicosis, the lung disease caused by years of inhaling coal dust, now lived there with his daughter and son-in-law who worked as a farm labourer. As the lane narrowed Helen drove more slowly. There wasn't usually much traffic to be encountered here, but one never knew whether a tractor or milk lorry might be

162

coming the other way, or, just around one of the many bends, a horse and cart or even a straying cow.

Half a mile or so along, the lane twisted into a steep dip where the hedges obscured her view; Helen pulled well into the side as she negotiated it, cursing as a low-hanging branch scraped her nearside. Just as well she had pulled in though – something was coming the other way. Helen slowed almost to a stop and a big black car rounded the bend.

Helen's jaw dropped as she recognised it. Cliff Button's taxi! As it passed she had a clear view of the driver who was looking straight ahead and concentrating on squeezing through the narrow gap and realised it was Cliff himself behind the wheel. She turned, looking over her shoulder to watch him disappear up the rise, infuriated and concerned. What on earth did the man think he was doing? It was only a matter of days since she had told him his epilepsy meant he must not drive. For a moment she hesitated, wondering whether to turn around and follow him, then deciding against it. There wasn't a great deal of point – so long as he didn't have a fit and crash the car – and she had a busy round to complete. But she'd have to have a word with him as a matter of urgency and warn him of the consequences if he ignored her advice again.

Helen sighed, dreading the encounter already. She hated having to be heavy-handed and she felt very sorry for Cliff. But, however unpleasant, she had a duty to do something about it. In his present condition Cliff on the roads was a danger to himself and everyone else. And whether he liked it or not she was going to have to tell him so in no uncertain terms.

'I've had one hell of a day,' she said to Paul that evening.

He had called in at the end of afternoon surgery as he so often did these days. In one respect Helen was always glad to see him. In some ways her relationship with the two partners had completely turned around. Dr Hobbs, whom she had assumed approved of her, since he had appointed her, had turned out to be somewhat difficult to work with – a slightly fussy, old-school doctor who often questioned

163

her closely about her diagnoses and treatments as if he didn't quite trust her, and had an annoying habit of coming into her room and flicking through the files on her desk as he spoke to her. He had pulled her up over quite a few things and though Helen would have been the first to admit he knew a great deal more about general practice than she did and was only too prepared to ask for advice if she felt she needed it, she was irritated and rather unnerved by his constant nit-picking over things she didn't feel mattered at all.

'Just be careful how you speak to Dorothea, my dear,' he had said on one occasion, his tone managing to be both avuncular and a little reproving. 'I know she can be difficult but she is a valued member of staff and you must try to humour her.'

'I thought I was perfectly civil to Dorothea,' Helen had replied, a little sharply, since Dorothea was often barely civil to her.

'You must remember she's been here a good many years and she doesn't like to be told how to do her job,' he said.

Helen had smarted, just as she had smarted when he had suggested that she would get through her surgery in far less time if she didn't allow patients to prattle on about their personal problems.

'They'll tell you their whole life's story if you let them,' he had chided and Helen had had to bite her tongue to keep from retorting that she thought that was the whole point – that you should know your patients well enough to be able to judge who and what to take seriously or dismiss as hypochondria or loneliness, and hazard a guess at where the root of their health problems lay. She didn't say it, of course – she didn't want to antagonise Reuben Hobbs by continually arguing with his criticisms, but her growing resentment made for a less than easy relationship.

Paul, on the other hand, had become her ally. Without being told – Helen would never be so disloyal as to talk to one partner about the other – he seemed to know the way Reuben Hobbs made her feel. He'd been in the same position himself once of course, she reasoned. Perhaps when he'd been young and new Reuben had treated him in the same rather patronising way. Whatever the reason, Paul was there for her, and she was glad of the unruffled easy-going nature beneath what Charlotte would have called his 'John Blunt' exterior. She was always glad to hear his broad northern accent greeting someone in the passageway outside her room; always glad when his square, rather rugged face appeared around the door. His presence reassured her, lifted her heart. And yet . . . and yet . . .

Helen was beginning to be worried that Paul's interest in her was a little more than simply that of a colleague. There was, after all, no need for him to come to the Hillsbridge surgery almost every day without fail, yet come he did, always looking in on her for a chat, perching easily on the corner of her desk like an oversized gargoyle; sometimes – as he had on the day when he had thrown Guy, oh so politely, out of her surgery – asking her out for a meal or a drink. She accepted him because she liked him and she had practically no other social contacts here in Hillsbridge. Lovely as Amy and Ralph were, they had their own lives to lead and she had very little in common with any of her other relatives in her age group in the town. Busy as she was it was still possible to feel lonely and she enjoyed Paul's company enormously. But at the same time she couldn't help worrying that he might be reading more into their friendship than she intended. He'd never made a move on her though, and she fervently hoped he would not. It would make things impossibly awkward if she had to refute some advance or other. The companionable relationship would be gone for ever and she would have lost a good friend.

Tonight she was especially glad that he was there to talk to.

'I really have had one hell of a day,' she said.

He settled his bulk against the small sink in the corner of the surgery, arms folded, raising his eyebrows at her.

'How come?'

'Well, for starters, I've made myself unpopular with the county doctor,' she said, cupping her chin in her hands. 'He saw one of my patients yesterday at her school and

165

told her he could find nothing wrong with her when she had a raging ear infection. The poor child has ended up with a perforated eardrum – and a very indignant mother, who was going to the school to say her piece – much to her daughter's distress – until I promised to have a word with him myself.'

'Oh God – so you took on the dreaded county wallahs!'

'I did. And it was a bit like bearding a lion in its den.'

'I bet it was. He had his reasons for not spotting the trouble, I imagine?'

'Wax, he said, as I knew he would. Drum obscured by a lot of wax. But the point is, Paul, he shouldn't have just dismissed her like that. It must have been perfectly obvious the child was in a lot of pain. They become so hard, those county doctors – that's the trouble.'

'Perhaps – but I dare say they've got a lot to make them.'

'If they refuse to listen to the patient and are incapable of summoning up an ounce of compassion they've no right to be in the profession at all.'

'You sound like a crusader, Helen. Riding out as the white knight to do battle.'

'I know – I know. I get too involved for my own good. There's another thing, though, I have to get involved in. Duty-bound, as they say.'

She went on to tell him about Cliff Button.

'Hmm, that is a sticky one!' Paul shifted his position slightly. 'What are you going to do?'

'Go and see him – have a word – tell him if he doesn't stop driving I'll have to report him to the licensing authorities. I don't like doing it. I'll feel an absolute bitch if I have to go that far. But quite honestly I don't feel I have any choice in the matter. Supposing he had a fit whilst he was driving and killed himself – or even worse – someone else? I'd never forgive myself.'

'You're right,' he said. 'You don't have a choice. Just hope and pray you can make him see sense without you having to get heavy-handed. Anything else?'

'Yes.'

'What?'

'A girl I had into the surgery this morning.' She paused, rubbing her eyes with her fingers, then pressing them against her temples, remembering. Such a pretty girl, so young – twenty-one years old, according to her records. A girl who should be standing on the very threshold of her life. A girl whose symptoms had caused her a good deal of concern.

'One of my patients?' Paul asked.

'Yes. Her name is Linda Parfitt. She lives at Tiledown. I'm surprised the family didn't transfer with you, actually. I mean, they're midway between the two surgeries.'

'The Parfitts wouldn't bother. They're the sort of people who are happy enough with whatever they're offered. And they don't often need a doctor, in any case. I think I've only seen them two or three times since I've been here. They're a pretty healthy family on the whole.'

'Linda's not healthy,' Helen said. 'Not any more.'

'What's wrong with her then? She's not pregnant, is she?'

'No,' Helen said. 'She's certainly not pregnant. I wish that was all it was.'

Paul frowned, looking serious. 'What is it then?'

Helen chewed her lip for a moment.

'I hope to God I'm wrong,' she said. 'But I think she's suffering from leukaemia.'

The next day Helen called on Cliff Button as soon as morning surgery was over.

Cliff lived in one of a neat row of cottages not far from the Market Place. His taxi was in its usual place, parked outside a lock-up garage on the opposite side of the road, but Helen could not make up her mind whether that boded well or not. At least he wasn't driving it – but then he didn't appear to have put it away for the duration either.

She went up the path, edged by beds of sweet william and snapdragons, and knocked on the door. It was opened by Cliff's wife, Hilda, wiping her hands on the skirt of her floral wrap-around overall. She looked taken aback to find Helen on her doorstep.

167

'Dr Hall! Whatever brings you here?'

'I wanted a word with Cliff,' Helen said.

'He's out in his garden,' Hilda said, looking anxious. 'You'd better come through.'

She led Helen through a small living room which smelled of lavender polish and a scullery where she was obviously baking – apples, peeled and cored ready for a pie, were simmering on a gas stove, and flour and partly rolled-out pastry lay on a wooden board on the linoleum-covered table.

'Cliff!' she called. 'You've got a visitor!'

Cliff, who had been nowhere to be seen, emerged from behind a tall row of runner beans, whose plethora of red flowers promised a fine crop in a few weeks' time.

'Dr Hall! What brings you here?'

'I think you know that, Mr Button,' Helen said.

Cliff held her gaze with an expression of innocent bewilderment which would have done credit to a naughty child trying to deny disobedience.

'You've got me there, Doctor.'

'Come on,' Helen said sternly. 'You and I both know that you have been driving. You passed me in Withydown Lane yesterday.'

'Oh.' Cliff's eyes fell away from hers, guilty now. 'That were you, were it, Doctor?'

'Yes,' Helen said. 'It was. Look, Mr Button, the last thing I want to do is report you to the authorities, but if you continue to drive your taxi, with or without passengers, I'll have no choice.'

'I'm sorry, Doctor.' Cliff looked utterly dejected now. 'I know you said I shouldn't, but I felt all right, and Mrs Coles wanted to get over to her daughter's at Withydown.'

'I'm sorry too,' Helen said, 'but whatever the reason, and however well you felt, you must not drive until we're absolutely certain your seizures are under control.'

Cliff was silent for a moment, then quite suddenly he nipped a runner off the beans with a savagery that surprised her.

'It's all very well, Doctor, but what am I s'posed to do 'til then? My car's my life! I've bin driving 'un since I was just a young lad. I shan't know what to do with meself all day.'

'Well – you've always got your garden,' Helen said, looking at the rows of cabbage plants and potato haulms hacked up and almost ready to dig, and the display of neatly sticked late peas, their fat pods shining amidst the pale leaf. 'You obviously get a lot of pleasure out of that.'

'Oh ah – I've always liked me garden,' Cliff agreed. 'But I've always kept it up together *and* drove me car. I haven't got enough to keep me occupied here all day long. And then there's the money. We'm going t' miss the money.'

'Surely you've got a retirement pension?' Helen said.

Cliff snorted. 'Could *you* live on nothing but a bit o' pension, Doctor? You wanna try it some time.'

Helen sighed, hating every moment of this, but knowing that was no excuse to shirk her duty.

'Couldn't you perhaps do a few gardening jobs for other people?' she suggested.

'Such as?'

'Well – I don't know. But there must be plenty of people who can't manage themselves who would be only too glad of your expertise.'

'Can't think of anybody,' Cliff said flatly. 'Who'd want a gardener who might fall down in the middle of the rhubarb with a bloody fit?'

The picture might have been amusing had it not been such a serious matter for Cliff. A fit and healthy man all his life, this unexpected illness had certainly got to him. Helen couldn't imagine that he would make any effort to find out if there was anyone who would pay for his services as a gardener – he was sinking too fast into a state of depressed hopelessness.

'Well, I'm sorry, Mr Button, but there it is,' she told him with finality. 'Falling down in a rhubarb patch would be a whole lot better than having an accident and killing someone, don't you think? Now – I must be going, but I have to warn you that if I find out you've been driving again, I shall have no option but to take the necessary action.'

'Don't worry, Doctor – he won't.' Hilda spoke up for the

first time. 'I'll make sure of that.' She turned on Cliff. 'Whatever were you thinking of, you silly old fool? If Doctor says you're not to drive, you're not to drive! As for the money – we'll manage. We've done it before and we'll do it again.'

For a moment Cliff looked from one to the other of them, a mutinous expression on his leathery face. Then: 'Women!' he muttered, and disappeared once more behind the beans.

'I'm sorry, Doctor,' Hilda said, tucking a strand of thick grey hair which had escaped from the bun at the nape of her neck back behind her ear. 'He can be a stubborn beggar sometimes.'

'I'm sorry I've had to upset him,' Helen said.

'You've got your job to do. Just get him better, that's all I ask. The last thing I want is to lose him.'

'It won't come to that, Mrs Button. Epilepsy . . .'

'Oh, it's not the epilepsy. I don't mean that. But when I think what might happen if he was to have a fit when he's driving . . . It doesn't bear thinking about. No, he won't be getting in that car again until he's better. You can depend on that.'

Helen thanked her, relieved to have her support, but as she left the house she realised some of Cliff's depression had rubbed off on her. I suppose I see myself as some kind of angel of mercy, she thought with grim humour. I don't like it when others see me as an authoritative monster instead! But there it was – being a doctor wasn't all a bed of roses. That was a fact of life she'd thought she'd come to terms with a long time ago. It was something of a shock to Helen to discover that she really had not.

Chapter Nine

Jenny was feeling bad-tempered and miserable.

As Helen had predicted, the course of antibiotics had made her depressed, and though the enforced break had given her plenty of time for reading the books of her choice she had found it difficult to sustain interest in them. As if to compound her mood, the weather had turned bad, rain beating incessantly against the windows and heavy cloud making everything look grey and bleak.

On the Saturday morning, when Carrie had gone to market, Jenny decided to ease the boredom by doing a jigsaw, but before long she lost patience with that too, throwing the box across the room in a fit of impotent frustration and bursting into tears.

Joe, who was treating himself to a half-hour with the *Daily Mirror*, since the weather was too bad for him to do any work in the garden, looked up from the paper.

'What's the matter, my love?'

'Oh, I don't know!' There was no way she could explain the edginess that was making her skin crawl. 'I'm just fed up with everything.'

'That's no good, you know!' She didn't answer, and after a moment, he went on: 'You want something to cheer you up, that's what.'

'There isn't anything, though, is there? I can't go out, the weather's foul, and I feel horrible!'

Joe was silent, his faded blue eyes thoughtful. Then a little smile tweaked the corner of his mouth. 'You never know. I expect something will turn up.'

Jenny looked up, as a sudden crack appeared in the storm clouds of her mood. She knew that tone! It meant her father was planning something.

'What?'

But Joe just smiled again. 'Oh, you'll have to wait and see, won't you?'

And nothing she could say would persuade him to say more.

When Carrie came home from the market, Joe waylaid her in the utility room. They were talking for some time, but though she pricked her ears, Jenny was unable to hear what they were saying. But she did hear the back door open and close again and when Carrie came through to begin putting her shopping away there was a funny little smile on her face too.

'Where's Dad?' Jenny asked.

'Oh – out in the outhouse, I think. Doing a bit of sorting out, seeing as he can't get out on the garden.'

'Oh.' Jenny felt inordinately disappointed without really knowing why.

About half an hour later she heard the kitchen door again and Carrie popped her head around the living-room door. The funny little smile was still there, a little broader if anything.

'Jenny – come out here a minute.'

'Why?'

'Never mind why. Just come out here.'

Jenny got up and went into the kitchen. Joe was there. He was wearing his gaberdine mac and there was a bulge underneath it, at chest level.

Jenny stared. 'What . . .?'

He pulled back the lapel of his mac and to her amazement Jenny saw a small silky brown head with pricked ears and moist brown eyes.

'Oh!' she gasped, almost unable to believe her eyes. 'It's a puppy! Oh, what a darling little thing!'

Carrie was beaming broadly now. 'Your dad thought it would cheer you up. It's one of those that Mrs Carter's dog had – you know, Mrs Carter down in the units. We talked about it before.'

'Oh, it's so lovely! Lovely! But poor little thing – she's shaking.' She was – trembling all over.

'Do you want to hold her?' Joe asked.

'Can I?'

'Course you can. She's ours.'

'Ours!' Jenny couldn't believe it. 'I thought you'd just brought her up to show me.'

'No, we've decided to have her.'

'Oh thank you! Thank you!'

'Don't thank me,' Carrie said shortly. 'Thank your dad. I talked about it, yes, but it was his idea to go on and do something about it.'

'Oh, Dad!' Jenny took the puppy from Joe, burying her face in its silky head, feeling the small body trembling against her.

'You see, Jenny?' Joe said, smiling his slow smile. 'There's always something to look forward to, isn't there, even if you don't know it. And now I'm going to have to go down to Hillsbridge to get a dog licence.'

'And some food. What does she eat? And what are we going to call her?'

'I think you'd better choose her name, Jenny,' Carrie said. 'But if it was up to me, I'd call her Sally.'

Naturally, Sally it was. Jenny adored her. She helped Carrie spread newspapers all over the kitchen floor because the puppy wasn't house-trained yet, and she helped clean up the messes Sally made. And when the puppy whimpered, missing her brothers and sisters, Jenny stroked her and cuddled her and spoke to her soothingly. At night she even sang her to sleep in the bed made of old blankets in the utility room. And the penicillin-induced depression began to lift. Who could be sad for long with Sally scampering around the place? Jenny felt that life had taken on a whole new meaning!

Jenny went back to school the week before they were due to break up for the holidays. Everyone, including Miss Vokes, was very nice to her, which was just as well since she still felt rather sorry for herself.

Rowena was full of the enormous fun had by all at the school camp, and the latest boy she had fallen in love with – a sixth former who was regarded as a heart-throb by his peers and the younger girls alike. Rowena was justifiably proud of having attracted his interest, but her smugness grated horribly on Jenny, who was torn between envy and resentment. As if it wasn't enough that she should have been asked to the pictures by this young Adonis, her mother was quite happy to let her go. It just wasn't fair, Jenny decided – and then was struck by yet another probable result of this new romance. If Rowena was going out with someone, she wouldn't have so much time for Jenny.

'Do you think Barry will ever go out with me again?' she asked Rowena wistfully.

'I don't know!' Rowena sounded impatient – she was as fed up with Jenny mooning over Barry as Jenny was fed up with the details of her conquest.

'Do you think he might?' Jenny persisted, unabashed. 'I mean, it's not as if we had a row or anything. It was just that dressed-up doll June Farthing getting her claws into him.'

'If he liked you, why did he let her?' Rowena asked, maddeningly reasonable.

'I don't know,' Jenny said. 'Oh, if he won't go out with me again, I just wish I could die. I bet if I'd died when I had that ear thing he'd be sorry.'

'He stood you up,' Rowena said patiently. 'How can you even want to go out with him again when he treats you like that?'

'I don't know. But I do!'

'It wouldn't do any good anyway,' Rowena said reasonably. 'I thought your mother wouldn't let you go.'

Jenny said nothing. She thought she would be prepared to go to any lengths of deception if only it meant she could go out with Barry again.

'I tell you who *is* sweet on you,' Rowena said. 'Jimmy Tudgay. He was watching you all through Maths. I saw him. If you want someone to go out with, I bet you could get him to ask you.'

Jenny felt a flush warming her cheeks. She'd been aware of him looking at her too, and though he hadn't gone so far as to ask her how she was, she had found herself remembering how kind he had been the day she'd first

174

been ill. But Jimmy Tudgay! He wasn't in the same league as Barry or Rowena's new boyfriend.

'I'm not that desperate,' she said. Then her face flamed even more hotly as she realised Jimmy and another boy were passing, almost within earshot.

Oh, don't let him have heard! she prayed. She didn't want to hurt his feelings.

Partly because she was worried about this and partly because she kept thinking of what Rowena had said, Jenny found herself watching Jimmy surreptitiously – and beginning to like what she saw. There was something powerfully attractive about someone who actually *liked* you – and that was not all. Jimmy had changed quite a lot, she realised. He might not have the film-star good looks of Rowena's boyfriend, but he wasn't at all bad-looking, with his strong-featured square face and a well set-up body that seemed to have grown an inch or so taller every time she saw him without thickening any more. Being the same age as her was a disadvantage, of course, But still, he really was rather nice.

With only a few days left to the end of term, serious lessons had been more or less abandoned. Curriculums for the year were completed, exams had been sat, and a sort of holiday air overtook everyone, even the teachers who were usually the hardest task-masters. The PE lesson was turned over to a game of Pirates, when all the equipment was set out at the same time and pupils played an elaborate version of tag, which immediately ended for any contestant caught by a pirate, or who fell into the sea – that is, touched the floor. Jenny was ridiculously pleased that she managed to be among the last half-dozen to be caught – she had at last managed to master the knack of climbing a rope, and by shinning to the top and moving from one to the other along the row that hung in the centre of the gym she evaded capture for quite a long time. In English they played Hangman, taking turns at the blackboard and setting a crossword-type clue for the rest of the form; in Maths there were number games, in Chemistry fun experiments, and in the period devoted to Art they were allowed to take their drawing blocks into the field that sloped away from the school and sit on the grass to sketch whatever they liked.

They congregated in that same field at lunchtime, sprawling contentedly under the huge spreading chestnut tree to find some shade from the relentless midday sun, boys and girls together now, because the days when they segregated naturally into single-sex groups were almost at an end.

On the day before the last day of term, Jenny was lying on her stomach, head resting on her arms, and almost asleep – the effect of the antibiotics still brought on drowsy spells – when she felt something tickling her neck. She released one hand and flicked at the tickling spot, thinking it was a fly or even a wasp, but there was nothing there and a few seconds the tickling came again. This time, as she slapped at it more vigorously, one of the others laughed and she rolled over to see Jimmy with a long blade of dry grass in his hand.

'Jimmy!' she said. 'What are you doing? I thought it was a creepy crawlie!'

Jimmy said nothing, just grinned at her, but unexpectedly she felt her tummy tip.

'Stop it! I'm trying to go to sleep,' she said, but there was a coquettish note in her voice. Jenny, who would have said she hadn't the first idea of how to flirt, was doing it naturally and quite unconsciously. There was even invitation in the way she plonked her head back on her arms – and of course, inevitably, he did it again.

'Jimmy!' She sat up, pretending outrage. 'I said leave me alone.'

'He'll stop on one condition,' Ginger Jacobs said. 'He'll stop tormenting you if you'll go out with him.'

Jenny blushed furiously; glancing at Jimmy she saw that he had gone red too – a flush that ran right down his neck under the collar of his grey school shirt.

'Ginger – you bastard!' he muttered.

'Well, it's true!' Ginger said, unabashed. 'He wants to go out with you. How about it? Put the poor bloke out of his misery.'

'I can't . . .' Jenny started to say, then broke off as she

176

caught sight of the tortured expression on Jimmy's face. She couldn't humiliate him in front of his friends by turning him down without a reason – and she couldn't explain either that she was not allowed, because that would humiliate her. And in any case . . .

I'd quite like to go out with him, Jenny thought. It would be nice to be with someone who liked her – and why should Carrie know? Jenny certainly wasn't going to make the mistake of confessing again.

'Why can't he ask me himself?' she said now, and the coquettishness, so new to her, was there again. 'I'm not going out with someone who has to get his friends to do his asking for him.'

She still didn't really think he'd do it. She thought he'd be too afraid of being made to look a fool if she said no. But to her surprise, a mulish look came over his red face.

'That's right, Ginger,' he said to his friend. 'I don't need you to talk for me.' And to Jenny: 'Can I have a date, Jen?'

Well, good for you, Jimmy! she thought, and smiled demurely.

'All right,' she said.

It really was very easy lying to Carrie, much easier than it had been to lie about Barry, because she still felt aggrieved about the way Carrie had behaved when she'd found out about it. It was also easier in practice, because she had a good excuse – all the school crowd had arranged to meet up almost daily at the open-air swimming pool at South Compton.

It was a wonderful pool – unheated, of course, and not really very big, but big enough, with a springboard and a high board that they could 'bomb' from, curling their knees up to their chins and leaping the ten feet into the shimmering ice-blue water beneath. Some of the boys even climbed on to the surrounding railing, or even the breeze-block wall beyond, and jumped from there, though if Mr Catley the pool attendant saw them, he shouted at them and they had to stop it or risk being turned out. In winter, Mr Catley was one of the council road sweepers, in charge of nothing more exciting than a broom and bin on wheels, and he relished the power that was his in the summer months.

The swimming pool was set in the long valley that ran between Hillsbridge and South Compton, and surrounded by fields. It was simplicity itself to have a quick dip, the girls screaming with laughter as the boys ducked them or pushed them in, then get dressed, meet Jimmy outside the turnstile gate, cross the wooden bridge and follow the stream through the cool green fields. As soon as they were out of sight of the others, Jimmy would take her hand or put his arm around her, and if they could find a hollow to sit down in he would kiss her. He wasn't as good a kisser as Barry had been, but then she supposed he was less experienced and it was very pleasant all the same.

One afternoon when she emerged through the turnstile gate, a gang of rather rough-looking boys was waiting to go in. Jenny went to hurry past them towards the bridge where Jimmy was waiting and she was surprised to hear her name called.

'Hey, Jenny! It's Jenny Simmons!' She glanced round and saw Billy Edgell sitting astride his old black Hercules bicycle. 'Hey, Jenny – come over here!'

Jenny felt her face going red. She didn't want anything to do with Billy and his friends. She turned away quickly but before she had gone more than a few steps the boys had surrounded her.

'Come on, darling – someone's talking to you . . .'

'Leave her alone.' Billy cycled slowly over, parking his bike right in her path. 'You been swimming, Jenny?'

'Yes.' She glanced helplessly towards Jimmy but he and his friends had climbed down over the bank to the river and he hadn't noticed what was happening. 'I've got to go, Billy.'

'What's your hurry?'

'Nothing. I've just got to go.'

'I'll walk you home if you like.'

'No, thanks.'

'Another time, then? How about coming out with me one night?'

'No. I've already got a boyfriend.'

178

One of the others laughed. 'You're getting the brush-off, Billy.'

'Am I?' Billy challenged her. 'I could show you a good time, Jenny. I know a thing or two – not like that lot of stupid kids.' He jerked his head in the direction of the river bank.

From somewhere Jenny found a courage she hadn't known she had.

'I wouldn't go out with you if you were the last person on earth!' she said scathingly. 'Now, are you going to get out of my way, or am I going to call Mr Catley?'

'Oh, you're really scaring me now,' Billy sneered, but he moved to one side anyway. As she slipped past he called after her: 'I wouldn't go out with you either. I was only winding you up. I wouldn't want to go out with a prissy-knickers like you!'

But he looked none too pleased, and Jenny guessed that she'd made him look a bit of a fool in front of his friends. She tossed her head to hide the fact that she was trembling a little and ran to the river bank, calling to Jimmy.

'Are we going for a walk or not?'

'Oh, you're there!' Jimmy joined her. 'I didn't know you were out yet. What's the matter, Jenny? You look all red.'

'Nothing.' She didn't want to tell him about Billy. He might go back and cause trouble. With a determined effort, Jenny put the incident out of her mind.

She always enjoyed her walks with Jimmy. He seemed to know so much about the countryside that she did not, in spite of having lived in it most of her life. He could identify the different trees, he could tell her about the wildlife that lived on the river, he could even catch tiddlers, though he always let them go again. When the herd of cows were in the field he would go right up to them, rubbing their noses while Jenny stood well back, half afraid. Carrie didn't care for cows and she had passed her fear on to Jenny. With Jimmy's encouragement, however, she had learned to con-quer that fear and even rub a hairy nose herself. The day one of the heifers actually licked her outstretched hand in return, Jenny had heard herself laughing with nervous delight.

All in all, it was a wonderful summer, one of those summers she would always remember in the years to come, when the reality of adulthood stole the magic of youth. But even as she enjoyed it, every sun-filled moment, every new experience, every languid lazy hour, an underlying feeling that was not quite a premonition nagged from a corner of her subconscious. She didn't want to acknowledge it and break the spell, but she knew all the same.

It couldn't last. Before long something would happen that would put an end to these halcyon days out of time, and they would be gone for ever.

Chapter Ten

Helen parked her car on the edge of the triangle of grass that divided Amy's front garden from the steep slope of Porter's Hill. She reached into the back seat for her medical bag, locked the car and headed for the garden gate. She should have begun to look around for a home of her own, she thought. She couldn't expect to stay with Amy for ever – wouldn't want to – but Amy was insistent that she enjoyed having her and hectic as life was at present it was an ideal situation for Helen. It was good not having to worry about laundry or shopping for the basic necessities of life – Amy's housekeeper, Mrs Milsom, took care of all that. And apart from the odd hasty glance in an estate agent's window, Helen simply hadn't had time to do anything about looking for property.

She pushed open the gate and made her way along the path between the burgeoning shrubs.

'Hello, Helen! I thought I heard the car!'

Amy emerged from behind a rose hedge, a pair of secateurs in her hand. She was wearing a collarless cotton shirt, linen trousers and a floppy straw hat to protect her fair skin from the still-warm sun. Once, Amy would have gone bare-headed whatever the weather – winter and summer alike. Now, at fifty, she knew better.

'This darned garden!' she said now. 'It's out of control.'

'I thought you enjoyed gardening,' Helen said.

'In moderation, yes. But at this time of year it suddenly goes crazy. Everything happens at once. You turn your back for a second and it's a wilderness. Just look!' She waved the secateurs towards a herbaceous border where clumps of forget-me-nots and the sort of spindly dandelions they had, as children, called wet-the-beds had sprouted almost overnight and the hedge which formed a

181

backdrop, thick with brambles, threatening to smother the whole lot. 'The trouble is, Roly just can't manage it any more. He's got terribly slow. And I haven't got the time, and neither has Ralph.'

Roly Withers had been their gardener for years now, and in that time had grown as old and wizened as some of the trees which had been there even longer than the house.

'I wonder . . .' Helen hesitated, not sure whether or not she should interfere. 'I think I might know someone who could help you out.'

'Oh, I couldn't put Roly's nose out of joint.' Amy dragged viciously at a column of ivy which had twined itself amongst the roses. 'He'd be so hurt if he thought I thought he was past it.'

'Oh well, never mind.' Helen looked at her watch. 'I was thinking of going to see Gran this evening. Why don't you come with me?'

'I've got my work cut out here,' Amy said. 'Mam wouldn't want me there, anyway, when she's got you. You and she are as thick as thieves.'

'She always asks about you,' Helen said.

'Does she?' Amy looked surprised.

'Well, of course she does! She is your mother, after all!'

'I know.' Amy sighed. Since she had grown up, she and Charlotte rarely saw eye to eye – because they were too much alike, Ralph said, and what he meant was that they were as spirited and stubborn as one another and could be equally difficult. Amy couldn't see it, though. She only knew that her mother was often sharp with her and almost always seemed disapproving. Amy, as different as could be from her placid older sister Dolly, would retaliate, and the visit would end with sparks flying.

'I'm going to get changed,' Helen said. 'I feel really sticky and horrible. Then I'll come and give you a hand until dinner, if you like. I'm no gardener, but at least I could pull a few weeds.'

'You don't have to, honestly.'

'It's OK – I'd like to.'

She went into the house, which was cool and dim after

182

the bright sunshine outside and smelled of roasting meat and roses, thinking about the patients she had seen today, and also about Paul Stephens. He'd turned up again this evening on some pretext or other just as she was finishing her surgery, breezing in as the last patient left and perching himself, as he usually did, against the sink.

'Good day?'

'OK. Apart from that I got the results back on Linda Parfitt's tests.'

'Not good news, I take it.'

'Uh-huh. They confirmed what I was afraid of. Leukaemia.'

Paul swore softly. 'Does she know yet?'

'I'm seeing her tomorrow and I'm not looking forward to it, I can tell you. Why, Paul? Why does it have to happen to someone like her? To anyone, come to that?'

'You know as well as I do, Helen, cancer is no respecter of youth.'

'It's so bloody unfair.'

'Life is, Helen. It's just that in our job we see more of it than most people.'

'I know . . . I know.' She ran a hand through her hair, which had flopped down over her forehead. However often she came up against something like this, she didn't think she'd ever get used to it. 'I'm getting her in to see Mr Brownlow as soon as possible, but . . .'

'But even he can't work miracles.'

'Unfortunately.'

'You won't tell her that.'

'Of course not! Never underestimate the power of the mind, my old tutor at med school used to say. But in the last resort . . .'

'Let's talk about more cheerful things,' Paul said. 'Are you going to Matthew Vezey's soirée?'

Helen did a double take.

'Soirée? What's a soirée?'

'You're asking *me?*'

'Oh – I know what a soirée is. I just didn't think people had them any more. And certainly not Matthew Vezey. Anyone less likely . . .'

'It's not so much Matthew as his sister. She suffers from delusions of grandeur. Haven't you had an invitation yet? Mine came this morning.'

'I don't know. I haven't had time to open my personal mail yet.' She reached into her briefcase and pulled out a handful of unopened envelopes, leafing through them. 'That looks like Matthew's practically indecipherable scrawl.' She slit it open with her paper knife. 'Oh yes. You're right. A soirée – on Saturday evening. It sounds very grand!'

'Knowing Enid it will be. She'll probably hire in catering staff all dressed in black and white and looking like penguins. Not my scene really, but there'll be enough booze to sink the *Queen Mary* and the sort of nibbles you wouldn't expect to meet face to face this side of the gates of Buckingham Palace.'

'You mean canapés. You can't have anything as common as a nibble at a soirée.' The effort to cheer up was working; she was feeling much better. 'I agree with you, it isn't my scene really either, but I suppose we shall have to put in an appearance.'

'In which case we might as well go together. No sense taking two cars. I'll call for you, shall I?'

'But it's out of your way to pick me up,' she protested.

'No problem. Let's see – it starts at eight. I'll be there about say . . .'

'Ten o'clock?' she suggested wickedly.

'Hmm. I take your point. But we'd better be on time. I expect the poor old boy will want us there nice and early so he can find out what's been going on in the practice since he hung up his stethoscope. How about I pick you up at ten to eight?'

'OK.' But she was feeling a little uneasy. If Paul was going to take her to Matthew Vezey's soirée that meant he would also be taking her home. Just the sort of encounter she was trying to avoid.

She thought about it again now as she changed out of her linen suit and into a cool cotton dress. As long as all he wanted was to be friends – fine. Anything more . . .

Her stomach clenched with the trapped feelings she

184

knew so well. What was it with her? Why did she always feel this way when she thought someone might be taking more than a passing interest in her? She hadn't felt it with Guy – but then Guy had been married and therefore technically unavailable. Sometimes Helen wondered if that was the reason she had been attracted to him. No ties. No pressure. No possibility of a permanent binding relationship. She'd longed for it, of course, hoped against desperate hope that he would leave that miserable wife of his for her. But if he had, if he actually had, what then? Would she have had the same reaction – wanted to run like a frightened rabbit? Sometimes Helen was terribly afraid she might, and the thought worried her. She wanted to marry and have a family. She didn't want to be alone for the rest of her life. Yet every time the vague, unstructured longing showed the slightest sign of being realised, she panicked. What the hell is the matter with me? she sometimes wondered. But at least her fulfilled life was too busy to spend much time worrying about it.

She went back downstairs and met Amy in the hall, hanging her sun hat on the antler stand.

'I'm calling it a day,' Amy said. 'Time for my G and T.' Amy had always liked her tipple but it didn't seem to have done her any harm.

'But I was coming out to do my bit!'

'Well, if you really want to. But . . . I was wondering, Helen, what did you mean when you said you thought you might know someone who could help out with the garden?'

Helen caught hold of the bannister knob, white-painted wood that felt smooth beneath her fingers.

'It was just a thought. Cliff Button – Herby's brother.'

'Herby! *My* Herby?'

'Yes. I've had to stop Cliff from driving and he's pretty fed up about it.'

'I bet he is. He was one of the first people in Hillsbridge to have a car! What's wrong with him? Why have you had to . . .? Oh, sorry! I don't suppose you can say.'

'Just as long as it doesn't go any further,' Helen said. 'He's suffering from epilepsy.'

'Poor Cliff.'

'He's a wonderful gardener,' Helen said. 'His garden is like something out of a flower show. I suggested it might be something he could take up to fill in his time – you know, doing a bit for other people – but it never occurred to me until I came home and found you struggling so that perhaps *we* . . .'

'Well, it's certainly a thought,' Amy said. 'Cliff Button. He and Roly must have been at school together. They'd probably have the time of their lives reliving the old days over the onions and dahlias. The only thing is – would they ever get any work done?'

Helen laughed. 'I can just picture it. And they say *women* are the ones who do all the talking!'

'Should I ask Herby to ask him to come and see me? Or would you rather put it to him?'

'I think it might be best if I did,' Helen said. 'I don't want him to think I've been talking about his problems to all and sundry.'

'I'll leave it to you then,' Amy said. 'Offer him seven and six an hour. That's what I pay Roly. On second thoughts – make it five shillings. After all, Roly's been here a long time.'

'That's still very generous, Amy. I think he'll jump at it.'

'Mmm. Oh – and Helen . . . I was thinking . . .'

'Yes?'

'Perhaps I ought to come with you tonight if the offer's still open.'

'Of course it is.'

'Maybe Mum and I will be civil to one another if you're there to referee.'

'Amy, she is just going to be so pleased to see you,' Helen said.

'Oh, David, I'm so frightened!' Linda said.

They were in her front room, not alone in the house tonight – her mother and father were in the living room – but they wanted some privacy anyway. As soon as he'd arrived this evening David had felt the tension like a living thing, making the atmosphere in the house as strained as the lingering heat of the day made it close. It pressed in on him, that atmosphere, claustrophobic and charged, quite the opposite of the usual feeling of cheerful, anything-goes that usually prevailed in Linda's home.

'What's wrong?' he had asked, apprehension prickling in the pit of his stomach.

For a moment no-one answered him, then Linda's mother said: 'She's got to see the doctor tomorrow.'

The load lightened a little.

'Oh . . . you don't know anything yet then?'

'Not yet, no,' Linda said. She looked very pale, but otherwise practically normal. In fact there was an almost translucent glow to her skin which made her look, he thought, even more beautiful.

'There was a note through the door,' Doreen said. 'Just a note, making the appointment.' There was a small tremble in her voice and without having to be told he realised the significance of what she was saying. The doctor must have had the results of Linda's tests back and wanted to see her urgently.

'Right,' he said, and the apprehension was back in the pit of his stomach.

'I don't like it,' Doreen said.

'Come on now,' Jim said soothingly. 'There's no sense getting in a stew. You might be worrying about nothing.'

Doreen averted her eyes impatiently. How can you be so calm about it? that look said. You might think I'm getting in a stew about nothing; I know different.

'Do you want a cup of tea, David?' she asked.

'No . . . no.'

'There's one in the pot. I've had the kettle on ever since I found that note. I don't know what I'd do without a cup of tea.'

'You'll turn into a tea leaf yourself, our Doreen,' Jim said with a heavy-handed attempt at humour. 'I don't know what colour your insides must be.'

'I don't want any, thanks, Mrs Parfitt,' David said, and Linda tugged at his arm.

'Let's go in the front room.'

Now they were there, however, her brittle façade had

187

crumbled and she clung to him, her face buried in his shoulder.

'I'm so frightened, David!'

He could feel the slight tremble that was shaking the whole of her body. In his arms she seemed very fragile. He thought that if he held her too tightly he could snap her in two.

'Don't, Linda,' he said, worried himself and at a loss to know how to comfort her. 'I expect your dad's right and there's nothing to worry about.'

'He's whistling in the dark. He always does that.'

'But at least wait until you hear what the doctor has to say.'

'I know what she's going to say.'

'How can you know that? *She* didn't know until she had the results of your tests, and she's a doctor!'

'I don't mean I know exactly. But I do know it's serious. *Know*, David, not just think, or fear. I can feel it in here . . .' She pulled away from him, pressing her hands to her midriff, then moving them to her temples. '. . . and here. It's like a weight, pressing down on me. I can't explain. But I know, all the same. I didn't need a note about a doctor's appointment to tell me. I knew already. There's something seriously wrong with me, David.'

Her conviction panicked him.

'But you seem so much better,' he said helplessly. 'You *look* better, really beautiful . . .'

'And I feel better. These last few days I've almost been my old self. But I think that's just an illusion. When you're really ill you don't necessarily feel a bit worse and a bit worse each day until one day you keel over dead. At least, I don't think that's how it is. There are bad days and there are better days. But you're still on the same track, like a runaway train that can't stop.'

'Linda!' he said sharply. 'For goodness sake!'

She gulped. 'I don't want to die, David.'

'Stop this talk of dying!'

She didn't seem to even hear him; she was sobbing softly now as she spoke.

'I don't want to die! I'm twenty-one years old! There are

188

so many things I want to do – so many! I want to get married, have my own home, children. I want to see them grow up, take them on holiday to Weston or Weymouth, fill their stockings at Christmas, make jellies and blancmange for their birthday parties. I want *you*, David, properly, not just in the front room when Mum and Dad are out, or in the back row at the pictures. I want to see the garden covered in snow, and the first crocuses when they come out and hear the birds and feel the sun on my face. I don't want to die! I'm not ready! Not nearly ready!'

'Shh, Linda. I won't let you die.' He said it fiercely, and she sobbed again, her body shuddering.

'What can you do? What can anyone do!'

'Linda, for God's sake, this is silly!' Helplessness was making him angry. 'Will you stop this silly talk?'

But she was past reasoning with.

'It just keeps going round and round in my head. All the things I want to do, all the things I'll miss. It's not fair, David. It's not fair! I had such plans! What I'd wear when we got married. I even cut a picture out of a magazine of the dress I wanted – white, ballerina-length . . . with little puff sleeves. I was going to have three bridesmaids – your Jenny, for one – and have them one in pink, one in blue, and one in yellow. Not green, because green's supposed to be unlucky. Unlucky! And we'd have a reception in the big room at the George and drive off for our honeymoon in a car with "Just Married" painted on the back and a string of tin cans trailing behind and . . . and now it's not going to happen. Any of it!'

'Linda!' he said.

Such a short time ago talk of marriage would have scared him rigid. Now, suddenly, he too was more afraid that it might not happen than that it would. 'Linda,' he said, 'you'll have your dream wedding, I promise.'

'How can you promise something like that?'

'Because I can. You'll have your dream wedding, whatever the doctor says tomorrow. I give you my word.'

She stopped crying, looking up at him with eyes that were puffy but full of dawning wonder.

'You mean . . .?'

'I mean I'm going to marry you, Linda, and no bloody doctor is going to stop me.'

'Oh, David!' she said.

He held her and kissed her, tenderly at first, then with growing urgency. And as he felt her fragile body pressed against his he prayed to a God he had not known he believed in that he would be able to keep his promise.

'Jenny! You look absolutely super!' Heather said.

Jenny flushed with pleasure at the compliment. She was wearing a seersucker dress with a design of tiny sprigs of mauve and blue flowers on a white background, very full-skirted from a nipped-in waistline, and a small stand-up collar. She was on her way to what had been billed as a 'Summer Spree' in the water meadow belonging to the church, ostensibly to help run one of the stalls, in fact to meet Jimmy. Over the past weeks, Jenny had become adept at gaining freedom to be with him by means of the most unlikely excuses.

The trouble was she wasn't sure she actually wanted to be with Jimmy any more. The first novelty had begun to wear off and she found that much as she liked him she didn't actually really fancy him. At first it hadn't mattered much; she enjoyed his company, he took her mind off Barry and gave her the status amongst her peers that came from having a boyfriend. But now she was beginning to feel restless and, worse, a little repelled by him – especially when he kissed her. As long as she could close her eyes and pretend he was someone else, it wasn't too bad, but pretending was becoming less and less easy and Jenny had begun to feel trapped.

I'll have to tell him, Jenny thought. I'll have to tell him I don't want to see him any more. But each time it came to the point, she couldn't bring herself to actually speak the words. The thought of the hurt look that would come over his good-natured face was more than she could bear. Tonight, she thought. I'll tell him tonight . . . And put off the moment by calling in to see Heather and baby Vanessa on her way to the church meadow.

'You like my dress then?' Jenny asked.

'It's gorgeous. Mum didn't make that, did she?'

'Yes, she did actually.' They exchanged a look and giggled. Whilst Carrie was a meticulous needlewoman, her creations were not known for either their flare or their fit – Carrie usually insisted on making garments a little on the generous side. 'You don't want it to pull,' she would say.

'You look champion, my old Dutch,' Walt said from the depths of his armchair.

'Is Vanessa in bed?' Jenny asked.

'She is – the little monkey,' Heather said, but she was smiling. Motherhood suited her. 'She's been into everything today.'

'Like what?' Jenny always loved to hear about the exploits of her niece.

'Pulling my gloving out all over the floor, mainly.' Heather indicated a large brown paper package stacked in the corner behind a chair. Since having Vanessa, she took in 'out-working' from the glove factory where she had used to be a machinist. 'Do you want to go up and see her?'

'Yes please,' Jenny said.

'Go on then – but don't wake her up whatever you do. It's such a job to get her to go to sleep these light nights.'

Jenny went upstairs to the small bedroom which always reminded her of a tree house because of the way it looked out directly into the branches of the tall old planes in the garden. She pushed the door open and tiptoed in.

Jenny stood for a moment looking down at Vanessa, feeling her stomach twist with an emotion she would have described as love had it not been for the fact that she believed love was what she had felt for Barry. Perhaps, she thought, tenderness was a better word. Jenny was very into words these days. Vanessa was so small, so vulnerable, so *perfect*. Jenny could well understand why Heather looked so content these days. One day, she thought, perhaps I'll be lucky enough to have a little girl of my own just like her.

One day. But not yet. Not for a long time.

She kissed a finger and laid it on Vanessa's warm soft cheek. Then she tiptoed out of the room.

Heather had the package of gloving on the table now, tying it with string ready to go back to the factory. She was humming to herself. Again, Jenny thought how lucky she was – a picture of contented motherhood.

She knows exactly what she wants from life, Jenny thought, and she's mostly got it. Not much spare cash, perhaps, not even a home of her own, but a nice husband and a beautiful daughter. No worries for her about exams and homework and boys and dates. No worries about deceiving Carrie.

Lucky, lucky Heather!

Stalls had been set out around three sides of the Church Field – trestle tables laden with books and home-made jam and bric-a-brac, interspersed with sideshows such as Roll the Penny and a complicated-looking contraption of loops and dips of wire around which a circle of wire on the end of a stick had to be passed without ringing a bell which signified that contact had been made.

Jimmy and some other lads who had volunteered to help with the Skittle for a Pig competition were already there, lounging around the sharp end of the makeshift board alley to return the balls as they thudded into the pile of sandbags and reposition the nine skittles in their traditional diamond pattern. They were all experienced at doing this; most of them earned a shilling or two pocket money each week sticking up in the local pubs and clubs, all of which boasted a skittle alley and ran at least one team in the skittle league.

Jenny skirted the stalls and joined the boys beside the bales of hay which had been piled up behind the sandbags to ensure no heavy skittling balls could go flying off like loose cannons into the field beyond. At once, Jimmy jumped up, grinning his pleasure.

'I was beginning to think you weren't coming!'

'I called in to see my sister on the way. How's it going?'

'OK. Are you going to have a go?'

'Me?'

'Why not? There's a ladies' prize and so far the top score is only seven.'

'I can't play skittles!'

'Course you can!'

A ball thrown by a sturdy-looking man came whistling down the alley, glancing neatly off the front pin and scattering the others across the board. The boy who was sticking up jumped for his life and a shout went up from the business end of the board: 'Spare!'

'See?' Jimmy said. 'That's how it's done.'

'Oh, I know how it's done,' Jenny said. 'It's doing it I'm worried about!'

'Go on!'

'Oh – all right. But you'd better take cover is all I can say.'

Laughing over her shoulder at him, she went down to where Alec Hall was taking the money and marking top scores on a blackboard with a knub of chalk.

'Fancy your chances, young Jenny?' he asked.

'No – but I'll have a go.'

'Top score for the ladies is only seven.'

'I've never got seven in my life! Anyway, I don't suppose the best players have been on yet.'

The pubs and clubs ran ladies' teams, too, and competition was as fierce as it was amongst the men.

'I'll have one go. Just one. That's all I can afford.'

She paid her sixpence and, as the stickers-up shied the balls back down the boarding, Alec caught them and stacked them ready for her.

'You can go up to that line if you like,' he said, indicating a white stripe beyond which, in competition, balls were not supposed to bounce.

'That's not fair!' a blowsy woman, smoking a cigarette, protested.

'Give the kid a break, Reenie,' Alec said.

'We're skittling for a prize here.' Reenie, at present in the lead, according to the blackboard, spoke with loud aggression. 'Rules is rules, Alec.'

'It's all right,' Jenny said to Alec. 'It's only a bit of fun. I wouldn't be able to hit those skittles if you let me go halfway down the alley!'

She picked up the first ball and threw it. It trickled to the left-hand side of the alley and ran off into the grass.

'See what I mean?'

She threw the second, overcorrecting on her first aim. The ball rolled off the right-hand side of the alley.

She laughed at herself, but knowing others were laughing at her too made her remember with a stab of discomfort the way she had used to feel in the gym and on the games field at school. Alec, always a kindly soul, sensed her discomfort.

'Come on, m'dear,' he encouraged her. 'That's one down each side. Go for middle for diddle now!'

Jenny bent into what her mother called a croupy position, keeping her eye on the middle pin. This time when she threw the ball her aim was firm and true. The ball ran an arrow-straight course down the centre of the alley, caught the middle pin and demolished five of the nine skittles.

'There you are, m'dear!' Alec praised her. 'That's the way to do it!'

Success made Jenny feel light-headed.

'Can I have another go?'

'If you've got another sixpence.'

Jenny fished one out of her purse. At the other end of the alley, Jimmy reset the skittles.

Her first ball took the front pin again and three of the four to its left, her second took all but one of the remaining skittles.

'Think what you'm doing now,' Alec advised.

Jenny looked down the alley, at the single pin that remained standing. Hitting it seemed an almost impossible goal, yet as she swung the heavy ball back she somehow knew she could do it. Some sixth sense was telling her how. She released the ball and watched it fly down the alley towards the skittle. It hit and thudded into the pile of sandbags, taking the skittle with it.

'You've cleared the board! Nine!' Alec sounded delighted for her. 'Looks as if we've got a new leader!'

'What's the ladies' prize?' Jenny asked, brimming with excited pleasure. 'What will I win?'

'A five-pound note. But there's a long way to go yet. We shall be skittling 'til it gets dark. You'll have to come back to see if you've won,' Alec said.

194

The blowsy woman named Reenie said nothing, just grunted, and lit another cigarette.

Jenny practically danced back to Jimmy and the other boys.

'I'm in the lead! I might win!'

Jimmy put his arm round her, grinning with pride, and the other boys made heaving noises. But for all that, Jenny sensed that beneath their loud ragging they were actually envious; she couldn't help noticing the way they looked at her, and suddenly she felt as strong and as sure of her sexual power as she had of her ability to hit that lone skittle.

'Do you want to go for a walk?' Jimmy asked.

'If you like.'

With the whistles and coarse comments of the other boys following them, they set off across the field.

The evening sun was still slanting through the branches of the trees along the river, making sparkling patterns on the water, but when they crossed a stone bridge where the river broadened out into a deep pool beneath a small weir the foliage was so thick that it was almost twilight.

'Did you know this used to be the town swimming pool?' Jenny said. 'See?' She pointed to a concreted area at one corner. 'That used to be the diving stage.'

'Fancy a skinny-dip?' Jimmy grinned at her.

'No! No *thanks*! My gran says it had to be closed because of the churchyard.'

'What d'you mean?' Jimmy looked puzzled.

'The churchyard. It's just up above here. Things . . . drain down . . . you know – nasty things. From the graves.'

'Oh!' Jimmy, about to dangle his hand into the water, withdrew it quickly. 'You mean . . .?'

'Yes,' Jenny said. 'When we were little we were told not to paddle here in case we had a sore on our feet or legs and got germs in it.'

'Ugh!' Jimmy turned away. The pool had lost its charm for him now; he wanted nothing to do with a place that might be contaminated by death. 'Shall we go on a bit further?'

They went back into the sunlight, following a track through the scratchy grass that ran parallel with the river for the length of the valley, Jimmy holding her hand. After a while they came to a place where the river looped, bare of trees and shallow, little more than a trickle over clean-washed stones. It was very quiet here, very secluded, no sound but the gentle gurgle of the water and the distant drone of a harvester.

'Let's sit down for a bit,' Jimmy said.

'I don't know if I should. My dress . . .'

'It's all right. The grass is dry as a bone.'

'I daren't get it dirty. It's new.'

'All right. You've heard of Sir Walter Raleigh . . .' Jimmy was unbuttoning his shirt, spreading it out on the ground. 'There you are! Sit on that.'

'Jim-my!' She was embarrassed by the sight of his bare chest; the sudden feeling of intimacy made her claustrophobic. But she sat down anyway. Not to do so in the face of such chivalry seemed churlish.

He sat down beside her and began to kiss her, and her feeling of claustrophobia increased. She didn't want him this close, especially when he wasn't wearing his shirt. His back felt hot and slightly moist beneath her fingers, his mouth, covering hers, made her feel as if she were being suffocated. But she kissed him back because it somehow seemed mean not to do so. When she felt his hand on her breast, though, her stomach tightened a notch with some-thing close to panic.

She tried to push his hand away, but he replaced it.

'Just a little feel, Jen. I won't hurt you.'

'No!'

But even to her own ears she did not sound very con-vincing and in spite of her misgivings there was something not unpleasant about the sensation that spread across her skin from his kneading fingers.

He was kissing her harder, his breath coming faster. She could feel the rapid rise and fall of it in his bare chest and when his hand crept up her skirt, touching the soft flesh of her thigh, any pleasure dissipated abruptly. She grabbed his wandering hand with her own.

196

'Stop it, Jimmy!'

But as fast as she removed it the hand was back and his mouth was stopping her protests.

She pushed him away, wriggled free.

'What do you think you're doing?'

'Only what everyone else does!' He sounded hurt as well as frustrated.

'Well, I don't! And you don't. Not with me.'

'Jen . . .'

She scrambled to her feet, brushing bits of grass from her skirt.

'Jimmy, I don't want to. Actually . . . I think we've been seeing too much of one another. I think we ought to give it a break.'

Still sitting there on the grassy slope he looked up at her, good-natured face furrowed suddenly with shock and disbelief.

'What are you talking about?'

'Us,' she rushed on, knowing now that this had been the catalyst and she couldn't face the thought of being in this position again, trapped, not wanting even to kiss him any more, let alone allow him intimate liberties, yet feeling oddly obliged to, as if it was all part of the deal. 'I don't want to go out with you any more.'

'Jen!' The furrows went slack, colour rushed to his cheeks and drained again; his lip wobbled. 'Jen . . . I didn't mean . . . I won't . . . If you don't want to . . .'

'You will. Boys always do. And anyway, it's not just that. I just don't want to go out with you. I'm sorry.'

He was on his feet. 'You don't mean that!'

'I do. I was going to tell you anyway. I was trying to think of a way.'

'Jenny, please!' To her horror she realised he was on the verge of tears. 'You can't do this to me!'

'I'm sorry,' she said again, feeling guilty, anguished, but more certain than ever that she was doing the right thing.

'But why? Why?'

'No reason, really. I like you, honestly I do. But . . .'

'Then why won't you go out with me?'

'Because.'

'I promise you faithfully I won't try anything again. Not ever. Say we can still go out sometimes. Please!'

This was worse, much worse than she'd dreamed it would be.

'Well . . . maybe sometimes.'

'Honestly?' He looked so relieved but still on the verge of tears – perhaps even more so – and Jenny knew in that moment that whatever he said, whatever she said, she wouldn't – couldn't – go out with him ever again. For the first time in her life she was the one with the power, the one with the ability to break hearts, and she didn't like it one bit. In its own way it was every bit as bad as being the outcast, the victim. Perhaps because she had been there too often she felt his pain as acutely as if it had been her own. But at the same time it diminished him in her eyes. Jimmy the tough guy, the hard nut with the soft centre that she alone had been able to touch, had become Jimmy the marshmallow, and with the revelation the last vestiges of his appeal for her melted away.

'Can I kiss you – just once more?' he asked, and though she felt she owed it to him to agree, she shrank from his touch, shuddered inwardly at the taste of his tear-wet lips.

As they walked back along the river Jenny felt not only awkward and villainously cruel but distinctly edgy – a sense of urgency she could not understand but was compelled by. In the gateway dividing the fields from the lane, Jimmy caught her arm.

'You *will* come out with me again, won't you?'

'I said so, didn't I?' She squeezed through the iron V-gate and started along the grass verge, Jimmy beside her.

The field was even more crowded than it had been when they had left it. People who had eaten a leisurely tea before heading for the fête clustered around stalls and ambled almost aimlessly between them. Then a figure she recognised seemed to leap out of the crowd and Jenny felt herself go cold and weak as the blood seemed to drain from her face and body.

There was no mistaking that matronly woman in the home-made cotton dress with pique collar and cuffs carrying a raffia shopping bag, with Sally, the puppy, pulling on her lead as she frisked along beside her.

Carrie.

Jenny, trembling now, understood that inexplicable feeling of urgency. Some sixth sense had told her to get back to the fête fast. But already it was too late. Carrie had seen her.

She came towards Jenny purposefully, face set in the expression of disapproval – anger! – that Jenny knew only too well.

'Mum!' she said helplessly.

'Where do you think you've been?'

'Nowhere . . . Here.'

'Don't you lie to me!' Carrie said furiously. 'I'm not stupid. You've been with this *boy*.' She invested the word with all the venom to make it an insult, jerking her head to indicate Jimmy whilst glaring from beneath beetling brows at Jenny.

'We've only been for a walk. We've only been gone a minute . . .'

'I've been here half an hour and more and there was no sign of you,' Carrie said furiously. 'I've been round and round looking for you.'

'I didn't know you were coming,' Jenny said miserably.

'I'm sure you didn't!' Carrie glowered at Jimmy, who looked as if he wished the ground would open and swallow him. 'It's a good job I *did* come, if you ask me! Well, now you can just come home with me.'

'Mum . . . I'm supposed to be helping on the Roll a Penny.'

'They seem to have managed so far without you. Come on, my lady. Home!'

Carrie, furious, was a force to be reckoned with. She marched up the hill in stony silence, pulling on Sally's lead impatiently whenever she stopped to sniff at a lamp-post. Jenny trailed miserably behind, knowing she had far from heard the end of it and also that she would have to pay for her misdemeanour for days to come, if not for weeks.

It was so unfair! She'd done nothing wrong; she hadn't even enjoyed herself. But she had been seeing Jimmy behind Carrie's back, and Carrie, with that uncanny intuition of hers, had somehow suspected and set out to catch her out.

'I had a feeling there was something going on,' she said when the front door closed behind them. 'I knew there was something not right.'

'How?' Jenny asked.

'I'm your mother, aren't I? You can't pull the wool over my eyes and get away with it for long, my lady. All I hope is you haven't done anything stupid.'

For a moment Jenny didn't know what she meant, then it dawned on her, and her face flamed.

'Mum!'

'Well, you wouldn't be the first, and you won't be the last. Not that you'll be getting the chance for a very long time. If you can't be trusted to behave yourself, you'll have to stay where I can keep an eye on you.'

'But I haven't done anything!' Jenny wailed.

'You've deceived me! Isn't that enough? Lied to me about where you were going and who with. Don't tell me it's the first time, because I'm not as green as I might be cabbage-looking. And I can tell you here and now I'll be keeping a close eye on you from now on.'

Why was she like it?' Jenny wondered wretchedly as she undressed and slipped between the sheets. Why couldn't she be more like other people's mothers, let her do all the things they were happy to let their daughters do? It was almost as if she was expecting trouble. Had she been so strict with Heather? The thought nudged another one – was it because Heather had been pregnant with Vanessa when she married Steve? But no, it couldn't be that. Carrie had always been strict, in all sorts of ways. For as long as Jenny could remember, now that she came to think about it, Carrie had dominated her, tried to keep her a baby, a little girl.

I'll ask Heather about it, Jenny thought. The prospect of talking to her sister was a comfort. But it was still a long while before Jenny fell asleep.

Chapter Eleven

Matthew Vezey's soirée was in full glorious swing.

As Paul had predicted, catering staff had been brought in from Bath – three ladies in black skirts and frilly white aprons – and they had set out a luxurious buffet on trestle tables in the big farmhouse-style kitchen – platters of cold ham and beef, dishes of tiny new parsley potatoes and salads, and in pride of place a whole salmon. With the strictures of rationing still all too fresh in people's minds it was an almost unimaginable feast. And as Paul had also predicted, there was enough alcohol to launch a battleship. Matthew himself was dispensing this to the undisguised disapproval of his sister Enid and his loud laughter and red face suggested that he had been taking a drink himself for every one he poured.

'You'd never think they were brother and sister, would you?' Helen said to Paul as they moved into the genteel but faded sitting room. 'Are you sure there's no secret scandal afoot here?'

Paul raised an eyebrow over his pint mug of Home Brewed.

'Do you really see Enid as a scarlet woman?'

'No. But you know what they say about still waters running deep. And opposites are supposed to attract, too. For all you know they could have been passionately in love once and unable to marry for some reason.'

'What do you suggest?'

'Oh – a husband or wife in the background perhaps?' But that was a little too close to home for comfort. 'Mentally ill – locked away in a lunatic asylum,' she hurried on.

'If Enid ever had a husband I think it's very likely he *would* end up in a lunatic asylum! I'm darned sure I would

201

if I was married to her! But no, sorry to disappoint you, Helen, they're brother and sister all right and neither of them has ever married.'

'If you say so.'

'I do! They'd never get away with that sort of thing in Hillsbridge. You must have learned by now that everyone here knows everyone else's business.'

'Mmm. I still find it hard to believe they had the same parents and the same upbringing. And how come they haven't fallen out long ago when they're so different?'

'Matthew isn't easily upset – though if he does lose his temper – look out! No, he just lets her have her say and then does exactly as he pleases, I imagine.'

'Like wearing that short-sleeved shirt when she'd like him in black tie.'

Matthew's outfit had been the first thing she had noticed when he had opened the door to them. She had never before seen him wearing anything other than a tweed suit with leather-patched elbows and matching waistcoat with a gold watch-chain straining across it, and a pair of highly polished but well-worn brogues. Tonight he was sporting a pale turquoise shirt, open at the neck, a pair of khaki-coloured corduroy trousers and buckled leather sandals, and in no way complemented his sister's chosen outfit of pink flounced blouse and calf-length black velvet skirt.

Now that she had met Enid, Helen could understand why the gathering had been dignified by the sobriquet 'soirée'.

Like her living room, Enid was all faded gentility with a nod towards the fashion of the day which somehow just managed to miss the mark. Her greying hair was swept into a smooth chignon, yet her fringe, soft and bubbly, looked as if it had just come out of curlers. Her lips were a fashionable pink, but she had applied a similar colour to her cheeks in well-defined patches that made her look oddly like a middle-aged Dutch doll. Her voice was girlish, her accent as mincing as her brother's was local. Her hands, with their bright pink nails, fluttered, her small eyes darted, her bright smile tightened into a grimace of disapproval each time her glance fell on Matthew.

Enid enjoyed being the doctor's sister, Helen imagined. It conformed perfectly to all her delusions of grandeur. But Matthew did not. No doubt she nagged him ceaselessly about his clothes, his behaviour, his way of speaking, but without the slightest effect. As Paul had said, Matthew would indulge her and ignore her, going his own sweet way.

'That chap hasn't bothered you again, has he?' Paul said unexpectedly.

'Chap . . .?' For a moment she was puzzled, wondering what on earth he was talking about, then as she realised she felt an uncomfortable flush begin in her neck. She'd hoped Paul had forgotten about the embarrassing incident when he had thrown Guy out of the surgery.

'No, I haven't seen him since.'

'Tell me it's none of my business if you like,' Paul said, casually conversational. 'But I couldn't help wondering.'

'It's none of your business,' she said lightly.

'Sorry.'

'It's OK. Just a bit of a sore point.' She didn't want to talk about Guy; didn't want to think about him even. It still hurt too much.

'I shouldn't have asked.'

'No,' she said. 'You shouldn't.'

Into the small awkward silence a voice from behind her boomed: 'Right, you two! So what's been going on since I left the fold?'

Matthew had seemingly abandoned the drinks table in his eagerness to be updated on the latest goings-on in the practice that had been his life for thirty years and more. Suddenly Helen was glad Paul had asked her about Guy. If he hadn't they might well have still been discussing Matthew and his sister.

'You see, Helen? What did I tell you?' Paul said. 'I knew this party was just an excuse for you to get the low-down on your former patients, Matthew!'

'D'you blame me?'

'No. OK, you old rogue, what do you want to hear about first? Flo Tranter's hypochondria – or the pretty young widow who's moved into Parsonage Lane and registered with me? No – don't tell me – the gypsy family down at Horler's Cross. The whole brood have gone down with impetigo, all fifteen of them. They're going round with purple-painted faces and frightening all the old ladies half to death. Now tell me you're not glad to be out of it!'

Helen glanced at him, at his cheerful grinning face and the wicked twinkle in his eyes. A moustache of beer foam had adhered to his upper lip and somehow it made him look a little vulnerable. She felt a sudden rush of warmth for the partner who had surprisingly become her ally. He really was rather attractive, too.

No, Helen told herself. The last thing you want at the moment is another set of complications.

She turned to Matthew.

'I could tell you all about how poor old Cliff Button has become epileptic and how I've fixed him up with a gardening job,' she offered.

And as the three doctors chatted, the awkward moment passed.

Walt Simmons was not feeling well. Truth to tell, he thought, he felt rotten. It had started this morning when he'd had a dizzy spell whilst peeling the potatoes, but he had taken the saucepan, bowl and knife into the backyard and finished them off sitting on the wooden bench and the spell had passed. Then, when he'd tried to eat his dinner, he'd been violently sick.

'I think I ought to get the doctor in,' Glad had said, but he had immediately protested.

'There's no need to bother the doctor,' Walt had said. 'I expect it's something I ate.'

'Well, I don't like it,' Glad said. 'It's not like you. And another thing – I'd like the doctor to have a look at your leg.'

'Whatever for? My leg's on the mend.'

And it was. The ulcer that had wept and mattered for the best part of twenty years seemed miraculously to be healing over.

'That's just it,' Glad said. 'I can't understand it. After all these years. It's a funny thing, if you ask me.'

'You don't call the doctor when something's getting better,' Walt said.

'You look a funny colour to me.'

'I'll be all right,' Walt said. 'When I've had a bit of a rest.'

He settled back in his chair with his head tucked between the wing and the back and his foot resting on the little three-legged stool – no sense not taking care of his bad leg even if it did seem to be improving – and sure enough when he woke again at about three he did feel better. Not right, but better.

He was glad about that, not only for his own sake, but also for Glad, Heather and Steve. The three of them were going out tonight. Steve had joined the local male-voice choir and Glad and Heather had got tickets to hear them sing in a concert in the Town Hall at South Compton. He knew they would be disappointed to miss it, but he also knew they wouldn't dream of going and leaving him alone babysitting Vanessa if they thought he wasn't up to it. Glad had already said as much.

'Heather can still go. I'll stop here with you.'

But he knew how much Glad was looking forward to the concert. She'd been very down this week, they'd had really bad news of David's girlfriend, Linda, that she had leukaemia and there was really nothing much that could be done for her, and Glad had taken it very hard. David had always been a great favourite with her – the only grandson in a family of girls. There was talk that they were going to get married, and this had upset Glad even more, knowing that David would be a widower before he was thirty, and with no chance of having children of the marriage. Going to the concert would take her mind off things, if only for a bit.

When teatime came and he managed to keep down a slice of bread and honey it gave him all the ammunition he needed.

'There you be! I told you I was all right. You get off and enjoy the concert. I can mind the babby.'

And so they had gone, leaving Vanessa tucked up in bed

and Walt in his chair, listening to the radio and looking at the evening paper which they had delivered every day except Sunday.

The truth was, though, he still didn't feel too good, and when the door had closed after them and he didn't have to pretend any more he acknowledged it to himself and even tried unsuccessfully to analyse it. He couldn't. He honestly didn't think he could remember ever feeling quite like this before – sick yet not sick, heavy yet floaty, and a pain in his stomach that might have been indigestion or a strained muscle from being violently sick and yet oddly felt like neither.

'You be getting old,' Walt said to himself. It wasn't a thought that worried him much. The only thing was he hoped he'd live to see Vanessa grow up. In his quiet undemonstrative way he adored his great-granddaughter.

Now he shifted in his chair, jiggling his feet and shaking his hands, which had gone to pins and needles. Perhaps he'd been here too long. It would do him good to move about a bit and besides, he could do with a cup of Bengers. The fact that he still felt queasy was probably down to the fact that he hadn't kept down more than a slice of bread and honey all day. He was empty – 'sinking' Glad called it – and that wasn't a bad description of it either.

He levered himself up out of his chair and went to the pantry, where he measured a cupful of milk into a saucepan. Back in the kitchen he lit the gas ring with a taper – Heather had bought them one of them new-fangled gas lighters with a battery which created a spark when you flicked a button, but he hadn't taken to it. Give him the old ways any day. And besides, he didn't think he'd have been able to manage that fiddly little button with his pincushion hands today even if he had wanted to.

The pain in his stomach was worse again now, shooting arrows in all directions. Walt gritted his teeth against it, spooned Bengers into the cup and headed back for the pantry with the tin. He hated muddle from things left about. 'There's a place for everything and everything should be in its place,' his mother had used to say. He had a sudden image of her, standing in the doorway, with her hair all piled up and wearing a black satin blouse and skirt that had been her Sunday best when he was a nipper. So clear it was it almost took his breath away.

'What are you doing here, Mother?' he asked aloud, then chuckled to himself, shaking his head. 'You'm taking leave of your senses, Walt,' he said, also aloud, but more softly, more to himself.

It was as he went through the doorway where he'd thought he'd seen his mother standing that he heard Vanessa crying. He stood under the bannisters for a moment or two, listening, his own aches and pains and sickness forgotten. Was she just crying in her sleep? Would she quieten down in a minute? But Vanessa's sobs were getting harder with an element of hysteria in them and he could hear her calling for her mummy.

'It's all right, my love, Grampy's coming,' he called, going along the hall and, with an effort, up the stairs. 'Grampy's coming now.'

He switched on the landing light and almost instantly Vanessa's sobs lessened. As soon as he went into the bedroom he could see why; the little red nightlight Heather always left on for her because she was afraid of the dark was out, the bulb had gone, he supposed. Or because it had still been light when Heather had put her to bed she'd forgotten to switch it on.

Vanessa had kicked her bedclothes into a tangle and her face was wet with tears and sweat. It had run into her hair too; damp strands and curls clung round her small round face.

'What's the matter, my old Dutch?' he asked.

'The moo-cows were chasing me.' Vanessa hiccoughed.

'Dear, oh deary me. Dreaming, was you? That's all it was, my love. You go back to sleep. There won't be no more moo-cows tonight.'

He bent over to tuck her in and she clutched his sleeve.

'Grampy . . . Nessa's frightened . . .'

'Come on, my ducks. Grampy'll leave the light on for you.'

Her fingers tightened their grip. 'Grampy stay!'

'Grampy can't do that.' He was thinking of the milk

heating on the gas ring, boiling over, perhaps, putting out the flame but leaving the gas to escape. But he was feeling pretty groggy again too. He didn't think he could make it down the stairs to turn the gas out and back up again. Well – not make it back up again, leastways.

'D'you want to come down with Grampy?' he asked.

''es! 'es!' She wasn't crying now, but the whimpery tone suggested she would be if he left her.

Walt turned back the covers and lifted her up. Her arms twined trustingly round his neck and she wound her plump little legs around his waist. Love surged through him and tenderness and pride. He thought he saw his mother again, in the shadowy corner beside the wardrobe.

'See, Mother?' he said, but silently this time. 'I didn't do so bad, did I? This here's my grandbabby!'

He carried Vanessa along the landing, holding her tightly and started down the stairs. He was two or three steps down, just rounding the curve, when the dizziness hit him again. He stopped, swaying, and let go of Vanessa with one hand to grab at the bannister, but it wasn't there. He hadn't reached it yet; here it was only a sham against the landing wall. He felt forward, his shaking hand grasping air, his fingers rasping on the wallpaper that divided the wooden struts, took another step and lost his balance. He heard Vanessa's cry of alarm, then there was nothing but the bump, bump, bump as he was propelled downwards, each stair thudding into his thin body, knocking the wind out of him, blotting out thought.

As he fell Vanessa fell with him, clinging on to him, too startled and frightened to scream again. It was only at the foot of the stairs that she began to cry once more as she lay trapped beneath him. But Walt could not hear her. He had been dead even before they reached the bottom.

The male-voice choir concert had been a great success. Heather and Glad had found seats right in the front row – why was it that people always filled up the middle first? – and Heather had been glad she had such a wonderful view of Steve, who looked smart and incredibly handsome in his dark suit, white shirt and red tie (the uniform of the choir), standing with the baritone section and singing his heart out.

There was something tremendously uplifting about the massed voices of the men, too; though their only accompaniment was an elderly woman on a somewhat tinkly piano, they *were* the music, singing in four-part harmony. The range of songs was enormously wide – 'Brigadoon' and 'The Desert Song' and 'South Pacific'; 'In A Monastery Garden', 'The Bells of St Mary's' and 'Ave Maria'. There were supporting artistes too – 'turns', as Glad called them – a fat tenor, resplendent in a black evening suit, frilled shirt and wine-coloured cummerbund, singing 'Granada' and 'O Sole Mio', and the local elocution teacher reciting Joyce Grenfell monologues.

Glad had enjoyed herself every bit as much as Heather, though for different reasons. She had met up with a lot of people she hadn't seen in a long time; she chatted with this one and that during the interval, almost regretting that the concert had to start again, and when it was over she took up where she had left off, hanging on in the hall whilst the organisers cleared away the chairs around her and then delaying on the pavement outside for a last lingering exchange of news and gossip.

Heather and Steve had almost begun to despair of ever getting her home at all. Steve had gone on to where the car was parked in the Island and Heather stood a few paces away from her waiting impatiently. Eventually her anxiety to get home to Vanessa got the better of her and she went back to Glad and touched her arm.

'Gran – look – I don't want to hurry you but I think we ought to be going home.'

'I'm coming. I'm just coming . . .'

But still she delayed, enjoying the chance for a gossip, even enjoying being able to regale her old friends with the details of Linda's leukaemia, for in spite of her genuine distress on David's behalf, her involvement in the drama made her feel not only important, but also like a tragedy queen.

By the time Heather eventually managed to propel her to the Island, Steve had the lights on and the engine

209

running. Heather installed her grandmother in the front passenger seat – sitting in the back made her queasy, she always said – and climbed in herself.

'I thought we'd lost you, Glad,' Steve said as he turned up the High Street in the direction of Hillsbridge.

'I was just talking,' Glad said, slightly huffy. 'I haven't seen Mrs Wilcox since I don't know when. I don't know why you had to drag me away like that, Heather.'

'Because I think we ought to get home,' Heather said. 'You know Grampy hasn't been well today.'

'Oh, he's all right,' Glad said dismissively. 'You don't want to worry about him.'

'Well, I do,' Heather said. 'Especially . . .'

She broke off. Especially since he's in sole charge of Vanessa, she had been going to say, but suddenly she didn't want to. Why she didn't really know, unless it was because the words would give form to the vague but unmistakable sense of unease that had been niggling at her for the last half-hour. But Glad wasn't listening anyway. She was still mulling over the titbits of gossip she'd gleaned.

'D'you know, Heather, Mrs Wilcox was telling me poor Connie Parker's gone funny again. She's in Wells . . .' Wells was the local mental hospital, or asylum as the old folk knew it. 'Gone down to Wells' in local parlance didn't mean a shopping trip or a visit to the Cathedral. It meant the equivalent of a fate worse than death.

Heather said nothing. She didn't know Connie Parker and she couldn't have cared less if she'd gone to the moon. All she wanted was to get home and make sure everything was all right.

Steve pulled up opposite the front gate to let them out then drove on around the block to the back lane where he had built a hard standing on the end of the back garden to park his car. Heather helped Glad up the steps, carrying her stick and her voluminous bag for her and noticing that a light was showing through the gap in the curtains of the small front bedroom – Vanessa's room. It wasn't the main bedroom light, it was too faint for that, but at the same time it was too bright to be Vanessa's little red light bulb.

210

She could only conclude it must be the landing light showing through, which must mean the bedroom door was open. The realisation gave her anxiety another tweak. She knew she'd pulled the door almost closed when she'd left as she always did.

She turned the knob and tried to push the front open – they never locked the front door until they went to bed at night, although they usually turned the key in the kitchen one when they'd finished outside. But the door would go no further than a few inches. She pushed again and again encountered solid resistance. And then she heard Vanessa whimper, no more than a foot or so away from her, behind the jammed door.

'Vanessa – is that you?' She was trembling suddenly from head to foot, ice water running in her veins instead of blood.

'Mum-my! Mum-my!'

'Vanessa – what are you doing? Let me in!'

'Mum-my! Mum-my!'

Heather dropped down on to her knees on the doorstep, placing herself at the level her child's voice was coming from, wriggling a hand through the narrow gap between door and door jamb. Her outstretched fingers encountered something that felt like thin human hair and beneath it flesh that didn't feel like flesh but cold and clammy. She withdrew her hand as if what she had touched had been searingly hot, gasping a scream as she did so.

'What in the world . . .?' Glad, who had been standing on the step looking only vaguely puzzled and still, for all the world, wrapped up in her wonderful gossipy evening, now sounded thoroughly alarmed herself. The panic in her voice went some way to calming Heather. Glad had had a bad heart for years.

'It's all right, Gran.' She bent forwards again, prepared now for what her groping fingers would encounter. And they did. A cold grizzled neck. The collar of a flannelette shirt. The sturdily made wool of Walt's cardigan.

'*Oh God, Oh God!*' she whispered to herself between chattering teeth, and then, louder: 'Vanessa – are you all right, sweetheart?'

211

'Mum-my! Mum-my!'

She couldn't move Walt or the door by so much as an inch. She should have known she wouldn't be able to.

'It's all right, Vanessa. Mummy's here. Mummy's coming.' She scrambled to her feet, tearing the knee of her stocking on the rough edge of the doorstep.

'What is it? What's going on?' Glad demanded again, panicky yes, but also, curiously, almost determinedly obtuse.

'I think Grampy's fallen down. In the doorway. I've got to get in. Is the front-room window open?'

She stepped on to the strip of garden beneath it, feeling at the surround with her fingertips in the almost total darkness. It wasn't open. Again, she should have known it wouldn't be, not at this time of night. Thinking it might be had just been a straw to grasp at.

In her panic she had almost forgotten that Steve would be approaching the house from a different direction – the back-garden path. It was only when she heard him rapping on the living-room window and calling her name that she remembered and flooded with relief.

'Steve!' she called desperately.

She heard his footsteps coming along the side passage between the house and the sheds.

'Heather?' he called over the solid wood door at the front garden end of the passage, which was also locked at nightfall to stop anyone who might want to take a short cut from the main road to the back lane by way of the gardens. 'Heather? What's the matter?'

'Can't you get in?' she called back.

'No – the back door's locked.'

'I can't get in this way either. Grampy's fallen down.' She still used the euphanism, though she knew in her heart it was more than that. 'He's right in the doorway. And Steve – Vanessa's there too, and she's crying!'

'All right. I'm coming.'

She heard him clambering on to the dustbin, then haul himself up on to the dividing wall and inched along it, sending a shower of small stones skittering down. Then he lowered himself to the ground, crunching into the lily of the valley bed that thrived in the shady corner.

'Steve – what are we going to do? The window's shut too!'

First he pushed at the front door with no more success than she had had. Then he went to the window and a moment later there was the tinkle of breaking glass.

'My window!' Glad said, outraged. 'You've broke my window!'

Neither of them answered her. Steve reached through the shattered pane, unhooked the window and hoisted himself up and through. Heather ran back to the front door and as she did so, heard Steve in the hall speaking to Vanessa, and a series of thuds and scufflings. At last the door opened and Steve thrust a sobbing Vanessa into Heather's arms.

'Take her . . . I can smell gas.'

He disappeared along the hall. Heather stepped over Walt's outstretched body, then, as she too smelled it, stepped back again into the fresh air.

'Wait there, Gran. There's gas escaping . . .'

A minute or so later Steve was back. 'It's all right. I've turned it off. It's not too bad – the lav window was open.'

Heather stepped over Walt's body again and pushed past Steve who was now kneeling beside him. Vanessa's chubby arms were wound tightly around her neck; in the light of the hall, Heather could see congealed blood in her hair.

'Steve – call the doctor!'

'It's too late. I think he's gone.'

'No – for Vanessa. She's hurt . . .'

Not waiting for Steve, she grabbed the phone herself, somehow managing to dial the number which she had learned off by heart in case of an emergency such as this, whilst still cradling Vanessa. As if from a long way off she heard Glad moaning and then the shrilling of the bell, over and over and over . . .

Helen was enjoying a plate of cold beef and ham when the telephone began ringing. She paused, fork poised halfway from plate to mouth, tensing slightly and listening, then consciously relaxing. This wasn't her house and it wasn't her phone. But some sixth sense was nudging her, all the same, and a moment later Matthew appeared in the doorway beckoning to Paul, who had been cornered by a large and ebullient lady who looked like nothing so much as a bejewelled tank.

A few moments later Paul was back, making his way to her side.

'We've had a call; can you come?'

Helen dumped her plate, found her bag and stole and followed him outside.

'What's happened?' she asked as she slid into the car beside him.

He told her.

'I think we might have a sudden death on our hands, and Vanessa's been hurt too.'

'Have they phoned for an ambulance?'

'I don't think so. We'll probably need an ambulance and the police, but we can assess the situation when we get there. They didn't give Dorothea many details, but she said Heather sounded very upset.'

Dorothea had been fielding calls and had Matthew's number in case of emergency.

Paul drove fast, negotiating the almost empty main road with skill and ease. The front door of the Simmonses' house was ajar, light spilling out on to the step and the peony bush sentinels and framed within it Steve, still wearing the blazer and flannels that made up his choir uniform, but with his tie pulled loose at the neck, could be seen looking out.

Paul took the steps two at a time and Helen followed.

'I'm sorry, it's a bit of a squeeze getting in,' Steve said and as they slid through into the hall Helen saw Walt sprawled on the floor. At a glance she knew he was past help.

'Where's Vanessa?'

'In the living room with Heather.'

Leaving Paul with Walt, Helen hurried along the hall. Glad was sitting in one of the fireside chairs, staring into space, Heather was on the sofa, cradling Vanessa in her

214

arms. The child was silent now; Helen guessed she had gone into shock. A faint smell of gas still lingered.

'Oh, Doctor, I'm sorry!' Heather said inconsequentially as she noticed Helen's finery. 'You were out somewhere and we've spoiled your evening.'

In the midst of mayhem and tragedy it was the sort of response that might have sounded ridiculous but Helen had heard it – or something similar – many times before – a not unusual attempt at almost banal normality.

'It couldn't matter less,' she said. 'Now – let's have a look at this little one.'

'What a night!' she said to Paul much later. 'So much for Matthew's soirée!'

'At least it gave us an easy get-out,' Paul said. 'Sometimes getting away from these things can be very difficult.'

Helen laughed. 'That is wicked of you! And I can't imagine the soirée is still going on now. Enid didn't strike me as the night owl type.'

They were driving back to Valley View House. The clock on the dashboard showed one thirty and the valley was silent and dreaming beneath the star-studded velvet of the night sky.

Helen had accompanied Vanessa and Heather to the hospital for X-rays and a thorough check on the little girl, whilst Paul had waited at the house for the police to arrive and then the removal team from the undertakers. By the time Helen got back from the hospital, Walt had been taken away to the mortuary to await the necessary post-mortem, for under the circumstances neither he nor Helen had been able to sign a death certificate. Helen was relieved to find him gone; she didn't want little Vanessa traumatised any further.

'It's the sort of experience that could mark her for life,' she said to Paul now. 'I only hope they'll talk to her about it and encourage her to do the same.'

Paul threw her a quizzical glance, steering the car into Mill Lane.

'She's too young for that, surely.'

'Old enough to know what happened. If they try to make her forget, maybe to all intents and purposes she will, but in fact all that will happen is that it will be driven deep into her subconscious. She'll never deal with it, Paul, just remember she was terrified and carry a child's terror into adulthood. There'll be a trigger – the dark, maybe, or stairs, or something equally innocuous that she associates with her terror and she'll never encounter that without it setting her off. Phobias are made of this.'

'You're getting a bit deep for me. I didn't do any psychology.'

'Neither did I. Well, not much, anyway. But believe me, I know from personal experience.'

'You?'

'Me. For as long as I can remember I was terrified of birds. Really freaked-out terrified. When I was little I had nightmares about them. I'd wake up thinking my hot-water bottle was a dead bird and I'd lie frozen, afraid to move a muscle in case I touched it. Afraid to get out of bed too, thinking I might step on one. Even when I grew up it wouldn't go away. I'd miss a bus rather than pass a pigeon and the seagulls.' She shuddered, remembering.

'Are you still afraid?' Paul asked curiously.

'No, that's the whole point. When I was at med school there was a guy who'd done a degree in psychology. We got talking and he asked if he could hypnotise me. I thought it was a load of rubbish, doubted he could even put me under, but I was intrigued. So I agreed.'

'And?'

'It took a couple of sessions before he found what he was looking for – and those sessions were an experience in themselves. I thought I was still fully conscious – relaxed, yes, but totally in control – and then I'd hear myself saying things in this little child's voice – really weird things, like: "Mummy said I didn't have to paddle today 'cos I've got a cold, but Daddy let me," and I'd be describing my dress and my sandals, even my pushchair.'

'Making it up to please him.'

'That's what I thought at first. But it wasn't that. It was – weird. And then we got to it. I'd been with Dad for a walk

216

in the woods at Alcombe. Some boys were there, shooting. They killed a rook. It fluttered out of the bushes, dying, right at my feet. I said in that same little child's voice: "It's dead! I don't want it to be dead!" And then I was crying, sobbing, tears streaming down my face. He told me there was nothing to be afraid of, that I was grown up now, and now that I understood, I'd lose my fear.'

'And did you?'

'Yes. Not immediately – I had to relearn years of responses. But gradually the terror went away. Now it's gone completely. And I can actually remember that fright with the reaction of an adult. So you see I am living proof of the damage that can be done. My mother had told me to forget it – it was over; she never talked it through with me. I don't want that to happen to Vanessa.'

They had reached Porters Hill whilst she was talking and Paul had pulled up beside the gate. The moon was bathing the valley in light so that the grass took on a silvery sheen and the houses on the far side of the valley were clearly visible. No lights showed at any of the windows; they might have been alone in a silent shadowy world. The sharing of the confidence had made Helen feel closer to Paul, she was surprised at the shaft of warm awareness as she glanced at him. He was looking straight ahead; his profile was strong and unexpectedly attractive. She caught at herself, caught at the sudden surge of emotion which was exciting her and making her feel oddly vulnerable both at the same time.

'I shall keep an eye on her, anyway,' she said. 'In fact, I might just have a word with Heather and tell her what I've just told you.'

'Be careful. People round here are very wary of anything that borders on the psychiatric.'

'Don't I know it!' She remembered her aunt Grace, her mother's sister, who had suffered so badly from the clinical depression which was described so cruelly hereabouts as 'going funny'. To go funny was almost a crime, certainly the cause for scorn and derision, as if the subject was to blame for their illness. Pneumoconiosis, hernias and heart disease were acceptable, nervous disorders were not.

'Heather's young though,' she said. 'I'm sure she would be more open-minded. We're not living in the Dark Ages any more, for goodness sake.'

'Hmm.' It was no more than a thoughtful expulsion of breath, followed by silence. Helen looked at him, puzzled.

'What was that for?'

'No reason.'

'It must have been! What were you thinking?'

Yesterday, much as she had enjoyed his company, she would never have pressed him for his private thoughts. That she did so now was a mark of the new intimacy.

'About Heather.'

'What about Heather?'

He glanced at her, running his fingers thoughtfully around the steering wheel.

'Have you looked at her records?'

'Yes. Why?'

'There's nothing before she came to Hillsbridge.'

'The family moved from Bristol during the war, didn't they? I assume Heather's records were lost in the bombing.'

'Possibly, I suppose. But all the others survived. It's my opinion that Heather's have disappeared for a reason.'

Helen was completely intrigued now.

'What do you mean?'

He was staring straight ahead again now, still fingering the steering wheel.

'I looked after Heather when she was having Vanessa. I delivered her in fact. Heather insisted Vanessa was her first child. But she wasn't. I didn't make an issue of it – there were no complications, no real reason to press Heather for details she obviously wanted to keep to herself. But Vanessa was not Heather's first pregnancy. There was absolutely no doubt in my mind. She'd had a baby before.'

Helen was silent, digesting this information.

'General practice is full of surprises,' Paul said with a grin. 'Never assume you know a patient, Helen. Most people have a cupboard full of secrets.'

'I know that,' she said shortly. 'I'm not totally naive.'

'I never thought you were. But you do tend to think the best of people.'

'Is that so bad?'

'No. Just typically you.'

'And what,' Helen asked mischievously, 'is typically me?'

He turned to look at her again. A corner of his mouth turned up; by the bright moonlight she could see it quite clearly.

'A bit fiery, a bit defensive . . .'

'Being a woman in a man's world has made me that!'

'And really altogether rather nice.'

'Nice!'

'A bit more than nice.'

'Oh.' She was embarrassed suddenly. 'You mean I'll do.'

'I reckon.' He paused. 'How would you feel about doing this more often?'

She knew what he meant; chose to be deliberately obtuse.

'Spend our evenings dealing with death and trauma?'

'Not exactly. I was thinking more of the social aspect.'

'Ah.'

'You're still involved with that Guy fellow.' He said it so quickly, so defensively, she realised that beneath the down-to-earth side of him which he chose to show to the world, he was actually rather vulnerable.

'No,' she said. 'No, I'm not. That's over.'

'Well then . . .'

'Is it wise?' she asked.

'When was wise ever worth bothering about?'

'True.' When had she been wise? She hesitated; threw caution to the winds. 'All right. Just so long as we don't get involved.'

'Did I ask you to get involved?'

'No.' *But you meant it. I know you meant it.*

'So what are you worrying about?'

A hundred and one things. Mostly how we would be able to go on working together if we want different things, want to move at a different pace.

'Paul, I . . .'

219

And then he kissed her. Afterwards she was never sure how it had come to happen. Only that she was in his arms and his mouth was on hers and it felt good. Very good.

'I suppose I shouldn't have done that,' he said, releasing her.

'No, you shouldn't,' she said. 'It's exactly the sort of thing I was afraid of.'

'I suppose that's why I did it,' Paul said. 'What were you just saying about confronting your fears? That if they're left to go inward they just get worse? I thought if you're into all this Freudian stuff it might be just the kind of therapy you needed.'

'I see,' Helen said. 'So it was a form of treatment.'

'If you like. Did it work?'

The moon was very bright. She thought afterwards it initiated a sort of madness.

'I'm not sure,' she said. 'Perhaps you should give it another try.'

He did.

'Any better?'

'Let me sleep on it,' she said.

Chapter Twelve

'I hear poor Walt Simmons has gone,' Charlotte said.

She was wearing her Sunday-best dress, sitting on one of the hardbacked chairs in Dolly's living room with her bag and a cup of tea on the table in front of her. She had been there for the half-hour since Dolly had cleared away the dinner things and replaced the tablecloth with one of the cream centrepieces Charlotte had crocheted for her and a glass jug and basin full of sweet william and snapdragons, waiting for Helen, who had promised to take her for a run in the car. But now that Helen was here, she wasn't sure she wanted to go out. It was a hot afternoon and there was so much traffic on the roads these days it worried her; even sitting in the back seat like a passenger in a taxi she found it difficult to relax, with motorbikes roaring past and other cars coming from all directions. It was a sign of getting old, she supposed, you felt more vulnerable, nervous of things you could have taken in your stride when you were twenty years younger. Besides, she wanted to talk to Helen and talking wasn't easy when the conversation had to be conducted over her granddaughter's shoulder.

'You went there when it happened, did you?' she asked now.

'They're my patients, yes.'

'So what was it then? A clot, I heard.'

'That's close enough,' Helen said. She didn't want to talk about it – though it was common knowledge now that Walt had suffered thrombosis she was still uncomfortably aware that she was discussing a patient. Even though it was only her grandmother she was talking to, even though it would go no further, she didn't want to give anyone the slightest chance to consider her guilty of breach of confidence. 'Dolly said . . . And her niece is the doctor . . .'

was all it would take. Like Caesar's wife, she must remain above reproach.

'Are you ready to go then?' she asked, changing the subject.

Charlotte sighed, finished her tea and got up. Her ankles bulged over the top of her shoes; even with a notch cut in the leather they felt tight.

'You're sure you'll be all right, Mam?' Dolly asked, coming in from the kitchen with the tea cloth still in her hand.

'Of course I'll be all right!' Charlotte said, a touch impatiently. If there was one thing worse than getting old it was having your children *treat* you as old.

Helen had parked her car in the lane behind the rank of houses; she armed Charlotte out and installed her in the back seat.

'I thought we'd go up to Masbury Ring. Or Deer Leap. What do you fancy?'

'Deer Leap would be nice.'

Helen had taken her there before; she liked to sit in the car and look down over the vista of countryside, green and unspoiled, though in truth nothing could match the way she had felt with her first sight of the Hillsbridge valley so many years ago. Then she had been a young bride, and to her the rolling fields, the rows of cottages stacked like the fingers of a hand into the hillsides, yellow lias and smoke-blackened grey, all in the shadow of the sentinel batches – the Black Mountains – had seemed an enchanted place. Lovely as it was, the acclaimed beauty spot could not even come close to stirring her as the Hillsbridge valley had stirred her then, but somehow it evoked the memory and as they drove home she said to Helen: 'I'd like to drive up to Greenslade Terrace. I'd like to see my old home again.'

There was something in her tone that caught at Helen and evoked a twist of anxiety. It was almost as if Charlotte had added the words: 'one last time'. Helen pushed the disturbing thought away.

'Of course. We'll make a detour up there if you'd like to.'

She headed down the main road into the centre of town.

The shops were all closed for Sunday, the blinds drawn and the sun awnings rolled up. Apart from a group of youths sitting astride their bicycles on County Bridge and a handful of people walking to chapel the streets were deserted. Helen turned the car into the steep hill alongside the George and was aware of Charlotte's sudden alertness as she looked from one side of the road to the other.

'Oh – the Miss Latchams have had their house painted! The spring's dry . . . of course we haven't had the rain this summer. Look at the state of that garden! Captain Fish would have a fit if he could see it now!'

Helen slowed at the approach to Greenslade Terrace. Cars could, and did, pass along the narrow lane between the backs of the houses and what had used to be the blocks of bake ovens, privies and coal houses, but if there were vehicles parked there it could be difficult to drive past and even more difficult to get out again. Some girls were playing hopscotch on a grid they had marked out, and a boy squatted outside one of the doors rolling marbles.

Helen drove slowly along the rank. Most of the people living here would be strangers to her now, but Charlotte was all avid interest and it was she who saw the estate agent's sign first.

'It's for sale! It's up for sale!' She sounded almost affronted.

'What?' Helen asked. Then she saw it too – garish green on white-painted tin.

'Well, fancy that!' Charlotte said indignantly. 'Over fifty years I lived there, and they're selling it again already! Well, I never!'

'I expect they have their reasons, Gran,' Helen said.

'Oh, I expect they do!' Charlotte retorted in disgust. 'They're looking to make a profit, I expect. I knew we let it go too cheap, but our Dolly was so worried about me being here on my own she couldn't wait to get rid of it. Oh, they had a bargain, all right.' She sighed. 'When I think of the happy times we had here! Summer nights we used to sit out on the steps, all of us, all along the rank – except the Clementses, of course. And the Christmases!

223

Singing carols round the piano, playing games – no television in those days. We made our own entertainment.'

So many memories were here – washing the menfolk's backs when they bathed in the tin tub in front of the fire after a shift underground; the day the Bryants' pig had escaped and rooted up the parsnips and Ted had been blamed for it; the end of the Second World War when she had heard on the radio that it was all over and she and Peggy Yelling had danced together in the street; the community parties with the children all sitting up at trestle tables eating tomato sandwiches and jelly and blancmange; Nipper, the stray dog Ted had adopted, scavenging for scraps at the dustbins.

Time had telescoped, somehow, events which had happened decades apart merging and blurring together though each one in itself was sharp as if it had been only yesterday; a lifetime encapsulated in a kaleidoscope of small scenes.

'I spent my whole life here,' she said. 'I always said they'd only get me out of here feet first in a box, and I wish they had.'

'Don't say that, Gran!' Helen protested.

'It's no more than the truth. I'm just a lodger at our Dolly's, biding out my time. She won't let me do anything to help.'

'She means well,' Helen said.

'I dare say she does. She was always a good girl. But oh, I don't know, it's no way to live. It's not like being in my own home.'

'Come on, Gran,' Helen said. 'I knew it was a mistake coming up here.'

'No,' Charlotte said, 'it was me made the mistake ever leaving.'

Helen slipped the car into reverse and backed away along the rank. Charlotte was silent now; glancing at her in the rear-view mirror Helen saw that she was crying. Her heart bled for her grandmother, and in that moment, she knew what she was going to do.

*

Next morning, as soon as surgery was over, she went to the estate agents.

'Number 11, Greenslade Terrace,' she said. 'It's for sale, I understand. How much are you asking?'

The girl at the desk fished the literature out of a file.

'Six hundred and fifty pounds. It's a very nice property, modernised, well-maintained . . .'

'I want to buy it,' Helen said.

The girl tried, unsuccessfully, to hide her surprise.

'You'd like to see over it? I could make an appointment for you.'

'No need,' Helen said.

A man in a tweed jacket, who might have been listening from the inner sanctum, appeared in the doorway and came towards her, holding out his hand.

'Don Basson,' he said. 'Can I help you?'

'I want to buy Number 11, Greenslade Terrace.'

'We have some very nice properties on our books. Perhaps you'd like to see some of those before you make up your mind.' He smiled ingratiatingly, suggesting that he had recognised her. *Much more in your class*, that smile said.

'I'm not interested in any other property,' Helen said. 'It's Greenslade Terrace I'm interested in. It hasn't been sold, has it?'

'I have someone viewing this evening . . .'

'But they haven't made an offer yet.'

'Not as yet.'

'Well, I am,' Helen said. 'I'm not even going to quibble over the asking price and I have nothing to sell. I can exchange contracts in the time it takes the solicitor to draw it up.'

'This is really very unusual, Doctor.' So he had recognised her. 'Don't you even want to see over the property?'

'I know it like the back of my hand. No, I don't want to see over it. I just don't want you to sell it to anyone else.'

'Well, in that case . . .' He seemed totally bemused. 'If you're quite sure, I suppose . . .'

'Oh yes,' Helen said. 'I'm quite sure.'

And she was. Never had she been surer of anything. Last night she had lain awake, not so much turning it over in her mind, for her mind was already made up, as relishing the idea, taking each aspect in turn and thinking how perfect it was.

She'd always intended to buy a house here, though not perhaps just yet, not until she was offered a partnership, but she already felt settled and thought that, barring some unforeseen catastrophe, the partnership would one day be hers. Property had to be a good investment and besides now that she was seeing Paul regularly she needed a home of her own, for a variety of reasons. She couldn't impose him on Amy and Ralph – hadn't even wanted to impose herself for too long, kind and accommodating though they were; couldn't – didn't want to – use his house as an extension of her own. That, perhaps, was even more of an influential factor. Since the night Walt had died she and Paul had a far more intimate relationship than previously but Helen was not ready to commit to anyone – and especially not Paul. She was still too raw and, in spite of herself, too much in love with Guy. Besides, all the dangers of a relationship with a colleague remained, as much of an obstacle as ever, and Helen thought that buying her own house, demonstrating her intention for continued independence was as good a way as any of keeping him at arm's length. They could be alone together there, but in *her* house on *her* terms.

It was possible, of course, that if the old family home had not been for sale she would have chosen something a little more upmarket, a little more the type of property Don Basson had expected her to be interested in. A cottage in one of the nearby villages, perhaps, small enough to be affordable, but with more privacy, and roses or creepers round the door. But Number 11, Greenslade Terrace held many happy memories for her too. And that was not the best of it. The best of it was that she would be able to take Charlotte home.

Jenny lay on the flat roof of the shed at the back of the grandstand in the town football ground. It was, she knew, an odd place to choose as a refuge, but for some reason she liked it there. It was one of her own special places.

226

What the shed was used for, she wasn't sure. It wasn't the team's changing rooms – they were in a spanking new concrete block building on the opposite side of the ground and just beyond the turnstile. It wasn't the refreshment hut – that was a wooden shed with a shuttered window a few yards away from the grandstand. Perhaps, she thought, it was used for storing equipment but what equipment Hillsbridge Town FC possessed she could not imagine. The only piece she had ever seen in use was the huge iron roller used for flattening the pitch, and over the bar of which the children turned somersaults, standing in line to wait their turn. It could be white paint for marking the lines, she supposed, but that hardly seemed to warrant such a spacious storage area.

Whatever, a few summers ago, when the grandstand had been in process of being renovated, she and the others had discovered the hut with the flat roof. In those days the boys had swung on to it by means of a rope attached to one of the grandstand girders and she had done the same – a little timidly, but gaining confidence each time and finding exhilaration in her daring. When the work on the grandstand was completed and the rope removed the boys lost interest in the hut, but Jenny continued to go there, climbing on to a water butt and hauling herself up. The roof was sheeted with asphalt which reflected the sun, but there was also shade from the tall side of the grandstand which dwarfed the hut and hid it almost completely from view. Jenny would take a book to read, or a pad and pencil to scribble the stories she had begun to write – lurid imitations of the paperback novelettes which came out monthly and which she saved her pocket money to buy. First it had been Schoolgirls' Own Library, with titles such as *Trixie's Diary* and themes that came straight out of her favourite comics, *School Friend* and *Girl*. But lately she had progressed to romances – *Yukon Adventure* one was called – and the stories she scribbled progressed accordingly. Carrie would have a fit, she knew, if she ever read Jenny's wildly imaginative stories – runaway teenagers and forbidden love, and even one about a pair of bigamists who married other people for their money but were really,

227

truly, in love with each other – and even more furious at the lurid descriptions of kisses and embraces, about which Jenny could now write from experience. But she wasn't likely to get the chance to read them. Jenny kept her notebooks close by her at all times, and at night slept with them under her pillow.

Today, however, she was neither writing nor reading. She'd brought her books with her but they lay spread out around her untouched. Her mind was too full of death.

First Grandpa. That had hit her harder than she'd imagined possible. Grandpa had been – just Grandpa. Never saying very much, a shadowy background figure, but always there, part of her world. Now he wasn't there any more and Jenny found she minded dreadfully. She'd never lost anyone close to her before, never thought about it very much. Well, she had lost Barry, of course, but that was different. He hadn't done anything as horribly final as dying. Now she felt as if the very foundations of her world had rocked, felt a terrible empty ache knowing he'd never be there again, ever; felt, too, fear. Grampy had gone and so would they all, one by one. Gran next perhaps, and then . . . the awful inexorable inescapability of it made her feel helpless and apprehensive. Who would be next?

Well, now she knew the answer to that. Linda Parfitt. David's Linda. Younger than Heather, even. Not much older than herself. Jenny shivered, feeling the chill of death in the heat of the sun.

She had only learned the terrible truth this morning. She had known something was going on; David had had long whispered conversations with Carrie in the kitchen, Carrie had done the same with Joe. But they'd always stopped when she had come into the room and when she had asked what was going on Carrie had said it was nothing to concern her. And then, this morning:

'David's getting married,' Carrie said. 'In three weeks' time, when they've had a chance to call the banns.'

Jenny had immediately assumed that this was a shot-gun wedding like Heather's; that explained the whispered conversations.

'Oh – I see,' she said.

'It's not that, Jenny,' David said, reading her mind.

Jenny looked at him, startled. His face was strained, and he didn't look at all happy.

'Then why . . .?'

And then they told her. Her first reaction was utter disbelieving shock and then she was angry as well. Why couldn't they have said something before? Why treat her like a child?

'Why didn't you tell me?' she asked.

'We didn't want it blabbed all over Hillsbridge,' Carrie said.

Typical! Jenny thought. Typical of Carrie to treat illness as something to be ashamed of.

'Do you really think I'd have gone round blabbing if you didn't want me to?' she retorted furiously. 'What do you take me for?'

'Don't be so stupid, Jen. I just didn't want to talk about it,' David said.

He was close to tears, her big brother, who never cried, and suddenly she wasn't angry any more, just sorry for her outburst and very, very sorry for David.

'I don't believe it!' she said, and she was close to tears herself. 'Oh, Dave – it's so awful! She's not really going to die, is she?'

She asked the same question now, sitting on the roof of the grandstand, staring up at the clear blue of the sky, and addressing herself to the unseen omnipresence.

She can't be going to die! Not Linda!

But there was no comfort in the voice that seemed to be speaking not only in her head but in every fibre of her being.

Linda *was* going to die. That was why David looked so ill himself, so totally devastated. Linda had leukaemia and there was no cure for leukaemia. Who could say for sure whether she would even make it to her wedding?

For a long while Jenny sat while the thoughts and emotions washed over her. She cried a little, for David, for Linda, even for herself and the rest of humanity who had no choice but to go along with the lottery of life – and death. She cried for Walt – the first time her grief at his

229

loss had actually found expression – and when at last the tears had dried, she sat some more whilst the thoughts and emotions rumbled around again, but less violently, as if they were the aftershocks of an earthquake or a thunderstorm rolling away into the distance.

When even they stilled, Jenny reached for her pad and pencil. Suddenly she wanted more than anything else in the world to write. Not her silly bigamy story (she didn't know how to finish it anyway), but something much deeper. She felt a compulsion to put what she was feeling on to paper, as if by so doing she could cleanse herself, ease the pain.

A strangely detached part of her mind was urging her to write it down *now* before she forgot. Some day – some day – she would look back and read it and say: 'Yes! *That's* how it was!'

She began to write, the words tumbling on to the page, and the overwhelming heaviness of heart began to leave her. It was a curiously uplifting experience.

When Jenny got home Carrie was cooking the dinner. Jenny smelled it as she went up the path – sausages frying. She realised how hungry she was, and was glad that Carrie's job in the school canteen meant that she was at home during the holidays.

When she went into the kitchen, though, Carrie was looking hot and bothered.

'It's not ready,' she greeted Jenny. 'I'm running late. That dog's led me a real dance this morning. First she messed all up the stairs and then I found her in the cupboard eating the cheese. A pound, I should think there must have been there, and she's had the lot.'

'Oh no!' Sally was indeed proving a bit of a handful; Carrie seemed to be shouting at her for one reason or another most of the time. Jenny lived in fear that she would say the dog had to go. 'Where is she?'

'Out in the garden. Shut out in disgrace.'

'I'll go and play with her for a bit,' Jenny said. 'She's just full of life, that's all.'

She went down the three steps from the alleyway into

the back garden, but couldn't see Sally anywhere. A feeling of foreboding filled Jenny. She called the dog's name and went down the path to investigate behind the runner beans – the only portion of the garden not in view – but of Sally there was no sign. She ran back into the house.

'Mum – she's not there!'

'What d'you mean – she's not there? She must be!' Carrie hurried out herself, calling for Sally and coming to the same conclusion as Jenny. 'Oh my Lord – she's got out! She must have gone over the fence!' Joe had erected chicken wire all around the garden so as to make it secure for the puppy. 'However did she do that?'

Jenny was panicking. 'Where is she? Suppose she goes down on the main road? She could get knocked down and killed!'

Carrie humphed with such feeling that it almost sounded as if she was thinking that such a catastrophe would at least mean the end of her trials. 'She'll come back when she's hungry.'

Jenny was close to tears. 'I'm going to go and look for her.'

'I suppose I'd better as well. Just let me turn the ring off under those sausages. You go down across the field, Jenny, and I'll walk up to the lane . . .'

They went out, splitting up and calling the dog's name loudly. Jenny ran down the path between the next-door semi and the units but when she reached the field she could see at a glance that it was ominously empty. The panic rose again, almost choking her. At that moment, she could not imagine seeing her beloved Sally ever again. She ran back again, face hot and damp with perspiration, hair flopping over it. A sense of nightmare had closed in, darkening the sunny day.

Jenny could see Carrie at the end of the road, still looking and calling. She looked around wildly, wondering what to do next. And then suddenly, there was Sally, trotting along the opposite pavement for all the world as if nothing had happened.

'Mum – there she is!' Jenny yelled. 'Sally! Sally!'

Sally ignored her. Frondy tail waving, she ran through the gateway into Joyce Edgell's garden.

Carrie was closest; she came hurrying back along the road, every purposeful step showing her annoyance. As she turned into Joyce's gateway, the front door opened and Joyce appeared, also clearly annoyed.

'What's going on?'

Sally, clearly in no mood to lose her new-found freedom so easily, trotted up the path away from Carrie, for all the world as if she intended going into Joyce's house. And Joyce aimed a spiteful kick at her. The dog skittered away, sufficiently unnerved by the unexpectedness of the attack to seek protection from her owner, and Carrie caught her by the collar.

'Get that bloody thing out of my garden!' Joyce yelled.

But Carrie, who a few moments ago had been angry enough to do Sally harm herself, was outraged.

'How dare you!' she blazed. 'How dare you kick my dog!'

'She was trying to come in my house!' Joyce blazed back. 'She'd have wrecked the place!'

'She'd have a job to do that!' Carrie retorted. 'It's a wreck already.'

'Keep your bloody mouth to yourself, Carrie Simmons! And keep that fucking dog under control, or I'll do more than kick it next time!'

She went in, slamming the door. Carrie dragged Sally back along the pavement.

'Bad dog. You bad dog!'

'She didn't mean it, Mum, she just wanted to go exploring.' Jenny was pleased, at least, to see how Carrie had leaped to Sally's defence. 'Don't be too hard on her.'

'Yes, well, she's got to learn,' Carrie said. 'She can't go wandering off like that, especially going into people's gardens. And why did it have to be Joyce Edgell's, I'd like to know?'

Jenny dropped to her knees, fondling the silky coat and ears.

'She hasn't got very good taste yet, Mum,' she said, lightheaded with relief.

'You can say that again!' Carrie agreed.

But inwardly she was wondering if she was fated to have spats like these with Joyce to the end of her days.

'I'm buying a house!' Helen said to Paul.

They were having a meal in a very new, very chic cellar bar in Bath; Helen had waited until they had finished their main course before broaching the subject. She had expected a barrage of questions which could be more easily answered if her mouth wasn't full of spaghetti Bolognese, but in the event, Paul seemed hardly surprised.

'I guessed you would, sooner or later. Where is it?'

She told him, explained her reasons.

'That's a really nice thing to do,' he said.

She looked at him, a little surprised by the reaction. She'd thought he might be a bit put out, or even suggest, as Amy had done, that it wasn't such a good idea.

'Are you sure you've thought what you're letting yourself in for?' Amy had asked. 'She's not the easiest person in the world to live with, you know.'

'We get along very well,' Helen had said, a bit sharply.

'And what if she's taken ill? Can't be left on her own when you have to go to work?'

'We'll cross that bridge when we come to it,' Helen had said, even more sharply. There could be difficulties, she knew, but she wasn't prepared to let them stand in her way. This was something she really wanted to do.

'Does she know yet?' Paul asked now.

'Not yet. I don't want to say anything until contracts are signed, just in case anything goes wrong. I'd hate to raise her hopes only to have her disappointed.'

'Well, I think,' Paul said, 'that is the nicest thing I've ever heard.'

He was looking at her with such undisguised admiration that Helen was embarrassed.

'It's for me as well. I'm not being totally philanthropic.'

'That's what I mean,' he said.

The waiter materialised at her elbow, brandishing leather-backed menus opened at the selection of sweets and puddings.

Helen glanced at Paul over the top of hers, uneasy

suddenly. The way he had said it belied his usual carefully casual attitude to their relationship. She had told him she'd go out with him as long as he realised there was to be no commitment and he had seemed to accept that. They were both to be free agents, even having other dates if they wanted to. Nothing was to be read into anything, not even the physical intimacy they shared when they felt like it.

'Just so long as you understand we're just good friends,' Helen had stipulated, and Paul hadn't argued.

'Suits me fine,' he had said, and Helen had congratulated herself that what she had thought might be a problem was actually no problem at all. *He's a confirmed bachelor at heart*, she had thought, relieved. *He doesn't want serious involvement any more than I do.*

Now she found herself looking at him and worrying. It wasn't what he'd actually said – in fact, a man with more than friendship on his mind might have been put out by the thought of an elderly grandmother on the scene. In a way it was worse. Helen had the most awful feeling that Paul had far deeper feelings for her than he was prepared to admit to. That he was in love with her, even. It was the very last thing she wanted.

I should never have agreed to go out with him, she thought in panic. *Even setting out the ground rules as I did, I've still managed to give him the wrong idea. Or encouraged him to think he's in with a chance. Or something.*

The trouble was how could she put a stop to things now without causing the sort of ill-feeling between them that was the very thing she'd been afraid of? She was trapped – had been, really, from the moment he had taken a fancy to her. Even then, she realised, it had been a case of being damned if she did and damned if she didn't.

Why the hell couldn't he have been happily married like Reuben Hobbs, so that no possibility of complications could have arisen to mar their professional relationship?

Men! Helen thought crossly. *Whichever way you look at it, they're nothing but trouble!*

But for all her annoyance, in spite of all the problems it could cause, Helen couldn't help feeling just a little bit flattered, and a little bit glad that someone like Paul might, just possibly, be in love with her.

It had to be a very quiet wedding. For one thing, there was no time to arrange anything elaborate; for another there was no telling how Linda would be on the day. But at least she was having her wedding.

Carrie had done her best to talk David out of it, using every argument she could think of, and putting them as forcefully as she always did. She felt sorry for Linda, but she was totally opposed to the ceremony which would, in all likelihood, make her son a widower before Christmas. She was already looking to his future, when, hopefully, he would meet someone else and forget all about this unhappy chapter in his life. In Carrie's book, having been married already made him that little bit less eligible.

But nothing she could say would change David's mind. He had promised Linda, and he wouldn't be swayed. Not that David ever could be influenced much once his mind was made up. There was a very stubborn streak in his nature.

In the end Carrie had to capitulate and make the best of it, as she said to Heather, and the implication behind her words was clear. She'd seen two of her children married, and neither of them under circumstances she would have chosen.

'I just can't see the point,' she went on. 'Going through all this palaver when she's only got weeks to live.'

'If that's what she wants,' Heather said, 'then it has to be worth it. I can understand her actually. And you should be proud of David. This must be a nightmare for him.'

'For all of us!' Carrie said, a little huffily. 'Well, I shall wear what I wore for your wedding. There's no time to make another outfit and I'm certainly not buying another hat. The one I've got hasn't been out of the cupboard from that day to this.'

Heather gave her head a small shake. Carrie would never change and in all likelihood the thing needling her most was that David was going against her advice.

On the day of the wedding, however, she did manage to smile as she, Joe and Jenny left the house and walked down

235

the garden path to where the hire car, with white ribbons fluttering on the bonnet, was waiting. Most of the neighbours had come out to their gates to watch, and even the children playing on the Green stopped their game and clustered round, some astride their bicycles, all ogling the spectacle. As the car pulled away there was a thud on the offside wheel arch and Carrie turned sharply, almost knocking her hat off as she did so, to see a football rolling away down the road.

'Little devils!' she muttered.

A few years ago, Billy Edgell would have been the perpetrator of an outrage such as this, but Billy no longer played on the Green. The sort of mischief he got up to nowadays was much more serious and took him further afield. Carrie had seen him coming and going late at night with a sack and an airgun under his arm, and suspected that he was poaching rabbits and maybe pheasants too from one of the nearby estates.

There was certainly at least one young Edgell amongst the youngsters on the Green, though – there were still enough of them left to carry on the family traditions!

Another crowd of onlookers had congregated outside the church, some who had come purposely, armed with boxes of confetti or even a horseshoe or wooden spoon with a bow of ribbon round the handle, others whose laden shopping bags and baskets bore witness to the fact that they had been passing by on their way home from market. Again, Carrie managed to smile, but her heart felt heavy. How could anyone possibly rejoice in this farce?

David and his best man, Tony Riddle, were waiting by the church door. They both wore carnations in the buttonholes of their smart suits, but David was very pale. Jenny gave his hand a squeeze as they passed and Joe clapped him on the back but it was all Carrie could do to keep a tight smile on her lips and she gave her head a small sad shake as they went through the porch and into the church.

The organ was playing and the sun shining in through the stained-glass windows threw multi-coloured patterns of light on the pews and aisle. But Carrie found it difficult to approve even so. Although she had lapsed from regular worship a long time ago she was still a Catholic at heart and she found the echoing vaulted space of the parish church unfriendly and lacking in reverence compared to what she had been used to. A church should have statues and shrines and holy water and be imbued with the smell of incense. Anything less just wasn't right.

After a few minutes David and Tony came in and took their places in the front right-hand pew, immediately in front of Carrie, Joe and Jenny. Carrie turned around to smile at Vanessa, who was wearing a frilly organdie dress and drumming her new anklestrap shoes on the pew in competition with the music, and caught sight of Linda's mother coming up the aisle. *She looks like I feel*, Carrie thought, *as if that smile is going to crack her face if she has to force it for a moment longer*. She nodded to her and Doreen nodded back, her chin nudging towards the back of the church. At the same moment the organ began to play the 'Bridal March'. Doreen had stayed with Linda until the last possible moment, Carrie realised, with a twinge of anxiety as to how Linda was today, how she was going to manage to carry this off.

The Linda who came up the aisle, however, did not look in the least like a girl under sentence of death. Though pale, there was a glow about her and to the entire congregation it was obvious that it was a glow of happiness. Somehow, in the short time she'd had, she had managed to get hold of a wedding dress that not only fitted, but suited her perfectly; the ivory lace was less harsh than pure white against her fragile skin, and the full skirt and puff sleeves concealed the fact that she was now painfully thin, whilst the nipped-in bodice emphasised her handspan waist. And it was ballerina-length, just as she had wanted. On her head she wore a coronet of diamanté and pearls and she carried a spray bouquet of pink roses.

Behind her came Wendy Young, her best friend, also in a ballerina-length dress of pink tulle. There had been no time to kit out the three bridesmaids she had planned.

As Linda took her place beside David at the altar Carrie saw the look that passed between them and felt her heart turn over. Had she been wrong after all to be so sceptical about the wedding? But it was a fleeting thought only. As the service progressed the words of the marriage service only reinforced all her misgivings.

How could they ever be of comfort one to the other? David might comfort Linda, but she would be unable to reciprocate. And there would be no children, either, to be raised in this union. Worst of all were the vows. When first David, then Linda, repeated the traditional words ''Til death us do part' the whole congregation seemed to hold its breath as one, so that the words reverberated from the ancient rafters and filled the whole church with a heavy bitter sweetness. There were no sobs – everyone had themselves too tightly under control for that – but there were a few sniffs and rustles as handkerchiefs were found in pockets and bags.

At last it was over.

'That's it then,' Carrie said to Joe as they waited for David and Linda to sign the register, and Joe said: 'It's what he wanted, Carrie. It's what they both wanted.'

'Something to want for, though!' Carrie muttered, almost to herself.

And then she was walking, arm in arm with Jim Parfitt, in the procession down the aisle, much more slowly than usual because already Linda was tiring. As they reached the door the bells began to peal, but for all the joy they brought to Carrie's heart, they might as well have been muffled and tolling.

'There's the church bells!' Charlotte said. 'Somebody must be getting married!'

'It's David Simmons and Linda Parfitt,' Dolly said.

'David Simmons? Not *Walt* Simmons' grandson?'

'Yes.'

'But Walt hasn't been dead any time at all! How can they have the bells?'

'It's special circumstances from what I can make out,' Dolly said. 'Oh – here's our Helen come to see you! Can you open the door for her, Mam? I'm all over flour.'

She was baking, as she always did on Saturday mornings

after getting home from market – a treacle tommy and a big jam tart.

Charlotte opened the door. Helen had pulled up so close that she almost fell inside as she emerged from the driving seat of her car, long-trousered legs first. Charlotte noted them with some disapproval. She was old-fashioned, she supposed, but she didn't like to see a woman wearing trousers.

Not that she'd say a word about that to Helen – unless of course she was asked, when she'd give her opinion straight!

'Hello, Gran! You're on the ball this morning!' Helen said, smiling.

'I had my orders,' Charlotte returned drily. 'This is a surprise, Helen. We don't usually see you on a Saturday morning.'

'Well, there you are – life's full of surprises.'

She looked like the cat that got the cream, Charlotte thought.

Helen ducked back into her car and reached for a bunch of dahlias, paper-wrapped, that were lying on the back seat. She handed them to Charlotte.

'For me?' Charlotte asked.

'For you – and Auntie Dolly, and anyone else who might appreciate them. I got them on the flower stall in the market.'

'I didn't think they were out of our Amy's garden!' Charlotte said drily.

'Amy's garden is actually looking very nice at the moment,' Helen said. 'She's got Cliff Button helping her out now.'

'So I heard. How is he?'

'He's OK,' Helen said. 'I didn't come to talk about Cliff Button, though. I want to talk to you about something quite different. And Auntie Dolly too.'

'Would you like a cup of tea, Helen?' Dolly asked. 'You'll have to put the kettle on if you do. I'm all over flour.'

'I know what I'd like,' Charlotte said. 'A nice glass of milk stout.'

'Mam!' Dolly sounded scandalised. 'Whatever will Helen think of you?'

'A bit of bread and nice tasty cheese and a glass of milk stout,' Charlotte repeated, enjoying every moment of her temporary notoriety. 'You know what they say – a little of what you fancy does you good. Isn't that right, Helen?'

'It certainly won't do you any harm,' Helen said, laughing.

'It'll spoil your dinner!' Dolly said severely. 'I've got sausages and Savoy cabbage with fat out of the pan – your favourite.'

'Spoil my dinner!' Charlotte scoffed. 'Anyone would think it was the children you were talking to! You're getting too bossy for my liking, Dolly.'

'You have a glass of milk stout if you want one, Gran,' Helen said. 'And I'll have one too.'

Pretending to ignore Dolly's disapproval, Charlotte padded defiantly to the pantry and emerged with two bottles and glasses.

'What did you come to talk to us about then?' Dolly asked as Charlotte rummaged in the kitchen drawer for the bottle opener.

'Well – I've got some news,' Helen said. 'You remember when we went up to Greenslade Terrace, Gran, we saw that your old house was up for sale?'

'It's never gone already!' Charlotte said, sounding shocked.

'Yes. Of course, it was a bargain, wasn't it?' Helen was so full of excitement she couldn't resist teasing a little.

'It was at that! When I think of all the things we had done! There was no electric when we moved in, you know, only the gas mantels. And no bathroom.'

'I know,' Helen said.

'All the same – gone already! Who's bought it, I wonder?'

'You'll never guess. In a million years.'

'What – you mean it's somebody I know?'

'You could say that, yes.'

'Well – who? You've come up here 'specially to tell me, I reckon. So don't keep me in suspense!'

'All right,' Helen said. 'It's me.'

For a moment Charlotte gaped at her, open-mouthed,

240

and Dolly stood transfixed with a circle of pastry suspended over her rolling pin halfway to the enamel pie-plate.

'*You!*' she said in the loud voice she adopted to talk to her deaf husband Victor.

'Me.'

'You never have!' Charlotte said. 'Fancy that!'

'You're a dark horse,' Dolly said. She sounded vaguely affronted. 'You never said a word!'

'I wanted to be sure I could get it,' Helen said. 'You never know with these things . . . there's so much that can go wrong. But now it's all signed and settled, I couldn't wait to share the news.'

Charlotte had forgotten all about her milk stout. It stood untouched on the little cupboard beside the sink.

'Well, I am pleased, Helen. I've always hated the thought of strangers in my house.'

Helen hesitated. This, she knew, was going to be the tricky part – asking Charlotte to come back and live in 'her' house. Ideally, Helen would have preferred to raise the subject when they were alone, but she didn't want Dolly to think she was going behind her back. Already she seemed a bit put out by not having known what was going on. It had been her home, too, once, after all. But the subject of where Charlotte would finish out her days was even more delicate. Dolly might be terribly offended that anyone should consider her mother might prefer to be anywhere other than with her.

'I did think, Gran,' Helen said carefully, 'that it would be nice for you. You could always come and stay.'

'I don't know about that.' Dolly had slapped the pastry on to the plate; now she ran a knife round the rim almost viciously. 'It would upset her routine.'

'For goodness sake, Dolly!' Charlotte said testily. 'Don't talk about me as if I wasn't here! And what routine are you on about, anyway?'

'Well – your All Bran in the mornings . . . your afternoon nap . . .'

'Why couldn't I have All Bran and a nap if I was staying with Helen?'

'Well, you could, I suppose. But it would be such a to-do, getting you there and back . . .'

'It would give you some time to yourself, Auntie Dolly. And you could stay for as long as you liked, Gran. When I'm out at work you can pretend nothing's changed and it's still your house, just like it always was.'

'It wouldn't be the same, though, would it? I should feel like a visitor.'

But Helen could sense the undercurrent of her excitement.

'Think about it anyway, Gran,' she said. 'And I shall be doing up your old room specially for you so you'd better not let me do it in vain.'

'Are you saying what I think you're saying?' Dolly asked suddenly, plonking strawberry jam into the tart and pointing the spoon at Helen. 'Are you asking Mam to go back there and live?'

'Well . . . if she wanted to there'll be plenty of room and I should be in and out and well able to keep an eye . . .' She broke off, aware that she was doing the same thing Charlotte had accused Dolly of doing – talking about her as if she wasn't there.

'Oh, Gran – I might as well come clean. There's nothing I'd like better than for you to be back where you belong. I know Auntie Dolly does a wonderful job of looking after you, but your heart's in Greenslade Terrace, and I'd be really happy if you moved back in with me – if that's what you want.'

'Well yes,' Charlotte said, 'there's not much doubt about where my heart is. What do you think, Dolly?'

'I haven't had a chance to think at all!' Dolly said. 'And nor have you, Mam. We need to sit down and talk it over – all the pros and cons. What if you should be taken bad? Helen would still have to go to work and I couldn't keep running over to look after you. I'm not as young as I used to be either, and I've got my own home and family to see to.'

Helen saw Charlotte's face fall but she was still very aware that she was treading on delicate ground. To say too much, and put Dolly's nose out of joint, would be counterproductive. The last thing she wanted was to cause a family rift.

'I think Auntie Dolly's right,' she said. 'Talk it over between yourselves. There's no rush. I'm not even going to get the keys for another couple of weeks. But at least you know the offer's there. If you want to move back into your own home, you know you can. If not – well, at least it's back in the family, isn't it?'

Charlotte nodded.

'You're a good girl, Helen.'

The tears were shining in her eyes again, Helen noticed with a sense of shock. In all her life she didn't think she could ever remember seeing her grandmother cry. Now, in the space of a few short weeks, it had happened twice – and both over the old home.

It means so much to her, Helen thought.

Everything else had changed – her children grown into men and women who were not just middle-aged but some of them verging on the old themselves – what a shock that must be, to look at a plump ageing woman and realise this was the metamorphosis of the tiny baby you had once held at your breast! Even her grandchildren were grown, with children of their own. James, with whom she had shared it all, was long dead. And the world had moved on. But Greenslade Terrace was still there, changed and yet oddly unchanging, the same bricks and mortar, the same narrow access lane to the back doors, the same plaster on the walls which had absorbed so many years of laughter and tears, seen births and deaths and marriages, survived two world wars, echoed with the living of a family at whose heart Charlotte had always been – who *was* its heart. For a brief, surprised moment tears constricted her own throat. Then Charlotte was holding out a glass to her.

'Don't let your milk stout go flat, Helen. Especially now we've got something to drink to!'

'I thought we were going to talk about it, Mam,' Dolly said.

'All right, Dolly, don't get your hair off with me! We do have something to drink to, whatever's decided.' She raised her glass. 'There's going to be Halls in Greenslade Terrace again. That's good enough for me!'

'Thank you,' Linda said.

She was in bed – the three-quarter-size bed that had been delivered from Bath because none of the local furniture shops could supply them with what they wanted in time, wearing her new filmy powder-blue nylon nightie. David, unknotting his tie, looked at her in the dressing-table mirror and felt his stomach tighten with love.

'What d'you mean – thank you? What for?'

'For today. For marrying a . . .' Her voice cracked. 'A lost cause like me.'

He turned. 'What are you talking about?'

She attempted to smile but it was wan, a pale imitation of the radiance of a few hours previously.

'David, don't pretend. You don't have to pretend.'

'I'm not pretending.'

'You went through today just to make me happy. And I want you to know how grateful I am. How much I love you for it. I just wanted you to know.'

'Linda, you're talking rot.' He crossed to the bed, sat down on the edge beside her and took her in his arms. 'I married you because I wanted to – all right?'

'Oh, David . . .' She nuzzled into his shoulder. Her hair felt like spun silk against his cheek. 'David, I love you.'

'And I love you.' His voice was hoarse with emotion, speaking the words he'd never expected to speak, let alone mean and feel with every ounce of his being.

He stood up, unbuttoning his shirt, unbuckling his belt, dropping his clothes on to the bright Readicut rug and turning back the covers to slip into bed beside her. She melted against him and as he felt the warm yielding curves moulding to his body he forgot momentarily that she was a sick – a dying – woman. She was quite simply just his Linda.

He slid his hand under the low frothy neckline of her new nightdress, cupping her breast, feeling the nipple rise and harden. With his other hand he rucked up the skirt, his fingers following the line of her thigh up to the jut of

244

her hip bone, then slipping back to bury themselves in the soft tuft between her legs. He crooked his leg so that his knee lay across her thigh, his whole body reaching out toward her, his love a thick knot of desire that blotted out thought and reason.

'Linda . . .'

He rolled towards her, at the same time taking her with him, his body probing now where his fingers had probed.

'Linda . . .'

At first he was too intent on his overwhelming need to notice her withdrawal, the tension, the slackening, the inertia. He covered her mouth with his, parting her lips with his tongue and she tore them away, turning her head to one side, her breathing laboured and ragged. Then and only then was he aware of a shaft of alarm.

He raised himself on his elbows.

'Linda – what's the matter?'

'I'm sorry,' she murmured. There was a sob in her voice. 'David, I'm sorry. I can't. I don't feel very well . . .'

His ardour was gone as swiftly as it had become aroused. He rolled off her, looking down at her anxiously, afraid he'd hurt her, afraid . . . afraid . . .

'I'm sorry,' she said again. 'I just can't. I really can't.' The tears were welling weakly in the corners of her eyes, trickling down her face. 'I'm so tired. So terribly tired. I'm sorry . . . I'm sorry . . .'

'Hush!' he said fiercely. 'Stop saying you're sorry! I'm the one who should be saying sorry!'

'It's our wedding night! But I honestly don't think I can . . .'

'It doesn't matter,' he said. 'Honestly, Linda, it doesn't matter at all.'

'It does . . .'

'No. You're my wife and we're together. That's the only thing that matters. I mean it, Linda.'

And it was true, he realised. Such a short time ago it had all been so different. Then it had been the physical thing that had mattered. Then he would have run a mile at the thought of marriage. That had all been turned on its head.

Just being with Linda – keeping her with him – was all that mattered now.

'There'll be other times,' he said softly, catching her tears with his fingers and wiping them away. 'We'll have other times, you'll see.'

He lay down beside her, holding her tenderly, listening to her breathing, shallow and regular, as she fell asleep. Through the long hours of the night they stayed that way; when dawn broke they were still in one another's arms.

Helen drove carefully along Greenslade Terrace and parked outside Number 11. It had been raining – the cobbles were slick and the doors of the houses on either side were closed. Helen was glad. She didn't especially want to run into any of her new neighbours today. She was too anxious to simply get inside the house and have a really good look around.

She fished in her bag for the keys – still on a little wire ring with a brown card label attached – and selected one. Then, with the key in the lock, she paused, savouring the moment.

Her first house. The first home of her own. It had been long enough coming! Thirty-two years was an inordinately long time to wait! But then, if she'd chosen a career which necessitated such a lengthy training, and chosen to get herself involved with a married man instead of finding a husband, she had no-one but herself to blame.

And it had been worth the wait. Not just any old house for her first home, but the one Grandpa had brought Gran to all those years ago; the house where her own father had been born and brought up. What an incredible chance that it had come on the market again now, just when she was able to step in and buy it!

Helen turned for a moment, looking out over the valley, gleaming wetly from the rain. From the wagon works down by the railway sidings the hooter sounded suddenly as it had every working day at midday for as long as she could remember. It evoked a twist of nostalgia in the pit of her stomach.

Helen turned back, rotated the key in the lock, and paused again. Then, with a smile, she went into the house.

BOOK THREE

1956–1957

Chapter Thirteen

In the summer of 1957 Jenny left school; in the autumn, with five O levels under her belt, she started a secretarial course at the Technical College in Bath. Each morning she caught the 8.12 bus from the centre of Hillsbridge, sitting in the little back seat on the top deck with her smart new hound's-tooth check vanity box on the seat beside her and practised page after page of shorthand symbols in her notebook using the special pen that would make both thick and thin strokes according to how much pressure you exerted on it.

She needed all the practice she could get, Jenny reckoned. Shorthand didn't come as easily to her as typewriting, which she loved, or even, surprisingly, book-keeping. The symbols and squiggles were all very well, very clever, but each time she thought she was beginning to master it, there was a new variation to learn and though she could write it quite well, reading it back was another matter. But master it she must. Jenny had set her heart on getting a job as a newspaper reporter, and the Head of Department at the college, a sharp little lady with a quavery voice, had said no editor would even consider taking her on with a speed of less than 120 words per minute.

She could do it, Jenny promised herself. If she could manage O levels in Latin and Maths and French, then she could learn to write shorthand at 120 wpm. Even if it meant practising until her wrist ached. And having persuaded Carrie to let her leave school and get on with doing the course that would help her achieve her ambition, she had to make a success of it!

Persuading Carrie hadn't been easy. Everyone had done their best to talk her into staying on and taking her

249

A levels – her teachers; the headmaster (he'd sent a letter to Carrie and Joe saying that to leave now would be a terrible waste of her potential); even Carrie herself, though Jenny knew that the financial position at home was no better than it had ever been and another two years in school would only have added to the pressures.

'The secretarial course is only for a year, Mum,' she'd said. 'I'm eligible for it because I've been to Grammar School. Then I shall be earning and I'll be able to help you out.'

'I don't want you to miss out on the opportunity to do well for yourself,' Carrie had said. 'I don't want you feeling all your life that you could have gone to college if only we were a bit better off.'

'I don't want to go to college,' Jenny had argued. 'What's the point? I'd never get to university – you've got to be really clever for that – much cleverer than I am – and college is really only for people who want to teach. I don't.'

'What's wrong with teaching?' Carrie had demanded. She rather fancied her daughter becoming a teacher. There was a lot of status attached to that.

'I don't want to do it! I want to be a newspaper reporter.'

Carrie had snorted in disgust. To her, a newspaper reporter was someone like Walter Evans, who wrote for the *Mercury*, the local paper. He had an office in the centre of Hillsbridge that was hardly worthy of the name, he wore an old tweed suit with patched elbows, drove a dreadful old banger of a motor car and seemed to spend most of his time standing on the doorstep of his office smoking roll-up cigarettes and gossiping to passers-by in the hope of picking up a titbit of information that would lead to a story. Not in the same league at all as teaching, by Carrie's reckoning.

'Everybody would look up to you if you were a teacher,' she said stubbornly.

'Everyone would look up to me if my name was on the byline of the *Daily Telegraph*,' Jenny said. 'And anyway, I don't care whether they do or not. As long as I'm doing what I want to. And looking after a lot of screaming kids isn't what I want.'

In the end, to Jenny's surprise, Joe had taken her side. He usually sat on the sidelines when such arguments were taking place, but when he did intervene, he could be unexpectedly forceful.

'I think you should let the girl do what she wants to, m'dear,' he said, and it was his tone more than his words which made Carrie take a step back. 'She's old enough to know her own mind and there's no point forcing her.'

'But I wanted to see her . . .' Carrie began.

'It's not what *you* want, though, is it?' Joe said reasonably. 'It's our Jenny's life and you can't live it for her.'

And so Carrie had conceded defeat, still not knowing whether to be relieved or disappointed – it was true that an extra wage packet coming into the house a year or so earlier than would otherwise have been the case would be very useful. Jenny had left school, bidding, in the end, a tearful goodbye to her friends. Most of them, including Rowena, were staying on.

Now, however, a few short months later, she felt as far removed from them as if they were inhabiting different worlds, which, of course, was not far from the truth. While they were still confined to school uniform, Jenny could wear what she liked, even a little make-up, which Carrie had at long last ceased to object to. Whilst they were living under the same regime of morning assemblies and dinner eaten in the school hall – albeit with a few privileges that came from being that elite Sixth Form – Jenny went straight to the desk that folded back to reveal her type-writer and ate sandwiches in the lunch hour in the coffee-bar style 'student's common room' before wandering around Bath window-shopping. It was an exciting time, opening a window on what life as an adult would be like, giving her for the first time a glimpse of real freedom. But to begin with it was also a little lonely. Jenny was the only one from the Hillsbridge area. All the others in her group had been to school in Bath – either the High School or the Convent or the City of Bath Girls' School – and she thought they considered her something of a bumpkin. And if not that, well, an outsider.

The first friend she made was called Susan – Susan Beauchamp – and she was a bit of an outsider too, being several years older and having gone from school to do a course at the Lucie Clayton School of Modelling. This might have made her impossibly glamorous, and in some ways Susan was, but she was also somehow embarrassing with her rather affected ways and her boomy 'posh' voice, and Jenny felt as reluctant to be paired off with her, as she had been, all those years ago, to be paired with bandy wombly Diane Whitcombe and fat Penny Presley. At least on her own she stood a chance of being accepted into one group or another. With Susan tagging along, she stood none.

It wasn't only with the other girls that her style was being cramped by having Susan in tow. Jenny had noticed that the coffee bar/student common room was often overflowing at lunchtime with interesting-looking boys. Most of them were on day release from the jobs they were apprenticed to and were therefore several years older than she was, which only made them more attractive – along with their hairstyles (including the DA which had been banned as totally unsuitable at school), their casual clothes (denim jeans and enormous fisherman rib sweaters) and their motorbikes (gleaming BSAs and Nortons and Triumphs drawn up in lines in the college car park).

There were engineers on Mondays and Wednesdays, electrical engineers on Tuesdays and Thursdays, and something known as Technical Trainees on Fridays. Amongst them, Jenny had spotted some Hillsbridge boys she knew vaguely – and would like to know better!

Shaking Susan off wasn't easy, but sometimes when she had no sandwiches she went into town for soup and a roll and Jenny took full advantage of her absence to go to the common room alone.

Such a short time ago, she realised, she would never have had the nerve! She wasn't sure she had now! But she hid her nervousness behind a façade of self-confidence and pit-patted in on her kitten heels, found a stool and tried to look pert and alluring at the same time.

It worked.

'Don't I know you?' one of the Hillsbridge boys – a Wednesday engineer – asked her, and soon they got talking and the others joined in. Jenny found herself the only girl in the circle – and found she was enjoying it too! Some of the older girls, the ones who wore short skirts and spiky stilettos, glowered at her, annoyed that she had muscled into what they regarded as their preserve, but the reaction amongst her own course mates, when they got to hear of it, was very different. They were impressed.

Jenny had never before thought of herself as a rebel or trendsetter; now with her reputation soaring, her confidence grew. The High School girls still thought themselves a cut above her, of course, but then they thought themselves a cut above everyone with the possible exception of Susan, but the Convent girls and the ones who had been to the City of Bath became noticeably friendlier.

Within a couple of months she had teamed up with three of them – Sandra, Marilyn and Jane – and was copying some of their more sophisticated city ways. She rolled her skirt over at the waistband so it was an inch or two shorter (though she had to roll it down again when she got off the bus in Hillsbridge each evening – Carrie would have had something to say if she didn't!) and wore a little more make-up. She began reading the magazines they read – *Melody Maker* and *Screenplay* and even, occasionally, *Vogue*. And soon she was meeting them at weekends too, taking the bus into Bath and walking round to the big estate where they all lived, listening to music and even (Carrie would have had a fit if she'd known) smoking the occasional Woodbine.

The first time she took a puff – in Marilyn's bedroom, up the chimney – Jenny thought she was going to pass out. It was a long time before she summoned up the courage to try again!

Her status in the group was finally sealed when one lunchtime one of the engineers asked her if she would like to go for a ride on his motorbike. It was a Triumph 500 Twin, as befitted its owner, a boy who could have been taken for the twin of James Dean, Jenny's current screen idol.

She clambered on to the pillion behind him, her tight black skirt hitched up above her knees, kitten-heeled shoes balanced precariously on the footrests, and wound her arms round his black leather-jacketed waist. He wasn't wearing his crash helmet because she didn't have one and he had made the very chivalrous declaration that if he was stupid enough to cause them to fall off he should be as vulnerable as she was. Jenny was charmed, not stopping to consider the doubtful logic of this, and they roared off, gently at first, manoeuvring the city traffic, then, when they hit the open road, zooming along with the throttle fully open. Jenny was exhilarated by the feel of the wind in her hair and the sensation of wild freedom. She soon learned not to be afraid to let herself go with the bike as he leaned it around bends, once or twice so low that sparks flew as the exhaust pipe scraped the tarmac.

All too soon it was over; a lunch hour didn't last long, especially as they'd eaten their sandwiches before leaving. By the time they got back a glance at her watch told Jenny her afternoon class had begun five minutes ago. She raced up the stairs and tore along the corridor. In her classroom Miss Lintern, who taught them French conversation, was in full flow. As Jenny threw open the door Miss Lintern looked up sternly over her horn-rimmed spectacles and the entire class, as one, turned their heads to look at her.

'Sorry I'm late . . .' Jenny scrabbled up the aisle to her desk, wondering why everyone was laughing. It was only later that they told her.

'Your hair's standing on end!'

'You look as if you've been dragged through a bush backwards!'

'Where have you been?'

Jenny went to the cloakroom, looked in the mirror. One glance was enough. Her hair was indeed standing on end – blown into a vertical shelf above her forehead and tumbled and tangled about her ears. In addition, the wind had made her mascara run into black smudges beneath her eyes.

'Oh my goodness – I didn't go into class like that did I?' she gasped.

'Yes, you did!' came the chorus.

But there was admiration in their laughter.

'She's not going to do it, you know,' Helen said to Paul. 'She's never going to do it.'

It was almost a year now since she had moved into Greenslade Terrace, but Charlotte was still living with Dolly.

'She keeps saying she'll come to stay, then she puts it off again,' Helen went on. 'I don't think she can bear the thought of being here if it's not permanent. And she won't commit to coming permanently because she thinks it would upset Dolly.'

'And you think she really wants to be here.'

'I know she does.' Helen chased the last bit of cottage pie round her plate, then put down her fork and pushed the plate away from her. 'Why does everything have to be so complicated?'

'It's understandable, I suppose.' Paul was mopping up the last of his gravy with a hunk of bread. 'This pie's too good to waste a mouthful! You're a terrific cook, Helen.'

'Who do you think you're kidding? It's just plain honest to goodness stuff I learned at my mother's knee. Hardly haute cuisine.'

'Who wants haute cuisine when they can have this? I stand by what I said, Helen – you're a fabulous cook. And believe me, I should know.'

'Oh yes? How?'

'Put it down to experience.'

She laughed, not sure what he meant, but thinking it didn't much matter anyway. There was a comfortable closeness between them which transcended such trifles and which had been growing steadily over the past year.

When she had moved into the house he had been on hand to help her – and not only by driving the van she had hired to transport her bits and pieces, though he had done that admirably, turning up at eight in the morning, dressed in a checked country shift and baggy khaki-

255

coloured cords. He'd helped her clean the house from top to bottom – the family who had moved out had apparently been founder members of the Society for the Preservation of Spiders, Helen had laughingly suggested – and stayed to share a fish and chip supper eaten out of the newspaper on the newly scrubbed kitchen table, which they had conveniently left behind.

In the weeks that followed, he had helped with the decorating too, though on occasion Helen had thought that might be a mixed blessing. Paul's idea of wallpapering was to get the strips up as quickly as possible, smoothing them into place with a suspiciously pasty rag and asserting cheerfully that the shiny streaks would dry out. They didn't, of course – Helen had known they wouldn't – but it seemed churlish and ungrateful to say to. And not only was it useful to have a man around to open jammed windows, fix electrics and drill holes for pictures and coat hooks, she was actually enjoying his company. Almost insidiously he seemed to be taking over that role in her life she had sworn he never would – and strangely she found she didn't mind at all.

'Would you like some pud?' she asked now.

'What is it?'

'Apple pie and cream.'

'Sounds good to me.'

She fetched it, warm from the oven, and put it on the table, a golden-brown crust with steam escaping through tiny sugar-coated vents and exuding a tempting aroma of cinnamon.

'When do you get time to make apple pie like this?' he asked admiringly.

She grinned enigmatically, cutting a large slice and passing it to him.

'Shortage of time is a poor excuse.'

'Hmm.' He poured custard on to it and tucked in. 'Going back to what you were saying about your grandmother . . .'

'Yes?'

'I wouldn't give up hope just yet.'

She looked at him, a spoonful of pie poised halfway to her mouth.

'What do you mean?'

'As a relative of the patient in question, I'm not sure I should tell you, but . . .'

'Paul – what are you talking about?'

'But since we both work for the same practice I don't suppose there's any harm in it.'

'In *what*?'

'I think there's an odds on chance your aunt Dolly is going to be in no fit state to look after your grandmother for a while.'

Her spoon clattered to the plate and she stared at him in alarm.

'What . . .?'

'Don't look so worried. It's nothing serious. But Dolly has been having a few problems of the variety usually referred to as "women's trouble". She went to see Harbutt-Lennox last week and he's recommending a hysterectomy.'

'Aunt Dolly?' Helen said, stupefied. 'She hasn't mentioned a thing about it to me!'

'My guess is you're the last person she'd talk to about it. But you and I both know a hysterectomy is going to mean a stay in hospital, followed by convalescence of at least three months. At her age and her weight, she's going to feel it. I think you'll find she'll be only too glad not to have to run around your gran for a while. In fact, Reuben will probably recommend she should have somebody to look after *her*.'

'I don't believe it!' Helen said. 'Auntie Dolly!'

'It's true, I assure you. So I suggest, Helen, you take the opportunity to get Charlotte here – if you're quite sure it's what you want.'

'Oh, I do!'

'Well, I'm looking after Reuben's patients whilst he's on holiday, as you know, and I shall make it my business to suggest to Dolly that she needs to shed as much of her responsibilities as she can. As her GP it's no more than my duty.' But his eyes were twinkling.

'Well, thanks for the tip-off – and for any assistance you feel obliged to render . . .' She hesitated, looking at him slyly. 'Is the apple pie good?'

257

'Better than my mother used to make – and that's saying something. You're a lady of many talents, Helen.'

'Well . . .' she smiled, her lips pursing mischievously, 'since this seems to be the time for confidences, perhaps I should confess. All *I* did was pop it in the oven to warm it up. It was actually made by one of my patients – a thank-you for getting her over a nasty bout of bronchitis. You actually have Mary Thomas to thank for the feather-light pastry.'

He grinned.

'As I said – a lady of many talents. Even if one of them is for being devious and deceitful. Don't tell me the cottage pie was made by a grateful patient, too!'

'No!' she said indignantly. 'Certainly not!'

He got up, came around the table and held out his hand to her.

'Come on – let's go and sit on the sofa to let it all go down. When you look at me like that it gives me ideas that don't include washing-up. And if your grandmother is going to be coming to live with you, my chances for putting them into practice might get rather restricted!'

Linda Simmons lay on the sofa in the front room of her parents' home with pillows piled behind her head and a tartan rug tucked around her body and legs.

Against all the odds, she had survived the winter and in spring she had surprised and delighted everyone by going into remission. Though the doctors had warned him it would almost certainly not last, David had allowed his hopes to rise. Every so often one heard of a medical miracle – why shouldn't his Linda be one of them? But then, quite suddenly, she was worse again, much worse, and his feverish optimism dissipated into a cloud of black despair.

She was so weak now that even lifting a hand to push her heavy lank hair off her forehead was too much effort for her, she only rolled her head restlessly against the pillow in an attempt to escape the irritation of the way it clung to her moist skin.

Dr Hall had suggested she should be in hospital but she had resisted, just as she had resisted taking to her bed upstairs. Tired as she was, weak and ill as she was, her spirit remained strong. If she went into hospital there was an odds-on chance she would never come out again; and the same went for retiring to the bedroom. Linda had faced the fact that she couldn't have long left to live and she was determined not to waste a minute of it. At least lying on the sofa she was still at the hub of the house, she could watch the comings and goings; listen to what was being said even if she couldn't summon up the energy to take part in the conversation.

Every morning before he went to work, David dressed her – a warm soft jumper or twinset and ski-pants, if she was having a good day, her quilted dressing gown if she was not – and carried her downstairs; every evening he reversed the procedure. During the day her mother was there to attend to her needs, she had a little transistor radio to listen to, and when the children's television programmes and the cartoons started at around teatime she was able to see the screen from where she lay. She couldn't read much – it made her eyes ache, and the effort of holding a book for long was beyond her – and she dozed quite a bit of the time because the exhaustion was like a drug, drifting her away.

But at least being downstairs gave some semblance of normality. At least there were times when she could almost forget for a little while that she was an invalid . . . worse, that she was going to die.

Today had been a bad day. A very bad day. As well as all other everyday and slowly worsening symptoms, she had a terrible headache, the sort that had started dully and worsened until it felt like a steel cap squeezing her skull, easing, relaxing a little, only to tighten again, worse than before. It weighed down on her eyes, making them so heavy she could only keep them open for a few seconds at a time and it pulsed in her ears. Linda who had learned to be so cheerful, so stoic, sank beneath it, whimpering weakly into the pillows, tears escaping from the corners of her eyes. Even they lacked the energy to roll down her face. They merely gathered in the hollows, tickling, drying where they lay.

For the first time in this whole nightmare, Linda lost the will to live.

When David came home he was shocked at the sudden deterioration, seeing anew the grey translucent pallor of her skin, the way it stretched taut over her cheekbones and fell away into the shadowed hollows beneath, the lack of lustre to her hair, her bloodless lips. But most of all, the expression on her face, the hopelessness, the resignation, the suffering. She looked like an old, old woman lying there. His Linda, his lovely, laughing Linda, had been lost without trace.

'We should get the doctor to her,' he said to Doreen.

'What can the doctor do?' Doreen asked.

'Well, give her something for the pain for a start,' he said.

'We'll have our tea and see how she is then,' Doreen said.

They had their tea and David tried to feed Linda a little soup, but she didn't want it, had difficulty swallowing, and when she did manage a mouthful, moaned that it made her feel sick.

'I'm getting the doctor!' David said resolutely.

'No – don't, please . . .' With an enormous effort, Linda grasped his hand, holding it with fingers that felt icy cold and trembling. 'Don't go. Just stay with me . . . talk to me . . .'

He couldn't think of a thing to say to her; his brain was swamped with anxiety, his whole consciousness concentrated on how dreadfully ill she looked. He sat beside her, holding her hand, and after a while she drifted into a fitful sleep. He stayed beside her, not wanting to disturb her or having her wake to find him gone, though his hand went numb with pins and needles and his leg, too, threatened to go into cramp.

After about half an hour, when she opened her eyes again, she seemed to rally a little.

'I'm so sorry, David. This isn't much fun for you, is it?'

'It's not much fun for you either. We're in this together, Linda.'

'Mmm.' She was silent for a moment, then she said: 'I

just wish we could have a proper life together. Nothing much – nothing special – just the sort of thing everybody else takes for granted. You know?'

'I know. But I wouldn't change a thing, Linda – except you being ill, of course.'

'I'd have liked a home of our own. Just you and me. So we could shut the door and just be by ourselves.'

'The door is shut,' he said. 'We are by ourselves.'

'Mmm.' Her eyes were closed. 'You'll have a proper home one day, though. With somebody else.'

'Don't talk like that!' he said fiercely.

'You will. You will. You deserve to be happy. I wish it could be me, I love you so much, but . . . it can't be.'

'There'll never be anyone else!'

'There will . . . there will.' Her voice was slurred, drowsy. 'Oh, David . . . I feel so ill . . . I can't . . . I can't fight any more.'

Something in her tone alarmed him, a cold, sharp shard of terror giving an edge to the constant state of anxiety and premature grief.

'Hold me . . .'

'Just a minute.' He got up, went through to the kitchen, keeping his voice low as he spoke to Doreen, though he could not disguise the urgency.

'Get the doctor. Now!'

He went back into the front room.

'Please, David, hold me!' she begged again.

He went down on his knees beside the sofa.

'I'm here.'

Then, as she had asked, he held her.

'That's the phone,' Helen said, unnecessarily. She dropped a handful of cutlery back into the washing-up water and stripped off her rubber gloves.

'You want me to get it?' Paul was drying the dishes she had already washed and stacked in the drainer.

'No, it's all right.'

She couldn't add by way of explanation that she didn't want to advertise the fact that Paul was with her, sharing supper. And in any case it might not be a professional call.

It could be personal. Amy. Her mother or father. A friend. Guy.

For some reason Guy had been on her mind lately. She kept thinking about him at odd times – and particularly when the telephone rang. She hadn't heard a word from him in more than a year, yet suddenly each time she lifted the receiver she expected to hear his voice on the other end of the line. Strange, really strange, but also very disconcerting, very unsettling. The wariness was there now in the pit of her stomach.

'Hello?'

'Doctor? I'm sorry to bother you, but Linda's worse.'

It wasn't Guy. It was Doreen, sounding desperately worried.

'I'll be with you right away,' Helen said. She went back into the kitchen. 'Sorry, Paul, I'm going to have to leave you to finish here.'

He raised an eyebrow and she qualified: 'It's Linda. She's taken a turn for the worse. She should be in hospital, of course, but . . . well, there you are. She didn't want to go in, not even for the end, and it's possible she's going to get her way. Can you cope here?'

He drew his breath in a sharp whistle. 'Oh – I don't know about that . . .'

'Paul, I'm sorry, I'm really not in the mood for jokes. I'll be back as soon as I can, but I can't promise when that will be.'

'OK. At some point I'll put the phone through to my house and let myself out.'

'If you would.'

She knew. In her heart she already knew. Strange how sometimes the sixth sense kicked in. Linda had already lived much longer than anyone had expected; if the present crisis passed she might rally again, go into remission again, for a little while at least. But somehow Helen knew this wasn't going to happen this time.

She had visited so often her car almost found its own way to the house. She parked outside, reached for her medical bag from the back seat.

The door was opened by Jim. He looked haggard – old suddenly, his face grey in the porch light.

'She's bad this time, Doctor, really bad,' he said. He stood aside for her to go in; she went along the hall and into the front room.

David was still sitting beside Linda, still holding her hand, one arm crooked around her head, stroking her hair. From time to time her eyes fluttered open and a brief half smile curved her lips, but it was immediately obvious to Helen that she was failing fast.

'Can I . . .?'

David moved reluctantly and Helen made a brief examination. Linda's breathing was shallow and ragged.

'Are you in any pain?' she asked.

Linda responded with an almost imperceptible shake of her head. Helen straightened, moved away, and David resumed his place at Linda's side.

'Can I speak to you?' Helen asked.

'I'm not leaving her.' His voice was low but determined.

Helen met Doreen's eyes, Doreen nodded and left the room. Helen followed.

'There's nothing I can do,' Helen said when they were out of Linda's hearing.

Doreen covered her mouth with her hand. Her eyes were brimming. Helen had never felt more helpless.

'All I can offer is pain relief. But she seems reasonably comfortable.'

Jim had followed them.

'She should be in hospital,' he said angrily. His grief was finding expression in aggression.

'There's nothing they could do for her either,' Helen said gently. 'And quite honestly, I think it's too late to think of moving her.'

'She wanted to be here, Jim,' Doreen said. 'She wanted to die at home.'

'Mum!' David called from the front room. There was urgency in his voice. Doreen made a dash for the door. Jim and Helen followed.

Linda had slipped into unconsciousness, her eyes half open, her head lolling against the pillow. Helen checked

263

her briefly. She was still breathing, but barely.

'She's going, isn't she, Doctor?' Doreen said, the tears held at bay by sheer effort of will.

Helen nodded.

'How long?'

'Impossible to say . . . but not long.'

David had Linda in his arms now, her head buried in his shoulder. He was murmuring to her softly, his voice too low for anyone else in the room to hear what he said. But that was as it should be. They were locked in their own private world.

Helen felt a lump in her throat. Standing by and watching someone die never got any easier.

At one end of the mantelpiece was a studio portrait of Linda as a child, a smiling little girl with curling hair wearing a smocked dress of white silk; at the other was a photograph of Linda and David on their wedding day.

Helen stared at it helplessly as Linda's life ebbed away.

He had never known such grief.

The church where they had married was packed, now, for the funeral. But surrounded by sombre and openly tearful relatives and friends, David felt utterly alone. The fog that enveloped him was impenetrable, through it voices were distorted, faces no more than a blur. He didn't know who was there; they might have been on a different planet. He answered when they spoke to him without knowing what they had said or what he replied. He followed Linda's coffin because his legs were obeying some unspoken inner command, but he was not even aware of the ground beneath his feet. His lips moved with the words of the hymns but no sound came out. His eyes never left the simple teak box, piled high with red roses that he could ill afford but had been determined she should have, but the images refused to translate accurately to his brain.

But he smelled the roses. The air was heavy with their perfume, just as the front room had been filled with the woody smell of chrysanthemums in the dozens of wreaths and sprays that had been arriving at the house all morning. They had been stacked around the walls in that room where Linda lay, her small face at peace above the frilled collar of her shroud, her hands crossed on her chest. She was still wearing her wedding ring; David had insisted it was not to be taken off.

He hated the smell of the chrysanthemums. The heaviness of it was typically funereal; it spoke of death. But the roses were different. The subtlety of their perfume spoke of love. The scent of them – and the choking smell of the chrysanths – would haunt him down the years, evoking blurred images from that terrible day.

For the rest of his life, his senses would never forget.

Chapter Fourteen

Hillsbridge was justly proud of its Scouts' Hall. Whilst most of the surrounding villages possessed a Scout Hut, there was no way that this imposing building could be demeaned by such a name. It stood in its own wooded grounds at the head of a long steep drive, which was in turn hemmed with trees, a large building which boasted not only the hall itself, with the sprung floor which made it an ideal venue for dances, but also the best stage in the district – a real stage, not merely a platform, with deep red plush curtains, ample wings with storage space above, and a room on stage right which could be used as a dressing room and which connected to the cloakrooms on stage left by means of a passageway behind the rear wall. The two inward slanted corners of the apron were decorated by oil paintings, ten feet high, depicting scouting scenes and, most impressive of all, the flooring in front of the stage could be removed to form an orchestra pit. There was also a trap door in the stage itself which enabled the Demon King to make the most startling entrances and exits when the local theatre group staged its annual pantomime. At the front entrance to the hall was a large kitchen with a shuttered hatch which facilitated its use as a bar, and a small committee room, which also served as a private bar when the hall was hired out for functions.

On this particular Friday evening in November the committee room was, as usual, well stocked with every conceivable type of spirit as well as a crate or two of beer, but only Bert Lines, who could never be separated from free booze for long, was inside, and even he lurked in the doorway, glass in hand, determined to get the best of both worlds. In the hall itself, a boxing ring had been erected and a series of amateur bouts, organised by the local ABA, was in full swing.

In the third row, with her back to the stage, her chair on the first tier of blocks that had been erected to ensure that everyone had a good view of the proceedings, Jenny could hardly contain her excitement, and the thrill she felt surprised her. Perhaps, in a way, she shouldn't have been surprised – she had been raised on boxing, for Joe tuned in to all the big fights on the radio, and since she had been knee-high to a grasshopper, Jenny had listened with him. But never before had she seen a live boxing match and now she was drunk on the atmosphere – the sweating boys in their trunks and vests, chewing on the gum shields, the fanfares that accompanied them into the ring, the shouts and groans, the thud of leather on flesh and bone.

She wouldn't be here now, she conceded, if it hadn't been for Marilyn. It would never have entered her head to go – or Carrie's to let her. But Marilyn had a boyfriend – Keith Hicks – who boxed for a club in Bath, and when she had heard a fight had been arranged for him at the Hillsbridge Scouts' Hall she had suggested to Jenny that they should go along.

'I've been promising I'd watch him box for ages,' she said. 'And with this bout being in Hillsbridge, you could come and hold my hand.'

'Why do you need someone to hold your hand?' Jenny asked.

'Wouldn't you, if it was your boyfriend being beaten to a pulp?'

'Isn't he very good then?'

'He's all right, I think. He seems to win as often as he loses. And he's been doing it for years, so I suppose he must enjoy it. But I can't think why. And I'm not very keen on the thought of watching someone hit him.'

'So why go at all?'

'I told you – because I promised I will. Only I keep putting it off. But if you'd come with me . . .'

'All right,' Jenny agreed. 'But just this once. Just because it's in Hillsbridge, and just because it's you.'

'Thanks – you're a pal! Now – will you comb my hair for me?'

Marilyn had thick dark shoulder-length hair and a fetish about having it combed.

Jenny had obliged, wondering what she was letting herself in for. An evening at a boxing tournament – she must be crazy! But instead of hating every minute of it as she had expected, she was loving it!

There must be something wrong with me! she thought as she sat beside Marilyn relishing every violent sweaty minute. *Perhaps in another life I watched the gladiators in ancient Rome, or a knight on a great blinkered horse carried my colours into the joust. It's just not right to feel so excited watching two men hitting one another!*

But it wasn't that. It was the whole thing – the skill of the footwork, their serious determined expressions, the seconds, working frantically in their corners with sponges whilst they talked incessantly, issuing instructions, the tension when the referee stood centre ring between the two boxers waiting for the decision of the judges, the moment when it came and the victor's hand was raised. There was something so primitive and yet so proud about the whole thing that Jenny felt almost like crying with excitement and a whole host of other emotions she couldn't even begin to identify.

Of course, she thought wryly, the contestants themselves might have something to do with it. It wasn't every day you got to watch a succession of fit, muscled young men wearing nothing but singlet and shorts and those flattering boots that managed to look softly pliant and tough both at the same time. There was something attractive about every one of those boxers, even the little ones – the flyweights – had that gritty look which Jenny found so appealing.

Marilyn's Keith had his bout fairly early on. He was boxing for the local boys – hand-picked from clubs within a ten-mile radius. Good as they were, quite a lot of them were losing to their opponents – a team representing the Armed Forces. Though naturally she supported the local boys, Jenny thought that in a way it seemed only right that the servicemen should be able to handle themselves so well – though they were using their fists, not guns, she felt she would sleep a lot more soundly in her bed at night knowing that such fine specimens would be defending England in the event of another war.

Keith's fight was a close one. Marilyn gripped Jenny's hand, hid her eyes, sobbed, screamed, shouted and held her breath until she turned puce. But in the end it was Keith's hand the referee raised and the whole hall erupted in a cheer of approval.

Between bouts Jenny looked round at the watching crowd – the officials of the Hillsbridge Amateur Boxing Club in their monkey suits and black dicky-bow ties, the local supporters, many of them men who had once been boxers themselves but had now either turned scrawny or gone to flab, and a handful of women who managed to make more noise than all the men put together. But there were also quite a few young men who had come along to support the Services team and several of them were very attractive.

One in particular caught Jenny's eye – a tall fair-haired lad with an angular chin and strong nose. From this distance she couldn't see what colour his eyes were, but she guessed they were blue.

In the interval, when Marilyn was hanging proudly on Keith's arm, she looked round for him, but he was nowhere to be seen. Jenny was disappointed; she hoped he hadn't left. When the boxing began again she took her seat but found she was more interested in scanning the crowd for him than she was in watching the fights. Then she saw him, standing by the door that led to the changing rooms, wearing a towelling robe, and a moment later, when the next fight was announced, he made his way between the rows of chairs to the ring. For just a brief second she could have sworn he looked directly at her, then he climbed up on to the canvas and ducked under the ropes.

'A middle-weight contest of three rounds,' the dinner-jacketed man with the microphone announced, 'between, on my right in the red corner, Ray Comer of Hillsbridge Amateur Boxing Club, and on my left in the blue corner, Bryn Thompson for the Armed Forces.'

269

Jenny's heart had begun to beat so hard she could feel the reverberations in her throat. The fair-haired boy – Bryn – took off his robe and she saw that he had the most wonderful lithe muscled body and sturdy boxer's legs. Against him, Hillsbridge's Ray Comer looked positively clumsy; shorter, thicker-set and bobbling agitatedly from foot to foot so that his red sash swung and bobbled too.

As the referee motioned the fight to begin she saw that Bryn moved easily and even with her lack of expertise she guessed that Ray would be no match for him. But she had reckoned without the local boy's strength and skill and the advantage that came from having the home crowd behind him. As the contest got under way she realised it wasn't going to be the walkover she had imagined. First it swung one way, then the other; whenever Bryn scored a good punch, Jenny cheered excitedly.

'I thought you were supposed to be supporting the local team!' Marilyn said in the break between rounds.

'Not this time – not this one!' Jenny couldn't take her eyes off Bryn, even now when he was slumped, legs splayed, on the little stool in his corner whilst his seconds sploshed water over his face and anxiously inspected what might be the beginnings of a cut over his left eye. 'He's gorgeous, isn't he?'

At last it was over. Jenny was on the edge of her seat as the referee called the two boys to the centre of the ring. Then, as he raised Bryn's hand high in the air, she whooped with delight.

'Yes! Yes!'

After that, the remaining fights were something of an anticlimax. When the last one was taking place she saw Bryn again, standing at the back of the hall, and once again she had the fleeting impression that he had been looking at her.

'Would you girls like a drink in the committee rooms?' Keith asked.

'The committee rooms, eh?' Marilyn said, pulling a face at Jenny. 'We are honoured! All right by you, Jenny?'

Jenny nodded. She had noticed some of the other team disappearing into the small smoke-filled room and the uppermost thought in her mind was: *Might Bryn join them? Or even be there already?*

They squeezed through the door and a small bald-headed man with a red face and wispy white moustache bore down on them. Stan Parker was the secretary of the Hillsbridge ABC.

'Keith! Well done, lad! You put up a good show out there.'

'Not bad.' Keith grinned modestly. 'This is my girl-friend, Marilyn, and her friend Jenny.'

'Oh, I know Jenny.' Stan beamed at her. 'What are you having to drink, then?'

'I'll have a pint of bitter,' Keith said.

'Girls?'

'Gin and orange, please,' Marilyn said.

'And you, Jenny?'

Jenny hesitated. She wasn't used to drinking. 'Rum and black, please,' she said, thinking it sounded marginally more sophisticated.

The drinks arrived and Jenny sipped hers standing a little apart because Marilyn was hanging on Keith's arm and everyone seemed to want to talk to Keith. She couldn't see Bryn anywhere and she was beginning to feel despondent when suddenly a voice said: 'Hello!'

She turned. He was standing right behind her. He had changed and his hair looked slightly damp as if he'd just washed it. She smiled.

'Hello.'

'I'm Bryn Thompson,' he said. 'I'm with the Armed Forces team.'

'Yes,' she said. 'I know.'

'Go on then,' he said. 'Your turn.'

'Jennifer Simmons. But my friends call me Jenny.'

'Can I call you Jenny?'

She tipped her head to one side, looking at him over the top of her glass.

'Why not?'

'So – what are you doing here?'

'Watching the boxing.' She wasn't trying to be clever, but it came out sounding pert anyway. She saw a light flush spread up his cheeks.

271

'No – I meant . . . who did you come to support?'

'Hillsbridge ABC, of course.'

'Ah – the opposition. Anyone in particular?'

She realised he was fishing and grabbed the opportunity to let him know she was unattached.

'My friend Marilyn's boyfriend – Keith Hicks.'

'Oh, I see.'

There was a small awkward silence.

'You're in the army then,' Jenny said.

'No. The RAF. I'm stationed at Colerne. I'm doing my National Service.'

So that meant he must be somewhere between eighteen and twenty.

'Did the RAF teach you to box?' Jenny asked.

'No – I've been at it since I was ten or eleven. I boxed for my county when I was a schoolboy. Kent.'

'Oh – right.'

'What do you do, then?'

She told him, thinking how boring it sounded by comparison. But he listened with apparent interest and the way he was looking at her was giving her a funny fluttery feeling in her tummy.

He finished his beer and looked at Jenny's glass. 'Can I get you another drink?'

She hesitated. The one she'd had already seemed to be going straight to her head, making her feel light and floaty to go with the butterflies. 'All right. Why not?' she said recklessly.

He took her glass and headed for the bar, which had been set out on a trestle table.

'You seem to be getting on all right!' Marilyn appeared at Jenny's elbow, smirking.

'Yes,' Jenny said.

'You want to watch it, though.'

'What do you mean?'

'Servicemen,' Marilyn said darkly.

Jenny looked towards the bar. She could just about see him. He was saying something to what looked like another of the Service team and they were both laughing. She felt a moment's doubt.

'You don't mean . . .'

'Here today and gone tomorrow. Just be careful, that's all.'

Bryn was coming back with the drinks. Marilyn winked and considerately turned her back. The second drink slipped down more easily than the first as they went on chatting. Then a big burly man – one of those wearing a dicky bow, suddenly descended on them, intent on talking boxing to Bryn, and Jenny found herself sidelined. They were discussing some future event from what she could gather, and then the burly man dragged Bryn off to meet someone else.

'Don't go away,' Bryn said to her.

But the minutes dragged by, he was still totally engrossed and Jenny began to feel awkward standing there alone. She looked at her watch – ten to eleven! She'd be in hot water with Carrie if she wasn't in by eleven. She waited a few minutes more and still Bryn didn't come back. She cornered Marilyn.

'I'm going to have to go.'

'OK. See you on Monday then,' Marilyn said breezily.

'But . . . Bryn . . . I don't to lose touch with him . . .'

'I did warn you,' Marilyn said.

'He got called away.'

'Oh yeah – as they do.'

'No – someone wanted to talk to him. Look, if he asks, will you give him my address?'

'OK. If he asks.' Marilyn's tone implied she was almost sure he wouldn't.

Jenny took one last despairing look at Bryn. His back was toward her and he didn't see. She buttoned her coat – her new peachy-coloured 'car-length' coat which she had bought out of the club Carrie had started running – and went out. She felt like crying.

It was a clear cold November night, the stars very bright above the tall whispering trees, the moon making their shadows dance and sway on the broad drive. She started down it, knowing she should run at least part of the way home and this, being downhill, would be the easiest, but not wanting to, reluctant even now to put distance between her and Bryn.

And then she heard running footsteps behind her and someone calling her name. She stopped, looked around, almost afraid to hope.

It was him.

'I told you not to go away!' he said, sounding almost hurt.

'I had to,' Jenny said. And then, because she didn't want to admit to a mother who insisted on a curfew: 'I thought you'd forgotten me.'

'They were trying to fix up my next fight. I couldn't get away.'

'Whatever's important to you,' Jenny said flippantly.

'I'm sorry – OK? Look, I'd offer to walk you home but our coach leaves in ten minutes.'

'That's all right.'

'I'll walk you to the bottom of the drive, though.'

In spite of the moon, in spite of the stars, when they left the bright floodlights of the hall behind the darkness closed in with the tall trees. He put his arm around her.

'Can I see you again?'

'Well – yes,' Jenny said, her heart leaping. 'But how . . .?'

'I've got a motorbike. I could come over one night. Are you on the telephone?'

'No, 'fraid not. My gran is . . .'

'I don't know that I want to phone your gran! Shall we say Tuesday?'

'If you like.'

'Where?'

Jenny thought for a moment. 'There's a pub not far from where I live. It's on the main road to Colerne. The Jolly Collier. It's got a butcher's shop on the side of it. You can't miss it.'

'Will you be all right going into a pub on your own?'

'Oh, I won't be *inside*,' Jenny said. 'I'll be outside. On the corner where my lane meets the road. There's a seat there.'

They were almost at the bottom of the drive now, the steep bit where cars got stuck in slippery weather. Ahead, the main road was brightly lit, with traffic going past spasmodically, but on the rise the shadow was still deep and made deeper by a high bank and retaining wall.

'I'll see you on Tuesday then,' he said.

And he kissed her.

She stood in the circle of his arms, with the nearness of him and the unaccustomed alcohol making her head spin, and the collar of her coat tickling her chin in a sensuous way, and felt she was floating ten feet above the ground. He kissed her twice, three times, and then he drew back, trying to get what little light there was to catch the luminous hands of his watch.

'I'm going to have to go or I'll miss the coach.'

She didn't point out that he couldn't miss it because the only way out of the Scouts' Hall car park was the steep narrow drive on which they were standing.

'See you then.'

He turned to walk back up the drive and she went out on to the main road. The warm glow of alcohol and happiness went with her.

On Tuesday evening she was a bag of nerves. They jumped in her stomach and skittered in her throat as she hurried down the steep lane to the Jolly Collier. She'd been ready for the last hour, changing into a clean jumper and skirt as soon as she'd had her tea, putting on fresh make-up and trying to do something about her hair. It was due a wash but there was no time for that. She puffed some Gem dry shampoo into it and brushed it out again, and was pleased with the fluffy, nice-smelling result. When she was ready, she tried to do a bit of shorthand homework whilst she was waiting time, but she couldn't concentrate. She kept watching the minutes tick by – so slowly! – and then suddenly the hands of the clock seemed to move all of a rush and she realised if she didn't go now – this second – she'd be late.

'What time will you be home?' Carrie asked.

'I don't know.'

'Well – no later than half past ten, I hope,' Carrie said. 'Your dad and I will want to go to bed.'

But at least Carrie allowed her to go out with boys now.

Thank goodness! She couldn't have stood to go through all that hole and corner stuff again.

She half expected him to be waiting but he wasn't. She checked her watch. Two minutes after half past seven. Her heart thudded uneasily. Marilyn had said he probably wouldn't turn up. But then, supposing he'd arrived on time or even early and *she* hadn't been there. He might have thought she wasn't coming and gone again, especially if he'd thought it was later than it was. Or what if something had happened to his motorbike – a breakdown – a puncture . . .

A leather-jacketed figure materialised around the corner of the pub building, coming towards her. Jenny's heart leaped again.

'Hi,' he said.

'Oh!' she said stupidly. 'Where's your motorbike?'

'I parked it around the corner.'

'Oh – aren't we going on it, then?'

'You don't want to go on it, do you?'

'I love motorbikes!'

'Mine's only a 350. Anyway, I can't take passengers. I haven't passed my test.'

'Oh.' She felt a bit let down.

'I never seem to have time to take it,' he said. 'What with training and everything.' He looked in the direction of the Jolly Collier. 'We could have a drink here, couldn't we?'

'Well yes, I suppose so.' Jenny thought she might feel a bit awkward so close to home.

The lounge bar this early in the evening was half empty. Bryn looked so handsome in his black leather jacket that Jenny actually felt a little disappointed that there were so few people there to see them. He bought her a rum and blackcurrant – *he remembered my drink!* she thought, pleased, and a pint of bitter for himself, and they sat side by side on one of the overstuffed leatherette sofas by the fire. And talked. And talked.

He told her his home was a village just outside Maidstone, that he was nineteen years old and his trade in the RAF was fitter. Unlike some, he didn't mind having to

276

do National Service, in fact he thought he might sign on as a Regular when his two-year stint was up.

'Unless I get an offer to go professional as a boxer. But if not, the forces are pretty good to sportsmen. They let you have time off for training and stuff – they like it when you can represent them and get them some kudos.'

She told him about her dream of writing for a top newspaper, and about the tragedy of Linda's death. That wasn't something she'd meant to talk about, it was hardly the sort of conversational gambit to make a first date go with a swing, but there was an ease between them – Jenny felt as if she'd known him all her life – that went far beyond physical attraction, strong as that was. As she talked, he covered her hand with his, gently stroking her fingers, and she thought that nothing before had ever felt so right.

'It must have been awful,' he said.

She nodded, staring into her rum and black.

'You just don't expect someone more or less your own age to die,' she said. 'It was bad enough when it was Grandpa, but at least he was old.'

'I know.' And he told her about a friend he'd joined up with who had been killed in an accident and again she felt that he understood, that they were communicating on the same level.

'Shall we go for a walk?' he asked when they had finished their drinks, and she got up without answering because she wanted to be alone with him, really alone, more than anything in the world.

He put his arm around her and she leaned against him, loving the feel of his strong body, loving the smell of his leather jacket, feeling a need she had never felt before and could scarcely put a name to, so strongly that it drove all other thoughts from her mind. As soon as they were off the main road, away from the lights of the pub and away from the passing traffic, he kissed her and immediately her body was pulsing with urgency and the desire to be close to him, closer than it seemed possible two people could ever be whilst still inside their own skins. And it seemed he felt the same, for he unzipped his jacket and folded them both

277

inside it, pressing the whole length of his body against hers. She could feel the swell of his desire in the hollow between her legs and the sweet sharp response it evoked in her was a delightful surprise. She pressed back against him and the sensation grew until it was almost unbearable in its sweetness and urgency. She opened her lips to his, tasting the softness, drinking it in. The world around was lost to her, the sounds of the night, the traffic passing a few feet away on the main road, an owl hooting somewhere in the distance, went unnoticed. They might have been alone, the only two people on the entire planet and the sweetness of the sensations of the flesh entered her heart, making it sing with happiness.

After a while they walked again, past the row of back-to-back cottages where the lighted windows behind their drawn curtains dotted the darkness with small oases of brightness, stopping frequently to kiss again because they could not get enough of one another. A cat leaped from a wall and crossed their path, a man in cap and muffler passed them, heading for the pub, and they only looked at one another and smiled, their eyes meeting in the private world made rosy by the glow of the street lamps.

The football field was deserted, the grandstand a dark cavernous shell. Beneath their feet the perimeter grass crackled with frost. Jenny could feel the cold sharp and aching on her face but the whole of her body was aglow. She showed him the hut with the flat roof that was her secret place and they kissed again, Bryn leaning against its wall, Jenny leaning against him.

'When can I see you again?' he asked.

'Whenever.'

'Thursday? I think I could get down again on Thursday.'

But Thursday seemed a lifetime away – two whole days when she wouldn't see him. She was missing him already.

'I'm going to have to go now,' he said. 'I have to get back. I'll walk you home.'

He walked with his arm around her and when they reached Alder Road Jenny worried a little that someone would see and tell Carrie. But there was no way she was going to tell him to remove it.

Outside her gate he kissed her again, but this time it was a light, chaste kiss, and Jenny, with one eye on the front-room curtains in case Carrie was looking out, was grateful if frustrated.

At the point where the path curved around the house to the side door she paused, looking back to watch him walking back along the road. She felt sick with happiness and excitement and slightly unreal, as if she was living a dream.

Jenny knew, without a shadow of doubt, that she was in love.

They met as often as they could, and Jenny felt as if she was living in a dream world where everything was wonderful and yet somehow not quite real. She had to tell someone – the way she felt she was bursting with it – and the person she most wanted to tell was Heather. Whenever she mentioned Bryn to Marilyn she acted strangely, pretending cool indifference, and there was no question of talking to Carrie. She'd already said she was of the opinion that Jenny was seeing far too much of Bryn and no good would come of it, and though she no longer actually prevented Jenny from going out with a boy, her disapproving manner cast a dark cloud. Once, Jenny had asked Bryn in for a coffee when he took her home after a date and Carrie's stiffness was almost as embarrassing as David, moping in the chair and contributing nothing to the conversation – David had moved back home following Linda's death. Jenny hadn't asked Bryn in again – the atmosphere only spoiled for her what had been a lovely evening. No, she certainly didn't want to tell Carrie about the way she felt. But Heather – Heather would understand. Heather would be pleased for her.

Jenny called to see her one evening on her way home from college.

Steve, who now worked at the RN depot at Copenacre with Joe, travelling to and fro on the same coach, was not home yet, and Glad had taken to her bed with a fluey cold, which meant extra work for Heather. But at least the sisters were on their own, except for Vanessa, who was

279

playing with the doll's house Steve had made her.

'You look full of the joys of spring,' Heather said as Jenny followed her into the kitchen where she was buttering bread for tea. 'You're really enjoying this course, aren't you?'

'Yes, but . . .' Jenny hesitated, torn, now that the moment had come, between wanting to share it and wanting to hug it to herself. Eventually her need to talk about Bryn won. 'It's not just that. I've met this boy, Heather. He's absolutely . . . oh, I can't tell you . . . just super!'

Heather smiled indulgently. 'Oh yes! Who is he? Someone at college?'

'No, he's . . .' Jenny explained, and to her dismay saw Heather's face change.

Inexplicably, her own reaction was anger. 'Oh, not you too!' she exploded. 'Can't *anybody* be pleased for me?'

'Oh, Jenny, if you're happy of course I'm pleased! Tell me all about him . . .'

Jenny did, but she felt defensive suddenly, so that she could hear herself sounding over-eager, anticipating the objections and over-compensating for them. It wasn't what she'd planned, and Heather's reaction wasn't what she'd expected either.

'You will be careful, won't you, Jenny?' Heather said, cutting another slice from the loaf.

Jenny frowned. 'You sound just like Mum!'

'Well, she has a point. I know she goes too far – tries to wrap you up in cotton wool – but it's only because she's thinking of your good. It's all too easy to get carried away when your feelings are this strong, and do something you'll regret. And it isn't like it's a local boy. You don't really know anything about him, do you? All you know is what he's told you. And he's a lot older than you. I mean . . . he could be married or anything. You wouldn't know.'

Jenny was staggered. 'Of course he's not married!'

'He could be. It's not impossible. He could be taking advantage of the fact that he's away from home to have a fling.'

'I don't believe this!' Jenny said. 'I wanted to tell you

280

because I'm so happy and all you're doing is trying to spoil everything!'

'No, I'm not. Honestly, darling, I want you to be happy more than anything in the world. I just don't want to see you hurt. And I certainly don't want to see you throw away the chance of really doing well, having the sort of career you really want.' She turned the gas on under the kettle and poured milk into a saucepan to warm for Vanessa. 'It's very important, Jenny, to give yourself the best chance in life.'

'I don't see what that's got to do with anything,' Jenny retorted.

'Well, it has. Look at me . . .'

'What's wrong with you? You've got a really nice life!'

For a brief moment there was an expression on Heather's face Jenny did not understand.

'I've been lucky, yes,' she said after a moment. The gas flared beneath the milk pan as she touched it with the ignition torch. 'Luckier than I deserve, perhaps. But you don't know the half of it. There are things I live with . . .' Her voice tailed away, then she seemed to gather herself together. 'Look – you've had a good education, you've got the chance to really make something of yourself. I never had that chance. I worked in a glove factory, on a machine, for a pittance, and now I do gloving here, when I'm dog tired, for even less. I don't even own my own home. But you . . . the world's your oyster. You can be anything you want.'

'What I want right now is to go out with Bryn. And everybody seems determined to spoil it!'

'That's not what we want at all, Jenny. We can see a bit further into the future, that's all. You've got a really good opportunity to really make something of yourself. But you've got to pass your exams and then put your whole heart and soul into getting where you want to be.'

'I can't see why going out with Bryn need make any difference.'

'It needn't, of course. All I'm saying is – be careful. Don't do anything you might regret.'

'You mean getting pregnant,' Jenny said. 'That's what you mean, isn't it? Why is everyone so sure I'm going to get

281

myself pregnant? Because you did, I suppose.'

Heather whitened. Her whole face went into a mask of frozen shock.

'But you were years older than I am now!' Jenny rushed on. 'And you and Steve were in love. He was the right one for you. So what did it matter? Anyway, I'm certainly not going to get pregnant. And I don't need you or anyone to remind me I need to get my qualifications. Going out with Bryn doesn't mean I won't still work hard. That matters to me too.'

But she knew, even as she said it, she wasn't being entirely truthful. Since she had met him nothing else seemed as real or important. Her homework *had* been taking a back seat.

'That's all right then,' Heather said. 'And truly, Jenny, the only thing I care about is you being happy. It's just that I'm scared for you. I know how easy it is to get carried away when you feel like that about someone.'

'I'm not stupid,' Jenny said. But again she admitted the truth to herself; it would be all too easy to give in to that overwhelming need she felt when she was with Bryn, to forget the possible consequences, forget everything, simply *not care*. Even now, away from him, a part of her was yearning to know what it would feel like to make love to him properly, go the whole way.

Heather turned to her, smiling now, and unexpectedly hugged her.

'Of course you're not stupid, Jenny! You're very bright – much brighter than me. You'll go far. And I'm really glad you're so happy.'

Jenny hugged her back, her annoyance forgotten. She hated quarrelling with Heather; could never stay angry with her for long.

'I am happy. Really, really happy.'

'Well, that's all that matters.' Suddenly there was a fizzing sound from behind them; Heather had forgotten all about the milk warming on the stove; now it was boiling over. A smell of burned milk filled the kitchen. She broke away from Jenny, wheeling round and turning the gas tap to the off position.

'Damn!'

A pool of milk was swamping the white enamel between the burners, the rivulets already beginning to crust over.

And suddenly Vanessa began to scream. Her cries were cries of pure terror, breathless, hysterical. Heather dived through the doorway into the dining room and Jenny followed. Vanessa was cowering against the wall, small knuckles pressed into plump cheeks, body rigid, eyes wide and staring. Minute items of doll's-house furniture lay scattered around her, knocked over or dropped when the panic attack had struck. Heather ran to her, trying to take her in her arms, but Vanessa beat her off in a frenzy of flailing arms and legs.

'No – no – no!'

'Darling – hush, it's all right . . .'

'No – no – no!'

'It's all right, darling – Mummy's here! Hush, darling . . .'

For seemingly endless moments the awful screaming went on, the panic-stricken flailing continued. Then gradually the screams became sobs and the tense body relaxed a little, though it still quivered in spasms of terror.

Jenny watched, shocked and horrified and uncomprehending. What had happened? Had Vanessa hurt herself somehow? But there was no blood, she certainly didn't appear incapacitated in any way, and nothing in the room was different, apart from the small items of furniture scattered across the floor. Nothing to account for this horrendous outburst.

Heather was holding Vanessa now, crooning softly to her; Vanessa's small arms wrapped tightly round her neck. But her eyes, visible over Heather's shoulder, were still wide and staring and her legs, knees locked around Heather's waist, shook with violent trembling.

'What's the matter with her?' Jenny asked, frightened.

'It's all right. She'll be all right in a minute. Jenny – could you clean away that burned milk for me, please? The cloth's on the draining board. Wash the cooker down – there should be hot water in the Sadia, and some soapflakes in the cupboard.'

'But . . .'

'Just do it, Jenny, please. Just get rid of that smell.'

Puzzled, worried, Jenny did as she was told. She stacked the metal guards in the sink and mopped up the top of the stove, rinsing it with hot soapy water. Then she scrubbed the metal guards with the pan scourer, flaking off the black bubbles of burned milk. When she had finished she went back into the dining room. Heather was sitting at one of the dining chairs, Vanessa on her lap.

'What happened to her?' Jenny asked.

'The milk,' Heather said over Vanessa's head. She spoke quietly, almost as if she didn't want the child to hear.

'The *milk*?' Jenny said. 'I don't understand.'

'The smell,' Heather said, 'when it boiled over.'

'But why . . .'

'Grampy,' Heather said, almost silently, mouthing the words. 'The milk. When Grampy . . .' Her lips squeezed shut, not speaking the word and Jenny added it in her head.

When Grampy died. The milk had boiled over when Grampy died. She understood then. Vanessa had experienced terrible trauma that night and the smell of burning milk had triggered a replay of the terror she had experienced then. Worse, perhaps, magnified by a thousand nightmares.

'Oh,' she said. 'The milk.'

'Don't talk about it,' Heather said fiercely. 'I want her to forget. She'll be all right once she's forgotten about it.'

'Right,' Jenny said, but she had an uncomfortable feeling that it wasn't going to be that easy. 'Heather – I'm going to have to go. Mum will wonder what's happened to me.'

'That's OK. You go,' Heather said. 'Vanessa will be all right now, won't you, sweetheart?'

'I'll just look in and say hello to Gran.'

Glad was sitting up in bed on a bank of pillows. Her nose looked red and sore and there was a resigned sort of expression on her face.

'Was that Vanessa having another of her turns?'

'Has she had them before then?'

284

'Yes. She has.' Glad was mashing one of Walt's big white handkerchiefs into a ball in her fist. 'Worries me to death.'

'Heather says she'll be all right.'

'*Heather* says . . . Oh, I expect she's right. But I don't like it. It's not natural.'

'Heather says it's because . . .' She broke off. She didn't want to upset Gran by talking about Grampy dying like that. 'I've got to go, Gran. I hope you'll be feeling better soon.'

'I expect so. I won't ask you to kiss me – not with this cold. You don't want to catch it.'

Jenny got her coat. But as she climbed the hill home, for the first time for weeks she had other things than Bryn on her mind.

Chapter Fifteen

Helen's day had been long and tiring. The sudden onset of cold winter weather had laid a lot of people low and the surgery had been overflowing with those seeking relief from coughs, colds, earaches and sore throats. In addition, the list of home visits requested had been so long as to be almost insurmountable, but somehow she had managed to get to every one of the addresses, where she had dealt with the influenza victims and even a case of pneumonia.

However late morning surgery finished, there was no way of cutting back on the home visits. In the main they were the most vulnerable of her patients, the very old, the chronically sick and the very young, those most likely to lose their battle with bugs and viruses and swell the ever-growing number of fatalities. The undertakers were being rushed off their feet too she knew and she had no intention of allowing any of her patients to require their services if there was anything she could do to prevent it. As it was, she was very concerned about the pneumonia victim – a middle-aged woman with a history of chest and heart problems, who had steadfastly refused to go into hospital in spite of the fact that she could scarcely draw breath. Even now, an hour or more after she had visited her, Helen couldn't forget the terrible rasping that had echoed through the house.

'I think I should go back and see her later,' she said to Paul.

They were sharing an evening meal, something which had become an almost daily habit, though today, because of the pressures of work, it was more scratch than usual – bacon, baked beans and some 'flat' chips made from potato slices browned almost to crisps in the frying pan.

'You look dead on your feet,' Paul said. 'There's nothing

more you can do if she's refusing to go into hospital.'

'I know. I just want to check on her – make sure she's getting the right nursing care. I don't think she's going to make it, Paul. If the crisis doesn't come to a head soon her heart won't take the strain much longer and I don't want to give anyone the chance to accuse me of neglect. She should be in hospital!'

'If she's that bad there's no guarantee she'd make it even if she was,' Paul said reasonably.

'But at least she wouldn't be my responsibility. Honestly . . .' she ran her fingers through her hair, which was overdue for a trim, 'it's really weird. You get some like that, so stubborn they just won't admit they're at death's door, and others who bang on about every little thing.'

Paul speared a last chip and used it to mop up the remaining tomato sauce.

'The heart sinks, you mean.'

'The heart sinks. The ones determined to waste my time. I had Ida Lockyear in again today.'

'Ah!'

'Don't say it like that! It's not funny.'

'No, of course it's not.'

They had discussed Ida before. She turned up at the surgery with monotonous regularity, always complaining of the same things – headaches, tiredness, dizzy spells, flu-like symptoms which never actually came to anything. Helen had run a whole series of tests to try to determine what was wrong with her but when they had all come back with negative results she had come to the conclusion that Ida's biggest problem was loneliness. Living alone in an isolated farm cottage she had too much time to exaggerate all the normal aches and pains that went with growing old. And when she wanted someone to talk to there was one person she could rely on to sit and listen to her – her GP.

Helen felt sorry for Ida – her husband had died suddenly a couple of years ago and her only son lived in London and didn't visit often, but when she was rushed off her feet with patients who were genuinely ill she found the constant demand on her time for what amounted to no

287

more than a desire for company irritating, to say the least.

Helen had tried, without success, to persuade Ida to join in with some activity in the local community – the WI, the Mother's Union, a knitting circle, a choir. But Ida maintained she wasn't up to it, couldn't get there with her bad legs, was so tired that she was ready for bed by nine, and Helen had given up. There was no way to help someone who wouldn't help herself.

'She was at the head of the queue again this morning,' she said now. 'There she sat with everybody sneezing and coughing germs all over her – she'll be going down with it next and wonder where she got it – complaining about the children and the hard seats in the waiting room and just about everything else. In the end I had to prise her out of my surgery like a sardine out of a can. It's sad really, but what can I do? I'm a doctor, not a social worker.'

'Sometimes,' Paul said, 'you have to be both.'

'You don't need to tell me that.' She was thinking now of little Vanessa. She had seen the child quite a few times recently, always with comparatively minor ailments, but considering what a healthy baby she had been, Helen couldn't help feeling they were stress related and a result of the trauma she had suffered the night Walt Simmons had died. She had suggested as much to Heather, citing the fact that Heather had mentioned that Vanessa sometimes woke in the small hours, screaming from what could only be nightmares, but Heather wouldn't have it.

'She's forgotten all that now. She never mentions it.'

'Just because she doesn't mention it doesn't mean she's forgotten,' Helen had persisted. 'It could well be that she's put it out of her conscious mind but I think it's probably still bubbling away in her subconscious, causing all sorts of problems.'

'She was too young to know what happened,' Heather said.

'Old enough to be terrified. There's evidence to suggest that even a bad birth experience can traumatise a child, and Vanessa was far beyond that stage. I'd like to arrange for her to see a child psychiatrist, see if we can't get to the bottom of it.'

'A child psychiatrist!' Heather was horrified. The words conjured up visions of mental illness and the poor people down at Wells who had gone funny.

'There's nothing to be alarmed about,' Helen reassured her. 'If there is a problem, a psychiatrist would be able to bring it to the surface and help her deal with it.'

'Remind her all over again, you mean,' Heather said. 'Drag it all up when she ought to be forgetting it. I'm sorry, Doctor, but I wouldn't be agreeable to that. And whatever would people say?'

'There's no stigma attached to emotional illness any more. We're moving into a much more enlightened age, thank goodness. I'm quite certain that in the next twenty years or so we shall see counselling become commonplace for adults and children alike, and the stiff-upper-lip attitude that has caused so many problems will become a thing of the past. The time is coming when people won't be ashamed to seek help. It has to.'

'Well, there you and I must agree to differ, doctor,' Heather said stubbornly. 'If we all went running to psychiatrists every time some little thing went wrong we'd never get anywhere. No, I'm sorry, but in my opinion if you've got a loving family to support you, you're better off just pulling yourself together and putting whatever it is behind you.'

Her tone was vehement, her pretty face almost hard. Once again, Helen found herself wondering about Heather, and she wondered about her now, remembering what Paul had said about Vanessa not being her first-born.

Had she lost a child? Suffered a miscarriage or still-birth? Had an illegal abortion or an illegitimate baby she had given up for adoption? Helen was quite sure that the vehemence was born of some deep, festering pain. It was as if Heather was trying to say: 'I've been through hell and I coped. I didn't have any truck with all this psychiatric nonsense, and I'm fine!' Except that she wasn't. Not really. Somewhere, deep inside, was a seething cauldron of suppressed emotion. Perhaps it would stay that way. Or perhaps one day, like a volcanic eruption, it would burst through the layers of restraint in a brilliantly devastating explosion that would change the surrounding landscape for ever.

Whichever, it wasn't an attitude that was going to help Vanessa, and Helen, concerned about the child's welfare, was helpless. She couldn't insist Vanessa go for treatment, the situation simply didn't warrant it. She could see no alternative to simply continuing to try to persuade Heather, but even that was fraught with danger. She didn't want to alienate Heather by harping on about it. Which left the only other option. Give up and hope that Vanessa would eventually overcome her trauma in her own way. It wasn't an option Helen cared for but at the moment it seemed the most politic.

'You remember me telling you about my bird phobia?' she said now.

'Uh-huh.'

'And how I was concerned something similar might happen to little Vanessa Okonski?'

'Yes.'

'I think it has . . .' She broke off mid-sentence. The telephone was ringing.

'You want me to answer it?' Paul offered.

'Would you?'

It didn't look as if it was going to be a quiet evening after all. No rest for the wicked! She stuffed egg and beans into her mouth, chewing rapidly.

Paul appeared in the doorway. He looked surprisingly grim. Her heart sank.

'Miss Freeman?' (The lady with pneumonia.)

'No. It's a personal call. A man.'

She knew. Instantly, absolutely, without the slightest shadow of doubt. Some sixth sense was telling her, even without tossing that grim look on Paul's face into the equation. She picked up the telephone. There was a flutter in her stomach and her hands felt unsteady.

'Hello?'

The voice confirmed it.

'Helen? It's me. Guy.'

'Guy.' She said it flatly, though her heart was racing. 'This is a surprise.'

'A pleasant one, I hope.'

Only Guy could say that, something so utterly facile and crass. Had he forgotten she had told him to get out of her life and stay out? Had he forgotten Paul throwing him out of the surgery?

'Why are you ringing me?'

'I need to talk to you.'

'I thought I'd made myself clear. How did you know where to find me, anyway?'

'Come on, Helen. It wasn't difficult. You are a doctor, after all.'

'I don't want to talk to you, Guy.'

She slammed down the receiver, stood for a moment collecting herself. The phone rang again. She hesitated, half-tempted to ignore it. But she couldn't. It might be a patient. She picked it up, wary, angry.

'Hello?'

'Don't hang up again, Helen.'

'Guy.'

'I've left her.'

The blood drained from her face. Instantly she was shaking all over, every bit of her. She couldn't speak.

'Listen to me, Helen. I've done it. I've left Marian.'

'I don't believe you.'

'It's what you wanted, isn't it? I can't live without you, Helen. I've moved out.'

'When? When did you move out?'

'What does that matter?'

'It matters to me.'

'All right. Today, if you must know.'

'Why?'

'You know damned well why!'

'I mean – why now?'

'Helen – I don't want to have this conversation over the telephone. I want to see you – talk face to face.'

She hesitated. *It's too late*, she wanted to say. *I wanted you so much for so long and now the moment's passed*. But she couldn't. Some perverse part of her was being drawn to him even now, the old longings too deeply ingrained to be denied.

291

'I could drive out to Hillsbridge,' he was saying. 'I could be with you in – what – three-quarters of an hour?'

'You mean – tonight?'

'Yes.'

'No,' she said, casting a glance at the living-room door, imagining Paul sitting there at the table, the picture of blissful domesticity. Except that the expression on his face when he'd returned from answering the phone had been anything but blissful. 'Not tonight.'

'Tomorrow then.'

Her thoughts and emotions churned in a whirlpool of indecision. When they'd first split up she'd felt like an amputee, missing him desperately. The void inside her had been enormous in spite of the fact that it had been her decision. Because of it, perhaps. But she'd fought the yearning for him and gradually the sense of loss had diminished. She'd filled the void with her work and now her life was on an even keel, a comfortable plateau. She shrank from the prospect of climbing back on to the roller coaster of highs and lows that their relationship had always been. And yet . . . if he really had left Marian, then she owed it to him to at least see him, talk it through, explain that things had changed – didn't she? Or was she simply kidding herself, grabbing with both hands the only excuse in the world that would allow her to see him again without going back on her promise to herself that it was over.

Into the silence he said, 'Helen? Please!'

If he'd said again that he'd done it for her, she might still have found the strength to say no. She was under no illusion on that score. If it had been for her and no other reason, he'd have done it long ago, when her life had been on hold for him, when their affair had been blazing most brightly, or when her desperate sense of isolation had been at its height. There were other factors involved, she was certain, and if he had tried to pretend there weren't she would have mistrusted his sincerity. But that 'Helen? Please!' came from the heart and she was remembering that other side of him that few people ever saw, the vulnerability beneath the apparent assurance, the fear of failure beneath the arrogance. Her heart lurched and she heard herself say, 'All right. If that's what you want.'

'You know I do.'

The momentary glimpse of the other Guy shuttered down again; he sounded almost smug, and some of her anger returned. He'd manipulated her – again! – and she'd let him. But it was too late now to change her mind. She'd agreed to see him.

She replaced the receiver and didn't know, honestly didn't know, whether she was glad or sorry.

Paul didn't mention the phone call. In fact he said practically nothing at all. His face said it for him. It had gone shut in, brooding. And the atmosphere had changed from relaxed to awkward.

'Sorry about that,' she said.

'No – not at all.'

'It was . . . an old friend.'

'So I gathered.' He didn't say he'd recognised the voice but she felt sure he must have.

'I do have them,' she said. She meant to say it lightly, humorously almost, but it came out sounding strangely defiant.

'Of course you do. It's none of my business. That was the deal, wasn't it?'

I've hurt him, she thought. *Damn and double damn!* This was exactly the scenario she'd feared and been anxious to avoid.

'Anyway, it's time I was going.'

'Already?'

'Things to do.'

'Right.'

'And I'm sure you have too.'

'Mmm. I suppose.' She couldn't think what they might be. Her mind was on a single track rail. 'Paul – tomorrow evening . . .'

'It's OK. You don't have to explain.'

'But . . .'

'No! I need to practise my cooking skills. I can't rely on you all the time.'

'Will I see . . . will you be in to the surgery tomorrow?'

'I expect so.'

But she knew he wouldn't be. She knew he would be avoiding her. Again she swore silently. Why had Guy had to ring just when Paul was here? Why had he had to ring at all? And – the million dollar question – why hadn't she hung up on him a second time?

When Helen got home the following evening a large silver-grey car was occupying her usual parking space on the piece of land between the outhouses where Charlotte had once grown sage, parsley and thyme. Her heart thudded uncomfortably and her mouth went dry. He was here already and she still felt completely unprepared.

Once again it had been a busy day, with full surgeries and a long list of home visits, and Helen's mood had not been improved by the fact that Miss Freeman had died during the night. Helen had gone to the house to see her and issue a death certificate. Whereas yesterday it had rattled with her painful gasps for breath, today the hush of death was broken only by the sobbing of the other two Miss Freemans, her sisters, who had nursed her through the last painful days. All very well to try to tell herself there was nothing she could have done; Miss Freeman weighed heavily on her conscience. She should have gone back to see her last night and had one more go at persuading her to go into hospital where at least she could have had her last hours made more comfortable. She *would* have gone – if Guy hadn't phoned. But he had and she hadn't and now it was too late.

Helen pulled her car as tight into the side of the road as she could so as to leave room for other cars to squeeze through and got out. Simultaneously, the driver's door of the silver-grey car opened and Guy slid out. He was wearing a waistcoat over an immaculate white shirt and he reached into the back of the car for his suit jacket, which was hanging on a peg, before coming to meet her.

'Helen.'

'Guy.'

'So this is where you live now.' He looked up and down

294

the rank, managing to convey his surprise without saying a word and she knew what he was thinking: a miner's cottage was an unusual choice of home for a GP.

She could have explained, but she didn't want to. Why should she? It was, after all, none of his business.

She found her latchkey and unlocked the door. She didn't want to have a conversation out here in full earshot of the neighbours. A few curtains had already twitched up and down the rank, she wouldn't mind betting.

She went in and he followed her into the scullery. Again she could feel his eyes roaming around, missing nothing. She took off her coat, hung it on a peg in the hall and went back into the living room.

'Do you want a drink?'

'What have you got?'

'The usual.'

'In that case I'll have a G and T.'

She found some ice in the freezer compartment of her little fridge and mixed them both a drink.

Guy looked oddly out of place in the small homely room, she thought, so handsome, so immaculate, the light from the wall lamps which she had switched on catching the flecks of silver in his dark hair and making them sparkle. She handed him his drink; as he took it the light caught his cufflink too, solid gold against the pristine white of his shirt, and the gold signet ring he wore on the third finger of his right hand. Was he still wearing his wedding ring? she wondered. But his left hand was out of sight and she could not see.

She sipped her own drink. The gin and tonic tasted good in her dry mouth and beat a path to settle a little uneasily in her empty stomach. But it was doing what she had intended it should – settle her jangling nerves.

'Well?' she said.

'Do you have to be so aggressive?' He half smiled.

'I'm not being aggressive.'

'That's how it feels to me. Don't let's quarrel again. Not now.'

'I've no intention of quarrelling. I never wanted to quarrel.' But she could hear the edge in her voice. She took another sip of gin and tonic and tried to sound less strung-up, more conversational. 'So – what's happened between you and Marian?'

'I told you. I've left her.'

'There must be more to it than that, Guy. I can't believe you just packed your bags and went.'

'There was . . . an altercation that brought things to a head. I think she had suspected for some time that there was someone else, but didn't want to believe it. Then when she was sorting out some suits for the dry-cleaners she found a hotel bill in a pocket – you remember when we went to London that weekend? – saw a show – what was it?'

She ignored the question. She didn't want to be trapped into becoming nostalgic. She wasn't even sure she believed this version of events. She found it difficult to credit that Guy had a suit – any suit – that hadn't been cleaned for so long.

'Did you tell her it was over?' she asked.

'You know Marian. When she loses it there's no reasoning with her. Anyway, I didn't want to. It was just the chance I've been waiting for. She said our marriage was nothing but a sham and I didn't argue. It's the truth, after all. To all intents and purposes it's been over for a long time.'

'So it wasn't so much that you left her – more that she threw you out.'

He tossed back the remainder of his gin and tonic.

'What difference does it make? The fact is – I'm free. We can be together – as long as we keep it discreet for a while.'

'Discreet. Yes. I thought we *had* been discreet. Now I suppose I'm likely to be cited as co-respondent in a messy divorce case.'

'That can be avoided. I'll call in a professional co-respondent and get the necessary photographs taken. There's no need for you to be involved.'

'Well, thank you for that.' Helen felt a twinge of guilt for her suspicion of Guy's sincerity. At least he'd thought about the likely repercussions for her if something like this got out in a small rural town. People here were less likely to be broad-minded than in the city; she could so easily have lost the respect of a good many of her patients and with it any chance of the partnership.

'Nobody will think twice about it,' Guy said. 'Everybody knows that stage-managed adultery is the quickest and easiest way of ending a marriage.'

'That's true, I suppose.' But the sordid overtones made her cringe inwardly. She mentally viewed a brief distasteful image of a half-naked Guy in bed with a strange woman – a hard-up out-of-work actress, a prostitute even, in some seedy hotel room waiting for an equally seedy private investigator to burst in and snap them, and wondered just how such things were arranged. But she didn't ask – didn't actually want to know.

'Where are you living?' she asked.

'I'm staying with George and Isobel temporarily.' George Carmichael was a surgeon friend and golfing partner of Guy's. 'Hopefully though it won't be long before I get a place of my own. I've looked at a couple of flats in Clifton, but neither of them is quite suitable.'

'You didn't waste much time,' she said. 'If you only left Marian yesterday.'

A faint colour infused his cheeks.

'I can't afford to waste time. It doesn't look good, not having an address of my own, and kind as George and Isobel are I don't want to impose on them any longer than necessary.'

'All the same . . .' She looked at him shrewdly, reading him like a book. 'You'd looked already, hadn't you?'

'Well – actually yes.'

The ice inside her began to melt.

'Oh Guy . . .'

'I told you, Helen, I can't live without you. I've tried, believe me, I've tried, for the sake of the children. But I'm not sure I was doing the best for them by staying. I wasn't much of a father . . .'

She couldn't argue with that, much as she would have liked to be able to. He'd spent as little time as possible at home; even when he hadn't been with her he'd made use of every possible excuse to stay out – work, conferences, golf, tennis, charity committees, every conceivable medical body. But he'd slept in his own bed at night. The fact that he had done so had, he had always argued, given his sons some sense of security.

'Are they all right?' she asked now. 'How have they taken it?'

'I'm worried about Giles. Thomas is very much his mother's son. He'll be all right I think.' He emptied his glass in one long swallow, the strain suddenly evident in the taut lines around his mouth, the way his eyes hooded.

Tenderness darted in her, a sweet treacherous barb.

'Do you want another drink?'

'I shouldn't. I had a couple before I left and I've got to drive home. At least . . .' his eyes met hers, dark eyes flecked with gold beneath those hooded lids '. . . I *suppose* I've got to drive home . . .'

Another treacherous dart, this time naked desire. *Oh Helen, why do you let him do this to you? Why can he break down your defences so easily?*

'One more won't do you any harm,' she said. 'I've never yet seen you drunk, Guy.'

She fetched the bottle and the ice, refilled his glass and her own. As she gave it to him, he reached out with his free hand, catching her by the arm.

'Helen – I need you.'

Unexpectedly tears sprang to her eyes.

'Don't cry, Helen,' he said. 'There's nothing to cry about. It's for the best. We can be together now, just as we always wanted.'

She gazed at him for a moment, emotions churning.

'I don't know, Guy.'

'What do you mean – you don't know?'

'This is all happening too fast.'

'We were together for five years, Helen. How can it be too fast?'

'But things are different now. Everything's changed.'

'In what way?'

'Every way. My life is here now. I'm not a junior hospital doctor any more. I'm sixteen miles out of Bristol with a busy country practice and my own home.'

'That's not insurmountable. It's hardly the other end of England. And later on, when the dust settles, you could always look for a practice in the city.'

The old resentment flared again.

'I don't know that I'd want to do that, Guy. I'm happy here.'

'All right, all right,' he said hastily. 'We don't have to make any decisions now. There's plenty of time for that. The important thing is we still have one another. Don't we? That hasn't changed, has it?'

'I don't know,' she said again.

His eyes narrowed.

'You don't know? How can you not know?'

'Guy, I put my life on hold for you for five years,' she said fiercely. 'When I left Bristol I cut you out of it. It wasn't easy. It was damned difficult. But I did it. And I'm happy. Happier than I was for at least half of those five years.'

'I thought I made you happy.' He sounded hurt.

'Well, you didn't. We had happy times, yes. We could have been happy. But let me assure you it's no fun being the other woman. Having to hide love away when you want to shout it from the rooftops. Alone at Christmas, and most nights as well. Knowing that you were with your family. Knowing I had no rights – not a single one. Snatching time together. Wondering if it would ever be any different. Hopes raised, then dashed again. Living in limbo. And always on the outside, looking in. It's soul destroying, Guy.'

'But it won't be like that now. You'll have what you wanted.'

She sighed. 'I'm not sure if I want it any more. All those years . . . Something dies. When I left I still wanted you, yes. But that was . . . habit. I've trained myself out of it now. And I can't just switch my emotions on and off like a tap.'

He groaned, his face going shut in but failing to hide the hurt within.

'Don't tell me it's too late, Helen. Please don't tell me that.'

'I'm telling you I don't know, and that is the truth.'

'All right,' he said. 'I accept you haven't always had a fair deal, but I do love you, Helen. I've never stopped loving you. I accept too that this has come as a bit of a bolt from the blue and I can see you might need a little time to accustom yourself to the idea that I'm free now.'

'You're not free,' she interrupted. 'Not by a long chalk.'

'But I will be. The biggest step has been taken. We *can* be together, and I won't ever hurt you again, I promise. It's been hell without you. Absolute sheer hell. Take all the time you need, Helen, but don't send me away.'

The treacherous longing tugged at her heart again. The hurts of the past, the hopelessness of it, what did they matter if he really meant what he said? What did anything matter? The old magic was still there, lurking just beneath the surface. *Step this way for the fairytale ending . . . Or the merry-go-round to heartbreak . . .*

'We can take it slowly, Helen. Get used to being together again. One step at a time. Can't we?'

His hands found her hands, those irresistible golden-flecked eyes found her eyes.

I shouldn't have drunk all that bloody gin! she thought, the last of her resistance draining away.

'Can't we, Helen?'

He was close enough now for her to smell his oh-so-subtle cologne, close enough to be aware of his body as a magnet to hers, energising every particle of skin, every pore.

'Just as long as you don't expect to just take on where we left off,' she said. 'Just as long as we really do take it slowly.'

But even as she said it, she was wondering how long *that* would last.

A nugget of anxiety had invaded Jenny's dream world worrying away at her happiness like a pearl in an oyster. The physical side of her relationship with Bryn.

Emotionally, everything had happened so fast, and where her emotions led, her body wanted to follow. Being close to him produced previously unimagined sensations which fired her with urgency and desire so powerful that it made her want to throw caution to the winds. Yet conversely she felt she was not ready. Making love was such an enormous step, and not only that, when it finally happened it had to be perfect. Nothing less would do. And there could not be any going back – not ever. The first time was the first time and could never be repeated.

But in the dead of night when she lay caressing her body and reliving the glorious sensations Bryn had aroused in her she found herself remembering Barry and the way he had dumped her for June – an older girl who, Jenny was sure, had been prepared to allow him to do things which she had not. Supposing Bryn did the same? They'd already gone further than she'd allowed anyone else to go, but she knew he wanted more, as much, if not more, as she did. She could feel the pent-up passion in his body, sensed the frustration that could find no release. If he decided he couldn't stand it any longer and abandoned her for someone who was easier . . . the dread washed over her in a cold tide, bringing tears to her eyes.

Tonight, as they so often did, they had walked round to the football field. The moon and stars were very bright, making it almost as light as day.

'Shall I show you my special place?' Jenny said.

'What d'you mean – your special place?'

'Where I go when I want to be alone – to write, or think, or whatever. Nobody else knows about it – or at least, they don't bother with it. See – up there!'

'The roof!' Bryn sounded horrified. 'You don't climb on the *roof*!'

'Yes I do. What's wrong with that?'

'It doesn't look very safe to me.'

Jenny laughed. 'It's perfectly safe! And getting up is easy – look, I'll show you!'

Before he could stop her she had scrambled up, unable to resist the chance to show that here, at least, she was not clumsy Jenny who could not vault a horse and who was afraid to turn somersaults over the bar of the iron roller.

'Come on – come up and see! It's a wonderful view!'

He scrambled up to join her and she danced to the edge.

'Be careful, Jenny!' He put his arms around her, pulling

301

her back, and then they were kissing and happiness filled her because Bryn was here with her in her special place, and for ever after it would be even more special.

He spread his coat down on the tarpaulin roof and they sat down and before long she forgot all about where they were as her body became sensitised under his touch. Even the cold leather of his jacket under her bare legs felt sensuous and she wriggled her hips to meet his so that his body nestled between her legs in the way that aroused her most.

'Oh, Bryn . . .' It was almost a sob.

He moved slightly and she pulled him back, not wanting the lovely sharp sensation to stop for even a moment. But to her surprise she felt his bare flesh, probing where a moment ago there had been only that sensuous bulge under his jeans.

'Jenny, I want you . . .' His breath against her face was ragged but suddenly all the inner turmoil was welling up.

Oh yes, she wanted him too – but they mustn't! Not here, not like this.

'Bryn – no!' She wriggled a little and he pulled back.

'Jenny . . .'

'No – please don't! Don't make me . . .'

For a moment she thought his passion was going to get the better of him. Then with a groan he threw himself off her and lay on his back, staring up at the stars. Fear trickled into the place desire was occupying. He was so still there, one arm lying across his face, his head turned away from her.

Oh God, she thought, *I've done it now! He'll hate me – he'll never want to see me again*.

'Bryn . . .' she whispered fearfully. 'I *do* want to – I really do – but we mustn't! Oh please, say you'll still go out with me! If you didn't want to see me again I couldn't bear it!'

For another long moment he lay motionless, then he turned his head to look at her.

'No, you're right, Jenny. I'm sorry. I shouldn't have . . .'

'You should! But just . . . not yet.'

'I know. I'm sorry.'

'Stop saying you're sorry!' Her lip trembled. 'I suppose

now you think I'm just a stupid baby.'

'Oh, Jen! You know I don't think anything of the sort! I just can't help wanting you, that's all. We'd better stop getting into this sort of situation, or I'll end up doing something we'll both regret.'

She swallowed hard. She hated the thought of not being in this sort of situation, but she could see that they were playing with fire. It wasn't fair on Bryn – she was leading him on and then slamming on the brakes. He was right. They'd have to change their ways until she was ready.

'Come on,' he said. 'I'd better get you home.'

But for Jenny the nugget of worry had grown so that it was no longer just an irritation but something which was overshadowing her world. It wasn't a problem that was going to go away.

'Can I have a word, Helen?'

Reuben Hobbs' head appeared round her door as she worked her way through a pile of repeat prescriptions after finishing morning surgery. His expression was unreadable but the body language and general vibes were not promising and Helen's first, slightly irrational, thought was that he had somehow discovered that Guy had spent the night with her, albeit in the spare room, when they had come to the conclusion that he had consumed too much gin to drive back to Bristol. But that was ridiculous; though no doubt some of the sharper-eyed neighbours would have noticed the big silver car on the parking space outside Number 11 Greenslade Terrace, none of them would have been likely to pick up the telephone (even if they had one, which few did) and call Dr Hobbs about it. Even if they had, it was none of his business. That such an idea should even cross her mind was, Helen realised, a sign of her own guilty conscience.

She capped her fountain pen and went along the corridor to Reuben's surgery. Another pointer to something less than pleasant in store was the way Reuben had disappeared immediately after summoning her. Something informal and he would simply have followed his nose into her surgery and plonked himself down on one of the consulting chairs.

'Nothing's wrong, I hope, Reuben,' she said, going into the big pleasant room which was, this morning, bright with winter sunshine.

Reuben looked up from his own pile of repeat prescriptions and gesticulated towards the chair which faced his across his ink-stained desk.

'Sit down, Helen.'

She did so, her heart sinking.

Reuben finished off a prescription with a flourish and laid his pen on the blotter.

'I've had a request from the Hillier family to transfer to Dr Honeybourne at South Compton.'

'Really?' Helen didn't quite know how to respond to this; the Hilliers, who were on her list, lived virtually right on the border between the two towns. 'Did they give a reason?'

'Well, yes.' Reuben looked directly at her over the rim of his spectacles. 'I don't like having to tell you this, Helen, but I feel I must. They said specifically it was because they were not satisfied with the way you've been looking after them.'

Helen's skin began to prickle. 'They said *that*?'

'I'm afraid so. I tried to talk them into simply moving on to my list, but they thought that would result in an awkward situation. They preferred to change practices.'

'Dr Honeybourne.'

'Yes. He'll snap them up, of course. The more patients he can get on his books the better, never mind that they actually live in Hillsbridge.'

'Only just . . .'

'Dammit, Helen, are you trying to be funny?'

'Of course not,' Helen said. Under the new National Health arrangements practices were paid per head of patients on their books. Dr Honeybourne's gain was Reuben's loss, financially as well as psychologically. 'What exactly was their complaint?'

'That when they brought their daughter Cheryl to see you, you refused to treat her.'

304

'That's ridiculous!' Helen protested. 'She had a heavy cold, that's all.'

'They maintain she had a sinus infection and was very chesty.'

'She had a bunged-up nose and a cough, yes. Nothing that wouldn't clear up on its own. They asked for antibiotics, which simply weren't appropriate – or warranted. I know penicillin is the new wonder drug, but you know as well as I do it won't do anything for the common cold.'

'If she had an infection . . .'

'I don't think she did. And in any case, I don't want to start prescribing antibiotics to a child when it's not necessary.'

'You could have given her something.'

'I did. A bottle of linctus. And I advised a steam kettle to clear her sinuses.'

'Well, they clearly weren't satisfied. I'm not going to question your diagnosis, Helen. You saw her, I didn't. But perhaps you could be a little more tactful next time and explain the situation more clearly. We can't afford to lose patients and in a small town like Hillsbridge word spreads like wildfire. It only takes the Hilliers to start talking – and they will – and we could suffer a major breakdown in patient confidence.'

Helen was shaken but seething.

'I'm quite sure I did all that was necessary and I'm equally sure I made my reasons clear. I didn't treat them any differently to any of my other patients.'

'Then perhaps you should give some thought to your bedside manner,' Reuben said smoothly. 'In general practice you can't employ the same tactics as on a busy accident and emergency department.'

Helen started to say she was aware of that, but Reuben cut across her.

'To more pleasant matters. At least – I hope they're more pleasant.' He smiled, a little smugly, Helen thought. 'Brenda and I are having a dinner party a week on Saturday. I hope you'll be able to come.'

'Thank you. I think I'm free that day,' Helen said stiffly.

'Good. Well, if you could confirm so that Brenda can get

her planning in hand.' He smiled again, but there was no warmth in it, just the finality of dismissal. 'I won't keep you any longer. I'm sure you're busy.'

Helen beat a hasty retreat to her own room, where she slammed papers around on her desk for a few minutes. It didn't help. The injustice of Reuben's attack on her was rankling, all the things she wished she had said running round inside her head now that it was too late. But there was an unpleasant sense of guilt and rejection too. Though she honestly didn't feel she had anything to reproach herself with, the fact remained she had lost the practice a patient family. Perhaps Reuben was right and she could have handled it differently. Perhaps she was to blame. And the thought of the Hilliers going round spreading some account of their dissatisfaction, enhanced and exaggerated, no doubt, was not a nice one. She had worked so hard at building up patient confidence, it was horrid to have it undermined this way. And all this coming on top of Miss Freeman's death, which was still making her feel uncomfortable and irrationally guilty.

Perhaps I am handling things all wrong, Helen thought. *Perhaps I have still got a busy hospital manner and I'm not connecting with the patients here.*

Under normal circumstances she would have talked to Paul, vented her tension and anxiety on him. But she rather thought Paul would be around for her less, and that too was a sadness. She had never been able to talk to Guy that way. For one thing he was never very interested in anything that didn't directly concern him, for another, in spite of the length of time they'd been together, she still had this absurd desire to impress him. Perhaps it sprung from the fact that he had once been her boss, perhaps it was just an intuition that anything less than perfection would fall short of the ideals he demanded, but Helen had never been willing to let him see her weaknesses.

And on top of everything else, Reuben had asked her to his wretched dinner party. She didn't like formal occasions at the best of times, and given that she was bound to be paired with Paul to even up the numbers, this one was bound to be awkward to say the least.

Damn, damn, damn! Helen thought.

But beneath all the surface anger lurked a sickening sense of failure. She had never felt more isolated than she did now.

Chapter Sixteen

Three weeks before Christmas Bryn was boxing again – in Bath at the Pavilion – and Jenny went in by bus to watch him.

This time the excitement was heightened to fever pitch by a mixture of nervousness and pride; it made her stomach turn over and the tension was a knot in her throat. When he came out in his towelling robe her mouth was dry and the palms of her hands moist, and her programme was rolled into a narrow tube between her trembling fingers.

It was a harder fight than the last time; once or twice his opponent had him on the ropes and she thought he was really hurt. She was almost weeping; screaming at him, 'Come on, Bryn! Come on!', amazed by the primitive responses she was experiencing. And then he seemed to come alive and it was the other man who was reeling on the ropes. A flurry of blows and a cut opened up over his opponent's eye. The gush of blood made Jenny gasp. Then the referee stepped in, signalling to the corners. It was all over. Bryn's hand was raised high, and then, once again, he was back in the ring, wearing his dressing gown and with a towel draped over his head, being presented with a small silver cup by an official in a black dinner jacket, frilly white shirt and dicky bow and the press cameras were flashing all around.

Tears of relief welled into the corners of her eyes, the adrenalin all released into trembling excitement. She watched in adoration and then he was climbing out of the ring, going, not towards the dressing room, but making straight for her.

'Well done!' she said, her voice a breathy little gasp.

And he gave her the cup. Placed it in her hands.

'For you,' he said.

It was one of those special moments Jenny would remember all her life.

When he came back, wearing his everyday clothes, he caught her eye and nodded towards the door. She wove her way between the seats to join him, clutching the cup to her as if it were indeed made of solid silver. She was aware of people looking at her but she had eyes only for him.

Outside it was a bitingly cold night but very dark, the moon and stars obscured behind a blanket of cloud.

'You were wonderful!' she said. 'And giving me the cup . . . can I really keep it?'

'That's why I gave it to you.'

'But don't *you* want it?'

'I've got loads of them.'

'I'll put it on my dressing table. I'll keep it for ever.'

He said nothing. His arm was around her shoulders, walking with her away from the lights. She glanced at him. His chin was hunched into the turned-up collar of his jacket and he was staring straight ahead.

'You're quiet,' she said. 'What's wrong?'

'There's something I've got to tell you.'

The seriousness of his tone cut a swathe through her delicious mood; suddenly she was filled with foreboding.

'What?'

He stopped walking and turned to look at her.

'I've got to go away.'

'You mean on a training exercise or something?'

'No. I'm being posted. To Norfolk.'

'Norfolk!' He might as well have said Singapore or Malta. It sounded like the end of the earth. 'When?'

'Next week. On Wednesday.'

'Wednesday!' Shock seemed to have robbed her the ability to do anything but echo his words.

'I know. It's a bugger.'

She'd never heard him swear before.

'But why?' she asked. 'You thought you'd be at Colerne for ages.'

'You don't ask why in the forces. You just do as you're told.'

'I don't believe it!' She was close to tears again but this time they were not happy tears. 'They can't do this! Can't you tell them . . .' Her voice trailed away. They could do it, of course. As he said, he belonged to them and they could send him anywhere they liked, whenever they liked. 'Is that why you gave me the cup?' she asked.

'Well – partly. I don't want you to forget me.'

'As if I would! Well, at least we'll have the weekend.'

'No, we won't. I don't think I'll be able to get down again before I go. Some of the time I'm on duty and then I've got all my packing up to do. This is going to be our last time, Jen.'

The finger of ice probed at her again, sending shivers of misgiving through her.

'Bryn, this isn't . . .' She swallowed. '. . . the end, is it? You will keep in touch?'

'Of course I will. I'll write as soon as I get there and I'll be back to see you, first chance I get.'

She nodded, unable to speak.

'And there's another hour before my coach goes,' he went on.

She thought of the last bus home, decided she didn't care. If she missed it, she missed it. 'Can we go somewhere quiet?' she said.

They walked until they found a secluded spot at the rear of the car park, where they melted into one another's arms. Jenny hardly noticed the raw cold any more; between them they were generating enough heat to insulate them in their own small world. She burrowed into Bryn's jacket, the sharpness of desire now made poignant by the impending separation, and his lips on hers and his hands on her body made her long for him with an over-powering intensity. He was going away, she didn't know when they'd be together again this way, and she didn't think she could bear it.

She slid her hands down his back, pressing his hips tightly against hers and relishing that fine-tuned ache deep inside that sometimes reached the physical equivalent of a scream.

'Jenny – don't make it so hard for me,' Bryn whispered

310

against her ear, and the raw edge of his need echoed her own.

'But I want you to,' she said. She heard the quick, ragged intake of his breath. 'I know what I said before but now . . . I want you to.'

'Are you sure?'

She nodded, her hair brushing his cheek. She was trembling with the enormity of her decision but she didn't want him to leave without them having been together properly. The time hadn't been right before, now it was. Perhaps tomorrow she would regret it; tonight it was the only thing in the world which mattered.

'Oh, Jenny . . .'

She could feel all the pent-up desire within him like a powerhouse of electricity reaching out to spark and fuse with her own, but his lips on hers were incredibly gentle, kissing her with a tenderness that was somehow even more evocative than the most passionate, bruising of kisses. Shyly she slid her hands round until they found the zip of his jeans and eased it down. His body, hot and swollen, surged forward into the palm of her hand and for a moment she hesitated, not sure what she should do, before she closed her fingers around it. She remained there motionless, enjoying the heat and the strength and the intimacy of the moment and then Bryn was rucking her skirt up about her legs, moving them both so that all that heat and strength was between her thighs.

'Jenny – are you sure?' he whispered again.

'Yes – oh yes!'

She'd heard the first time could be painful, but it wasn't. He slid inside her with unbelievable ease and she felt only full and complete. She buried her face in his shoulder, her arms wound around him so tightly that their hearts seemed to be beating as one and their breath rising and falling in unison. Then, as he moved within her, his breath came faster and faster and she tipped her head back, seeing the stars and the orange-tinged hue of the city lights in the night sky through a dewy mist. At the last he cried out her name and, as he slipped out of her and she felt the sticky wetness between her legs, she experienced

311

the most enormous rush of tenderness and warmth. Strangely, her own sharp sensations of response had gone away the moment he had entered her and though they returned now, teasing, the overwhelming emotion was one of satisfaction that she had given herself to him, heard his cry of delight.

'Oh, Jenny, I'll never forget,' he said.

And that, she thought, was the most important thing of all.

She couldn't stop watching for the postman. She waited at the landing window, dashing into her bedroom or the bathroom if anyone came into the hall because she didn't want them to know how eager she was. But they were in no doubt. The moment the mail dropped on to the mat she was down the stairs, almost falling over herself in her eagerness, pushing Sally out of the way. Sally had ears like radio receivers. She could hear the postman's bicycle coming from way down the road and ran into the hall to attack the letters with a frenzy of barking. They were in no doubt either as to Jenny's disappointment. She would deposit the mail on the dining-room table and disappear upstairs again, the picture of dejection.

It was almost two weeks now since Bryn had gone and she couldn't understand why she hadn't heard from him.

'Forget about it and it will come,' Carrie advised. But Jenny couldn't forget. She thought about it every waking moment and her dreams were overlaid with a sense of gathering despair.

Why hadn't he written? He'd promised! She hugged the silver cup, gazed at it, willing him to write, but still the longed-for letter didn't come.

'It's the Christmas post, I expect,' Carrie said, but she sounded more consoling than confident, and Jenny knew her mother thought that Bryn had probably forgotten all about her and was secretly glad it was over.

The post, it was true, was becoming more and more erratic. Sometimes now it didn't come until lunchtime or even later, delivered by fresh-faced students with long striped woolly scarves, out to earn some pin money during the holiday. Jenny had tried for a job, but by the time she'd thought about getting round to it they'd all been snapped up. Her holiday was not as long as what Carrie called 'proper colleges', and meant university.

For her part, Jenny couldn't believe that Bryn had forgotten about her, but the worry that he might have done was growing insidiously with every disappointment, and she veered between hope and despair, a roller coaster of emotion that was reducing her to a nervous wreck.

Supposing he'd had an accident on his motorbike? He could be in hospital, dead even, and she wouldn't know. She said that to Carrie, because the fear was so intense she couldn't keep it to herself, but Carrie pooh-poohed the suggestion.

'It's not very likely, is it? I don't think it's that for one minute.'

And truth to tell, neither did Jenny. The chance of Bryn having been killed was very small and if he was simply injured, there was nothing to stop him writing. Unless, of course, he was unconscious, or had both arms in plaster, or . . . Jenny realised she was stretching credibility, looking for an excuse. She also felt that if something terrible had happened to Bryn, she'd have known somehow, really *known* deep inside, as opposed to the imaginings of anxiety.

Whether she wanted to believe it or not it was actually far more likely that he'd simply used the posting as an excuse to finish with her. Perhaps he hadn't even been posted away at all, just made that up as an excuse because he didn't want to see her again. But it didn't make sense – why would he have given her the cup if he hadn't cared about her? Unless of course it was just a way of easing his conscience. Tears pricked her eyes as she remembered the way he'd said: 'I've got loads of them' as if perhaps they meant nothing to him at all.

Round and round on the carousel of hope and despair she went, sometimes trying to forget him, tell herself at least now she could concentrate on passing her exams with really good grades and getting started on the career she'd always wanted. But it did no good. The terrible hollow ache was still there inside her and it refused to go away.

On the Saturday before Christmas she went to see Heather and Vanessa. Vanessa was highly excitable, unable to keep still for two seconds, and whilst Heather went to shop Jenny trimmed the tree that Steven had bought and stuck it in a bucket of sand. She let Vanessa help her but had to keep shouting at her to be careful with the ornaments – candleholders into which tiny candles would be stuck, glass icicles and incredibly fragile coloured balls, concave on one side, with pretty contrasting frosted linings. Inevitably, some of them had shattered since last year, which made Jenny feel even more sad. She remembered each and every one of the baubles from her own childhood; Heather had inherited them since Carrie, who hated the mess made by falling pine needles, had treated herself to one of the little artificial trees that were beginning to appear on the market. Jenny hated it – it was spiky and ugly and lacked the lovely scent of a real tree. It was also too small to trim properly.

'Have you heard from that boy of yours yet?' Heather asked when she got home from shopping and was unpacking her basket. Jenny shook her head.

'Don't upset yourself about it,' Heather advised. 'There's plenty more fish in the sea.'

Jenny turned away wretchedly. That wasn't what she wanted to hear at all, and it didn't help one bit. There might be plenty more fish in the sea but there was only one Bryn. If she never saw him again she didn't think she could bear it.

As she made her way home though, back up the hill past the Jolly Collier and the butcher's shop where cockerels and pheasants, still wearing all their feathers, hung above the window from a row of meat hooks, she suddenly felt better. There was no logical explanation for her change of mood, it was just that somehow the fog had lifted and the sun come out. Jenny walked along Alder Road with a spring in her step, humming 'While Shepherds Watch'.

The boys were playing their inevitable game of football on the Green, their socks in untidy concertinas round their ankles, coats discarded, in spite of the chill December air, to mark the goal posts. The ball came hurtling towards her and before she could stop herself she had kicked it back to them. Not a bad kick either, covering at least half the distance, though it stopped short against the kerb. The boys came whooping to collect it and Jenny went up the path actually grinning.

The house smelled of cooking chips – chips and Spam was a Saturday staple, though sometimes for a treat they had fish and chips from the shop. The trouble with that was by the time they got them home they were cold and had to be heated up again in the oven, which always spoiled them, to Jenny's mind. The other Saturday staple was sausage and mash, but since Jenny didn't like Carrie's mashed potato, which was rather stodgy and un-interesting, she was glad it was chips.

Carrie was standing on a chair, hanging newly arrived Christmas cards on a length of twine which stretched along one wall dangling in loops between the holly-decked pictures. She looked round as Jenny came in and waved her hand towards the table.

'There's something for you there.'

Jenny's heart leaped, but somehow she wasn't surprised. Deep inside she'd known. All the way home she'd known.

Jenny picked up the envelope with her name on it, a small square envelope addressed in a hand she didn't recognise. She clutched it to her as if she'd never let it go and went upstairs without even stopping to take off her coat.

It was quite a short letter. His name, service number and address, written in neat capitals in the top left-hand corner, took up almost half the first side, and he began without any flowery preamble: 'Dear Jenny'. There was a bit apologising for not having written before, a bit about what he'd been doing, and that was more or less it. But he finished: 'I miss you. Please write soon. Love, Bryn' and she melted inside just looking at his name. It didn't matter that he hadn't written much. It didn't matter that there were no declarations of undying love. The letter had come. He hadn't forgotten her. That was enough.

*

David was dreading Christmas. The brightly-lit shop windows, the decorated tree and the festoons of streamers and cards at home, and the general air of festivity only served to sharpen the terrible sense of loss which had closed in around him since Linda's death. This should have been their first Christmas together as man and wife, instead he was living at home again just as if his marriage had never happened. Linda's name was rarely, if ever, mentioned. David couldn't bring himself to talk about her, hugging his grief to himself, and Carrie, typically, seemed determined to deny her existence, as if pretending it had all been just a bad dream would somehow make it so. The thought of sitting around on Christmas Day, opening presents and singing carols as they always did, was unbearable to him. Not only would he be missing her with the ache of sorrow that tore his guts out, he would also resent the way the family were celebrating. That they were sorry she had died he did not doubt, but they didn't feel it as he did and Carrie would make sure the shadow of her death did not mar the festivities. That, David felt, was the ultimate betrayal. At this time, more than any other, he wanted to mourn her – *needed* to mourn her. And he wanted to do it alone.

'I'm not going to be here for Christmas,' he said.

The family were having Sunday lunch – roast lamb and onion sauce – and *Family Favourites* on the radio was playing one sickly love message after another from separated sweethearts. Love you – Miss you – Can't wait until we can be together again. He and Linda would never be together again.

Carrie put down her knife. 'What d'you mean – you won't be here for Christmas?'

'I'm going away.'

'Going away! Where?' Carrie sounded outraged.

'I don't know yet. I thought I might go camping somewhere.'

'*Camping!* You can't go *camping* in the middle of December! I never heard anything like it! You'll catch your death of cold!'

'Mum – I used to be in the army, remember? I've

camped in worse conditions than this.'

'Nowhere will be open this time of year. All the sites will be shut up for the winter.'

'I'll find somewhere. And if I can't – well, I'll just pitch my tent in the woods or something, like we used to on exercises.'

'I won't hear of it!' Carrie said. 'Spending Christmas on your own – it's the last thing you want to do.'

'Leave the boy alone, Carrie,' Joe said. His tone was level but unusually authoritative, the tone that, because he so rarely used it, always brought Carrie up short. 'He knows what he wants.'

'Do you think *I* could enjoy my Christmas knowing he was on his own in the wilds, in a tent, in December?' Carrie retorted defensively.

'This isn't about you though, is it, m'dear?' Joe said mildly yet firmly. 'If that's what he's decided he wants to do then it's not for you to interfere. Nor start making him feel guilty on top of everything else.'

'What do you mean – make him feel guilty?'

'He's got enough to worry about without you making him think he's going to spoil your Christmas.' He turned his faded blue eyes on David. 'If you want to go away, my son, you do it. And don't you think twice about us. We'll be all right. We've all got one another.'

David nodded. 'Thanks, Dad.' There were tears glittering in his eyes. His father's understanding had brought to the surface some of the emotions he fought so hard to keep under wraps. But he was grateful, all the same. Joe might stay in the background most of the time, but when he did intervene he was able to put Carrie in her place better than anyone else could!

In the middle of the afternoon of Christmas Eve, when the house was full of the smell of mince pies baking and singed cockerel as Carrie burned the feather stubbles off the bird in preparation for the oven, there was a knock at the front door.

'Can you get it?' Carrie called from the kitchen.

Jenny went to the door. The postman was standing

there, a proper postman this time, not one of the students. Jenny was surprised. She'd thought the post would have been and gone by now.

'Couldn't get this through the letter box,' he said, handing her a thin white parcel. 'Happy Christmas!'

'Thank you. Happy Christmas!' Jenny said.

She recognised the writing on the box at once – she had read Bryn's letter so many times that the unfamiliar was now totally familiar.

'What is it?' Carrie called. 'If it's those carol singers again, tell them I haven't got any more change.'

'No, it's the post. For me.'

'The post? This time of the afternoon?' Carrie came into the living room wiping her hands on her apron. 'What is it?'

'It's for me,' Jenny repeated.

She tugged at the sticky tape with eager fingers and opened the box.

Inside was the most beautiful card she had ever seen – rabbits and robins and a huge padded red satin heart in the middle of which sat a brooch made of imitation pearls and bits of diamanté. *To The One I Love* was the inscription.

'Oh!' Jenny said.

'Well!' Carrie said, looking over her shoulder. 'Well!'

She sounded a bit cross, Jenny thought, but she didn't care. She took the brooch off the card and pinned it to her jumper. It looked a bit odd, sitting there on the dark grey wool, but she didn't care about that either.

Like the cup, she knew this was something she would treasure all her life.

'Well, I don't know, this is a treat and no mistake!' Charlotte said.

She was installed in the fireside corner of the living room of her old home, and Helen, gratified, thought she had seldom seen her looking happier.

The furniture was different, of course – her own had been sold with the house and Helen had put in a modern cottage suite. But she had managed to find a wing chair in a second-hand shop that was very like the one that had been Charlotte's favourite, and it was in that she now sat, beaming at the family who had congregated to spend Christmas Day in their old family home.

Jack and Stella had come up from Minehead and were staying in Helen's room whilst she had moved temporarily into the small spare room, sleeping on the camp bed that was the only piece of furniture it could yet boast. Charlotte was in the second bedroom and the others had all arrived during the afternoon – Amy and Ralph, who had driven over to collect Dolly en route, Barbara and Huw and their children Hope and Neil, Maureen and a young man she had met at college and brought home for Christmas. There would be another wedding in the family before long if she wasn't very much mistaken, Helen thought, and permitted herself a wry smile. Most of her cousins were younger than she was and they were all beating her to the altar!

I must seem like a confirmed spinster to them! Helen thought.

'You're not having any of your own friends here on Christmas Day, then,' her mother had said, and Helen had known what lay behind the apparently casual remark.

'I know what you're getting at, Mum,' she had said. 'You're asking me if you can buy yourself a new hat – and the answer is no. I'm afraid you'll have to wait a bit longer.'

'I'm not asking anything of the sort!' Stella had said hastily but the flush of colour in her cheeks gave the lie to the denial.

Perhaps, Helen thought, it was just as well Guy had opted out. She had invited him, feeling duty-bound to do so since if he had left Marian he would be likely to be spending Christmas alone, though even as she issued the invitation she had been concerned she might be giving him – and her family – the wrong idea. Though she had been seeing him fairly regularly she was still sticking by what she had told him – that she didn't want to rush into anything and find herself back in the same position as before. But it wasn't easy; already she had felt herself being drawn in, the web that was spun as much from her own emotions as anything Guy did or said ensnaring her insidiously but relentlessly.

319

And in fact, though she had had her reservations about inviting him, she had actually been a little hurt when he had refused.

'You'll have a houseful with all your family there,' he had said. 'Don't worry about me.'

Perversely her first reaction had been: *He doesn't want them to get the idea we're a couple either*.

'You can't spent Christmas on your own,' she had said.

'I don't suppose I'll be on my own,' he had replied. 'Anyway, by the time I've gone in to the hospital, dressed up as Father Christmas and distributed a few presents, the day will be gone.'

She'd laughed, shaking her head. Guy dressed up as Father Christmas, touring the wards, was so out of character as to be almost unimaginable. But it was a tradition; she should be used to it by now.

'We'll have our own Christmas when they're all gone home again,' he said. 'I'll arrange to take a few days off and . . .'

'We won't actually be able to be on our own here, Guy.'

He frowned. 'What do you mean?'

'I'm having Grandma with me whilst my aunt Dolly has a hysterectomy. I'm hoping she'll go on living with me afterwards.'

His frown deepened. 'To *live* with you?'

'Yes. This used to be her house. I told you. I know she'd like nothing better than to see her days out here. And Aunt Dolly will be in no fit state to look after her for some time.'

'Surely though . . .' *There must be someone else who could look after her*, he had been going to say, and she knew it.

'I want her here, Guy.'

'Oh well . . . if you *want* her . . .'

She didn't like his tone; couldn't help comparing his attitude to Paul's. And she could read him like a book; having a grandmother living with her would put paid to any ideas he might have had about moving in with her himself for the odd night. Grandmothers were likely to have old-fashioned ideas about extra-marital cohabitation.

Today, however, Helen was not going to let such petty

annoyances as Guy's selfishness spoil things for her. It was Christmas, the family were all together in Greenslade Terrace. And Helen was determined that she and they were going to enjoy every moment of it.

Billy Edgell had not had a good Christmas. In fact, he thought, it had been his worst ever.

Christmas to Billy usually meant getting roaring drunk – one year he had fallen down in the middle of the road on his way home from the pub and had to be taken home in a passing police car. He was never sure whether it had been the spirit of goodwill to all men which had entered the policeman and made him decide on this course of action rather than taking him to the police station and locking him up in a cell for the night or whether his primary motive had been avoiding all the ensuing paperwork so as to get off duty in time to see his children open their Christmas stockings. Whichever, Billy had spent the night in his own home – albeit on the front-room floor because his legs refused to carry him up the stairs, and his hang-over had lifted enough the next day for him to be able to enjoy his mother's Christmas dinner.

This year he had not been so lucky. This year he *had* spent the night in a cell, locked in at lights out by a warder with a big jangling bunch of keys and with no opportunity whatsoever to partake of the Christmas spirit.

Billy had been found guilty two months earlier of being involved in a warehouse robbery. A large quantity of stolen cigarettes and bottles of whisky had been found stashed away in his mother's outhouse and Billy had been sentenced to a spell in prison.

It wasn't the first time he'd been inside. He'd served a couple of spells in youth custody, first at an approved school and later in Borstal, which hadn't been much fun either. He didn't mind the long runs across muddy fields in the rain, but he did object strongly to having his hair, of which he was very proud, cropped short to his neck, and he loathed the discipline. But at least he'd never had to spend a Christmas there and now he was kicking himself, not for breaking into the warehouse, but for being stupid enough

321

to get caught – again. It wasn't as if he'd been attempting the Great Train Robbery, for God's sake, just a poxy warehouse. And he couldn't even get away with that.

They knew him, the police, that was the trouble. As soon as there was any job done locally they were there on his back. He'd never be able to get away with a bit of honest thieving as long as he lived in Hillsbridge. He'd have to branch out into the world outside, somewhere he wasn't known. Trouble was, his mother made it too comfortable for him at home. Food on the table, his underwear washed – when he remembered to change it – and no questions asked.

Billy shifted on his bunk, tossed aside the girlie magazine he had been ogling, and reached for the supply of chewing gum he kept there, hidden away from the thieving hands of other inmates.

'What a way to spend Christmas!'

'Could be worse,' came the voice from the bunk below.

'Oh yeah? How?'

'You could be on the streets. At least you get a Christmas dinner in here.'

'You been on the streets?' Billy asked.

'Was last year.'

'Why was that?'

'My old lady's new boyfriend and me didn't get on. This has to beat a shop doorway in Broadmead.'

'S'pose so,' Billy acknowledged grudgingly. 'You come from Bristol, then?'

'Yeah.'

'I come from Hillsbridge.'

'That's over Bath way, isn't it?'

'Well – sort of.'

It was the first conversation Billy had had with his new cell mate. His previous mucker had been released for Christmas and all he knew about the new arrival was that his name was Dallimore – Sean on his birth certificate, Ticker to his friends.

'That's where the coal mines are, right?' Ticker said.

'Yeah.'

'There used to be coal mines round Bristol, too.

Fishponds way, I think. Long time ago, though.'

Billy didn't bother to reply. To him, coal mines were a way of life and hardly worthy of comment. He picked up his magazine again, flipping a page and ogling the model pictured there.

'I knew a girl went to live over your way,' Ticker offered. 'Went to school with her. Heather, her name was. Can't remember her other name. Don't s'pose you know her, anyway.'

'Might do.'

'She'd be older than you. She's my age.' He paused, thinking. 'Simmons – that was it. Heather Simmons.'

Billy looked up from his magazine.

'Heather Simmons – I know her.'

'Never.'

'Yeah. Her parents used to live across the road from us. Still do. She got married. To a Pole.'

'Well, bugger me! Small world, in't it?'

They both considered this.

'She was a bit of all right,' Ticker said after a moment or two. 'Tits that came round the corner half an hour before she did and legs up to her armpits. She put it about a bit, though. They reckon she was knocked up when she left. That's what her mates said, anyway. The story was her family had gone to get out of the way of the bombing, but her mates reckoned that was only the half of it.'

'She was in the club, you mean?' Billy asked.

'That's what was going round at the time. One or two of the boys in our class were sweating, I can tell you, but nothing ever came of it. Her mother wanted to keep it quiet, I s'pose. They were like that. Toffee-nosed. Fancied themselves.'

'Well, I'll be buggered!' Billy said, a grin spreading from ear to ear. He had nothing against Heather – scarcely knew her really – but he'd never forgotten the way Jenny had given him the brush-off, and he'd always disliked Carrie. When he'd been younger she'd been forever shouting at him and he could still remember the night he'd peed over her garden wall in revenge and she'd looked out of the window and seen him doing it. He could

323

remember the hiding he'd had off his mother too after Carrie had come over and knocked on the door to complain about it. Joyce had given her an earful, but after she'd gone he'd been for it!

Carrie didn't shout at him any more, but she wouldn't acknowledge him either. If he passed by on the pavement she'd look straight through him and the expression on her face was as if she'd smelled a bad smell. Now it was gratifying to find out that for all her airs and graces she was no better than anybody else. Her daughter in the club when she was still at school! That was a good one!

'Often wondered what became of her,' Ticker said. 'Heather, I mean. What she did about the nipper an' that. P'raps she got rid of it.'

'Well, there was certainly no kid when she lived opposite us,' Billy said. 'Just her and her brother and sister. She's got one now, I think, with her husband – the Pole. Though now you come to mention it . . .' he paused, wrinkling up his puggy nose as he tried to remember something which had been of no interest at all to him at the time, '. . . there was some talk then that she had to get married.'

'I wouldn't be surprised,' Ticker said. 'If she was at it when she was fourteen or fifteen . . . Can I have a borrow of your magazine if you've finished with it?'

'I haven't,' Billy said, but he handed it over anyway. Then he lay back on his bunk with his hands above his head, staring at the ceiling and thinking about what Ticker had said.

'Are you all right, Jenny?' Carrie asked. 'You're not eating your dinner.'

'I am!'

'Well, you don't look as though you're enjoying it. It's a lovely bit of cockerel, too. You'd better make the most of it, we shan't be having another one 'til next year.'

'She does look a bit peaky,' Glad said.

They were all sitting around the table in Glad's home, tucking into their Christmas meal. All except David, who, meeting his mother's concerns halfway, had booked himself into a bed and breakfast in the wilds of Dartmoor.

'I'm fine,' Jenny said, but truth to tell she wasn't. She didn't feel very well, though she couldn't exactly put her finger on what was wrong. There was a strange hollow niggle in the pit of her stomach and she felt vaguely . . . not nauseous, exactly, that was too strong a word for it . . . well, just *odd* in a way she couldn't remember feeling odd before.

'She's in love,' Steve said, teasing her from across the table. 'That's what it is.'

Carrie snorted, Jenny blushed and Heather smiled at her conspiratorially.

'You don't want to be thinking about that sort of thing yet!' Glad said. 'Not at your age!'

'I'm sixteen, Gran.'

'Sixteen!' Glad shook her head. 'I wish I was sixteen again!'

'Sweet sixteen and never been kissed!' Steve said, still teasing.

Jenny's blush deepened.

'Leave her alone, Steve,' Heather warned. 'You're embarrassing her. No wonder she's not enjoying her dinner, with you sitting there making fun.'

'She doesn't mind, do you, Jenny? What's mistletoe for, I'd like to know?'

'Don't take any notice of him, m'dear,' Joe said, shaking yet another spoonful of salt over his meal. 'You eat up and enjoy your dinner. Brussels and potatoes out of my own garden . . . what could be better?'

Having Bryn here, Jenny thought. But she said nothing. And however much she tried, the meal wouldn't go down the way it should.

Chapter Seventeen

As always, after the bright oases of Christmas and New Year were over, it seemed that winter would last for ever. According to the calendar, the days should be gradually lengthening; instead they seemed shorter, for sometimes the light was no better than dusk from daybreak to nightfall. Drizzle and sleet fell from a leaden sky, the wind howled in the trees and the headgear of the pits, and the fields and hedges were barren and brown. Last year's dead leaves lay in sodden drifts in corners and alleys and the smoke from the chimneys hung in a hazy cloud over the ranks of houses on the hillsides.

At the surgery the queues grew ever-longer as rheumatics and persistent chest infections joined the ranks of colds and influenza. Helen, rushed off her feet, had little time to worry about her strained relations with Paul, and less to spend with Guy. He was also busy as the hospital was full to overflowing and for that, at least, she was grateful. It gave her the breathing space she needed to try to sort out her feelings, though by the time she fell into bed at night she was usually too exhausted to think of anything but falling asleep and hoping that she would not be woken by the telephone for an urgent night visit.

During those dark and miserable weeks the telephone interrupting her sleep was an all too frequent occurrence. Sometimes she became aware of it as part of a dream, sometimes she reached to switch off her alarm before realising it was not the clock at all but the telephone, sometimes she even came to wondering where she was, so exhausted and disorientated was she.

Perhaps it was just as well that Charlotte had not as yet moved in, she thought, shivering uncontrollably as she struggled into her clothes. Dolly's hysterectomy had been postponed due to pressure on hospital beds and she had insisted Charlotte should stay with her until she went into hospital. Helen had felt frustrated by the delay – who knew whether Charlotte would be one of those to succumb to the unrelenting winter weather? – but in the bitter small hours she was forced to concede that at least with Dolly her grandmother was getting an undisturbed night's sleep. And quite honestly she herself was better off without the added pressure of having to look after her.

One morning in early February Helen was still wading through a procession of patients who had been well enough to come to the surgery when the telephone on her desk rang. She reached for it, slightly surprised. Because of the pressure of work, Dorothea Hillman was fielding all calls; she never put one through when the doctor was with a patient unless it was something that could not wait.

Dorothea herself was on the other end of the line.

'I'm very sorry to interrupt you, Doctor, but I've just had a call from Charlie Gregory, the Co-op baker's rounds-man. He's just called on Ida Lockyear and found her collapsed.'

Helen experienced a twist of foreboding.

'Has he called the ambulance?'

'I don't think so. He was ringing from the cottage next door and called us first. I've said I'll get the ambulance, but from what he says I think it may be too late for that. I thought you should know, Doctor.'

'Thank you, Dorothea. I'll get over there right away.'

The foreboding thickened into very real anxiety. It enveloped her in a fuzzy cloud as she hastily got rid of her patient, who was suffering from nothing more serious than an attack of sinusitis, and drove over to Ida Lockyear's cottage.

From what Dorothea had said it sounded as if Ida might already be dead – but why? It could be she'd had a stroke or a heart attack, of course – at her age that was by far the most likely explanation. And yet . . .

Helen thought of all the times Ida had visited the surgery, all the times she'd dismissed the woman as a 'heartsink patient'. Was it possible there had been something seriously wrong with her all the time and Helen had missed it? Dorothea suspected as much; that was why she had warned Helen before calling the ambulance. And Helen knew that deep down she thought so too. That was the reason she was trembling with anxiety.

As she turned into the lane – little more than a track – where Ida lived, Helen saw the Co-op bread van parked outside. It was one of the new motorised ones; though horses and carts were still used for deliveries on some rounds, motorised vans now served the more outlying districts.

Charlie Gregory and Annie Tiley, the neighbour to whose home he had run to use the telephone, were on the path. Annie had thrown a coat on over her working dress and pinafore and Charlie's hands were thrust into the pockets of his donkey jacket.

Helen pulled up behind the bread van and they came down the path to meet her.

'Thank goodness you'm here, Doctor!' Charlie's face was red and his eyes watering from the cold; a heavy dew-drop hung pendulously from the end of his nose.

'Not that there's much you can do,' Annie Tiley put in. 'She's gone all right and the place is full of fumes. That's why we'm out here in the cold. I reckon we should be treated an' all, after what we breathed in in there.'

'It's her boiler,' Charlie supplied. 'That's what's done it, all right. Goodness only knows when she last had the thing seen to.'

Helen felt sick as all her worst fears came back to haunt her. The boiler. Carbon monoxide poisoning. It added up. That was what had been causing Ida's symptoms. And she had dismissed them as the psychosomatic results of an old woman's loneliness.

'I'd better have a look at her,' she said.

'Mind how you go in there, Doctor! Though it shouldn't be so bad now. We opened all the windows.'

As Helen passed the front door she noticed how the brass knob and knocker gleamed against the sun-faded paintwork. Ida must have polished it quite recently – perhaps as recently as yesterday – and Helen realised with

328

a pang of guilt just how little she really knew about the woman who had been her patient. She'd never been here, to Ida's home, before. Ida had always come to the surgery – and even then she hadn't really listened to her, simply tried to sort out her symptoms and then dismissed them because they had seemed so innocuous and insignificant, nothing more than an attempt to secure attention.

The back door was ajar – obviously Charlie had gone in this way when he had knocked and got no reply. It led directly into a kitchen-cum-living room. One wall housed the sink and a motley collection of cupboards, all of different levels, a tall kitchen cabinet faced her, its pull-down working surface open. In the middle of the room was a table, covered with well-scrubbed oilcloth, and three dining chairs with tall backs and leatherette seats.

Ida was in an easy chair beside what must be the offending boiler. Her head rested against one of the wings, her hands were folded in her lap and her legs splayed out in front of her as if she had simply fallen asleep. But one glance was enough to tell Helen she was not asleep. Ida was dead, and had been for some time.

Helen made a cursory examination but there was nothing the body could tell her that the fumes still lingering in the room could not. She went back outside, glad, for once, of the chilling fresh air. She felt slightly sick and her legs were trembling as they sometimes did when she was upset.

Charlie and Annie looked at her expectantly and she answered them with a small shake of her head.

'I knew it,' Charlie said. 'Soon as I looked at her, I knew she'd gone. Knew even before that really. She's always on the lookout for me. I mean, there's a lot of folk just leave their money on the side and I'll take it and put their pound loaf or their lardy cake or whatever down where 'twas and never set eyes on 'em. But Ida, she'd always catch me, whether she wanted anything or not. Always wanted a word.'

'Oh, that were Ida,' Annie agreed, but she looked a little shamefaced and it crossed Helen's mind that she, too, might be feeling a little guilty, wishing, perhaps, now that it was too late, that she had given more of her time to her admittedly irritating neighbour.

A clanging bell announced the arrival of the ambulance, closely followed by a police car. Dorothea had wasted no time in making her phone calls to the emergency services. The two ambulance men started purposefully up the path. Helen stopped them.

'I'm sorry, but you can't touch her.' She turned to PC Dowding, young, fresh-faced and eager. 'This is one for you, I'm afraid.'

'Sudden death?' Dowding ran his fingers through springy ginger hair, pausing to scratch his head in a way that reminded Helen incongruously of Laurel and Hardy. For a horrible moment she teetered on the brink of totally inappropriate laughter, and knew that it was reaction.

'I can't issue a death certificate. You'll have to inform the coroner.'

She nodded briefly to Charlie and Annie, returned to her car and started the engine. Then, with much revving and jerking, she squeezed out of the space between the baker's van and the ambulance, reversed into a gateway opposite, and drove away 'As if,' Annie said later when she recounted events to her husband, Len, 'all the little devils in hell was on her tail!'

Carrie saw the mortuary van when she was on her way to work. It passed her in the steep part of the lane and she recognised it at once.

Somebody must have died, she thought, and briefly wondered who. But it didn't occupy her mind for long. That was too busy with other things. Namely Jenny and her very unsuitable romance.

From the beginning, Carrie had had deep misgivings. She hadn't cared at all for the idea of Jenny going out with a serviceman – here today and gone tomorrow – and about whom she, or anybody else for that matter, knew anything. But Jenny was sixteen now, she'd always said she'd allow her to go out with a boy when she was sixteen and, for all her reservations, Carrie was a woman of her word.

It wouldn't last, she'd told herself. She'd see him once or

twice and that would be it. She only hoped Jenny wouldn't get hurt. When the boy had been so-called posted somewhere in the wilds of East Anglia Carrie had felt enormous relief and vindication. She had been sorry for Jenny but not surprised when at first no letter had come. It was just as she'd expected. The letter and the flashy card with the cheap-looking brooch had been something of a set-back, but she had still not been overly concerned. Perhaps the posting had been genuine and not just an excuse, but Carrie felt confident that with him so far away it would all peter out in time.

The trouble was, it hadn't. Letters had continued to come at the rate of one or two a week and Jenny had even asked if this Bryn could come down to stay for a few days. Carrie hadn't known what to say. She didn't want him in her house, didn't want the two of them under one roof, but didn't know how to refuse. She'd hedged: 'We'll see, when the better weather comes,' but Jenny had taken that as a yes and thanked her so effusively, with hugs and even tears, that Carrie had been completely thrown.

She still didn't know what to think, and this morning, when yet another letter had arrived, she had succumbed to temptation.

Jenny left just before eight in the morning to catch her bus to college and the post didn't usually arrive until quarter or twenty past. When the letter with the East Anglian postmark had fallen on to the mat along with the electricity bill she'd taken it in and propped it up on the table as usual, ready for Jenny to find when she got home in the evening. But it had seemed to be mocking her. She couldn't take her eyes off it, and in the end her curiosity had got the better of her.

Trying to justify her actions by telling herself she was only doing it for Jenny's good, she had boiled a kettle and steamed the letter open.

The trouble was she hadn't made a very good job of it. The paper had wrinkled a bit and there were a couple of tiny tears where the glue had held. But Carrie had gone ahead anyway – it was too late now to give up – and what she had read when she extracted the three sheets of cheap ruled paper from the envelope had made her hair curl.

Whatever next! Carrie thought as she read the endearments and too-personal-for-her-liking sentiments. *Dear oh dear! I don't like the sound of this at all!*

It was as she tried to reseal the envelope that the idea came to her – and really she had no option, she told herself. If she gave it to Jenny looking like this, Jenny would know at a glance that it had been tampered with. Carrie hesitated, looking at it and wondering if she dared tear it up and throw it in the fire. That way Jenny would never know – she'd come to the conclusion in the end that this particular letter had been lost in the post.

But somehow, for all her bad feelings about it, Carrie couldn't quite bring herself to destroy the letter. She thought some more, then took it upstairs and hid it in her underwear drawer. At least that left her options open. If she changed her mind she could always retrieve it on a Saturday when Jenny was here, take it downstairs and pick it up with the rest of the post. Then if Jenny was suspicious about it having been opened, she'd think it had been done elsewhere – even at the post office, perhaps – and the date stamp would prove it had been delayed.

But Carrie was still thinking about it as she walked down the steep lane towards the Jolly Collier, still worrying, still busy justifying herself – though the word guilt would never have crossed her mind. She'd do her best for Jenny, just as she always had, guide her away from all the pitfalls by persuasion, heavy-handed ultimatums and, if necessary, guile and deception. The ends justified the means, especially when she knew she was in the right, Carrie always thought.

She could be a very determined woman.

'There'll have to be a post-mortem, of course, possibly an inquest,' Reuben Hobbs said.

He looked and sounded grimly displeased.

'I realise that,' Helen said. 'I'm no happier about what's happened than you are, Reuben. I keep asking myself whether there was something I could have done. But I ran all the usual tests and they came up negative. The fact that her symptoms might indicate carbon monoxide poisoning in small frequent doses never crossed my mind. Like the rest of us, I thought she was malingering.'

'That's no excuse.'

'I realise that too and I don't think I shall ever forgive myself.'

'Hmm.' Reuben turned his pen over between his fingers, looking at it with intense concentration. 'This is always the danger, of course, in general practice. Becoming complacent.'

Helen bridled slightly.

'I don't think I've become complacent. If I thought that, I'd give up the profession tomorrow.'

Reuben let this go without comment.

'Well, we'll just have to play it by ear. I suggest you go over every detail of Mrs Lockyear's case now, whilst it's fresh in your mind, and compile some sort of statement. As I said, I think it's quite likely there will be an inquest and it's as well to be prepared. Then try to put it out of your mind. You don't want to be so preoccupied that you give your other patients less than your full attention. We don't any more disasters.'

He didn't add that this sort of thing was very bad publicity for the practice, but he didn't need to. Helen was already all too aware of the implications. Quite apart from word of mouth, the whole tragic incident would receive full press coverage in the *Mercury* – already Walter Evans had been on the telephone looking for a comment to add to the story that would no doubt be the front-page story on Friday. Dorothea had fobbed him off for now, but if there was an inquest he'd be there, with his pencil sharpened and his quick inquisitive mind missing nothing. Feeling as she did herself, that somehow she had failed Ida Lockyear, Helen didn't see how she could blame others for reaching the same conclusion.

For the first time Helen wondered miserably whether she was in the wrong job, and wondered whether Reuben thought so too. He hadn't been exactly supportive. She'd felt his criticism hanging heavy in the atmosphere between them. And he had every right to be critical.

However one looked at it, a patient had died because she hadn't investigated fully enough. And who was to say it couldn't happen again?

The full weight of responsibility settled heavily upon Helen's shoulders, and she felt bowed down by it. Later, she would think about the possibility that this unhappy episode might scupper her chances of the partnership she hoped for. But for the moment her thoughts were all with Ida, who had put out a cry for help and been misunderstood – a misunderstanding which had cost her her life.

She tried to ring Guy. Usually so self-sufficient, on this occasion Helen desperately needed to talk about what had happened to someone who would understand. But Guy was unavailable, and his secretary, who was based at the private clinic from which he sometimes operated, was evasive.

'If I could take your name and address I'll pass the message on.'

'No, it doesn't matter,' Helen said, ashamed, already, of having run to Guy for support, and also wary about giving the woman her name. Guy had his own flat now, in Clifton, but they were still being discreet.

'That's not Susan, is it?' the secretary enquired.

'No, it's not.' Helen almost, but not quite, fell into the trap. Crafty secretary, using a trick like that to try to get her to disclose her identity. 'I already said – it's not important. I'll catch up with him later.'

She put down the phone and picked up the list of house calls Dorothea had left on her desk. Reuben had been right to say she must not let this unfortunate business distract her from giving her other patients her full attention. But it wasn't easy to concentrate on sorting the wheat from the chaff with something like this hanging over her.

Somehow she got through the day, the usual mish-mash of infections and minor complaints interspersed with the occasional more serious one. But now she felt less than confident about the simplest diagnosis and imagined, too, that she saw doubt in the faces of her patients. If she felt like this now, what would it be like when the story got around – particularly if the coroner decided some blame should be attached to her. Helen's face burned as she imagined the word negligence being bandied round.

By the time she finished afternoon surgery she was shaking with fatigue. The constant worrying seemed to have drained all her last resources.

Helen sighed, pulled herself together and looked at her watch. Six thirty. Perhaps this would be a good time to call Guy again. He should be home by now. She dialled the number, imagining him relaxing with a gin and tonic, perhaps in the bath even, soaking away the smells of the hospital. But the phone rang and rang and suddenly she realised she wouldn't have known what to say to him anyway. Wasn't this just what she had always tried to hide from him – her doubts, her insecurities, her failures? Just hearing his voice would have been a comfort, of course, but when had he ever been there when she had needed him? Tears of self-pity pricked in the corners of her eyes. For as long as she could remember, it seemed to her, she had fought her battles alone.

She blinked fiercely, annoyed with herself for her weakness. If she was alone, it was her own fault. Her choice. Maybe the first time around she hadn't known what she was letting herself in for, getting involved with him. She'd been too naive, too trusting, too much in love. But this time she hadn't been under any illusions. She'd thought she was battle-scarred enough to cope, that she'd just play along and see how things developed. She'd let him flatter and cajole his way back into her life, and pretended to herself that she was the one in control. But all the time she'd been walking back into the same peat bog, falling into the same trap. All over again.

Who did you think you were kidding, Helen?

Too weary and depressed to be able to make the effort to clear up and go home, Helen folded her arms on her desk and lay her head on them. The events of the day were still going around in her mind, overlaid now with depression about her feelings for Guy – such unwanted, treacherous feelings, yet so totally out of her control – but they were blurring, becoming oddly distant and confused.

She could hear the rain beating on the window and the wind moaning softly, she could hear the murmur of voices, but they too were distant, muzzy.

Exhausted from overwork, broken nights and too much emotion, Helen slept.

The sound of the door being opened jolted her awake. She raised her head sharply, jarring her neck. Her vision was slightly blurred and her mouth tasted stale.

'Helen? Are you all right?'

It was Paul, standing in the doorway.

'Yes – yes, I'm OK. I must have fallen asleep.' She massaged her sore neck, squinting at him.

'Strange place to choose.'

'I didn't choose it, I just . . .' She rubbed her eyes, leaving a dark smudge of mascara on her lower lid, 'I was just sitting here thinking and I . . .'

'I saw your car was still here – and your light on,' he said, by way of belated explanation. And then: 'Do you want to talk about it?'

'Ida Lockyear? You've heard then?'

'Reuben phoned me.'

'I cocked up,' she said bluntly.

'You did, didn't you?' He came in, closing the door behind him. 'You shouldn't be too hard on yourself, though. It could happen to anyone.'

'Carbon monoxide poisoning. It never even crossed my mind . . .'

'It's pretty unusual. You weren't to know the state of her boiler. If anyone's to blame it's her son for not making sure it was safe. And it has to be said, Ida herself must take some of the blame. She'd bunged up all the ventilation in that kitchen with rags. To keep the warmth in, I suppose, and the draughts out.'

'But she's dead,' Helen said. 'And she was my patient. I should have thought!' She hesitated. 'Reuben thinks so, too. He's furious with me.'

'Of course he's not furious. Just worried. He is the senior partner in this practice, after all. The buck stops with him.'

'Well, I got the very definite impression that I was not exactly flavour of the month.'

'I don't suppose you are, but . . .'

'And I've blown any chance I might have had of being offered a partnership here.'

The moment the words were out she could have bitten off her tongue.

Paul was looking at her with an expression that was both startled and quizzical.

'You want a partnership? Here?'

'Oh, I know I'm being presumptive. I know I haven't been here very long and I've no right . . . but yes, actually, that's what I've been hoping for ever since I came. Surely that's what every GP works towards? And this is my family's home town, remember.'

'Well, yes, but . . .' He swung back on the cupboards. 'I had the impression you'd be wanting to get back to Bristol when the time was right.'

Her face flamed. He'd made some enquiries, of course, and now he knew not only exactly who Guy was, but also that he had a wife and children to account for. It wouldn't have been difficult. Guy was well known in medical circles.

'I never wanted to go back to Bristol,' she said. 'I plan to make my home here. That's why I've bought a house, why I'm hoping to get Charlotte to come and live with me. And naturally I hoped I might get a partnership eventually. Yes, I admit it. But I guess that'll be out of the window now.'

He swung forward again, regarding her steadily.

'I don't think Reuben would hold it against you. Provided he's satisfied with you in every other respect.'

'Mmm.' She thought, but didn't say, that she had the very definite impression that Reuben was not entirely satisfied with her. Recently everything had seemed to be going wrong – Miss Freeman dying of pneumonia at home, not in hospital as Reuben would have preferred; the family who had defected to Dr Honeybourne at South Compton because they were unhappy about her treatment of their daughter; a hundred and one little things when she'd seen his eyebrows go up and his mouth tighten.

'I have a say in it too,' Paul reminded her.

Yes, and I alienated you by going back to Guy, she thought.

'Look, Helen, you've really got to stop crucifying yourself over Ida Lockyear,' he went on. 'It could have happened to any of us. I'd probably have come to exactly the same conclusion. We talked about her – remember? You told me all about her symptoms and I didn't cotton on either.'

'That's true . . . we did talk about her, didn't we?' Helen said, brightening a little.

'We did. And like you I thought it was nothing more serious than a case of extreme loneliness. We're doctors, Helen, not clairvoyants.'

'But if I'd visited her at home I might have realised . . .'

'Did she ask for a home visit?'

'No, but . . .'

'There you are then. You did all you could reasonably be expected to do.'

She was silent, chewing her lip.

'And now,' he said, 'I really think you should go home and try to get some rest while you can. This has been a long winter and it's not over yet. You look all in.'

'I am,' she admitted.

'Have you had anything to eat today?'

'Toast at breakfast. I didn't feel like anything at lunchtime.'

'You must eat.'

For a moment she thought he was going to suggest they got fish and chips as they had sometimes used to, and to her surprise she felt her heart lift. She'd missed him; she'd really missed him. But he didn't suggest fish and chips.

'Go home, get yourself a good supper, have a hot bath and go to bed,' he said. 'Doctor's orders.'

She smiled, wearily and a little sadly.

'OK, I will.'

'And stop worrying – right?'

'Right.'

At least, she thought, as she drove home through the dark, rain-slick streets, some good had come out of tragedy. At least she and Paul had gone some way to mending their bridges, and for that she was grateful. But to lose a patient in such a way was a high price to pay for it.

'Was there any post for me today, Mum?' Jenny asked.

Carrie, straining potatoes over the sink, kept her eyes fixed on the pan.

'Post?'

'Yes. A letter for me – from Bryn.'

Carrie gave her head a small non-committal shake.

'Haven't seen anything.'

Out of the corner of her eye she could see Jenny's face. She looked not only disappointed but worried somehow.

'You were expecting a letter, were you?' she asked ingenuously.

'Well – yes. I usually hear every two or three days. It's been five.'

Carrie snorted in a good imitation of scornful amusement.

'Five days!'

'I know it doesn't sound much,' Jenny said defensively. But it's a long time for Bryn.'

'I expect the shine's wearing off,' Carrie said.

'What do you mean?'

'It's been a bit much of it, writing every two or three days. You can't expect him to keep that up, especially when you haven't seen him for months and you hardly knew him in the first place.'

'That's an awful thing to say!'

Carrie turned to replace the saucepan on the hob and saw that Jenny's eyes had filled with tears. She experienced a pang of guilt but quickly smothered it. She'd done what she'd done for Jenny's own good. But she wished Jenny didn't have to be hurt in the process.

'Oh, I expect you'll hear by the end of the week,' she said, an attempt at comfort which came out sounding impatient. 'In the meantime, just try and forget about him. Nothing's going to come of it in the end. It won't last, Jenny.'

'Oh yes it will,' Jenny said. The tears were still glittering in her eyes and there was a small uncontrollable tremble at the corner of her mouth. But there was a certainty in her voice that made alarm bells ring in Carrie's gut. 'Oh yes it will, Mum. As far as I'm concerned, it's going to last for ever!'

Chapter Eighteen

Jenny was almost beside herself. It was three weeks now since she had heard from Bryn. And that was not the worst of it. She was horribly, sickeningly sure that she was pregnant.

The realisation had not come as a shock to her. In a strange sort of way she felt as if she had known right from the very first day. Somehow, without being able to explain it, she had felt different.

At first she had tried to explain it to herself as the result of being in love – making love for the first time – being parted from Bryn so soon afterwards. The strange niggly sensation deep inside could be nervous excitement, so might that feeling of not-quite nausea. Even missing a period could be put down to the same thing – everyone knew that tension and the like could upset a cycle. But as the days became weeks and still her period didn't come she began to acknowledge as fact what she had known all along.

At first her moods veered between dread of what Carrie would say and excitement. If she put all the practicalities to one side, the thought of having Bryn's child was actually an intoxicating one. She missed him so much! If she was pregnant they'd get married. Then they'd be together – wouldn't they? – a proper family, she and Bryn and the baby. She wasn't actually sure whether National Servicemen were allocated married quarters or not, but he wouldn't be doing National Service for ever. Somehow they'd manage to be together. It was all she wanted now, and she felt confident it was what he would want too.

Yet she mentioned nothing of this in her letters to Bryn. Several times she began to write of her suspicions, each time she tore the page up and began again. This wasn't something she wanted to commit to paper. She wanted to tell him face to face, have his immediate support and reassurance. And supposing her letter went astray or was opened by someone else? It was such a private thing, telling a man you were going to have his child. They'd talked about him coming to stay – she'd even asked Carrie about it and got a tentative agreement, but if she reneged on that, Jenny was fairly sure she could persuade Heather to allow him to stay with her. She'd wait a while. There was still plenty of time.

And then his letters stopped coming.

Every day Jenny rushed home, eagerly at first, and then with growing desperation. She kept reminding herself of those first few weeks after he'd gone, when she'd gone through the same sort of experience. It had been all right then; it must be all right now. There must be a reason for him not writing. But none of the scenarios she came up with really held water. Jenny's anxiety became so acute that she couldn't forget it for a single moment of a single day. It was with her from the moment she woke each morning, and it invaded her dreams so that they were overlaid with an aura of nightmare.

She began to feel as if she was constantly trembling – though her hands were steady, her insides felt like jelly and there was a tight knot in her stomach, a dull ache that made her think, several times a day, that her period was going to come after all. She'd rush to the toilet and sit there, willing the blood to come. Once it did – a sparse, brownish flow and she trembled again with the elation of relief. But after a few hours it tapered off again and the anxiety returned, so overwhelming she was almost crying from it.

She wrote again, begging him to get in touch, saying that she had something very important to tell him.

'You won't forget to post it, will you, Mum?' she said, propping it up against the teapot before she left to catch her bus to college.

Carrie almost always took care of the mail. She had to pass the post office on her way to work.

'Of course I won't forget,' Carrie said impatiently. 'I

don't know why you keep lowering yourself to write to him, though. You shouldn't do the chasing. It won't do you any good. Men like to make the running.'

'I'm not chasing,' Jenny objected.

'Well, that's how it looks to me. If he wants to write to you, he'll write. But I expect the truth of the matter is he's got tired of it. I expect he's met somebody else.'

Jenny didn't argue. For one thing, she didn't have time – if she didn't leave right this minute she'd miss her bus – and for another, she was beginning to wonder herself whether this might be the case.

'Will you please post it anyway?'

'All right,' Carrie agreed, 'but I think you're being very silly, Jenny.'

Jenny ran all the way down the hill and when she got to the bus stop she felt so sick she thought she was going to throw up, right there in the road.

So far she had told no-one about her predicament. When she'd mentioned to Marilyn that she hadn't heard from Bryn lately she'd received no more sympathy than she had from Carrie. Marilyn had taken much the same attitude – a sort of smug 'I told you so' which did nothing to help. What she would say if Jenny told her she was going to have a baby didn't bear thinking about. Defending to herself what she had done was one thing; explaining it to Marilyn quite another. And although she couldn't honestly say that if she had her time over it would be any different, the truth was that Jenny did feel a bit guilty and ashamed. At the very least she'd been naive and trusting, at worst easy. Neither was something she was happy about admitting to. But keeping her secret to herself made it seem all the more daunting, a huge weight she carried around with her.

That February evening as she hurried up the hill on her way home, Heather was watching out for her. As she drew level with the house, the front door opened and Heather appeared, waving and calling out. Jenny's heart sank. She was anxious to get home and see if today's post had brought her a letter.

She crossed the road and went up the steps.

'Hiya.'

'Hiya, Jen. Can you take some cakes up to Mum for me?'

'Cakes?' Jenny said blankly.

'Yes. Rock cakes. You know how Dad loves a rock cake with his sandwiches.'

'OK. You got them ready?'

'You're in a hurry tonight,' Heather said. 'They won't be a minute.'

'You mean they're not ready.'

'They'll be out of the oven any minute now. Aren't you going to come in? Gran's next door having a cup of tea with Mrs Freak. It's only me and Vanessa.'

'I suppose.'

'Well, you don't want to stay out there, do you? Come on, I want to shut the door. I'm letting all the cold in.'

Jenny went in with bad grace. The house was full of the smell of baking. It filled her with aching nostalgia for her lost childhood. Carrie hardly ever baked. But the smell also made her feel a bit sick again.

Vanessa was at her small desk, playing with plasticine.

'Auntie Jenny! I'm making a pig – look!'

'Oh yes,' Jenny said, without interest.

Heather looked at her curiously.

'What's the matter with you, Grouchy?'

'I'm not grouchy.'

'Bad day?'

'No. Stop asking me stupid questions!'

'Not grouchy, eh,' Heather said sarcastically.

'I just don't feel like talking,' Jenny said. 'I don't feel very well.' And promptly burst into tears.

'Jen!' Heather said, concerned. 'What's the matter?'

'Nothing. Nothing!'

'Something is. Come into the kitchen – come on!'

Reluctantly Jenny followed her. Heather opened the oven, took out a tray of nicely browned rock cakes and set them on the table.

'Now – tell me what's the matter.'

Jenny shook her head.

'Come on – it can't be that bad!'

'It is.'

'Well, tell me then.'

344

'No – I can't.'

'Jenny – it's *me* – Heather. I'm not Mum. Whatever it is, you can tell me.'

Jenny just cried harder, her fist pressed against her mouth.

'Oh, Jenny – don't . . . You'll make yourself ill. Please, tell me what it is!'

Jenny gulped, opened her eyes and looked at Heather over the top of her bunched fist.

'It's . . . oh, Heather, I don't know what to do.'

'I can't help you if you won't tell me, Jenny.'

It was still a few moments before she could bring herself to speak. The need to share her anxiety was intense now and Heather was just the right person. But once she'd said the words she couldn't take them back. Her secret would be out. And she was so ashamed.

'I . . . I . . .'

Heather waited.

'I . . . oh, Heather, I think I'm going to have a baby.'

Now it was Heather who was lost for words. Jenny looked at her through blurry, tear-drenched lashes and saw the look of blank shock. It was as if Heather's face had been carved in stone, frozen in the expression of concern it had worn for the past few minutes. Then she closed her eyes briefly, exhaled in an audible sigh, and became familiar, caring Heather once more.

'Oh, Jenny,' she said. And then: 'Are you sure?'

Jenny nodded. 'Almost. I haven't had a period since Christmas and I feel . . . oh, really horrid most of the time.'

'Sick?'

'Well – yes. And peculiar . . . right here.' She pressed her hands against the lower part of her abdomen.

'You haven't been to the doctor, have you?' Jenny shook her head. 'Well, there could be some other reason for it. You never know . . .' But she didn't look as if she believed it. '*Could* you be pregnant? I mean . . . have you been with anybody?'

Jenny nodded silently, the tears welling again.

'That RAF boy, I suppose,' Heather said. 'Does *he* know?'

'No – that's the other thing. That's why I'm so worried. I haven't heard from him – not for weeks now. I don't know why . . .'

Heather's mouth tightened. *I could make a good guess*, that look said.

'No!' Jenny said, anguished. 'No, you're wrong! He wouldn't do that, Heather! He wouldn't leave me in the lurch.'

'So why hasn't he been in touch?'

'I don't know! But it isn't because of the baby. I haven't told him.'

'He might have a jolly good idea,' Heather said tartly. 'He knows what he did, after all. And unless he's thick he knows what the consequences might be.'

'Oh, don't say that, Heather, please! He wouldn't! I'm sure he'd never do that.'

Heather, on the point of making a sharp retort, bit it back. Jenny was upset enough. 'I take it you haven't said anything to Mum?'

'No! She'll go mad! I don't know what she'll do . . .'

'Look,' Heather said. 'The first thing is to find out if you really are pregnant. If you're not, there's no need for Mum to even know you've been silly. I'll ring the doctor for you, see if we can make the appointment instead of having to queue up in the surgery. And I'll come with you.'

'Would you? Would you really?'

'I'll do it tomorrow. Call in on your way home and I'll tell you what I've been able to fix up. In the meantime, don't say anything to anybody. And try not to worry.'

'Oh, Heather – you're a star!'

'Oh, don't talk daft! Come on now, dry your eyes, there's a good girl. You look a fright.'

'Mum will wonder why I'm late . . .'

'Just tell her I kept you talking. But she'll know there's something the matter if you go home looking like that. So go and wash your face and then try to cheer up.'

Footfalls on the steps outside the kitchen window.

'Go on – quick now! That's Gran, coming back. I won't say anything to her, don't worry, but do go and wash your face!'

Jenny went. She felt as if a load had been lifted from her shoulders, even if only temporarily. Just sharing her worry was the most enormous relief.

Her mood lasted as she hurried up the hill, the rock cakes in a paper bag smelling good to her now. So light-hearted did she feel she could almost believe there would be a letter from Bryn waiting for her beside her plate. But there wasn't, and once again Jenny felt the sense of night-mare closing in.

She'd shared her trouble, but that didn't mean it had gone away. Heather was on her side, but not even Heather could work miracles. Nothing had really changed, except that she wasn't quite alone any more.

Helen felt a sense of foreboding as Jenny came into the surgery accompanied by her sister. She'd had it, in fact, ever since Heather had telephoned.

Not that a sense of foreboding was unusual these days. With all the things that seemed to be going wrong lately Helen, usually optimistic, had found herself half expecting the worst of any given situation. And this was certainly a little out of the ordinary. When Heather had telephoned she had asked to come in before evening surgery rather than queuing in the waiting room in the usual way, but refused to elaborate.

'You could do that,' Helen had agreed. 'Or it might be better if you came after surgery, in case I get held up with something on my afternoon rounds.'

'No – before would suit us better,' Heather had said. 'Jenny can skip her last lesson at college and get an earlier bus. We'll take a chance on you being held up.'

'If we say twenty to five then,' Helen said, 'and I'll do my best to be there.'

But intuition was working over time, putting two and two together and guessing that the reason behind the rather complicated – and on the face of it unnecessary – arrangements was so that Jenny's mother wouldn't know she had a doctor's appointment. The whole thing seemed overlaid with pitfalls of the kind she was anxious to avoid and she decided she didn't like this one little bit.

Now she swivelled round so that she was facing the patient's chair.

'Sit down, Jenny. And Heather . . . if you'd like to take a seat over there.' She indicated another chair, set a little apart.

Heather hovered, as if unwilling to be separated from Jenny by so much as a foot, let alone a yard. Then she did as Helen had asked, sitting forward, her bag clasped on her knees. Jenny, who was pale and clearly nervous, set her vanity case down beside her chair, then picked it up again, hugging it to her as if she was in need of the sense of security it gave her.

'So,' Helen said. 'What's the problem, Jenny?'

Jenny stared at her vanity case, head bent, not answering, then, as Helen waited, cast a quick pleading look at Heather without raising her head.

'She's worried,' Heather said. 'She hasn't had a period since Christmas.'

'I see. Is it unusual for you to miss periods, Jenny?'

Jenny nodded.

'I see.'

'She's afraid she might be pregnant,' Heather said, hesitant at first, then all of a rush. 'I know there can be other reasons for missing periods, but . . .'

'Could you be pregnant, Jenny?'

Again Jenny nodded. Some colour came into her pale cheeks, too hot, too low, and she looked on the verge of tears.

'OK.' Helen nodded. 'Well, you're right, of course, Heather. There could be other reasons for your periods to stop, Jenny, but if there's a possibility you might be pregnant then it would be a good idea if we checked that out first. If you'd like to hop up on the couch, Jenny.'

Jenny stood up, placing her vanity case on the chair she had been sitting in and casting another frightened look at Heather.

'Go on, Jenny,' Heather said, encouraging but unsmiling.

Helen turned her back, slipping on a pair of surgical gloves to afford Jenny some privacy whilst she undressed.

A strange consideration, in view of the fact that in a moment she would be examining her intimately but she knew that patients were often embarrassed about taking off their underclothes. When she turned back, Jenny's skirt, stockings and panties were in a neat pile on the floor beside the couch and Jenny was perching nervously on the edge, uncertain as to her next move.

'Lie down for me now and try to relax.'

As she examined Jenny, Helen's heart sank. It was, quite honestly, no more than she had expected, but she would have liked to be able to set the girl's mind at rest rather than . . .

'OK. If you'd like to get dressed, we'll have a chat.'

'Am I . . .?'

'I'm sorry. Yes. I don't think there's much doubt. I'd estimate you're about three months pregnant.'

Jenny bit her lip but said nothing.

'You're quite sure?' Heather asked.

'As I've just said, I don't think there's much doubt. I'll get some tests done, but I'm confident they'll confirm my opinion. What was the exact date of your last period, Jenny?'

Jenny told her and she made some calculations.

'I'd say your baby will probably be born around the end of August, beginning of September. The third, to pluck a date out of the air.'

Jenny was dressed now, sitting once again in the patient's chair. Her forlorn expression and the way her hands knotted tightly in her lap confirmed what Helen had suspected – this was not welcome news.

'I assume your mother knows nothing about this yet?' she said. 'And what about the father? Is he in the picture?'

'He might be,' Jenny said defensively. 'When he knows . . .'

'He doesn't know yet either.'

'No. But . . .

'He's been posted away and she hasn't heard from him for weeks,' Heather said.

'So there is no possibility of him marrying you, Jenny?'

'I don't know . . .'

'I think it's unlikely,' Heather said. 'To be honest, Doctor, she hardly knows him.'

'That's not true, Heather . . .' Jenny was becoming distressed. 'And he will write, I'm sure of it, especially when he knows.'

Helen's heart went out to her. She'd seen it all before, boys who got what they wanted and disappeared before having to face the consequences. Jenny might think he was in love with her – giving that impression, unfortunately, was all part of the game – but unless he was one in a million there was no point including him in the equation at this point.

'You're going to have to tell your mother, Jenny – or your sister is, though I think it would come better from you,' she said as gently as possible. 'Then perhaps you'll make another appointment so that I can talk to you together and we can look at the options open to you.'

'The options,' Heather said, looking at her directly.

'About where and how Jenny is going to have this baby. Whether or not she's going to keep it.'

'There's no possibility, I suppose, that she could have an . . . ?' Heather stopped mid-sentence, unable to bring herself to say the big 'A' word. Helen said it for her.

'Abortion? As far as I'm concerned, absolutely not. Quite apart from anything else, it's illegal. And it would be a very misguided person who went to the back streets to try and find someone willing to do a termination. Don't even think about it, Jenny. I've seen too many girls messed up – dead even – because they didn't heed that advice. Abortion, as far as I'm concerned, is out of the question.'

'So what are the alternatives?'

Helen looked at Heather sharply, remembering how Paul had said he was certain Vanessa was not her first child; remembering, too, her missing notes. Was Heather pretending innocence as part of an elaborate charade, intended to throw everyone – Jenny included – off the scent and conceal the fact that she had once been in a similar situation herself? Or was she asking in all seriousness because she thought things had changed since she herself had given birth to an illegitimate child?

'Well, obviously the first thing is to decide whether Jenny is going to keep the baby or have it adopted. If there really is no prospect of her marrying the father, that is. Obviously, from a purely biological point of view, keeping the baby is advantageous for Jenny, and would save her a lot of heartache. But there are the practical considerations, too, and if you tend more towards them, then you might feel it would be better off with adoptive parents. There are a lot of couples who can't have a child of their own who would jump at the chance and provide a wonderful home for a baby. If you do decide to go down that route, it may be that you would prefer to go away, to a mother and baby home, perhaps, for the birth. You'd be there in all for about three months – six weeks before the birth and six weeks afterwards.'

'Six weeks *afterwards*!' Heather said, sounding shocked. 'That seems an awfully long time!'

'Local authority homes like to give their mothers the chance to be sure that adoption is right for them. If you still want to go ahead after the six weeks is up, then it will be arranged. Of course, there are privately run homes that would accept you earlier, Jenny, and arrange for an immediate adoption, and the same would apply if you should decide to simply go into hospital from your own home, or that of a relative. But the thinking is that it can cause a lot of psychological problems if you don't at least have the opportunity to care for your baby in the first weeks of its life yourself.' She paused. 'You really do need to talk all this through with a counsellor in order to decide on the best option for you. And as I say, until you've had the chance to discuss it with your mother and your boyfriend, if you can get hold of him, it's all a bit academic. Now, I suggest you come back to see me in about a week. Give me a ring to check on the test results in a couple of days, and we'll fix another appointment. Out of usual surgery hours like this one. That would be more comfortable for you, wouldn't it?'

'Yes, Doctor. Thank you, Doctor.'

'In the meantime, try to drink plenty of milk and eat good fresh vegetables and fruit. OK now?'

Jenny nodded and once again, Heather thanked Helen. *For what?* Helen wondered. *For being the messenger of doom?*

This wasn't an ideal situation for any unmarried girl to find herself in. Knowing what Carrie could be like when roused, Helen thought that perhaps Jenny was in for as rough a time as any of them.

'Oh, Jenny!' Heather said as they left the surgery.

'I know, I know. What am I going to do, Heather?'

'Well, stop worrying for a start,' Heather said, making a big effort to pull herself together and be strong for Jenny. 'That won't do any good at all.'

'That's all very well to say! But Mum – she's going to kill me!'

'You might be surprised,' Heather said. 'Sometimes there's more to Mum than meets the eye.'

'I just don't know how I'm going to tell her!'

'Let's get this test over first. Come into my house and do it and I'll post it off for you first thing tomorrow.'

'I don't know what I'd do without you, Heather. You've been . . . the best sister in the world!'

'Don't be ridiculous,' Heather said shortly. 'I haven't done anything special. The one thing I wish I *could* do something about is that bloody Bryn!'

Heather scarcely swore. Jenny was a little shocked.

'I'm sure there's a reason for him not writing,' she said desperately.

'I'm sure there is. Not the sort of reason you're hoping, though.'

'Oh, don't say that, please!'

'You have to face facts, Jenny. The chances of him having fallen under a bus or something just aren't very high. You might as well accept it.'

'When he knows I'm having his baby, he'll stand by me. I know he will!'

Heather said nothing. It didn't seem the right moment to ask Jenny if that was what she really wanted – a shotgun wedding, a reluctant husband and father, the end of all her ambitions. Time enough for that when they knew for certain.

In her heart though, Heather, like Jenny, was already sure, and the first-hand knowledge of what Jenny had to go through made her feel sick with dread. History was repeating itself. In spite of all she and Carrie had tried to do to prevent it, Jenny was going to have to face the same dilemmas, make the same choices, none of them ideal, as she had had to face at much the same age.

And worse, whatever she decided, she would have to live with the consequences for the rest of her life.

When the last of her patients had been seen, Helen dashed home, freshened up and changed, and headed her car towards Bristol for dinner with Guy.

It would be the first time in several weeks that she had seen him and she was surprised by how unenthusiastic she felt. In the past, however much she had despised herself for it, there had always been a frisson of excitement and expectation; tonight she simply felt weary and resentful.

Why was it she who had to drive to Bristol and not the other way around? As usual, Guy's reasoning had been perfectly plausible – there were no decent restaurants in Hillsbridge, and should there be an emergency at the hospital, he would be reachable. Helen, for once, had a night off – Paul would be taking her calls – so she had no excuse to offer. But as she drove towards Bristol, straining her eyes to follow the line of the unlit road in her less-than-penetrating headlamps, she found herself thinking how pleasant it would have been to simply curl up in front of the fire with a book or the radio for company, treat herself to a long hot bath and slip between the sheets early for one of those rare unbroken nights.

Too late now, though – she'd agreed to meet Guy and she hated reneging on arrangements without good reason.

The road dipped down towards a valley which followed the line of the brook, and as Helen saw the mist lying like a layer of thick white cloud beneath her she realised what hadn't occurred to her before – the reason her headlamps seemed even less efficient than usual was that it was actually a bit foggy. Her heart sank another degree. She loathed driving in fog. Ice, snow, driving rain she could cope with, but fog was so trying – the constant dipping of the headlights, then flicking back on to full beam and back yet again to dipped as one struggled to get the best possible view of the road ahead, the way things loomed, suddenly and scarily, the disorientated claustrophobic feeling that came from not being able to pinpoint your exact progress no matter how familiar you might be with your surroundings. Fog changed everything, there were bends and curves you never normally noticed, straights that seemed to go on for ever, an alien landscape to be passed through with agonising slowness. As yet it hadn't come to that, but the signs were all there. Again Helen almost succumbed to the temptation to turn around and go home, again she kept on driving. She couldn't let Guy down because of a bit of river mist.

The restaurant was one they'd used before – it served also as the à la carte dining room for one of the most prestigious hotels in Bristol.

Helen found a space to park and went inside, fully expecting to find Guy there already. He was not. The booking had been made in his name, however, and an overly attentive maître d' showed her to a table where candelabra, fresh flowers and heavy silver adorned the starched white napery. A waiter brought her a gin and tonic and she sat sipping it rather too fast, watching the door and feeling her irritation growing. She'd driven all this way whilst he was almost literally just up the road – if she could be on time why couldn't he? But then, that was typical of Guy, always striking a pose. Sometimes it was the considerate, perfect gentleman, sometimes the busy consultant, implying by his lateness that his time was actually far more valuable than yours. So tonight it was to be the latter scenario, Helen thought, growing crosser by the minute.

She glanced at her watch, glanced up again, and there he was, handing his coat to a hovering waiter. She waited to experience the quickening of her pulses that his suavely handsome presence usually generated and felt nothing but the irritation.

'Helen – I hope you haven't been waiting too long. I was

called back – an emergency. Things are ridiculously fraught at the moment.'

'And as always you were indispensable.'

She didn't know why she'd said that; it was petty and rather stupid of her. She knew from first-hand experience there were often occasions when he *was* indispensable.

He raised an eyebrow, sat down opposite her.

'I'm sorry,' she said. 'I've had a heavy day too.'

'Well, we're both here now so you can relax. Have you looked at the menu?'

'Not yet. I've been enjoying my gin and tonic.'

'I'll have one too. A large one.' He beckoned the hovering waiter. 'A large gin and tonic and the menus.'

They ordered; Guy chose pâté de fois gras and salmon en croute. Helen found herself contrasting his choice to the plain wholesome pies and roasts that Paul loved and finding it somehow pretentious by comparison.

'It seems a very long time since I saw you, Helen,' he said, reaching across the table to cover her hand with his.

'It's only a few weeks.'

'Too long. When are you coming back to Bristol?'

'I am in Bristol. Now – this minute.'

'You know what I mean. When are you coming back for good?'

'I don't know, Guy. I'm not . . .'

And then she was thinking of all the things that seemed to be going wrong in Hillsbridge. Perhaps she would have to come back to Bristol. Perhaps she would have no choice. The hollow feeling the thought generated made her realise just how little she wanted to lose her new way of life. Fraught with problems it might be, but it was what she wanted – what she had always wanted. Not the frenetic turnover of patients at the hospital, not the abdication of sole responsibility. And certainly not formal dinners in formal restaurants with a man who somehow always managed to make her feel he was her superior, favouring her with his attention.

Oh, she was being unfair. And stupid. He'd begged her, hadn't he?

And yet the impression remained. Throughout the meal

355

Helen continued to feel uncomfortable and slightly resentful. She was not, she admitted to herself, enjoying it one bit.

'I don't think I should be too late,' she said as they drank coffee from tiny bone-china cups – Paul would irreverently compare them to eggcups, she thought.

'You're coming back to the flat.' It was a statement, not a question.

'No, actually, I don't think I am. I'll be having another busy day tomorrow and I really need a good night's sleep.'

'Oh!' He looked surprised – and hurt – that vulnerability that lurked beneath his suave confidence and which could usually make her heart turn over, showing itself. 'I thought . . .'

'Another time, Guy.'

'Helen . . .' The dark, gold-flecked eyes sought hers and again she glimpsed the vulnerability. 'You're not trying to tell me something, are you? Because if you were I couldn't bear it.'

'Guy.' She glanced round, slightly embarrassed, but the tables were set at a discreet distance apart and no-one appeared to be even remotely interested in their conversation. 'It's nothing I haven't said before.'

'Helen – I'm free now. Things are different.'

'And so am I.'

'I love you, Helen. I won't let you do this. I'm warning you . . .'

'Pay the bill, Guy. Let's go.'

'It's a terrible night, sir,' the maître d' said as he escorted them to the door. 'You haven't too far to go, I hope. The fog is very thick.'

'Not far,' Guy said shortly.

The maître d' was quite right – whilst they had been inside the fog had thickened to a dense blanket punctuated only by the faint blurred glow of the lamps which lined the drive. They floated, disembodied, in the opaque night, and there was a bite to the clammy wetness which suggested that if not already freezing, it was not far off.

'You can't drive home in this,' Guy said. 'You'll have to stay, Helen.'

'I have a surgery in the morning.'

'You can leave early. At least it would be daylight. This is lethal stuff.'

Reluctant as she was, Helen had to agree. Driving all the way home to Hillsbridge in this would not only be stressful and unpleasant, it would actually be quite dangerous. Again she found herself wishing she had never agreed to come tonight. But it was a little late now for that.

'I think you might be right,' she said.

'I know I am. Do you want to leave your car here and I'll bring you back to collect it in the morning?'

'No, I'll follow you.'

'If you're sure you can cope . . .'

'Of course I can cope! Where is your car, anyway?'

He showed her, a dark shape she was unable to recognise until she was almost right on top of it.

There was little traffic about; Helen managed to stay on Guy's tail lights through town. Though she had been to his new flat before, she thought that in this murk she might have had difficulty identifying it if she lost sight of him. The tall old houses – even the streets – looked almost identical.

She managed to park, followed him up the path and into the hallway – all elegant tiles and stained glass. His flat was up two flights of carpeted stairs where the walls were hung with framed prints. Inside, however, it was curiously bare; it had been let as partially furnished and he had not bothered to add to the decor. The omission Helen found vaguely surprising – Guy was a man who liked his comforts. She could only assume he had left all but his most personal possessions in the marital home and not got around to buying more, but the fact that he had not stamped his personality on the flat in any way gave it an odd feeling of impermanence.

He went around switching on lights – standard and table lamps whose shades had once been elegant silks but which now were faded and sad – and put a record on the radiogram, a classical piece she recognised but could not put a name to, though she thought it might be Mozart.

'Drink?'

'No, thanks. I've had enough. I'd really like to go to bed. I have to be up early in the morning to be back in time for my surgery. Where am I going to be sleeping?'

'You'd better have my room. I'm not sure if the bed in the spare room is aired. I don't think it's even made up.'

'What about you?'

'Don't worry about me.'

'But I am worried! You don't want to sleep in a damp bed either.'

'I was hoping . . .' he said, looking at her slyly, 'that perhaps you'd be prepared to share.'

'Guy . . .'

'It wouldn't be the first time, after all.'

'That was when we . . . it was different.'

'I find your attitude really odd, Helen. You were quite happy to sleep with me when I was with Marian. Yet now I'm free . . .'

She hesitated. Put like that it did sound rather ridiculous. She felt guilty, too, consigning him to either a damp, unmade-up bed or the rather cramped overstuffed sofa in his own home.

'There's sleeping with and sharing a bed with,' she said after a moment. 'If we share a bed, I want you to be quite clear it is just that.'

'I would have thought you knew me well enough to know I have never, and would never, force myself on someone who doesn't want me,' he said smoothly, but she sensed the slight smugness of triumph and experienced another qualm of misgiving.

He wouldn't force himself on her. Quite right. It wasn't his style. But when he was lying beside her, when she felt the warmth of his body as she had used to feel it, smelled the intimate blend of cologne and skin odour, heard him breathing in unison with her as always seemed to happen when they lay close, heads sharing the same pillow – how could she be sure that she would not invite him to be with her as once they had been?

She pushed the thought aside, angry with herself. Was she really so weak that after being irritated by him all

358

evening she could now even contemplate being tempted to make love? And became even angrier as she realised the answer was yes. The physical attraction between them had always been strong. It had been the instigator of their affair, now it was not beyond the bounds of possibility that it was still potent enough to rekindle a spark from the ashes.

'You realise I didn't come prepared to spend the night,' she said. 'I haven't got a toothbrush, much less a change of underwear.'

He smiled briefly.

'I think there's a new toothbrush in the bathroom cabinet. And you can borrow a pyjama jacket to wear to bed. I'm afraid I can't do anything about the underwear.'

'Do you mind if I go and find the toothbrush and use it right away?'

'Be my guest.'

She went through to the bathroom. Avocado green with matching chenille bath mats. Helen smiled to herself. Hardly Guy's style. She opened the small mirrored cabinet and the sight of his shaving brush and razor twisted more bitter-sweet chords of memory. She averted her eyes from them. There was indeed a new toothbrush, still in its plastic wrapping, on the top shelf. She pulled it and something rolled out and landed at her feet. A small black tube embossed with gold. A lipstick.

She bent automatically to pick it up but it was only when it was in the palm of her hand that the significance of it occurred to her. A lipstick. In the bathroom cabinet of Guy's bachelor flat. She slid off the cover. The lipstick was a bright shade of pink – shocking pink, the fashion columns called it. It was hollowed from use beneath its chiselled tip, but smooth and creamy still. She sniffed it. It smelled fresh and slightly perfumed, in no way stale.

She replaced it on the shelf where it had been. Her hand was trembling slightly. She tore the wrapping from the toothbrush, half expecting to find the bristles moist from recent use though she knew that was a ridiculous notion. She cleaned her teeth using Guy's toothpaste and thought that her face, reflected in the mirror, looked pale and drawn. After a moment's thought she opened the cabinet again and palmed the lipstick.

Guy was flipping through a stack of records in the storage cupboard of the radiogram. A glass of golden liquid stood on top. Brandy – his favourite nightcap, though not in one of his elegant balloon glasses now, just a cheap-looking tumbler.

'Has Marian been here?' she asked.

'Marian?' He looked at her blankly.

'Marian. Your wife.'

'Of course not.'

'No, I didn't think so.' She'd known, the moment she'd seen it, that the lipstick wasn't Marian's. She couldn't imagine Marian wearing that shade in a million years.

'What are you talking about?' Guy asked.

'This.' She opened her hand. The black and gold case lay in her palm, accusing him. 'Who does this belong to, Guy?'

She saw the flicker of guilt in his eyes before the shutters came down and it confirmed what she already knew.

'I've never seen it before,' Guy said. 'Where did you find it?'

'In the bathroom cabinet.'

'It must have been left there by a the previous tenant.'

'You are a liar, Guy,' she said.

She was angry now, as much with herself as with him. A few short minutes ago she had been contemplating sleeping with him, the man who had supposedly left his wife for her, the man she had given five years of her life to, whom she had loved so much. And all the time . . .

'You didn't leave Marian because of me, did you?' she said. 'She didn't throw you out because of me. I couldn't understand it. It didn't add up. I mean – a couple of years ago, yes. When we were . . . but not now. Not when we hadn't seen one another for months. There's been someone else, hasn't there? Someone who uses shocking-pink lipstick. Who is she?'

'Helen, I . . .' For once Guy seemed totally lost for words.

'I'll bet that hotel receipt Marian found didn't have anything to do with me either. I thought it was odd, after

360

all this time. You send your suits to the cleaners every few weeks. You can't tell me you hadn't had that particular one cleaned since we went away together. I don't believe it. There's been someone else, someone you went away with, someone who's been here.'

'And what if there has? You can't expect me to live like a monk, Helen. If you . . .'

'Come off it, Guy! It's got nothing to do with me and everything to do with you. You deceived Marian to have an affair with me, and if we were together, I'd get the same treatment. You'd have to have someone else to butter your ego.'

'That's rubbish!'

'Is it? You like a bit on the side to make life exciting, Guy. Only this time it got out of hand. Marian found out and threw you out. You didn't leave her for me. You didn't leave her at all. She just decided she'd had enough.'

'If that's what you think of me,' Guy said, cold suddenly, 'you'd better go.'

'Don't worry. I'm going.' She picked up her coat from where it lay across the back of a chair, shrugged into it, feeling in the pockets for her keys. 'Don't bother to see me out. I'll find my own way.'

'Helen.' He followed her to the door. 'You can't drive home in this fog.'

'I'll be all right.'

'If anything happened to you . . .'

'You'd never forgive yourself. I know. Don't worry, I won't lay that on your conscience, too.'

Outside the fog was as thick as ever. She got into her car, sat there for a moment, trembling. She thought she could see him silhouetted in the doorway but she couldn't be sure, didn't even want to know. God alone knew, he could probably make her change her mind and stay even now. Then the light in the hall, time controlled for three minutes after it had been switched on, went out and the house – the lower floors anyway – was in darkness.

Helen started the car and drove. She drove slowly, with all the immense concentration the appalling conditions demanded and afterwards she was never sure whether the

361

visibility was really the same for everyone that night or whether, for her, it was made worse because she was looking through a haze of tears.

The result of Jenny's tests was back on Helen's desk within forty-eight hours. As she had expected, it was positive. Heather rang during evening surgery. Helen heard the deathly silence at the other end when she passed on the news.

'Get her to come and see me as soon as possible,' she said. 'There's no point delaying things and I shall want to advise her about diet and so forth, and her entitlements.'

But brisk and cheery though she forced herself to sound, Helen was in no doubt. However she decided to play it, Jenny was in for a rough passage.

Chapter Nineteen

Jenny was living a nightmare she couldn't wake up from. A horrible all-pervading nightmare that hung around her like a shroud. At least she wasn't alone in it any more. At least she had Heather's support. But Heather couldn't work miracles. She couldn't make the nightmare end.

It could have been so different if only Bryn was with her. It wouldn't be ideal, of course. No-one actually wanted to start their life together this way – there would still be all manner of practical problems to overcome. Life would still change for ever and not necessarily for the better, Carrie would still have to be told and her disappointment and anger faced, but at least they would be together. As it was, Jenny was betwixt the devil and the deep blue sea – responsibility for deciding the future of an innocent baby on the one hand, grief at Bryn's apparent faithlessness on the other. Wherever she looked, she saw nothing but blackness; the blackness of a dark night with no hint of the promise of dawn.

Heather waylaid her on her way home that evening and Jenny could tell from the look on Heather's face that the news was bad. But didn't she know that already?

'It's positive,' she said flatly.

'I'm afraid so.' Heather's voice was equally expressionless. 'Come in for a minute, Jenny. Gran's next door again, and we need to talk.'

Glad seemed to be making a habit of having tea with Mrs Freak. The two women – both widowed – were becoming very friendly and when they weren't having tea together they were gossiping or playing cards – two-handed whist and sevens.

Jenny followed Heather in.

'She's taken Vanessa with her,' Heather said, and Jenny

guessed that Heather had wangled it so that they could be alone.

'What am I going to do?' she asked wretchedly.

'Sit down, for a start.' Heather moved a pile of gloving, packed up and ready to go back to the factory, from the sofa. 'You look awful. You're going to have to start taking care of yourself, Jenny.'

She perched on the sofa and Jenny sat beside her, hunched and miserable.

'You still haven't heard from that boy, I suppose?' Jenny shook her head. 'No, I thought not. Well, you're going to have to have this baby adopted, Jenny.'

She saw Jenny wince.

'I know . . . I know. You don't like the thought of it. But you've got to be sensible. You're sixteen years old with your whole life in front of you. You can't let this mess you up for ever.'

'I'll have finished my course before it's born,' Jenny said, grasping at straws. 'I'll be qualified as a secretary. I can get a job and . . .'

'Don't talk silly!' Heather said fiercely. 'Do you really think they'll let you sit in class when you start to show? And even if they did, even if you managed to pass your exams with all this on your mind, what then? You won't earn enough for ages to support yourself, let alone a baby too. You'd even have trouble getting a decent job, I shouldn't be surprised.'

Jenny stared at the floor. Heather was probably right; she'd thought the same thing herself, going over it and over it when she should have been practising her short forms. No employer was going to want to take on an unmarried mother with all that it implied. Certainly not the sort of employer she'd hoped for. She'd no longer be able to offer the sort of commitment they would demand, even supposing they were prepared to overlook the fact that she was a moral outcast, which they probably wouldn't. Whatever qualifications and qualities she had to offer they wouldn't be enough to make up for the stigma.

'You're sixteen years old,' Heather said again, emphasising each word. 'There's no way you can bring up a baby

364

on your own. It wouldn't be fair on either of you. And I know Mum will say the same when you tell her.'

Again Jenny cringed.

'You know what she's going to want, don't you? She's going to want this kept quiet. She won't want anyone to know you've let yourself down.'

'You mean she's going to want me to go away to one of those homes the doctor talked about,' Jenny said.

She didn't need to be told that, either. It was something else she'd thought about – forced herself to think about – Carrie's reaction. She couldn't hope for any support from Carrie, she knew. She could remember all too clearly the fuss there had been when Heather had had to get married in a hurry – and she had been grown-up, with a steady boyfriend prepared to stand by her.

'I know all that,' Jenny said wretchedly. 'But I just don't know if I can do it, Heather. *My* baby – mine and Bryn's.'

'Never mind him!' Heather said, and there was something of Carrie in the harshness of her tone. 'It's *you* we're talking about – *your* future – your whole life! You can't throw it all away. You're going to be a journalist, remember?'

'That was before . . .'

'And it will be again.'

'No,' Jenny said. 'All I want now is to marry Bryn and keep the baby.'

'Oh, Jenny, that isn't going to happen.'

'But to give my baby up! Never see it again!'

'Look – I've been thinking.' Heather twisted on the sofa so that she was directly facing Jenny. 'There is a way.'

Jenny's eyes, full of hope, met hers.

'What?'

'If I pretended it was mine.'

'You!'

'It could work,' Heather rushed on. 'If I started telling people I was pregnant, made myself fatter – you know, padded myself out . . .'

'Heather!'

'I don't see many people. I'm sure I could get away with it. Then I'd go off on holiday – the baby is due in the

365

summer – pretend it had come early . . . I honestly don't think anyone would be any the wiser. There might be a few questions asked, but they'd soon forget it.'

'You mean . . . *you'd* bring my baby up as if it were yours?'

'That's exactly what I mean. You'd be able to watch it grow up.'

'Thinking *you* were its mother!'

'Yes.'

'And I was just its auntie!' The horror was in her voice, written all over her face.

'Isn't that better than giving it up to a stranger? Never seeing it again? Never knowing what it looked like – whether it was happy, well, dead or alive even? You'd *be there*, Jenny. At least you wouldn't lose it altogether. Wouldn't that be better?'

'No!' Jenny said. She was shaking all over, trembling with the fiercest emotion she had ever experienced. 'I think it's a terrible idea! I don't know how you could even think of such a thing!'

'I'm thinking of *you*, Jenny. And the baby. And yes, me too. I don't want this baby to go to strangers any more than you do. Because . . .'

She reached for Jenny's hands; Jenny snatched them away.

'I can't believe you're suggesting this! *My* baby – thinking *you* were its mother! Just imagine what it would be like! I'd have to watch it come to you instead of me. I wouldn't have a single say in how it was brought up.'

'Of course you'd have a say! I'd make sure you did.'

'No!' Tears were pricking her eyes. 'I thought you were going to say you'd help me – look after the baby while I went to work or something. That would have been fine.'

'Mum would never have that. People knowing you had an illegitimate baby. The shame would kill her.'

'And it would kill *me* if my baby grew up thinking you were its mother. What do you take me for? What sort of person could do something like that?'

Heather turned away. She looked older suddenly, haunted and sad. There were tears in her eyes too.

'It was only an idea, Jenny. I didn't mean to upset you.

But think about it. Please. And talk to Mum. See what she says. You've got to talk to her, anyway. She's got to be told.'

'Don't you think I know that?' The tears spilled over and ran down Jenny's cheeks as the terror of telling Carrie eclipsed all else once again. 'I'd better go, Heather. She'll be wondering where I am.'

'So tell her now. Tell her tonight.'

'I'll try.'

She meant to. She really meant to. But when it came to the point she couldn't. There was always some reason for putting it off. Just as she'd screwed up the courage something would happen to prevent her going ahead – David or her father would come in, or one of Carrie's customers from the Kays Club she ran would come to the door with their weekly contribution or to pick up a parcel. There were twenty customers – well, twenty 'turns' anyway to cover the twenty weeks; some people, Carrie herself included, had two turns – so the Club caused a lot of comings and goings. But even when the house was quiet and Carrie was on her own in the kitchen, Jenny lost her nerve at the last minute.

Once the words were said they could never be unsaid. Jenny went cold, literally, when she imagined them leaving her lips, and the thought of Carrie's reaction filled her with dread. She remembered all the times she had incited her mother's wrath, and realised she was afraid of Carrie. Not physically, of course – she could only remember Carrie ever striking her once – a slap on the back of her legs when she was about five or six. Carrie had been wound up about something and Jenny kept dancing around, annoying her, and refusing to keep still. Jenny remembered the occasion very well simply because it *had been* an occasion – the day Carrie had slapped her. The one and only. But Carrie had other ways of showing her displeasure that were far worse, in Jenny's experience, than a slap. The sending to Coventry, the cold tone of displeasure when she did speak, the way she had of making you feel that to go against her was a personal affront which hurt her deeply. Basically she was a good mother, strict but kind and generous, always ready to do almost too much for you, so that when she made it plain you'd upset her you felt so horribly guilty. So horribly, terribly, dreadfully guilty. Jenny loved Carrie very much and respected her and she wanted Carrie's love and respect in return. How much of either could she count on when she confessed to that most heinous of sins – 'Letting herself down'.

And so she put the moment off, praying all the while that she would get a letter from Bryn, though hope had faded now, and let in despair.

She wrote one more time, to tell him she was pregnant, and gave it to Carrie to post. She hated herself for what he might see as blackmail on her part but she told herself he had a right to know – and admitted privately that was just an excuse for this one last attempt to get a response from him. If it didn't work this time, she promised herself, she wouldn't humble herself by writing again. Or contacting him. And if, when she told Carrie, her mother wanted to know where to find him so as to make him face up to his responsibilities, she wouldn't tell. Unless, of course, Carrie already had the address copied down somewhere. Jenny wouldn't put that past her.

But she wouldn't willingly allow Bryn to be forced into anything. Frightened and wretched though she might be, she felt that somehow it was her problem and hers alone.

In moments when she felt strong, Jenny made herself a promise. Whatever happened, she'd manage. Somehow.

Helen was beginning to be concerned. It was more than two weeks now since she had confirmed Jenny's pregnancy to Heather and asked that Jenny should make an appointment to see her, but so far that hadn't happened. There had been no word from any of the Simmons family. Helen wondered how long she should let it go on before she did something about it. She was anxious to examine Jenny properly, give her advice about her ante-natal care, help work out some plan of campaign. Mother and baby homes got very booked up – if they didn't soon do something about it, she might have difficulty finding Jenny a place. But the situation was delicate to say the least. Presumably Carrie didn't yet know, or she would have been in the surgery banging the table and having her say, if Helen knew anything about it.

Which meant she was sitting on a time bomb and whatever she did or didn't do, was likely to upset at least one of her patients. If she spoke to Carrie she could be accused of breaking Jenny's confidence; if she didn't she could be seen as colluding with Jenny to hide the facts from her parents with whom she still lived and who were still, in some areas, legally responsible for her.

The law of majority was a total mess, Helen decided. You could marry at sixteen with the permission of your parents or the courts but had to wait another year before ceasing to be a child in legal terms; you could fight – and die – for your country at eighteen but not vote or come into an inheritance until you reached the magic age of twenty-one.

A total mess. And where did it leave her? Helen decided this was a case which could benefit from being discussed with at least one of her partners. But first she wanted to get over the other thing that was hanging over her head like the sword of Damocles. The inquest on Ida Lockyear.

It took place on a Wednesday afternoon at the beginning of March in the room in the Victoria Hall which was used as a magistrates' court. Helen, who had been called to give evidence as she had expected, arrived early, smartly dressed in a grey costume with a pleated skirt and a small fitted jacket, and wearing, for once, a hat. It was only a small hat – scarcely more than a band of felt and feathers – but it clipped tightly just above her ears and made her feel uncomfortable. She left it on, nevertheless, feeling that the solemnity of the occasion warranted it, just as it warranted a pair of wrist-length cotton gloves.

Helen took her seat in the front row of chairs which were lined up facing the bench and waited. She nodded to the policeman who had attended the scene, PC Dowding, and to Charlie Gregory, the baker man, and Annie Tiley. Walter Evans, the *Mercury* reporter, was already installed too, with a notebook on his knee and an expectant expression on his rather red face. He looked as if he was in two minds as to whether or not to come over and speak to her and Helen dissuaded him by looking away. She looked away, too, when a man and woman she guessed were Ida's son and daughter-in-law came in. The man looked to be in his middle forties, slightly built, and wearing a dark suit which, judging by its cut, had been bought for his wedding twenty or more years ago, a white nylon shirt, a cheap black tie and a black band fastened around his arm just above the elbow. The woman, too, had made some effort to appear in mourning. She wore a tight black costume which pulled uncomfortably round her bosom and stomach. Both wore sombre expressions.

Perhaps, Helen thought, the grief concealed guilt. If they had visited more often and made sure Ida's home was safe for her to live in she might not have died. But the thought only served to stir up her own feelings of guilt. Whatever Ida's son might or might not have done, it was she, Helen, who had been Ida's doctor. She had been on the spot when they had not and she had misinterpreted Ida's calls for help.

At precisely two o'clock, the policeman standing guard at the second door – the one nearest to the bench – opened it, peeped round, and cleared his throat.

'All rise for HM Coroner.'

The coroner's name was Harvey Benson. He was a small rotund man with a fringe of hair surrounding a shiny dome, and with a pair of half-glasses perched precariously on the end of his rather bulbous nose.

Harvey Benson liked his courts to be as informal as possible. Chatting to witnesses rather than interrogating them was much the best way to get to the truth, in his opinion. He said as much as he opened the proceedings and, as each witness added a little more to the story, Helen thought he was probably right.

'What do *you* think happened?' he would ask conversationally, sitting back in his chair and looking over the top of his glasses, and one by one they opened up, putting flesh on the bare bones of the tragedy.

Helen, however, did not escape so lightly. As he questioned her she felt his censure; benign he might appear, but Harvey Benson had no patience with professionals who failed to do their job properly.

'So the symptoms were all there,' he said when Helen explained how Ida had come to the surgery.

'They were.'

'But you didn't diagnose them as carbon monoxide poisoning.'

'No. With hindsight I should have done, but as you yourself know, all these complaints could be attributed to a number of other things, from influenza to depression. They could even have been imagined.' She felt bad saying that, casting aspersions on Ida's character when she was not there to defend herself.

'So you dismissed Mrs Lockyear as a hypochondriac.'

'She had a history of hypochondria, yes. But I didn't dismiss her. I ran every test I could think of to determine what was causing her symptoms and drew blanks on every one.'

'But you didn't do a test for carbon monoxide poisoning.'

'No. I have to admit it never occurred to me. I wish it had – but it didn't. I find it very difficult to accept that if it had occurred to me, I could probably have saved Mrs Lockyear's life.'

For the first time Harvey Benson seemed to relent.

'Don't be too hard on yourself, Doctor. You're not the first to miss something like that and you won't be the last. Without inside knowledge of Mrs Lockyear's circumstances you couldn't reasonably be expected to consider carbon monoxide poisoning. It is, after all, very unusual. Indeed, in my experience, rare indeed. I don't think that any blame can reasonably be attached to you.'

'Thank you,' Helen said. But it didn't actually make her feel any better. She could have saved Ida's life and she hadn't. A fatal mistake. A professional failure. Simple as that.

Eventually all the witnesses had been heard and the coroner summed up.

371

'In all circumstances, I find that Mrs Lockyear's death was accidental.'

Helen stared at her hands, knotted together around her black cotton gloves in her lap. She was enormously relieved but it did nothing to ease the sense of guilt. She got up, turning away from Walter Evans, who was heading in her direction, and walked past the rows of seats to the rear door without looking to left or right. As she stepped out into the small lobby, a voice behind her said: 'Just a minute.'

She turned, not sure whether it was she who was being spoken to. Ida Lockyear's son, Clarence, was behind her, his wife behind him.

'You got away with it then,' he said.

'I beg your pardon?'

'You got away with letting my mother die.'

'I'm sorry . . .' she began.

'And so you should be! If you'd treated her properly she'd be alive today. You should be struck off!'

'Mr Lockyear . . .' The viciousness of the attack had made her begin to tremble. 'You heard what the coroner said . . .'

'Oh yes, I heard all right. He covered up for you. You lot all stick together, don't you? I shouldn't have expected anything different. Well, I'm not leaving it there. My mother is dead because of you.'

'Now just a minute.' There was someone else at the doorway behind the Lockyears. As she recognised the familiar voice, Helen started with surprise. Paul! She hadn't realised he had been in the court. He must have been in one of the back rows, hidden behind others. Now, in spite of his smart suit and tie, he looked for all the world as he must look to the attacking forwards on the rugby field – solid and rather threatening.

Ida's son hesitated, taken by surprise. Then, like a terrier squaring up to an Alsatian, he snapped: 'Mind your own business!'

'It is my business. That's my colleague you are talking to.'

'Oh – another of the clique!' the man sneered. 'You

372

should be ashamed, all of you.'

'Didn't you hear what the coroner said?' Paul said tartly. 'He exonerated Dr Hall of blame. There was no way she could have been expected to know your mother's boiler was emitting toxic fumes. The verdict was accidental death.'

'Negligence, more like.'

'On whose part?' Paul asked.

'Well – hers, of course.'

'Perhaps,' Paul said smoothly. 'I should point out that the coroner also said that if the boiler had been properly maintained, this tragedy would never have occurred.'

'My mother was an old woman!'

'Exactly. So don't you think there might be others who had a duty of care to make sure the house was safe for her to live in?'

'What a thing to say!' That was Mrs Lockyear junior, determined to put her oar in. 'My husband has just lost his mother and you're trying to put the blame on him!'

'Not at all. But I think, don't you, that we should all accept a share of responsibility for what happened. When did you last visit your mother, for instance?'

'I'm a busy man!' Clarence Lockyear retorted. 'I can't keep driving up and down from London.'

'And Dr Hall is busy, too. She has a great many patients besides your mother to look after. She can't be expected to do the things one would normally expect members of the immediate family to do. For our part, I assure you we regret what happened very much, and lessons will be learned. But it's totally wrong to try to shift the blame for what happened on to Dr Hall. She did her very best for your mother.'

'And it wasn't good enough,' Mrs Lockyear junior was determined to have the last word. 'Trying to blame my Clar! I never heard the like!'

'I think we shall have to leave it there,' Paul said. 'If you wish to make a complaint to the GMC then of course you have every right to do so.'

'And what good would that do? They'd stick up for you lot just the same!'

'They would look at the facts and come to a balanced conclusion,' Paul said, adding, with emphasis: 'Just as the coroner did.' He touched Helen's arm. 'Shall we go?'

She was shaking from head to foot.

'Oh my God, Paul, that was awful!'

'It was guilt, Helen. He feels guilty and he's trying to shift the blame so as to ease his conscience. He hasn't been near his mother for months.'

'But he had a point. I should have known, Paul. I should have taken it further.'

'We've been through this before, Helen.'

'And I still feel terrible about it.'

'Look.' He took her arm. 'From time to time, Helen, you are going to miss something.'

'Misdiagnose, you mean.'

'If you'd known about the boiler, you wouldn't have misdiagnosed. You need facts to help you, otherwise you're only guessing – taking shots in the dark. You ran every test I'd have run and they all came up negative. Unfortunately it never occurred to you to run the one test that might have uncovered the truth.'

'And my patient died.'

'Little as we may like it, we have to accept it. We're human beings, Helen, not God Almighty, all seeing, all wise, whatever our patients might like to think.'

'At this moment I feel like chucking it all in and doing something where lives aren't at stake.'

'Don't talk such nonsense. You're an excellent doctor. Think of all the lives you've *saved*.'

'Right now I can only think of the one I lost. You don't know how I feel, Paul.'

He was silent for a moment. Then he said:

'Believe me, Helen, I do know. I lost a patient once because I missed something. A young woman, with a young family. She had a three-month-old baby when she came to me complaining of a painful lumpy breast. I diagnosed mastitis; she took my word for it. She didn't come back to me for another six months. By that time it was obvious to me that it wasn't mastitis. She had breast cancer. Raging breast cancer. I sent her straight to hospital and they operated but it was too late. The cancer had spread to her lymph system and her spine. The baby was fifteen months old when she died, and her other children two and four years old. It's a long time ago now. Her husband remarried and her children are all at secondary school. But I've never forgotten her, never stopped blaming myself for not spotting what was wrong in the first place and not following up to make sure the "mastitis" had cleared up. If I'd been on the ball I might have been able to save her life. But I wasn't and she died, aged just twenty-nine. So you see, Helen, I do know exactly how you feel.'

'Oh God,' Helen said. 'I'm sorry, Paul. But . . .' she laughed bitterly, 'it doesn't actually help. It only makes the point even more clearly the awful things that can happen if we mess up.'

'It comes with the territory,' Paul said. 'You have to put it behind you and go on. Hopefully you learn from your mistakes. And the job has its compensations. If we weren't doing it, putting our own necks on the block, a lot more people would die.'

'Well at the moment my neck feels very vulnerable indeed.'

'I'm sure it does. But ride out the storm, Helen. You'll get over it.'

'I certainly hope so,' Helen said.

They were back at the surgery now.

'Why did you come to the inquest?' she asked suddenly. 'I didn't know you were there.'

He smiled crookedly.

'I thought you could do with a little moral support. And now, if I'm not mistaken, you could do with a large drink.'

'I could, but I've still got a surgery to take.'

'Afterwards?' he said. 'Would you like to meet up for a drink afterwards?'

She nodded. It was only later that the thought occurred to her; perhaps some good had come out of this whole horrible business. At least she and Paul were back on good terms. Of that she was very glad. But even thinking that she might have benefitted in some way from Ida's death made her feel guilty all over again. Helen thought that it would be a very long time before she was able to put it behind her.

Carrie stared at the letter Jenny had asked her to post for her and felt her stomach churning. Jenny was going to have a baby. There it was, in black and white, in Jenny's own handwriting.

I knew it! Carrie thought. *I knew there was something wrong with her! Oh, the stupid, stupid girl! After all I did to try and make sure something like this didn't happen, the minute I let her have a bit of rope she goes and hangs herself with it.*

As she so often did when she needed to settle herself down, Carrie went into the kitchen and put the kettle on. A cup of tea was definitely called for.

One of Jenny's Pitman magazines lay on the table and Carrie flipped it open. The page was filled with lines of symbols for translating. They meant nothing to Carrie but Jenny was good at it, she knew. It was unthinkable that all that should go to waste. And it might very well do, even now, if she posted the letter. The boy might stand by her and Jenny would end up in married quarters somewhere, tied to a husband she hardly knew and a baby to bring up when she was scarcely more than a baby herself.

But why hadn't she said something? She'd been going around looking like a wraith these last few weeks and Carrie had known deep down that it was more than simply heartache over that boy. There had been times when she'd almost confessed – Carrie could see it now – the times when she'd hovered, looking nervous as well as wretched, trying to summon up the courage to begin, most likely.

It's a good job I decided to have a look, Carrie thought, justifying to herself the appalling invasion of privacy she had committed. *It's a good job I didn't just put it in the drawer with the others. Goodness only knows when I'd have found out the truth if I'd done that.*

She reread the letter and in spite of herself, in spite of everything, felt a stab of sympathy. Jenny was obviously going through hell. But then, you couldn't expect to have your fun and not pay for it. Jenny wasn't the first young girl to find that out and she wouldn't be the last. *Stupid, stupid girl!* she thought again, angry now as well as upset. *No wonder she was so anxious to get in touch with him.*

Briefly she asked herself if she had done the wrong thing keeping them apart. Perhaps she had. She'd asked herself the same question more than once over the weeks, but somehow her course of action had been like a snowball rolling down a mountain slope and gathering its own momentum until it became an avalanche.

After the first time when she'd hidden Bryn's letter to Jenny, it had been easy, too easy, to hide the next, and to refrain from posting Jenny's letters to him too. The first guilt had been swallowed up in what had become a crusading spirit – it was for Jenny's own good. When she thought it was over she'd forget him, get on with her life, and then, one day when the time was right, meet someone more suitable. Carrie could see it clearly in her mind's eye – Jenny with a good job, marrying some nice local boy.

By the time she saw how unhappy Jenny had become and experienced a few more pangs of conscience it really was too late to change her mind. One letter might go astray – a whole series of them, in both directions . . . well, you didn't have to be a Scotland Yard detective to work out that was highly unlikely. She'd worried about it a bit, imagining them comparing notes, putting two and two together and making four. And then the boy's letters had stopped coming and she'd begun to breathe more easily. That was it, then. All she had to do was wait for the dust to settle and things to get back to normal.

And now this. Carrie stared at Jenny's letter, feeling as if she was being carried along by a flood tide over which she had no control.

What now?

Again the thought occurred to her that if she posted this letter the boy might yet come back on the scene and Carrie couldn't see that it would really solve anything. Simply make complications.

I don't want her tied down yet, Carrie thought. *That's not what I want for her. She's worth more than that. We'll work something out. We did before. Look at Heather now – really happy. It would have been a very different story if she'd ended up with that no-good lad in Bristol who got her into trouble. And our Jenny's got an even brighter future in front of her. We worked it out then and we'll work it out now. Ourselves. As a family.*

The other letters she had omitted to post were hidden in her underwear drawer. Just in case she should change her mind. But this one . . .

The contents were so abhorrent to Carrie she couldn't bear for them to exist, even. She tore the letter into little pieces and threw them on to the living-room fire.

Then she made herself that much-needed cup of tea and sat down to work out what she was going to do next.

She tackled Jenny that same evening – no sense letting things go on any longer. David was out with his friends – since his lonely Christmas, which, to Carrie's surprise seemed to have done him good, he'd taken to going out on a Friday night with the same crowd he used to get about with before he married Linda – and when Joe put on his muffler and went out for his pint at the Working Men's Club, she and Jenny were alone.

Carrie pulled up the fireside chair so she was facing the one where Jenny was supposedly reading – supposedly since Carrie hadn't seen her turn the page once. She got her knitting out of her tapestry work bag and clicked her needles for a few moments. Jenny was staring down at her book, chewing her lips. Her eyes flicked up once, and when they met Carrie's she looked quickly away.

'Is there something you want to talk to me about, Jenny?'

Jenny's eyes flicked up again, full of apprehension.

'What do you mean?'

'I think it's time you and I had a little chat, don't you? Come on, Jenny, you might as well tell me the truth.'

Jenny had gone very red.

'You . . . know?'

'I've got a fair idea.'

'Did Heather tell you?'

'Heather?' Carrie was shocked. 'Does *Heather* know about this?' Jenny did not answer and Carrie thought quickly. She didn't like the idea that Jenny had talked to

378

Heather behind her back, but if she had and if she thought Heather had talked to her, then she wouldn't wonder how Carrie had known. 'I want to hear it from you,' she said.

'Oh, Mum, I'm so sorry . . .'

'You're in trouble, aren't you? You're going to have a baby.'

Jenny nodded.

'Oh, Jenny, how could you let yourself down like that?'

'I'm really sorry . . .'

'It's a bit late for sorry, isn't it? I tried and tried to stop something like this happening. I've seen it coming ever since you . . .' She broke off. There was no way she could say what she meant – ever since Jenny had lost her puppy fat and turned into an attractive young woman. To say that would be to admit she had been something of an ugly duckling before, something Carrie had always strenuously denied. And in any case, it wasn't strictly true. She'd seen it coming for much longer than that. Getting pregnant outside marriage wasn't the prerogative of attractive girls. Quite often it was the plain ones, the fat ones, the ones with low self-esteem who wanted so desperately to be loved that they fell into the trap of giving themselves to the first man who paid attention to them. No, it had nothing to do with looks and everything to do with personality and character, and right from the word go Jenny had been a prime candidate, even leaving aside the wild streak that must be in her genes as it was in Heather's.

'Well, it's no use crying over spilt milk,' Carrie said shortly. 'What's done is done. But we'd better get some plans made – and made soon. You don't want to be still round here when you start to show.'

'But . . .'

'You don't want to get yourself talked about, do you? You want to be able to walk down the street with your head held high. You've done so well and everybody round here thinks you're a nice girl. We don't want them knowing any different, do we? Then, when it's all over, you can come back and go on as if nothing had happened. That's much the best thing.'

Jenny wanted to argue, wanted to demand some say in what happened. It was her body, after all, her baby. But the habit of the years was too strong. Carrie had always been the one who made the decisions. She knew best, or so she thought, and the rest of the family accepted her own valuation.

Besides . . . if Bryn were here, Jenny thought, she'd find the strength from somewhere to fight her mother. But Bryn wasn't here. He had deserted her when she needed him most. The only person she could rely on to help her sort out this whole terrible mess was Carrie.

'Is that you, Joe?' Carrie called out as she heard the front door closing. She knew it was, of course – who else would it be at this time of night? – David was usually much later than this. In any case, Sally had been waiting by the door for the last five minutes – she always seemed to know instinctively when Joe turned the corner of the road.

'It's me, m'dear,' yes.' Joe came in, unbuttoning his sports coat – he had already taken off his overcoat in the hall and hung it on the bannister.

'Oh, I'm so glad you're home,' Carrie said. She was sitting in the fireside chair, but her knitting lay in the tapestry bag beside her, the needles sticking out untidily, and a ball of wool had rolled out on to the floor unnoticed.

'Whatever is the matter?' Joe asked.

Carrie shook her head in distress. 'Something terrible's happened, Joe. I don't know how to tell you. It's our Jenny. She's got herself in trouble.'

'Our Jenny? No!' Joe's placid face furrowed.

'Yes. I got it out of her tonight. That RAF boy's the father.'

'Oh dear, oh dear!' He could see now why Carrie was so upset – he was upset, too. Jenny was the apple of his eye; this was the last thing he'd have expected.

'She'll have to have it adopted,' Carrie said. 'There's nothing else we can do.'

'D'you really think so? Couldn't we . . .?'

'No!' Carrie said shortly. 'I've been thinking about it ever since I found out, and it's the only way. But oh, my goodness, this is something I could have done without!'

'What about the boy? Perhaps if he knew he'd . . .'

'Marry her? Is that what you want for her, Joe? I know I don't! No, it's far the best that she has it adopted and tries to make a fresh start.'

'Well, I suppose you know the best, m'dear,' Joe said. He was too shaken by the news to argue with Carrie. Truth to tell, he didn't even want to think about it. His little Jenny – pregnant at sixteen. He'd seen her blossom, taken a quiet pride in the way she'd turned out, but he'd never thought it would turn out like this, not even knowing as he did what boys that age were like. He'd thought his Jenny was too special for something like this to happen. Now the taste of the beer he'd drunk at the club turned sour in his mouth, making him feel sick.

'I'll start sorting it out tomorrow,' Carrie said. 'It's not going to be any picnic, mind. Not for any of us.'

Joe said nothing. He couldn't bring himself to. But Carrie was certainly right there – this certainly wasn't going to be any picnic.

As good as her word, next day Carrie made an appointment to see Helen to discuss options. The day after that she contacted a social worker. By the time the week was out she had arranged for Jenny to go to a Catholic-run mother and baby home, not six weeks before the birth, but three months. Jenny would work there, helping out in the kitchen and doing domestic chores. The Church would arrange an immediate adoption so that Jenny could be back in Hillsbridge within two weeks of the birth. The home was within the catchment area for a secretarial college – if she could manage to continue her studies on her own initiative, she would be able to sit her examinations there.

Jenny went along with it all, numbed by the enormity of what was happening to her, regressing, almost, to the child she had so recently been – submissive, anxious to make amends, wanting only to be told what she should do. Heather made no further mention of taking on the baby herself but the fact that she had suggested it and Jenny's

381

violent reaction to the plan made an awkwardness between the sisters for a while.

As for Joe, he withdrew into himself, spending more time than ever pottering in the garden and in his shed. At the moment, it upset him just to look at Jenny, for seeing her reminded him that his innocent little girl had gone for ever. Jenny found his absence hurtful, but instinctively she understood, and was almost grateful, for she was as embarrassed in his presence as he was in hers. They both needed time to come to terms with what had happened – was happening – but she was in no doubt but that when the chips were down he would be there for her as he always had been. For the moment, he needed to do nothing. Carrie had taken charge, as she always did.

Chapter Twenty

'Haven't you done with those steps yet, Jennifer?'

Jenny sat back on her heels, tucking a strand of hair behind her ear with damp puffy fingers as Sister Anne bore down on her. The strand of hair felt lank and needed cutting but she had resisted letting the sisters get their hands on it. She'd seen how they 'barbered' the other girls' hair – a pair of scissors that were practically shears and a pudding basin. A visit to a proper hairdresser was out of the question, so she scraped it back with a rubber band and hoped they wouldn't notice it was longer than the regulations insisted upon.

'I've nearly finished, Sister.'

'Get on with it then. That's the trouble with you girls – you're born lazy. If you'd been brought up properly and taught how to keep yourselves busy you wouldn't be in the mess you're in now.'

Jenny wished she dared answer back, retort that she wasn't lazy, just tired, tired, tired – more drained and exhausted than she'd ever been in her life – and bending double over a scrubbing brush gave her a cramp in the stomach, but she knew better than to argue. It did more harm than good. The sisters – especially Sister Anne – had ways of punishing girls who were insubordinate or cheeky and the sisters were all-powerful. The best course of action was to remain meekly silent and try to ignore the unfair and hurtful things they said. But inwardly Jenny burned with resentment.

Though her family hadn't been practising Catholics for years she had been brought up to respect the Church and to think of nuns as gentle, kindly creatures who spent their days on good works or in prayer. As far as this lot were concerned nothing could be further from the truth. Most of them were hard and cold, embittered perhaps by their proximity with a procession of young girls who had achieved what they never could – motherhood.

To them, these girls were sinners, wild girls, wicked girls, girls with no morals, girls who had brought disgrace on themselves and their families. They had cheapened themselves, desecrated the temple of their bodies, lost the precious gift of their virginity in some back alley for a few moments' pleasure – or because they were so lacking in moral fibre they had been unable to refuse some greedy man his pleasure. They had not only let themselves and their families down, they had let down their sex, if not the whole of humanity. They were the damned, and the Sisters were determined not to let them forget it.

The penances they extracted were harsh. To those who complained they would reply, with the fierce zeal of the evangelist, that they were saving souls. And perhaps they believed they were doing just that, Jenny thought – but oh! how they enjoyed the process! Jenny hated them, every one, with the possible exception of Sister Agnes, old and wrinkled as a walnut, frail as a sparrow, who worked in the kitchen and seemed kindly. But Jenny didn't think Sister Agnes would be at the home much longer. The others were impatient with her, and Jenny guessed they thought she lacked the authority to deal with the constant stream of fallen girls. If she didn't die first, Sister Agnes would probably be sent off to a convent before long. And then there would be only the wardress nuns, as Jenny thought of them, for they reminded her more than anything of prison warders.

She had been here now for a month and hated every last moment of it. Up until that time she had continued going to college, wearing a tight strapping under bloused dresses that Carrie made for her to hide what there was of her bulge. Not that there *was* much, just a thickening around her waist, too high to shout pregnant from the roof tops, and on her mother's instructions Jenny simply moaned to everyone that she was getting fat. Whether the deception had worked she wasn't sure – Marilyn in particular, had given her some odd looks – and she wondered if when she

384

had disappeared suddenly from the scene on the pretext of illness and a necessary recuperation with relatives at Bournemouth, they had guessed the real reason. But it scarcely mattered. Bath was eight miles away from Hillsbridge and it was very unlikely that anyone would ever know for sure.

And so she had come to the home, driven there by Steve and accompanied by Carrie. Jenny thought that the loneliest moment of her life had been when she had watched them drive away, leaving her with her pitifully small attaché case in the echoey entrance hall.

Sister Anne had been briskly reassuring whilst Carrie was still there.

'Don't worry about her, Mrs Simmons. She'll be all right with us.'

But the moment they had gone her manner changed.

'Right then, Miss. I'll lay down the ground rules for you. We stand no nonsense here, and the sooner you realise that the better.'

Jenny shared a dormitory with three other girls. One, Lisbee Smith, cried herself to sleep each night; another, Pauline Warren, was what Carrie would have described as hard as nails; and the third, Myra Cottle, gave birth to her baby a week after Jenny arrived at the home. As long as she lived, she would never forget Myra's moans, and the cruel way Sister Anne spoke to her.

'Now you see what you get for being wicked. The pains of hell. All I hope and pray is that you have learned your lesson.'

Myra was left for hours in the dormitory, examined from time to time (unnecessarily roughly, Jenny thought) by Sister Claude, who was supposed to be a midwife, but who reminded Jenny of a man in drag. Jenny suspected it was done on purpose to frighten the other three girls as much as to punish Myra and if this was indeed the case, the nuns succeeded. Eventually, in the small hours, Sister Claude pronounced the time right and Myra was made to walk to the waiting ambulance carrying her own bag and stopping every few paces to double up in pain. Then days later she was back – alone. Sister Anne never left her side

385

whilst she fetched her belongings and waited for her parents to collect her, and there was no opportunity for any of the girls to talk to her. But word was that the baby had been taken by his new adoptive parents direct from the hospital.

The brush with the reality of what was to come frightened and upset Jenny. She felt utterly helpless and completely at the mercy of these people who had taken charge of her life and her future. They made the decisions here – she and the other girls were moved about like pawns on a chessboard.

Although she had thought it had been agreed she could take her exams in shorthand and typewriting, Sister Anne had quickly disillusioned her. She gave no real explanation as to why it would not be possible and Jenny was too intimidated to press her. Though disappointed, Jenny was not totally disheartened. She could always take her exams in November when this was all over, and she would be better prepared then. It wasn't like O levels, where the set books and curriculum changed each year – Pitman's shorthand would still be Pitman's shorthand in six months' time, and typing would still be typing. Besides, she didn't have the opportunity to keep her speed up now, or the energy to study. The hard manual work she was expected to do saw to that.

From morning to night, it seemed, the nuns kept Jenny and the others busy. There were potatoes to peel, dishes to wash, stacks of bed linen to be ironed. There were acres of floorboards to polish, dozens of statues of the Blessed Virgin, Saint Joseph and the other saints to be dusted, hundreds of candles to be trimmed. And worst of all were the flagstone floor and steps which had to be scrubbed daily. Although it was summer, the weather was unseasonably wet – it rained almost every day and no-one coming in seemed to wipe their feet properly. Already Jenny had come to hate the scrubbing brush and pail with a fierce loathing. Her hands quickly became as red and work roughened as a Victorian housemaid's and the skin at the side of her nails peeled back in hang-nails. The only consolation was that it wasn't winter, at least she didn't have what Carrie called 'cuts', deep splits which Carrie got in the tips of her fingers from hanging out the washing with hands not properly dried. Jenny had seen these cuts bleeding, seen Carrie, that most stoic of women, wincing if she knocked them on the corner of a cupboard or drawer and set up the painful throbbing.

But at least all the hard physical work helped to keep Jenny's mind off things.

Sister Anne stood now, watching critically for a moment as she worked. Jenny could feel the malice in her gaze without even looking at her.

'When you've finished, Jennifer, and cleared away after yourself, come to my office,' she said at last. 'I want to talk to you.'

As she passed Jenny she managed to tread on a clean, but still wet, patch with her sensible lace-up shoe. The mark she left made Jenny want to weep. *She did that on purpose*. But that was her right.

At least I'll be leaving this place soon, Jenny thought. *She won't be*. The thought was some small comfort to her.

The home had once been a small manor house and it had seen very little in the way of renovation. Narrow corridors, twisting staircases with rooms branching off at mezzanine levels to create a hotchpotch effect, wood panelling, creaking stairs. It was rumoured there were priest holes behind some of the wood panelling, and also that the building was haunted by the ghost of a young nun who had been walled up in one of them when she had become pregnant by a priest who had fallen in love with her. It was also said that sometimes a ghost baby cried in the dead of night and there was some speculation that this baby had actually been born after the nun had been walled up. The story, gruesome enough under any circumstances, was particularly upsetting to the girls who now spent the last weeks of their own pregnancies at the home.

Sister Anne's room was panelled; Jenny thought of the story as she went in, and shivered.

Sister Anne was sitting behind her desk, leather-tooled and polished to a high sheen by one of the girls. She did not

387

invite Jenny to sit too but left her standing like a naughty schoolgirl called to the headmistress's study.

'I have some news for you, Jennifer. Suitable adoptive parents have been found for your baby. A good Catholic couple who are unable to have children of their own. Provided, that is, that the baby is a girl.'

Jenny's stomach fell away. 'You mean . . .'

'The baby can be adopted as soon as the hospital is satisfied with its progress. Provided, as I say, that it is a girl. The couple in question are very clear on that point. They don't want a boy.'

She spoke the word 'boy' as if it were somehow not quite nice, as if, in fact, she was in whole-hearted agreement. Who in their right minds would want a *boy*?

'Who are they?' Jenny asked.

'You should know better than to ask me that. I can't divulge any information, let alone identify them. Suffice it to say that we are satisfied they would make excellent adoptive parents. They have their own attractive home and they will be able to give your baby all the things that you cannot. That is all you need to know, and you should be grateful for it.'

Jenny couldn't answer. Her voice seemed to have disappeared into a lump in her throat.

'That's all. You can go and get on with whatever it is you have to do.' Sister Anne glanced at the clock, dark-cased, which hung on the wall to one side of the desk. 'Sister Claude will be expecting you in the kitchen. Off you go, now. And don't forget to say a rosary to thank our Blessed Lady for sending these people to us. It's more than you deserve.'

From somewhere Jenny found her voice. 'Thank you, Sister.'

But she wasn't at all sure that when she said a rosary it would be a prayer of gratitude. Jenny rather felt that her rosary would be to implore anyone who might be listening that her unborn child would be a boy.

Helen was far from happy with the arrangements Carrie had made for Jenny. She had heard things she didn't like

388

about mother and baby homes run by the Church – that they were over-zealous and punitive to the point of cruelty. But the matter had been out of her hands and beyond giving advice and looking after Jenny until she left Hillsbridge, it was not her place to interfere.

Truth to tell, she didn't like the idea of adoption at all. It went against all her instincts. But she could see that in Jenny's case it was probably the best option. The girl was little more than a child herself and she had obviously been taken advantage of by a here-today-gone-tomorrow RAF man. If Carrie had been prepared to support her then perhaps keeping the baby would have been a possibility, but clearly Carrie had no intention of doing that. Her greatest concern had been that nobody in Hillsbridge should find out, and Helen had mixed feelings about this too. She had a dislike of secrets, which had a nasty habit of coming to light at the least convenient moment. But she could see that whilst it was all very well to say that it would be a nine-days wonder and soon forgotten if Jenny had been older and able to marry the father, under the circumstances the reality would be very different. People could be very narrow-minded, especially in a small town like Hillsbridge. For the rest of her life Jenny would be judged by this one mistake. She would continue to be known as 'the girl who had a baby before she was married' for years to come. To make things worse, the chances of anyone being willing to take her on with a baby were pretty remote. Employers and potential boyfriends alike would regard her with suspicion, and the child as a liability. It wasn't right, but that was the way things were and Helen couldn't change that. No, adoption probably was the best solution, giving Jenny the chance of a fresh start, but it was a tragedy all the same, and one that both she and her baby would have to live with for the rest of their lives. Helen could foresee that she might have to be the one to pick up the pieces at some time in the future.

For now, however, she had other patients who needed her attention, and the added responsibility of her grandmother. Dolly had at last gone into hospital for her hysterectomy, and Charlotte had moved in to Greenslade Terrace.

Helen loved having her; wasn't it just what she had wanted for so long? But it meant her free time was no longer her own in quite the same way it had been. Now, when she got home, Charlotte was there, often with a meal waiting for her, the kind of old-fashioned homely food she cooked so well, but which, as a staple diet, Helen found slightly too stodgy, or fatty, or both. She couldn't complain, though – Charlotte's feelings would have been hurt and Helen wouldn't have hurt her feelings for the world.

Then there was Dolly to be visited – Charlotte insisted on that, and Helen complied. Dolly's feelings had to be considered too.

From being a free agent she suddenly found she had a great many family obligations and she wasn't sure how well she was coping with them. She just wasn't used to having to think about anyone but herself! Realising just how set she had become in her ways was quite a salutary experience.

There had been no further repercussions over Ida Lockyear's death – Walter Evans had slanted his report in the *Mercury* towards warning of the importance of making sure heating and cooking appliances were safe rather than dwelling on Helen's failure to identify the symptoms of carbon monoxide poisoning, and Ida's son had gone quietly away, presumably not wanting to draw attention to his own neglect of his mother. But Helen still felt that Reuben considered her culpable. Too often he asked seemingly casual questions about this patient or that and she felt that the reason behind them was that he no longer totally trusted her judgement. The resulting tension made her worry that before long some kind of slip-up was inevitable.

At least her relationship with Paul had improved, though. It wasn't quite back to where it had been before Guy had come back on the scene, but it was almost there. Paul often joined her and Charlotte for supper and seemed to thoroughly enjoy Charlotte's solid home cooking. There were, of course, no cosy cuddles on the sofa afterwards, and even when Charlotte took herself off to bed, leaving them alone (on purpose, Helen guessed) Paul made no move to reinstate that side of their relationship. Whether he felt uncomfortable with Charlotte in the house, or whether he simply didn't want to, Helen was unsure. But she did sense a lingering reserve that had been missing in the pre-Guy days, and decided his reluctance was made up of a little of each. It suited her not to be rushed, but she regretted, all the same, the lack of the old total ease between them, and regretted too that she might have hurt him. Paul wasn't one for displaying his emotions but that didn't mean he didn't have any, and his feelings were as easy to hurt as the next person's.

One evening in June, when he called in to see Reuben following afternoon surgery as he did at least once a week, he popped his head around her door as he passed.

'You're not going to run away, are you?'

'I wasn't thinking of it, no.'

'I mean – I've just got to have a word with Reuben, then I was going to come in and see you.'

It was there again, that hesitance – uncertainty almost – liberally dusted with an almost too-studied casualness.

'You don't have to make an appointment to see me, Paul,' she said, smiling to temper the slightly caustic tone. 'Anyway, Reuben still has a patient with him I think. Mrs Price from Waterside Cottages.'

'You're well informed.'

'I know because I could hear him shouting at her. She's deaf as a post and he's going to syringe her ears. We'll know if it's been a success or not when it all goes quiet. If it all goes quiet!'

'Mmm.' He cocked his head, listening, then smiled as Reuben's voice, raised and deliberate, carried through the closed door of his consulting room. 'OK – I'll ask you now. I was wondering if you'd like to go out for a drink this evening. There's a friendly skittles match on at the Prince of Denmark – Regulars versus Casuals – and they've asked me to make up number for the Casuals.'

'I didn't know you played skittles!'

'I don't. But the proceeds are going towards a fish tank for my surgery, so I suppose they thought it might be an added attraction to have me along, making a fool of myself.'

'What do you want a fish tank for?'

'Rosie Jenner has got it in her head it would help the patients relax.' Rosie Jenner was the district nurse at Purldown. 'It'll be in the waiting room, of course – not my surgery.'

'Well – yes. I have heard they're good, though. Very therapeutic.'

'You reckon? Personally I don't think I could take to all that gushing water and bits of seaweed, never mind the fish.'

'So what time is this skittles match?' Helen asked.

'Eight o'clock start. I could pick you up if you like. But if it's too early for you, you could always come along later under your own steam.'

Helen hesitated, pleased that Paul had asked her, thinking how nice it would be to be collected and taken home afterwards, but aware that by the time she and Charlotte had eaten and cleared away she might have a problem with being ready for seven thirty or so.

'Perhaps it would be best if I made my own way. Just in case of problems.'

The door of Reuben's surgery opened, voices carried in from the corridor. Mrs Price was leaving – still hard of hearing by the sound of it.

'See you later then?' Paul said. 'You know the Prince of Denmark, don't you?'

'The pub just outside Purldown on the Bath road.'

'That's it.' He raised his hand in salute and disappeared out the door.

Helen packed her things together and headed for home. She was surprised by how pleased she was that Paul had finally overcome some of his reserve with regard to them being alone together and also by how much she was already looking forward to the evening. A skittles match – friendly or otherwise – was hardly her scene; perhaps it was because it was so long since she had been anywhere socially.

She parked her car and opened the back door of

392

Number 11, balancing the paraphernalia of the day against her chest. Usually the smell of cooking greeted her – chops baking in the oven, or a stew simmering on the hob. Today she could smell only the kipper that Charlotte had poached for her breakfast.

'I'm home, Gran,' she called.

No reply.

'Gran?' She pushed open the living-room door with her foot.

Charlotte was sitting in the big armchair.

'Oh, Helen, I'm glad you're home.'

'What's the matter, Gran?' Helen asked, alarmed.

'I had a bit of a funny turn.'

'What sort of funny turn?'

'I came over giddy and the next thing I knew I was on the floor.'

'You fell down, you mean?'

'I suppose I must have done. I haven't done anything about your tea, Helen. I didn't feel up to it.'

'Never mind the tea,' Helen said, dumping her bag and files on the table. 'You'd better let me have a look at you.'

'Oh, I'm all right now.'

'If you're having giddy turns and falling down there's a reason for it,' Helen said briskly. 'I'm going to find out what it is.' She looked more closely at her grandmother. There was something not quite right about her mouth, which was slightly drawn, and the corner of one eye was drooping slightly and allowing a trickle of moisture to run down on to her cheek.

'Show me your hands,' Helen said.

Charlotte raised one; the other, the same side as the twisted mouth and drooping eyelid, remained in her lap.

'It's gone to sleep,' Charlotte said. 'I've been sat here too long, Helen.'

Helen said nothing. She knew, and Charlotte knew, she was sure, that it was more than that. Charlotte was just making light of it because she didn't want to face the truth. Helen unclicked the clasps of her medical bag and took out her blood pressure gauge.

'Can you roll your sleeve up, or do you want me to do it for you?'

'You do it.' For the first time since she had moved back to Greenslade Terrace, Charlotte sounded unsure of herself and frightened. 'What's the matter with me, Helen?'

'I think, Gran,' Helen said, 'that you may have had a slight stroke. But you already know that, don't you?'

There would be no skittles for her this evening. But that wasn't important. All that mattered was being with Charlotte and looking after her. A bit of a busman's holiday it might be, but Helen had known when she had asked Charlotte to come and live with her that it might come with the territory. All she was glad of was that she, and not some stranger, was in a position to help.

When Billy Edgell was released from prison it never occurred to him to go anywhere but home. He arrived back in Alder Road in mid-June, when the red clay gardens were full of spindly French marigolds and the children were using the circular road around the Green as a cycle race-track.

Joyce welcomed him home with a cup of tea, a lecture on mending his ways, and a running commentary on recent events in general and her own doings in particular.

'It's been all go, really,' she said. 'I hope you've noticed we've got a television now.'

'Yes, I saw.'

'Oh yes, we've come up in the world! Unlike some. There's something funny going on over at Number 27 if you ask me.'

'Who's Number 27?' Billy asked in a bored voice. He wasn't the least bit interested in gossip about his neighbours.

'The Simmonses, of course. Carrie Bloody Simmons, who thinks she's a cut above everybody else. Her Jenny's disappeared off the scene and there's something fishy about it if you ask me. She looked as if she was putting on weight just before she went. So putting two and two together I reckon she's got herself into trouble.'

'Jenny!' Billy said, surprised and a bit shocked. 'In the club?'

'Jenny,' Joyce repeated with satisfaction. 'It's always the quiet ones, the ones that look as if butter wouldn't melt in their mouths. I can see her now when she was a little girl – fat and plain but full of herself. Carrie used to put white ribbon bows in her hair. You remember, I expect. The others were always poking fun of her.'

Billy was silent. It was the other Jenny he was thinking about, the Jenny who had turned into a stunner, the Jenny who had made him look a fool in front of his mates that summer day at the swimming pool. So somebody had got inside her knickers, lucky sod, and she wouldn't even give him the time of day. The rejection was a slow sullen anger burning away at what mattered most to him – his male ego.

'I bet Carrie's doing her nut,' Joyce went on, enjoying herself. 'It's prize, really, when you think about it. Her precious daughter in the club!'

'Well, it won't be the first time, will it?' Billy said maliciously.

Joyce's beady little eyes narrowed. 'What are you talking about?'

'The chap I was banged up with knew them in Bristol. He reckoned somebody got their leg over Heather when they were at school. Well – he reckoned quite a few did, but one of them must've shot their bolt and knocked her up. He didn't know what had become of her, of course, because according to him the whole family did a vanishing act.'

'Well I never!' Joyce was cock-a-hoop. 'When did you say this was?'

'I don't know exactly. In the war sometime. When Heather was about thirteen or fourteen. How old would she be now?'

'The war,' Joyce said, thinking. 'That's when they came here. I remember Carrie starting work down at the canteen. What a stuck-up cow! Well, she's got her come-uppance and no mistake! Both her girls getting themselves in trouble! And fancy you finding out about it, Billy.

It's a small world, all right.' She chuckled. 'Oh my goodness, she'd have a fit and die if she thought anybody round here knew about it! You've made my day, Billy.'

'I'm glad I've done something to please you,' Billy said, grinning. If he knew his mother, she'd make the most of this. Well, it served Jenny and her snotty family right. She wouldn't be making a fool of *him* again in a hurry.

Billy wasn't far wrong. Already Joyce was turning the information over in her mind and relishing it. From the window she could see Carrie's house on the opposite side of the street, neat as a new pin, but hiding goodness-only-knew-what secrets behind its prim lace curtains. Well, at last she had the ammunition to take her down a peg or two. And how she was going to enjoy doing it!

Helen was feeling uncharacteristically down and she couldn't really put her finger on the reason for it.

Charlotte was recovering well from her stroke – Reuben, whom Helen had called out for a second opinion, had confirmed it had been slight, and between them they had decided on a course of treatment to help her along and lessen the likelihood of a recurrence. It remained a possibility, of course – if someone had a tendency that way, the chance of having another, more serious stroke, was considerably increased. If that should happen and Charlotte was really incapacitated then it would throw up all sorts of problems about her care. But Helen had never been one to worry about what might never happen – there was enough of the phlegmatic Hall about her to make her feel the future was best left to look after itself.

She hadn't made any more serious errors at work either, nothing that Reuben could hold against her, and her position as assistant was beginning to look more secure again. Goodness only knew how much damage she'd done to her chances of being offered a partnership, of course, but here too she was hopeful of rebuilding the trust that would one day mean that Reuben would decide she was the right person for the job.

She hardly thought about Guy, which was good, and when she did it was with anger, not mourning. She regretted that she had wasted so much of her life on him, but it was over now, and she could look forward to the future without constantly wondering if she had done the wrong thing in cutting loose from him. As for Paul – they were on friendly terms. There had been a distinctly frosty nip in the air immediately following the missed skittles match, but when she had explained the circumstances, he had been kind and concerned. Of course she couldn't leave Charlotte alone any more than was absolutely unavoidable for the time being. But for all his protestations to the contrary she couldn't help wondering if he thought she was glad of the excuse and she regretted too the fact that they couldn't go out alone together and give themselves a chance to rebuild their relationship.

Even so, none of these things was really enough to bring about the sense of impending disaster which haunted her. When she felt apprehensive for no good reason, it worried Helen. She felt apprehensive now, and it hung over her like a storm cloud waiting to happen.

One Friday evening in late June Joyce went across the Green and knocked on Carrie's front door.

Ever since Billy had told her about Heather she had been mulling over various ways she could use what she knew to get at Carrie. She could, of course, simply spread the story around, adding her suspicions about the reason behind Jenny's absence, but that wasn't quite satisfying enough for her. She couldn't be sure the gossip would get back to Carrie and even if it did she wouldn't be there to see her discomfort. Joyce hadn't waited all these years to get her own back to waste the opportunity now it had arisen. She wanted to make the most of her moment of revenge.

It was when she saw Carrie going from door to door that Friday that the idea came to her. She knew what Carrie was doing – collecting her catalogue club money. She had used to do it every week, now it was once a fortnight – Joyce had no idea why and could only suppose that Carrie had been granted some kind of high-grade credit.

Carrie's customers were hand-picked, people she was

friendly with and could trust to pay regularly even when their turn fell early in the twenty-week cycle. Joyce had never been approached and knew she never would be even if it hadn't been for the bad blood between them. That, Joyce thought, smiling to herself, was why her plan was such delicious irony. Not that Joyce used the word irony of course. It simply wasn't in her vocabulary. 'Ripe' was the word she used. *Oh, that'd be ripe. Real ripe!* she thought to herself, and laughed out loud.

Sally came barking to the door and Carrie answered it wearing a flowered dress and cardigan that looked as if it had come straight from the pages of the catalogue. The skirt – unpressed pleats – did nothing for her big hips. In spite of it being quite a warm evening, she was wearing stockings with her flat sensible sandals. When she saw Joyce, she frowned, and Sally, who had never forgotten being almost kicked by Joyce, growled threateningly.

'Can I have a word?' Joyce asked, ignoring the dog.

She, too, was wearing a cotton dirndl and a cotton top with three-quarter sleeves, but her legs were bare and her feet, with their bright-red varnished toenails looked none too clean.

'What about?' Carrie asked suspiciously.

'Aren't you going to ask me in?'

Carrie looked to be on the point of refusing, but manners got the better of her. She stood aside, letting Joyce into the hall.

'Well?'

'You run a club, don't you?' Joyce said. 'Kays, is it?'

'Yes, that's right.'

'I'd like to join.'

Carrie looked startled. 'You?'

'I want some sheets and pillow cases but I can't afford to pay all at once. With the club you pay weekly, don't you?'

'Yes, but all twenty turns have gone for this time around.'

'When d'you start again?'

'It's only about halfway through. Anyway, all my customers will want to go on again.'

'What about Mrs Watson?'

'What about her?'

'She's moved, hasn't she? You won't want to go all the way over the other side of Hillsbridge to collect her money.'

'I haven't decided yet,' Carrie said. 'In any case, there's a waiting list.'

This was exactly what Joyce had expected; she was ready for it.

'Are you making excuses, Carrie Simmons? Don't you want me in your club, is that it?'

Carrie, who hated scenes, refrained from saying that was exactly it.

'There's no room on the list.'

'Not good enough for you, am I?'

'I don't want to quarrel with you, Joyce.'

'You always did think yourself somebody, Carrie. Why, I don't know. Well, at least none of my children have let themselves down like yours.'

Carrie began to tremble.

'What! With your Billy just out of prison?'

'Our Billy's just a rascal. The police have got a down on him. But none of my daughters have got themselves into trouble. That's more than you can say.'

'What are you talking about?' Carrie demanded, but her flaming face was all the encouragement Joyce needed.

'You know very well what I'm talking about – your Heather. Oh, you might have thought moving out here from Bristol you could keep it quiet. But things have a way of getting out. Your Heather had a baby when she was still at school. And you've got the nerve to look down on me! But that's not the end of it, is it? That's where your Jenny comes in. And we all know about Jenny, don't we?'

She'd hit the nail squarely on the head. All the colour had drained from Carrie's face and she looked defeated and old.

'You don't know anything, Joyce,' she said, her voice shaking. 'You couldn't know about that. We were so careful! Jenny's *ours*, mine and Joe's . . .' She broke off, her eyes going wide with horror and in that moment Joyce knew. In a flash it all came clear. The big gap between David and Jenny. The reason they'd all moved here from

Bristol. Carrie and Joe and Heather and David. And Jenny, just a baby when they'd arrived. A tiny little baby.

Unwittingly she'd uncovered far more than she'd expected, far more than she'd ever dreamed was there to be uncovered. It was all there in Carrie's horrified eyes. Joyce's triumph was complete.

'Whatever is the matter?' Joe asked.

He had been in his garden, picking the tops out of the runner beans, when Carrie appeared, clearly distraught.

'Something terrible's happened! Oh, Joe, I don't know what we're going to do!'

Joe transferred the latest bean shoot from right hand to left and put his arm round Carrie's shoulders. She was trembling violently; he couldn't remember when he'd last seen her so upset. 'Come and sit down and tell me about it,' he said soothingly.

He led her back to the house, depositing the bean shoots neatly on top of the compost heap en route.

'Now then,' he said when he had closed the kitchen door after them. 'What's upsetting you, m'dear?'

'Joyce Edgell knows about our Jenny.'

'Well, that's not the end of the world, is it?' Joe hadn't been happy about Jenny's pregnancy, it wasn't what he wanted for her, but these things happened and he couldn't see the sense in all the secrecy really, he merely went along with it because Carrie placed so much importance on it. 'It'll all be over and forgotten in no time when our Jenny comes home and everything gets back to normal. You'll see.'

'No!' Carrie was verging on hysteria. 'I mean about Heather – and Jenny!'

Joe thought for a moment, frowning.

'No. She couldn't know. How could she know about that?'

'I don't know. But she was saying awful things – terrible – and hinting . . .'

'There you are then. She doesn't . . .'

'And then I let the cat out of the bag. If she didn't know before, she does now.'

Joe looked amazed. 'What did you say then?'

'Oh – I don't know – I can't remember exactly. I was so shocked it just sort of came out. Whatever are we going to do, Joe? We can't move again. Not now. And Heather . . . I mean, this is her home now. But if it gets round – and it will . . .'

'You're making mountains out of molehills. It'll be just talk, that's all.'

Carrie turned on him furiously.

'Oh, for goodness sake, will you take things seriously for once!'

'It's no good getting worked up about it.'

'How can you say that! Can't you see what it means? It's not just people talking, though that's bad enough . . .'

'You worry too much about people talking.'

'It's our Jenny. She'll get to hear, won't she? Somebody will make it their business to say something to her, you can be sure of that. Oh, Joe, I'm going out of my mind with worry!' And she burst into tears.

Joe sighed. He hated to see anyone cry, but most especially Carrie.

'I always thought you were making a rod for your own back doing what you did.'

'It was for the best! We agreed!'

'No, m'dear – you decided. I just went along with it for the sake of peace.'

'That's the same thing, isn't it?' Frantic anxiety was making her aggressive. 'Our Heather was just a bit of a kid! It *was* for the best. I'd have done the same for Jenny if I was younger.'

'And have this all over again? Lying's not right, Carrie. You always get caught out in the end.'

'A fat lot of help you are!' she snapped. 'What are we going to do, Joe?'

'I don't know, m'dear. But I think you'd better have a drink and calm down. Getting in a state won't help anything.'

He went to the cupboard, hesitating over the quarter-bottle of brandy kept there for emergencies, changed his mind and went upstairs. He had a miniature of gin hidden

401

in the drawer where he kept his odds and ends. He'd been keeping it for Carrie for when she heard that Jenny was in labour – remembering what she had been like when Heather was giving birth, he'd reckoned she'd need it. But as emergencies went, this was just as pressing.

He took it downstairs, fetched a glass and a bottle of bitter lemon. After drinking it, Carrie seemed to recover some of her equilibrium.

'Well,' she said, pressing her fingers to her mouth and looking as tragic as if she had just faced the fact that the world was about to come to an end, 'I suppose the first thing is I shall have to go down and talk to our Heather.'

Joe felt an enormous sense of relief. If Carrie was back to making plans, the worst was over.

'There you are, m'dear. I told you you'd work something out.'

'Well, somebody has to!' Carrie said, rather scornfully.

Joe ignored the jibe. He had accepted long ago that Carrie could be more domineering than he would have liked, and he was used to her organising ways. It was Carrie helpless that he really couldn't take. In a strange way he found it deeply disturbing, as if a sleeping giant was waking and shaking the foundations of his world.

'It'll all come out in the wash,' he said comfortingly, ignoring the look of exasperation which Carrie shot at him.

David and his friends were drinking in the Miners' Arms. He did a lot of drinking in pubs these days, but it didn't seem to help him much. To the less perceptive, it might look as if he was getting over Linda's death, but that was simply because he'd stopped moping about and on the surface at least returned to some sort of normality. But in his heart it was still winter, bleak, never-ending winter. Sometimes, when he overdid the drinking, he could find oblivion for a little while, but next day the darkness of the soul was back, worse than ever. David thought it would never end.

Tonight he'd hidden the way he felt inside, downing a couple of pints of bitter whilst he and his mates had played a game of shove ha'penny, followed by a game of darts, and now they had decided to move on to the club, where there was a jukebox. As they emerged from the spit-and-sawdust bar, another gang of lads was coming up the steps. David fell back into the lobby to let them in, not taking much notice, until a cheeky voice said: 'Oh look – it's David Simmons! Evening, David!'

It was Billy Edgell. David nodded, but otherwise ignored him.

'Too big to speak to me, eh?' Billy taunted, planting himself right in front of David. 'What have you got to be so full of yourself about?'

'Get out of my way, Billy,' David said quietly. 'I'm not looking for trouble if you are.'

'*I'm not looking for trouble if you are,*' Billy mimicked. 'Quite the gent, aren't you? But what's it feel like to have two fucking whores for sisters? That's what I'd like to know.'

'You *what?*' David said. '*What* did you just say?'

'You heard. A pair of fucking knocked-up whores.'

He never got any further. David's fist connected with his jaw and he went head first and backwards down the steps. For a moment he lay there, half-stunned, and David bent over him threateningly.

'If you ever – *ever* – say anything like that about my sisters again, I'll break your bloody neck, Edgell.'

Then, his friends staring after him in amazement, he marched off along the street.

'I gave Billy Edgell a bloody nose tonight,' he said to Carrie.

Her hand flew to her mouth. 'Oh my Lord! You did *what*? But why?'

'I don't think you'd want to know,' David said.

'Oh, you shouldn't have! I mean, you shouldn't fight with anybody, but especially not those Edgells. They can make a lot of trouble for us. I think I ought to tell you . . .'

'Mum, don't,' David said. 'There's things in this family you want swept under the carpet, that's up to you. Just leave me out of it. I know what you're talking about – or I can have a good guess, and I've done my bit. But I don't want anything to do with the tangles you've got yourself in. I've got enough to worry about without that.'

'Oh, David.' Tears sprang to Carrie's eyes. She knew David didn't always approve of the way she stage-managed family life and his good opinion was very important to her. 'You shouldn't upset Billy Edgell, though,' she said anxiously. 'He's trouble, just like his mother, and he won't forget it.'

'Shall I tell you something, Mum?' David said. 'I've been wanting to give somebody a good hard punch ever since Linda died. Well, now I have, and I'm bloody glad it was that bloody Billy Edgell!'

Chapter Twenty-One

'There's someone to see you, Jennifer.'

Jenny, on her knees trying to retrieve the last bit of fluff that lurked beneath the old claw-foot bath, looked up at the sound of Sister Theresa's voice, hope flooding through her like warm spring sunshine. Someone to see her! She had had no visitors since coming to the home – visitors were discouraged as unsettling for the girls. So who could it be unless . . . *Bryn!* her heart shouted.

'Where?'

'In Sister Anne's office.' Sister Theresa was one of the younger nuns; she had a kind voice and a nice smile, but Jenny had noticed that when she showed any incipient friendship towards the girls the stricter nuns gave her black looks. Sister Theresa was probably given a talking-to and some kind of penance once they were out of earshot judging by the fact that after such an incident it was always a long time before she showed any signs of being friendly again.

Jenny followed Sister Theresa out on to the landing, tidying her hair as best she could. There were no mirrors in the home – mirrors smacked of vanity – but Jenny was uncomfortably aware that she did not look her best. The untidy hair, the puffy red hands, the lack of even the lightest touch of make-up and worst of all, the ungainly shape her body had become beneath the ugly voluminous grey smock that all the girls were expected to wear.

Her feet flew her down the stairs and along the flagged corridor, each stone of which she had personal acquaintance with so often had she scrubbed it. The door to Sister Anne's study was ajar; outside Jenny hesitated, then knocked.

'Come!'

She pushed the door open, her stomach knotting with anticipation. Not Bryn in the hidebound visitors' chair. Had she really imagined for a moment it would be?

Heather.

Jenny's initial rush of disappointment was quickly replaced by pleasure. Tears pricked her eyes and she stood motionless for a moment. Then Heather was on her feet and the two girls were in one another's arms, oblivious of the disapproving gaze of the old nun.

'Oh, Jenny . . . Jenny . . .' Heather was close to tears too, overcome with emotion.

'What are you doing here?' Jenny asked, frightened suddenly that Heather had come to break bad news.

'Control yourself, Jennifer,' Sister Anne said tartly. And to Heather: 'Jennifer can show you to the library. You can talk there.'

Jenny couldn't let go of Heather's arm for even a moment. She hung on to it like a lifeline as she led Heather back along the stone flagged corridor.

'What a weird place!' Heather said with a small shiver as she took in the oppressive atmosphere of the wood-panelled walls and the small statues on their plinths in the various niches, the mingled smells of incense and carbolic, the queer-shaped patches of light that crept in through the small vaulted windows and only managed, somehow, to make the surrounding dimness deeper and more shadowy.

'It's supposed to be haunted.'

'I'm not surprised! Are you all right here, Jenny?'

'All right.'

She wanted to say it wasn't the ghosts she was afraid of. It wasn't the ghosts that made her existence here such an ordeal but the flesh-and-blood women whose sole purpose in life seemed to extract a penance from her and the other girls for their sinful behaviour. But she didn't want Heather to know how unhappy she was. In any case, it wasn't quite true that the ghosts played no part. They added to the aura of oppression – and not simply the spirits of the long dead, either. Since the manor had become a mother and baby home, the thick walls and the wooden panelling had seen too much unhappiness and despair, soaking it up like a sponge so that the atmosphere was thick with it.

The library had once been a drawing room. Shelves filled with religious and improving books lined three walls. The fourth was given over to a massive old fireplace surrounded with more dark panelling. No fire was ever lit here, even in the depths of winter, and the library was little used. Once or twice Jenny had tried to read here, but that same oppressive atmosphere which pervaded the entire house was intensified here by the smell of musty paper and disuse.

Heather and Jenny sat down side by side on the worn leather sofa.

'Are you getting proper medical care?' Heather asked.

'The doctor comes once a week.'

'And you're keeping all right? He's happy with the baby?'

'He's never said that he's not. Did you know they've found a couple to adopt the baby – as long as it's a girl? I wrote and told Mum.'

'Yes, she told me.'

There was a small silence; Heather looked increasingly uncomfortable.

'It's lovely to see you,' Jenny said, 'but I never expected . . . I mean, Sister Anne doesn't like us to have visitors.'

'I know.'

'So – is there any special reason why?'

Heather dropped her eyes, catching her lip between her teeth and biting hard.

'It's not Mum or Dad, is it?' Jenny asked, worried. 'Nothing's happened to them?'

'No.'

'Gran, then? Or David?' It didn't occur to her to add Vanessa to the list. If anything had happened to Vanessa it wouldn't be Heather who was here.

'No – it's nothing like that, Jen. But I do need to talk to you. There's something I have to tell you before you come home and hear it from someone else.'

'You're not splitting up – you and Steve?'

'No – no. It's, oh Jenny, I don't know where to start.'

407

Jenny waited, puzzled and apprehensive, and after a moment Heather said: 'You remember when you first found out you were pregnant? And I suggested maybe I could bring your baby up – pretend it was mine?'

'No!' Jenny said. 'If you've come to try to persuade me to change my mind, the answer is no. I couldn't. It would be even worse than . . .' She broke off, gulping; her fingernails – what was left of them – were digging uneven crescents in the palms of her hands as she contemplated the awfulness of what was to come. 'Don't ask me, Heather, please.'

'I'm not asking you.'

'That's all right then, because . . .'

'Jenny, you're making this so hard for me!'

She was close to tears again. Jenny gazed at her, puzzled.

'What do you mean?'

'Being so against the idea . . .'

'I can't help it, Heather. I know you'd do your best but I couldn't. I just couldn't.'

'. . . because it's what I did.'

'What?'

'Oh, Jen, I know this is going to come as an awful shock, but . . . well, the same thing happened to me when I was . . . well, younger than you, actually.'

'You mean . . . *you* had a baby?' Heather nodded, not speaking. 'You! But what happened to it? You had it adopted like I'm going to?'

'No.' Heather's mouth worked but no more words came.

'Then what? Did it die?'

'No. Oh, Jenny . . .' And suddenly the tears were coursing down her cheeks and she reached blindly for Jenny's hands, squeezing them so hard that it hurt. 'No, she didn't die, and she wasn't adopted. Well, not the way you mean. Oh, don't you see? Do I have to spell it out to you? Oh, Jenny . . .'

'No!' Jenny said. She couldn't – wouldn't – believe the thought that was occurring to her. It couldn't be! She was mad to think it for even a moment. 'No! No! Tell me I'm going crazy! It's not . . . Heather. You're not saying . . . are you . . . that *I* . . .?'

408

Heather didn't need to answer. It was there in her eyes, written all over her face.

'Heather! Tell me!' Jenny was screaming now.

Heather was crying in earnest, her face crumpled, the sobs coming from deep inside.

'Yes, Jenny, it's true. Mum's not your mother. I am. *You* were my baby, Jenny. I'm not your sister. I'm your mother.'

'Oh God!' Jenny whispered. The room was spinning round her, she thought she was going to faint. She tore her hands away from Heather's, seeing her through the mists, seeing not the familiar, the loved, but a stranger. A stranger who had lied to her, deceived her, for the whole of her life. A stranger who was now taking away from her everything that formed the foundations of her world – her parents, her very identity. 'Oh God! Oh God! Oh God!'

'Jenny, please . . .'

'Oh God! Oh God!' In shock, she repeated those same two words over and over again, as if she had been wound up like a clockwork toy. She could hear them escaping her lips, monotonous and inevitable, meaningless yet filled with every emotion she could imagine and some she could not. And she simply could not stop.

'Jenny – is it so bad? Please, I love you! I've always loved you! You don't know how many times I've wanted to tell you, but I couldn't. It wouldn't have been fair to Mum. Not after all she did . . . I was just a child, Jenny. It was either give you up completely, or this. I didn't want to give you up! And Mum didn't want it either. It was her idea. She said she'd bring you up as her own, so we moved out from Bristol, away from anybody who might have guessed. And she did. And I . . . Well, at least I hadn't lost you. Not completely. I could watch you grow up – be there for you. I could even pretend sometimes when I was looking after you that everything was the way I wanted it to be. You were my little girl. My darling little girl. And you were with your real family – not with strangers . . . Jenny, it's not that bad, surely? That I'm your mother? Oh please, Jenny, tell me you forgive me.'

Jenny leaped to her feet. The atmosphere of this horrible room was suffocating her, there was a thundering noise in her ears, she thought she was going to be sick.

'How could you?' she ground out through chattering teeth. 'How could you live with a lie like that?'

'Jenny . . .'

'Go away, Heather! I never want to see you again!'

She turned and ran from the room. All the ghosts and unquiet spirits, all the whisperings and tumult, all the roaring and shaking of a world disintegrating, went with her.

Sister Theresa came to her room.

'Jennifer? You can't stay up here. You must come down.'

Jenny turned her face into the pillow, not replying.

'Jennifer? Did your sister say something to upset you? It's all right, she's gone now. Look – you must come down. Sister Anne . . .'

'I don't care about Sister Anne,' Jenny muttered. 'What do I care about that silly old crow?'

Sister Theresa pretended not to have heard.

'Dinner is ready. It'll be getting cold.'

'I don't want any dinner. I feel sick.'

'Should I fetch the doctor?'

'No. I don't want the doctor.'

'Then you must try to calm down. This is very bad for you and for your baby.'

'I don't care.'

'Don't care! About your baby! Come on now, you mustn't be so selfish.'

'Why not?' Jenny muttered, and she meant it.

She felt like being selfish, if that was what thinking about yourself first meant. She couldn't think of anything but herself. In the most fundamental way. Like – who was she? For all of her life she had known – or thought she had known. Now the things she had taken for granted had been stripped away and she no longer knew. Not just who she was now – but who she had ever been. Jennifer Simmons ceased to exist. She was in a vacuum and it was the most terrifying thing that had ever happened to her.

Mum was not her mother at all but her grandmother. Dad – not her father but her grandfather. David, her uncle. Vanessa, her sister. Heather . . .

Hatred welled up, choking her. How could Heather have done that to her? How could any of them? It was the fact they'd kept it from her she couldn't stomach. That they'd known, all of them, something so completely fundamental about her and she hadn't. As a betrayal it ranked with the worst. All her life they'd pretended. All her life, nothing had been as it seemed. Nothing! And they'd known it and she hadn't. They had conspired to keep it from her and the conspiracy made a unit of them somehow, a unit of which she was no longer a part. She'd been Jenny Alone all the time and she'd never known it. Separated from them by the enormity of a truth she'd never so much as guessed at. A lie. It had all been a lie. Everything. Always.

It explained a great deal, of course, like why Carrie had always been so protective of her. Carrie had been desperately afraid that she, Jenny, would go the same way as Heather. Not following in a sister's footsteps, but taking after her mother.

And she had. She had! That was the supreme irony of it. For all Carrie's precautions she had ended up just like Heather. Just like her mother.

She wanted to scream. She wanted to cry. And she could do neither. She simply lay staring at the ceiling while the emotions rolled over her in relentless waves, leaving no room for coherent thought.

Maybe if they'd told her before this she could have coped with it. But not now. The enormity, in her heightened emotional state, was simply too much. And Jenny couldn't imagine she would ever get over it, ever feel any differently.

Afterwards Jenny was never quite sure at what point she decided what she was going to do. She was never quite sure, come to that, if it was a conscious decision at all, or just a reaction. Of only one thing was she perfectly, absolutely certain. The whole of her family had become strangers. Only one living being in the whole world was hers and hers alone.

Her baby. Not her baby and Bryn's – he, like the rest of them, had abandoned her, deceived her, let her down. But the baby, the tiny helpless life inside her . . . it was the one constant she could cling to. Whatever it took, Jenny was decided on one thing. Nothing in heaven or on earth would persuade her now to part with her baby.

Joyce Edgell liked the fact that her kitchen window overlooked the Green. Some might say it was a topsy-turvy sort of house, and they would have preferred the living area to overlook the front garden rather than the rows of cabbages and potato haulms that most people grew in the vegetable plots to the rear, but since the Edgells' gardens, both front and back, were identical – uncultivated wastelands of weeds and rubble left over from the time when the houses had been built, with sparse patches of field grass that had sprouted from seed blown in on the wind and a rusty bicycle and old gas cooker as ornamentation, this was hardly a consideration where she was concerned.

Having the kitchen at the front meant that when she was working at the sink, which in spite of her slovenly habits she had to do surprisingly often since she did not own a washing machine, she was able to watch all her neighbours' comings and goings.

One Saturday morning in late June as she plunged socks and underwear into a sink of soapy water she saw Joe come out of the Simmons house and ride off on his bicycle and a little later Carrie and David emerged and got into David's car, which he kept parked on the Green.

Joyce didn't agree with people parking their cars on the Green. Once upon a time, when they had first moved in, only Tom Glass at Number 22 had owned a vehicle – a small blue van that he used in his business as a jobbing builder. Now the cars were springing up like mushrooms and for some reason their owners had taken to driving them up over the low kerb and on to the grass, where they left ugly tyre tracks and got in the way of the children who wanted to play football. Served them right if the cars got scratched or had a window broken, Joyce thought, and she always smiled with satisfaction when she heard the thud of a football on metal.

This morning she had seen David paying close attention to one of his wheel arches – a dent perhaps – and Carrie too had a look before she got into the front passenger seat. She had her shopping basket with her and Joyce guessed David was taking her down to market.

At this distance Joyce had been unable to see the expression on Carrie's face, but she could picture it. Worried. Carrie always looked worried these days – and with reason. Joyce pulled a handful of socks out of the water and wrung them out with gusto. How she'd enjoyed that altercation with Carrie! She only wished she could think of a way of getting more mileage out of it. As yet, she'd said nothing to anyone, not spread the gossip at all. Once it was common knowledge she would lose the lovely sense of power that came from being the only one who knew. She was not ready to relinquish that until she was sure there was no better way of eking out her pound of flesh.

She rinsed the socks, sniffing them to see if they had lost their cheesy smell, and took them through to the back garden where her washing line looped and sagged between two poles. Her basket of pegs was on top of the old cooker. She hung out the socks and went back inside. Nothing for it, she'd have to do the sheets next – a chore and a half that was! Joyce never washed sheets if she could help it. A quick airing on the line usually did the trick, but every so often the time came when they had to be introduced to soap and water, and unfortunately she didn't think she could put it off any longer.

She was hauling a sheet in and out of the sink, swishing it round a bit so that the dirtiest patches came into contact with the soapy water when she heard a motorbike in the road outside. She looked up and saw it stop outside Number 27. She didn't recognise the lad riding it – at least, the crash helmet and leather jacket were unfamiliar to her – and when he removed his crash helmet, balancing it between seat and tank, she didn't think the rider looked like anyone she knew. He had fair hair cut quite short, a good deal shorter than was fashionable, anyway, and he looked tall and well built. Curious, Joyce watched as he went up the path of Number 27 and knocked on the door. After waiting a few moments he knocked again, then retreated back down the path between the borders of French marigolds and snapdragons, looking up at the windows of the house.

Unable to contain herself a moment longer, Joyce went to her own door. The young man had come back out on to the pavement and was standing beside his motorbike, hovering uncertainly and still looking back at the house.

'There's nobody in,' Joyce called.

He didn't hear her and she called again.

'They're all out!'

This time she had attracted his attention, and to her gratification, he came across the Green towards her. Encouraged, Joyce went down her path to meet him.

'Who was it you were looking for? The Simmonses?'

'Yes.'

'I think they've gone to shop. Well, Carrie and David have, anyway. And Joe went off on his bike. Or was it *Jenny* you wanted?'

'Jenny – yes.'

Joyce experienced a thrill of triumph. She'd known it! The minute she'd seen him, she'd known it! He could have been a friend of David's, but her first gut feeling hadn't let her down.

'Oh – she's away,' she said smugly. She saw his face fall and added: 'She's been away a month and more now.'

'Away? Away where?'

'Well, none of us knows that for sure. It's all a bit of a mystery. But . . . well, there's talk.' She folded her arms across her chest and made a knowing face, hoping he'd ask her what kind of talk, but he didn't.

'You a friend of hers, are you?'

'Yes.'

'You're out of luck, then. No, judging by the talk that's going round, it'll be another month or more before she's back here. You know what I'm saying, don't you?'

'No. No – I don't.'

414

'Ah. Well . . .' Joyce twisted her face into a knowing expression, 'let's put it this way. When a girl disappears like Jenny has, you can more or less say it'll be that the nine months is up before you see her again.'

'Nine months . . .?' He sounded puzzled but she could see from his expression that he understood her all right. Only his brain hadn't quite caught up with itself. He was shocked and in denial of what he was hearing.

'Well, there you are,' she said triumphantly. 'It's always the quiet ones, isn't it? That's what I always say.'

She broke off. David's car had turned into the road and she could see Carrie sitting up in it. She hadn't been long at market today!

'Here they are now,' she said. 'Carrie and David, anyway. They'll be able to put you right about it all.'

She stood her ground, smiling and nodding to Carrie with false friendliness. Carrie ignored her. Instead she was looking at the young man. And the expression on her face spoke volumes.

She's not pleased to see him! Joyce thought. *He's the last person she wanted to see, by the look of it!* As she turned to go back to her house, she was smiling.

'What are you doing here?' Carrie demanded, getting out of the car. She was shaking all over; how was it that she always seemed to be shaking these days? It took only a word or a look or the slightest little thing going wrong to set her off and in an instant her whole body would be a quivering jelly.

'I've come to see Jenny.'

'She's not here.'

'So your neighbour said.'

'Well, there you are then – you may as well go again.'

'If she's not here, can you tell me where I can get in touch with her?'

'Why do you want to do that?'

'I want to know why she hasn't answered my letters.'

'Well!' Carrie said tartly, 'if she hasn't answered your letters I should think it's pretty obvious. She doesn't want any more to do with you.'

'I'll believe that when I hear it from her.'

'You've taken your time anyway, haven't you? Following her up?'

'I've been abroad – Malta. But she knows that. I wrote and told her.'

Carrie said nothing.

'So can you give me an address, please?' he said, polite but persistent.

All manner of thoughts were chasing through Carrie's head. But the only one making itself heard loud and clear was that if Jenny and this boy got their heads together it wouldn't take them long to work out the truth as to why each of them had thought the other had broken contact. A whole series of letters had gone astray and were burning a hole in Carrie's underwear drawer. For the first time in her life she was ashamed of herself, and frightened by what she had done. She didn't want Jenny to know. Jenny would never forgive her. Coming on top of the devastating news Heather had had to break to her, it would be the last straw. She had not heard a word from Jenny since Heather had gone to see her, and neither had Heather. If she found out Carrie had put paid to her affair with this Bryn as well as letting her think all these years that she, and not Heather, was Jenny's mother, then in all likelihood she'd never want to see her again.

'It's no use,' Carrie said, facing him out squarely though the trembling was so bad she felt her legs were going to buckle and let her down at any moment. 'I'm not going to tell you. She's better off without you.'

'She's having a baby, isn't she?' he said. He was pale and the strain was showing in every line of his face but he, too, was determined not to back down. 'The woman across the road told me. Well, if she's having a baby, it's mine. So I've got a right to see her and you can't stop me.'

'Oh, can't I, my lad? We'll see about that! I'll have the police on you if you don't leave her alone!'

'You can't do that. She's over sixteen.'

'I don't care how old she is. She's my daughter, and I'm telling you to leave her alone. Now – clear off. Do you hear me?'

Argument was clearly useless. The only purpose it was serving was to bring neighbours to their doors and windows in the houses all round the Green.

'I'll find her,' Bryn said. 'If you won't tell me, I'll have to try other ways. But I will find her!'

He put on his crash helmet and turned away.

'What did you do that for, Mum?' David asked as the motorbike roared away.

'I don't want to talk about it,' Carrie said shortly.

She marched down the path, setting her basket down against the wall whilst she unlocked the door. By the time she was in the hall David had locked the car and followed her.

'Mum – there's been too many secrets in our family. And if he's the father of our Jenny's baby . . .'

'There's no doubt about that, I hope!'

David ignored the bitter innuendo.

'All this sweeping things under the carpet does more harm than good. He's got a right to know.'

'He has no rights at all!'

'Mum – you know how upset our Jenny has been because she hasn't heard from him. And if he wants to take responsibility, then surely he ought to be given the chance. It might solve a lot.'

'What are you talking about?' Carrie, who was still shaking all over, now vented the resulting aggression on David.

'I wouldn't be surprised if he wouldn't be prepared to marry her.'

Carrie banged her purse down on the table. It came open, spilling coins over the polished wood. 'And you call that solving things?'

'Well, yes . . .'

'Then a fat lot you know. I don't want our Jenny tied down at her age. It would blight her whole life.'

David, who thought Carrie was far too fond of organising all their lives according to what she thought was best for them, sighed.

'Don't you think she ought at least to be given the

417

chance to make up her own mind what's going to blight her life? I'd have thought having her baby adopted and never seeing it again might do that.'

'She'll get over it,' Carrie said shortly. 'In time.'

'That's what you said to me. About Linda.'

'You will. You might not think so now, but you will. And our Jenny will get over this baby. Once it's gone to a good home she can make a fresh start. And I don't want anything to stand in the way of that. So if you're thinking of telling her that Bryn was here, you can forget it, or you'll have me to answer to.'

'All right, all right,' David said hastily. Generally, like his father, he liked the quiet life.

Satisfied, Carrie began unpacking her basket, turning custard cream biscuits into the barrel on the sideboard and crumpling the paper bag into a ball.

'What if he goes to see our Heather?' David said unexpectedly.

'What?'

'He said he'd find Jenny somehow or other. What if he goes to see our Heather – or Gran?'

'Your gran wouldn't say anything and neither would our Heather. Anyway, I don't suppose he knows where they live. He only went out with our Jenny a few times.' Carrie was beginning to feel a bit more like herself. 'All I wish is,' she went on, 'he hadn't spoken to that blooming Joyce Edgell.'

But she was even beginning to think that Joyce wasn't quite the danger she'd seemed to be. There had been no repercussions from the fact that Joyce had discovered her well-kept secret and Carrie was more than halfway to persuading herself there wouldn't be. Who would listen to anything a trollop like Joyce said anyway? Without a shred of proof? It would just sound like sour grapes and hopefully nobody would believe such a thing of a well-respected family like the Simmonses.

No, all in all, Carrie was daring to hope she was in control again.

Helen was driving up Porters Hill.

She had been to visit Amy, who had telephoned to say

she had a first picking of peas from her garden, courtesy of Cliff Button, who was still working wonders with his green fingers, and would Helen like some to share with Charlotte? Helen had stayed longer than she had intended, chatting about Charlotte's progress and a good many other things besides whilst enjoying a glass of sherry with Amy at the picnic table on the lawn.

Usually she, like Amy, used the lane that ran along the valley past the mill rather than the steep and rutted hill, but today a tractor was moving slowly along it, scything the hedges, and rather than be stuck behind it or have to drive on to the verge and risk scratching her car, she had opted for the alternative route. She pulled out past the iron foundry – quiet today, no rollers trundling off behind lorries, and drove down towards the Jolly Collier, glancing to her left to look at the new road of bungalows that was being built in the field below Alder Road. More council housing. At last the economy seemed to be picking up after the rigours of war, but although she knew the houses were badly needed, Helen couldn't help regretting that the open spaces within the boundaries of Hillsbridge were fast disappearing.

Just as she reached the junction with the steep lane, a motorcycle came roaring down. Shocked, Helen realised he had no intention of stopping. She stood on her brakes and at the same moment the motorcyclist seemed to become aware of her and did the same. As she veered wildly, her car objecting to the sudden stop, she saw the motorcycle skid in the loose gravel which had accumulated on the junction after the recent tar-spraying. With almost comic grace, car and motorcycle floated towards one another and there was a crash and a thud as they collided.

Helen leaped out and ran round to where the motorcycle and rider lay beside her front nearside wing. She turned off the ignition and dropped to her haunches beside him.

'Are you all right?'

'My leg . . .' He tried to get up, but his leg was pinned beneath the machine.

'Don't try to move. I'm a doctor.'

The crash had been heard inside the Jolly Collier; three or four men who had been enjoying a lunchtime drink appeared in the doorway, pints in hand, with Ken Coles, the licencee, behind them.

'Can you help?' Helen asked.

Two of the men obliged, lifting the motorcycle clear and propping it up on its stand. It looked relatively none the worse for wear, with only a few scratches on the tank and a shredded handgrip to show for evidence of the accident.

Helen made a quick examination of the rider. He, too, seemed virtually unscathed – apart from his leg, which had taken a nasty knock.

'I think we ought to get this X-rayed,' she said. 'I'm not convinced you haven't got a fracture there.'

'I'm all right.' The young man sounded more impatient than shocked.

'I'd like to be sure of that. I'll drive you over to the cottage hospital myself and check you out there.'

Helen could be quite assertive when she chose, and she was backed up by Ken Coles.

'Doctor's right. You do as she says, mate. We'll put your bike on the forecourt of the butcher's shop for you. It'll be all right there.'

The motorcyclist looked on the point of arguing, but Helen opened the passenger door of her car and he reluctantly got in.

'You shouldn't just have come out on to the main road like that,' Helen said, starting the engine. She was a little shocked herself, and it made her sharp. 'This is the main road, you know.'

'Yeah. I wasn't thinking.'

'I don't know you, do I?'

'No, I'm just visiting. This won't take long, will it? I've got to be back at base tonight – I'm in the RAF – and I've got things to do round here first.'

'Provided there's a radiographer on duty, and provided you haven't got a fracture, you shouldn't be held up for long. Where are you stationed? Colerne?'

'Not now, no. I'm in Norfolk.'

'Norfolk! That's quite a trek! What's your name, by the way?'

'Bryn Thompson.'

'And I'm Helen Hall. Dr Hall. We'll need to exchange details formally and get the accident reported to the police, but let's get you seen to first.'

Hillsbridge town centre was bisected by two sets of railway lines; Salisbury Hill emerged between them. To reach the hospital Helen needed to turn to the left, but the crossing gates were closed on that line for a train which stood at the station, steam gushing out from the locomotive as the fireman took on water from the tanks at the end of the platform. Helen pulled up in the queue of traffic waiting to go through and glanced at Bryn. He had been silent for some moments now and she wondered if shock was setting in.

'Are you OK?'

His eyes were narrowed thoughtfully. After a moment he returned her glance.

'You're a doctor here, in Hillsbridge, are you?'

'That's right.'

Another momentary hesitation. Then: 'You're not Jenny Simmons' doctor, by any chance?'

'Yes,' she said, surprised. 'As a matter of fact I am.'

'So you'd know . . . could you tell me where I can find her?'

The engine was moving over the level crossing, its retinue of trucks clattering behind. Steam billowed across the windscreen of the car, thick enough to obscure Helen's view. She looked at Bryn again, adding together the fragments of the puzzle and coming up with an almost complete picture.

An RAF serviceman, previously stationed at Colerne and now in a posting on the other side of the country. In Hillsbridge with something very much on his mind, and looking for Jenny. It could mean one thing and one thing only.

'You do know where she is. You must!' he said, turning in his seat so he could look directly at Helen.

Helen made a great show of concentrating on moving

421

with the line of traffic. Her mind was racing over all the possibilities and pitfalls of this chance encounter.

'Why are you trying to find her?' she asked, turning into New Road.

'Why?' He sounded surprised she should ask.

'It's a simple enough question, surely?'

'Because I want to see her, of course. After I was posted to Norfolk, they sent me to Malta for a spell and we somehow lost touch. I can't understand why she stopped writing. I haven't heard from her now since before Christmas. She must have found somebody else, I suppose, but I couldn't just let it go like that, so I came down here to see her first chance I had. I thought – well, if she didn't want to have any more to do with me, I'd have to accept it, but it seemed strange. Anyway, she's not here, and her mother won't tell me where she is.'

'Why do you think I'd know?' Helen asked.

'Because . . .' He was silent for a moment, grimacing, whether in pain from his leg or for some other reason Helen did not know. 'I talked to one of her neighbours. She told me she thought Jenny's pregnant. If she is, and you're her doctor, well, you'd know, wouldn't you?'

'Do *you* think Jenny is pregnant?' Helen asked.

'I suppose she could be. But if so, why didn't she write and tell me?'

'If she is pregnant, you think the baby is yours?'

He jumped as if she had hit him. She sensed his hurt.

'Why are you asking all these questions? Why can't you just tell me where I can find her? I've got to see her, Doctor, surely you can see that?'

'What for?'

Then he really did explode. 'What the hell do you mean – what for? Because I want to marry her, of course – if she'll have me! I love her – can't you understand that?'

They were at the gates of the hospital. Helen felt nothing but relief at the reprieve.

'Let's get your X-ray done first. Then . . .'

'You'll tell me?'

'We'll talk about it,' Helen corrected him.

*

She didn't know what to do. She honestly did not know what to do. As she waited for the plates to be developed so she could examine them for evidence of a hairline fracture, she kept turning it over and over.

The boy seemed genuine, there was no doubt in her mind. If he said he was the father of Jenny's baby, then in all probability he was. Jenny wasn't a promiscuous girl, and the timing would be just right. But the stumbling blocks were there all the same. *One*. Jenny had stopped writing. Hadn't even let him know she was pregnant. *Two*. Confidentiality between doctor and patient was one of the cornerstones of her professional etiquette. To tell him that Jenny was indeed pregnant, let alone where she was, would be a serious breach of that confidence. If she got it wrong, she would be finished in Hillsbridge – perhaps finished as a doctor full stop.

And yet . . . and yet . . . She kept seeing Jenny's frightened face and hearing Carrie's bossy voice as she took charge. Jenny had had no say as to what she wanted – Carrie had made the decisions and Jenny had gone along with them because she thought she had no choice. Now it was possible she did have a choice.

As for the letters – it was always possible, if he was moving from place to place that they had not caught up with him. And then, feeling rejected, Jenny had stopped writing, retreated into a position from which she could not be hurt any more.

The boy was clearly anxious to stand by her, which was a good sign. It would have been all too easy for him to do a runner at the first mention of the word pregnant if he had wanted to.

The radiographer appeared with the plates. Helen checked them, struggling to keep her mind on the job. They looked fine.

'No fracture,' she reported back to Bryn. 'You'll be in some discomfort for a couple of days, and I'll give you a painkiller for that, then I'll take you back to the Jolly Collier for your motorbike.'

His eyes met hers, steady and determined. 'What about Jenny?'

Helen made up her mind. 'I can't give you information just like that. But what I will do is speak to her and see if she's willing for me to tell you what you want to know.'

'But I told you . . . I have to go back to camp tonight.'

'We'll stop off at my surgery,' Helen said. 'I'll make a phone call from there.'

Sister Anne was feeling spiteful.

This morning she had had a most unsatisfactory conversation with Jennifer – a girl she particularly disliked since she seemed not to appreciate anything that was being done to help her out of the predicament in which she had found herself. She had called Jenny to her office with what she had believed to be good news.

'We have found alternative adoptive parents for your baby,' she had said, looking with distaste at Jenny's swollen body. 'As you know, the first couple stipulated a girl. This couple have no strong preferences either way. All they are asking for is a healthy baby.'

She looked up at Jenny, saw the way her face set suddenly into lines of mulish defiance.

'Well?' she demanded. 'Isn't that a relief for you?'

Jenny swallowed hard. 'No.'

'What do you mean – no?'

Again Jenny swallowed, as if she was nervous but determined not to be intimidated. 'I've changed my mind, Sister. I don't want my baby adopted.'

Bitter gall rose in Sister Anne's throat like the indigestion to which she was a martyr.

'It's a little late for that, Jennifer. The arrangements have been made.'

'I haven't signed anything.'

'You have made a moral commitment. In any case, your mother . . .'

'She's not my mother,' Jenny said. 'She's my grand-mother. And she can't make me do what she wants. None of you can.'

'Young lady,' Sister Anne said severely, 'you are not in a position to assume responsibility for a baby.'

'I'll find a way!'

'I think not.'

'I will!'

'Don't talk nonsense! It has been decided that the best course of action for you and your baby is that it should be adopted. A lot of hard work has gone into making arrangements. And let me tell you, it will be so, whether you like it or not.'

'You can't . . .'

'A few years ago,' Sister Anne said, 'a very few years ago, girls like you would have been committed to an asylum. You are more fortunate than that. But you *will* do as we say. Believe me, your mother and I between us will make sure of that. Now, go to your room and think about what I have said.'

Jenny's lip was trembling but still she faced Sister Anne out defiantly.

'You can't take my baby! I won't let you!'

'When you are suffering the hellfire of childbirth,' Sister Anne said, coldly furious, 'I think you will find that you are not in a position to argue. Now – go. And I think, in preparation for penance, you should miss your lunch.'

Jenny had gone, but Sister Anne's bad mood had lingered. Just who did girls like Jenny think they were? Hussies – all of them. Little better than prostitutes! But with the nerve to argue with her – her! – Sister Anne!

At lunch, she had the satisfaction of noting that Jennifer had not tried to disobey her on that edict at least. Her place at table was empty. Perhaps when she got hungry enough she would begin to see the error of her ways.

It was about two in the afternoon when the telephone on Sister Anne's desk rang. She reached for it and was surprised to find Jenny's GP on the other end of the line.

'You want to speak to her *now*?' she said coldly. 'I'm not sure that it's convenient.'

The GP – a woman – refused to take no for an answer. Sister Anne put the call on hold and rang the bell to summon Sister Theresa.

'Would you go and fetch Jennifer, please? Her doctor wants to speak to her urgently.'

Five minutes later Sister Theresa was back. She looked flushed, flustered and frightened.

'She's not in her room, Sister! I can't find her anywhere. And her things seem to be missing.'

Until she had seen for herself, Sister Anne simply refused to believe it. But when she had inspected the dormitory there was no denying what Sister Theresa had said. Jenny had gone.

Chapter Twenty-Two

The town square, which had been busy with Saturday afternoon shoppers, was growing quiet and more deserted. Couples and family groups, like birds at sunset, were heading home. The long shadows, sharp against the bright patches of sunlight, concealed the debris of the day – chocolate wrappers, crisp packets, cigarette butts. There it would lie until morning when the road sweepers pushed their bins around the deserted streets and swept it all away.

In the bus station café on a corner of the square, Jenny huddled over a mug of luke-warm coffee, her hands cupped tightly around it in an effort to stop them from shaking. The emptying streets had awakened a feeling of panic. All those people wending their way home while she had nowhere to go! Soon the streets would be empty and then the night-lifers would move in. And still she would be here, on her own.

Think. She must think. Where to go. What to do. She hadn't stopped to consider for so much as a moment when she had walked out of the home. The only thing on her mind had been getting away – away from Sister Anne's tyranny, away from everyone who wanted to take her baby away from her. She had thrown her few belongings into the old brown leather attaché case and fled, terrified that she would be apprehended and hauled back. But there had been no-one to see her creep down the stairs – they were all at lunch. She could hear the clatter of cutlery on pottery, but no murmur of voices. Mealtimes at the home were silent affairs. The heavy old door creaked as she opened it and her heart beat hard against her ribs. But no-one came and she stepped out into the sunshine.

All she could think about then was putting as much

distance as possible between her and the nuns. She half ran down the drive and into the village street, then slowed down, aware that too much haste would only draw attention to her, and aware too, painfully, of a stabbing stitch in her side.

There was a bus at the stop opposite the post office store with a few passengers getting off and a few more waiting to board. Jenny didn't even stop to wonder where it was going. She joined the queue, glancing anxiously back towards the gates of the home, but still no-one came.

'Where to?' the conductor asked when he worked his way down the aisle to the back where she had flopped down, her case on the seat beside her.

'As far as you're going.'

She could sense his curiosity as he rolled out her ticket, swaying with the movement of the bus as a master mariner might sway with the rocking of a boat, but he didn't say anything. He was a solid, ruddy-faced little man, and when she counted out the money he averted his eyes, embarrassed, no doubt, by her condition.

The journey lasted for almost an hour and Jenny watched the hedges and fields roll past in a kind of heavy trance. At last the countryside gave way to houses and the houses to office blocks and shops. The bus turned into the square and the driver killed the engine. She had to get off. This was the end of the line.

Heat came off the pavement in waves as she walked aimlessly, burning through the soles of her shoes and a fine sheen of sweat formed across her back. The baby was a leaden weight, exhausting her, and the stitch had become a niggle of discomfort low in her back. Where was she going? She didn't know. Lisbee Smith, with whom she had shared a dormitory for a while, lived in this part of the world and she had given Jenny her telephone number before she left, but if Lisbee had been packed off to the home to have her baby, Jenny couldn't imagine that she would be greeted with open arms if she turned up on the family doorstep!

The first elation was beginning to give way to anxiety now, sending her thoughts into chaotic turmoil, and time, too, was playing peculiar tricks. On the one hand it moved so slowly as to seem to stand still, on the other it rushed by, minutes becoming hours in the blinking of an eye.

As the shadows began to sharpen, both the heavy discomfort in her lower back and her sense of panic and isolation grew. All very well to run, but with nowhere to go it seemed less and less of a good idea. The future which just this morning had seemed so ominously imminent was now a lifetime away, playing the same tricks as the hands on her watch. First there was today to get through and, more importantly, tonight. Having nowhere to sleep and next to no money to pay for accommodation would have been bad enough under any circumstances, as it was, with a baby to think of, it was even more worrying.

Scouring the streets, Jenny found a couple of small commercial hotels offering vacancies, but when she enquired the cost of a night's bed and breakfast she realised it was beyond her means. One night and all her money would be gone with nothing left over for anything to eat. She couldn't possibly make herself penniless in one fell swoop. Dare she use the accommodation and leave without paying? The very thought was anathema to her, raised as she had been to be strictly honest. And supposing she couldn't get out in the morning? For all she knew the proprietors might lock and bolt the door. If she was caught trying to leave without paying the police would be sent for. In any case, the B & Bs probably required payment up front, or at the very least a hefty deposit.

So it was beginning to look as though she'd be sleeping rough after all. At least – thank heavens for small mercies – the weather was good. From the windows of the bus Jenny had noticed a small park on the outskirts of town, with swings and an iron roundabout for the children, and a bandstand. There were sure to be covered benches too which would afford her some shelter.

By now Jenny was hungry, thirsty and exhausted. She made her way back to the bus station and spent some of her precious little money on a sausage roll and a cup of coffee. From here, she thought, she could retrace the route the bus had taken and find the park again. But not just yet. Someone might notice her lurking and turn her out. She'd wait a while. But even sitting down the ache in the seat of her back was still making her squirm, a discomfort as persistent as a nagging toothache.

At least her brain was beginning to function again, though. The panicky spirals were straightening out, forming straight lines. The trouble was they led nowhere. Or, perhaps more accurately, they all led to the same conclusion. Her situation was totally hopeless. She might be free of the home and the nuns, but she had no money, no way of getting any, nowhere to go, no real plans beyond the next few hours. She couldn't survive this way alone, much less with a baby. She'd behaved with incredible foolishness, made things worse rather than better. And yet . . .

Maybe, just maybe, the fact that she had run away from the home might make Carrie realise how desperately she wanted to keep this baby. Had the nuns notified them yet that she was missing? Were they worried about her? If they knew, they certainly would be worried. That they cared about her, very much, had never been in question. It was just that they'd cared too much about other things too – propriety and what people would say, to name but two. Perhaps they even cared too much about *her*, thinking about her future, coming up with the wrong decisions for all the right reasons and imposing them on her because they believed they knew best.

Well, she wasn't going to go along with their decisions any more, she had made up her mind about that. She wasn't going to have her movements mapped out for her as if she was still a child. Whatever happened she was going to keep this baby and bring it up. But if she was to convince them that she was a fit person to be a mother she must show some sense of responsibility now. Sleeping rough in parks, endangering her own health and the health of her unborn baby was not the way to do that. She had to prove to Carrie that she was sensible enough – grown-up enough, to cope. Then, perhaps, she would help.

And then Jenny remembered what she had been unable to forget since Heather had come to see her, but which had

430

somehow fallen out of the equation as she tried to work out what to do, where to go. Carrie wasn't her mother. Heather was.

A sudden rush of love and longing for the girl she had always thought of as her sister overwhelmed her. When Heather had broken the news to her, the shock of it had made her recoil. She had been able to think of nothing but the deceit practised on her, the growing-up years when nothing had been as it seemed. The sense of rejection, coming from a quarter where she had never expected to find it, had made her determined that her own child should never experience such a rejection, and she had retreated into a hard shell of bitterness, shutting herself off both physically and emotionally from the family she felt had betrayed her.

Now, for the first time since she had learned the truth, she found herself remembering the closeness of her relationship with Heather; the little things and the big; the way Heather had always been there for her, the love she had shown.

Heather had been even younger than she herself was now, Jenny reminded herself, even less able to resist Carrie's relentless overpowering way of making all the family decisions. No doubt it had been her idea to bring Jenny up as her own, and Heather had gone along with it.

I, of all people, should be able to understand how it was for her, Jenny thought. *How frightened she must have been, how helpless she must have felt. And how it has been for her all these years, too. I glimpsed that when she offered to take on my baby. But I was too shocked to consider her feelings. How I must have hurt her!*

And had it been such a bad thing that Heather had done? However misguided, she and Carrie had both acted out of love.

I've known that love all my life, Jenny thought. *At least I have been with my family, not with strangers. And I can't believe, honestly, that they will turn their backs on me now.*

It wasn't true that she had nowhere to go, tonight or any other night. Whatever the problems, somehow, as a family, they would find a way to overcome them. Carrie's desire for secrecy might be blown out of the water, but it

431

seemed to Jenny that the time for secrecy was over. There were other more important considerations now. Her mind was made up. She was going home.

'Where can she *be*?' Heather said. 'Where would she go?'

She had been asking the same questions over and over again, every few minutes, ever since she had heard that Jenny was missing, pacing the floor in an agony of anxiety, trying to control the wilder excesses of imagination and not quite succeeding.

'The stupid girl!' Carrie said. 'What a stupid thing to do! In her condition!'

She, too, had become repetitious and as usual her anxiety was finding release in irritation. It had been like this all afternoon.

Heather had been at Number 27 Alder Road when Dr Hall had come knocking on the door. Steve had taken Vanessa to the swings in the football fields and Heather had gone to collect a pair of curtains which had shrunk in the wash and which she had promised Carrie she would try to let down for her.

They were at the window, hanging a replacement pair, when the car pulled up outside the gate.

'It's the doctor!' Carrie said as Helen got out. 'Whatever does she want?'

'I expect she's got the wrong house,' Heather said. She could see a young man in the front passenger seat. 'There's somebody with her.'

Carrie pressed her nose against the glass, peering out, then exclaiming in disbelief.

'No! I don't believe it . . .'

The doorbell rang.

'Do you want me to go?' Heather asked.

'No.' Carrie was breathing hard now, chest puffed out like a turkeycock. 'I'll go. She's got that boy with her! Keep the dog in, will you?'

Heather grabbed Sally's collar. 'What boy?'

'The one that got our Jenny into trouble! I've sent him packing once today, and I'll do it again!' She flounced down the stairs and threw open the door.

Heather followed.

'Yes, Doctor.' Carrie's greeting was short, snappy.

'Mrs Simmons. Can I come in?'

'Not if you've come to talk to me about *him*, no!' Carrie nodded her head abruptly in the direction of the car.

'It's not . . . well, only indirectly. Look – I really think it would be better . . .'

'He's got no rights. None at all!'

'Just a minute,' Heather interrupted. 'Did you say that's Jenny's boyfriend out there?'

'He's already been here bothering once today,' Carrie said. 'I sent him off with a flea in his ear.'

'Well, I'd like to talk to him,' Heather said.

'Over my dead body!'

'Mum – if he's come here looking for Jenny, we have to talk to him.'

'I don't want her unsettled.'

'Can I get a word in, please?' Helen said. They both looked at her. 'The fact that Bryn is in my car is incidental. I'm here because I've just learned some very disturbing news I didn't want to tell you on the doorstep but you leave me no choice. Jenny is missing.'

'Missing? What do you mean – missing?' Carrie demanded.

'She's disappeared from the mother and baby home. And her things have gone too. From what I can make out, pressure was being put on her with regard to the adoption . . .'

'It's only what we agreed was for the best!'

'And it's upset Jenny enough to make her decide to run away.'

'Oh my Lord!' Carrie said. 'Perhaps you'd better come in after all, Doctor.' She saw Helen glance towards the car and the young man and her mouth hardened. 'Not him!'

'Mum!' Heather said. She was upset, yet more in command than Carrie had ever seen her. 'Isn't it time to put a stop to this?' She turned to Helen. 'He came to you looking for her, did he?'

Helen let that go. She didn't want to waste time explaining about the accident.

'He's very anxious to get in touch with Jenny. And he's very upset about her disappearance.'

'*He* knows? Before *we* did?' Carrie was outraged.

'He was with me when I found out, yes.'

'He's no right to know before us.'

'For heaven's sake, Mum!' Heather yelled, turning on her mother. 'If he's the father of Jenny's baby, he has every right!'

'Hasn't he done enough?'

'Jenny thinks the world of him, Mum, you know that as well as I do. And now she's missing and all you can think about is who knew first! I can't believe you! I'm going out to speak to him!'

She pushed past Carrie, who could only stare, open-mouthed. It was the first time Heather had openly defied her over any of her decisions regarding Jenny. With a resigned shake of the head she gestured to Helen to follow her into the house.

'So what's this all about?'

Helen told her all she knew.

'Oh, the stupid girl! Everything planned and she has to go and upset it all!' Carrie said. 'Whatever is she thinking of . . .' She broke off as Heather came in, accompanied by Bryn. 'Now see what you've gone and done!' she shot at him. 'All the trouble you've caused!'

'Stop it, Mum!' Heather said. 'You're not helping anyone. Bryn is as worried about Jenny as we are.'

Carrie responded with an angry snort.

'He wants to go up to Gloucester and try to find her,' Heather said.

'You've told him where she is!'

'We don't *know* where she is!' Heather snapped back. 'She's wandering around somewhere all on her own in heaven only knows what state. You should be glad he cares! I'd go myself if it wasn't for Vanessa.'

'I'm not sure there'd be any point in going up there,' Helen said, trying to calm the situation. 'The sister in charge was going to call the police and report her missing and I'm sure she'll soon be found.'

'I'm going anyway,' Bryn said.

'I thought you were due back at camp tonight,' Helen said.

'I'll ring them – put in for compassionate leave.' He turned to Carrie. 'I'm sorry if you think I'm to blame for all this, Mrs Simmons, but I do love Jenny. I still can't understand why she stopped answering my letters and I can't understand why she didn't write and tell me about the baby.'

Heather frowned. 'But she did! I know she wrote! She told me!'

'It must have gone astray,' Carrie said quickly – too quickly.

Heather looked at her incredulously. 'Mum . . .?'

A dark flush rose in Carrie's cheeks. 'If he's been abroad anything could have happened to it.'

'Look, I really have to be going,' Helen said. 'I'll give you a lift back to where you left your motorbike, Bryn. And what about you, Heather? Do you want to go home and make some telephone calls?'

'I think so – yes.'

'I'll come too,' Carrie said.

'No, Mum,' Heather said. 'I think you should stay here. This is Jenny's home address, remember. If the Hillsbridge police get a message they'll come here. I'll find out what I can and then come back.'

Carrie had no choice but to agree.

'I'm so sorry about all this,' Heather said to Bryn as they rode down the hill in Helen's car. 'I just hope and pray Jenny hasn't done anything silly.' She was silent for a moment, then she added: 'If you find her, you will let me know?'

'I'll let *you* know.' His tone left her in no doubt how he felt about Carrie. 'She thinks a lot of you.'

Heather swallowed hard, tears knotting suddenly in her throat. 'Find her, Bryn. Make her come home.'

'Oh, I'll find her,' he said.

When she had made the necessary phone calls, Steve ran Heather back up to Alder Road. She was none the wiser, no-one had seen Jenny since before lunch. But the police had been notified and were searching for her. For the moment there was no more they could do. Heather opened the door and went in without knocking.

'Mum, I want to talk to you . . .' She stopped in the doorway of the living room, hardly able to believe her eyes. Carrie was at the table, leafing through a stack of letters. She looked flustered – and very, very guilty.

'Mum?'

Heather crossed to the table, unable to believe her eyes. Envelopes addressed to Bryn in Jenny's handwriting, sheets of paper, some unfolded to reveal closely written lines in an unfamiliar hand – and at the top, preceding the sender's address, a service number. When Carrie had been so quick to claim Jenny's letter about her pregnancy had gone astray the thought had flashed through Heather's mind that she might have known more about it than she was prepared to admit. But this!

'Don't look at me like that!' Carrie snapped.

'What have you done, Mum?' Heather sounded more incredulous than accusing.

'It was for the best.' Carrie was trying to bundle the letters together. 'He wasn't right for her. I wanted to put a stop to it.'

'But you had no right. Mum, how could you?'

'I was only trying to protect her. She was far too young to be getting serious with a boy she hardly knew. I thought it would all die a natural death. I never knew she was . . .' She baulked at the word pregnant. 'I wasn't to know how it was going to turn out!'

'It's a terrible thing to do!'

'I did what I thought was right. That's all I've ever done. The best thing now is to get rid of them. I should never have kept them in the first place.'

'You can't get rid of them!' Heather said, shocked. 'They belong to Jenny.'

Carrie grew even more flustered. 'She mustn't see them! She'll . . .'

'Never forgive you? No, I don't expect she will. To be honest, I shall find it very hard to forgive you myself.'

Carrie's jaw dropped. 'What are you talking about?'

'I trusted you with her, Mum. I trusted you to give her a better life than I could . . .'

'And she's had it! Nothing but the best.'

'You've kept her in a gilded cage! You were so worried she'd turn out like me you ruled her with a rod of iron. I can't tell you how many times I've had to bite my tongue over the way you've been with her. But I told myself I'd forfeited my right to interfere. I suppose in a funny sort of way I still thought that you knew best. I took you at your own valuation – respected your judgement – because you are my mother. But this . . . you've gone way too far this time. And look what's happened as a result!'

Carrie's face crumpled suddenly, the confidence rushing out of her like air from a punctured balloon. She knew she'd meant well, just like everything she'd ever done it had been for the best and for their own good. But how to make the others see that? She had never known Heather so angry, never experienced such scorn, directed at her by her own daughter.

'Whatever is going on?'

So engrossed had they been in their argument, neither of them heard Joe come in. He stood now, looking from one to the other, troubled and puzzled. Carrie's lower lip sagged, trembled, fought a losing battle at holding back the tears.

'Oh, Joe – it's our Jenny! She's run away, and we don't know where she is.'

'Wherever have you been, Helen? I was getting worried to death about you!'

Charlotte was out by the door, leaning heavily on her stick, when Helen eventually pulled up outside Number 11, Greenslade Terrace.

'Oh, Gran, don't even ask!' Helen couldn't face going through it all again. She was too worried – though she was trying to console herself that thanks to her chance meeting with Bryn and her telephone call to the home, Jenny's absence had been discovered hours before it might otherwise have been, and the search for her begun. 'I'm really sorry, though, leaving you on your own all this time.'

437

'Oh, I'm not on my own,' Charlotte said. 'I've got company.'

'Company.'

'Me.' Paul appeared in the doorway. 'We've been getting along just fine without her, haven't we, Gran?'

'Gran!' Helen managed a smile. She thought she had never been more pleased to see anyone in her life.

An hour and a half after Helen dropped him off, Bryn was knocking on the door of the home. His leg was paining him quite badly and hunching over the handlebars of his motorcycle he had discovered that he had strained a shoulder muscle too. But he gritted his teeth against the discomfort. Something so trivial wasn't going to stop him finding Jenny.

The door was opened by Sister Theresa. She stood barring his way, her face apprehensive beneath her veil. Men always made Sister Theresa nervous, their rough ways and loud voices set her nerves jangling and this young man, in his leather jacket and crash helmet, looked more threatening than most.

'Can I help you?' she asked timidly.

'Has Jenny been found?'

'Jenny?'

'Jenny Simmons. Has she come back?'

'No – we don't know where she is.'

'Have the police been told she's missing?'

'Yes, yes, of course. We're very worried about her. She's due to have her baby at any time.'

'What is going on here?' Sister Anne appeared in the doorway. Sister Theresa explained, still fluttering.

'You'd better come in,' Sister Anne said. 'It's all right, Sister, he's not going to attack you.'

'I take it you are the young man to blame for Jennifer's condition,' she said severely when she and Bryn were alone in her study.

His eyes met hers square on. 'I am. Yes.'

'I can tell you very little, except that Jennifer walked out of our care soon after midday today. As I'm sure you must be aware, the girls are not prisoners here, and we cannot

438

be responsible for their well-being if they choose to absent themselves in this way.'

'Where could she have gone?' Bryn asked. He had no intention wasting time with apportioning responsibility or blame.

'I really have no idea. As I told the police . . .'

'Where do you think she might have gone?' Seeing Sister Anne about to deny all knowledge once again, he added: 'I want to find her, and I should think you'd want that too.'

'I should be pleased to know she is safe, of course,' Sister Anne conceded. 'Though whether we would be prepared to take her in again is another matter entirely. This kind of thing is very bad for our reputation and the sooner the police cease to be involved, the better.'

'So where could she have gone?' Bryn persisted.

Sister Anne thought for a moment. 'We're very isolated here. She *could* have walked, I suppose, but in her condition it's not likely she would get very far. I think the most likely thing is that she would have caught a bus in the village. They run into town every half an hour. Unless of course she hitched a lift in a car.'

Bryn's anxiety was a knot in his stomach. The thought of Jenny vulnerable and alone in a car with a stranger was not a pleasant one. As for the bus . . . if she had gone into the city she could be anywhere by now. But at least it was a starting point. The only one he had. And the voice of intuition, though he was almost afraid to listen to it, was telling him he might be on the right track. He tried one last question.

'She hasn't made any friends around here that you know of?'

'None of the girls she has met live in the vicinity. And if they did, they would be in no position to help her.'

Bryn moved towards the door. 'I'll just have to look and keep looking then,' he said.

For the first time, a small crack appeared in Sister Anne's concrete-hard façade. 'You will let us know if you find her?'

Bryn didn't reply. He was already on his way.

'I'm afraid you've gone too far this time, m'dear,' Joe said, shaking his head. His tone was worried and sad, but it also had that edge that Carrie dreaded.

'I did it for the best.'

'That's your trouble. You always do. But to keep her letters like that – you shouldn't have done that, you know. You've really upset the apple cart this time.'

'Never mind the letters!' Carrie snapped defensively. 'Where's our Jenny, that's what I want to know. I'm worried to death about her, Joe.'

'So are we all, m'dear. But she'll turn up. She's a good girl, our Jenny. The thing is, when she does, you're going to have to own up about all this.'

Carrie pressed a hand over her mouth. Beneath it, her chin wobbled dangerously.

'Whatever is she going to think of me, Joe?'

'Well, she's not going to be best pleased with you, that goes without saying. But I reckon the best way to make it up to her is to give her the chance to make up her own mind what she wants to do about the boy – and the baby. We should never have sent her away at a time like this. She should be here at a time like this, in her own home.'

'But everyone would have been pointing the finger . . .'

'You shouldn't worry your head so much about what people think. If she's run away from that place, she must be unhappy there. When she turns up, and she will, let her come home. And if she wants to keep the nipper, whether that boy's on the scene or not, then we should let her. Only leave it to *her*, Carrie. Stop trying to make her mind up for her.'

Carrie bit her trembling lip. What Joe was suggesting would blow all her carefully laid plans out of the water. But perhaps he was right. For all that he seldom expressed his opinions, he often was.

'Let's just find her first,' Carrie said jerkily. 'Let's just find her and make sure she's all right, and then we'll worry about all the rest of it.'

'It wouldn't do any harm to be thinking about it while we're waiting,' Joe said firmly.

440

Jenny was studying the timetables, covered with sheets of clear plastic, that punctuated the edge of the square outside the bus station. She was trying to work out the best way of getting home. She was hungry, her head ached and her back was niggling unbearably. Because her eyes were blurring it wasn't easy to make out the small print on the timetables, much less decipher which buses ran, or didn't run, on Saturday evenings. She was worried as to whether she had enough money for the fare, even more worried about the reception she would get when she arrived home. Should she telephone – ask if David or Steve could come and get her? But that would give them the chance to take her back to the home.

A bus rolled up to one of the stops, disgorging a gang of girls, obviously Saturday night revellers. They were giggling and chatting and the reminder that such a short time ago she had been just like them deepened Jenny's despair. She looked away quickly, out across the square, and suddenly her heart was pounding, racing.

The young man walking down the opposite side of the square was exactly like Bryn! Fair hair, black leather jacket. She must be going mad, seeing things like a mirage in the desert. But she couldn't tear her eyes away. It couldn't be him. It wasn't possible. But . . .

It was! It was Bryn!

Terrified of losing sight of him, Jenny plunged off the pavement. The bus that had just finished unloading the Saturday night revellers was backing up. Jenny was totally unaware of it and the driver never saw her step into his path.

'Bryn!' she shouted. And at the very moment he turned and saw her, she went under the bus.

'She'll be all right, Helen,' Paul said. 'What can possibly happen to her?'

'I don't know. She's a sensible girl, but . . .' Helen broke off, unwilling to admit she had this really bad feeling.

'Look – why don't we go out? Reuben's on call, your gran's on the mend, and you could do with taking your

441

mind off all this. There's nothing you can do.'

'I know.' But she knew that as long as Jenny was missing she wouldn't be able to forget. 'Well, if we do go out, can we at least call round first to see if there's any news?'

He pulled a face. 'If you want, I suppose.'

'I do want.'

'You, Helen,' he said, 'are one of the most caring GPs I've ever me.'

She pulled a face back. 'I hope it makes up for my other shortcomings. I'm losing far too many patients one way and another.'

'This one will turn up, I promise you.'

'I hope you're right.'

But the bad feeling persisted.

'Jenny! Jenny – can you hear me!'

His voice seemed to be coming from a long way off, a million miles away, above the singing in her head, above the thick whirring background noises. She tried to move and could not. She was wedged firmly and her leg was doubled awkwardly beneath her. And there was pain – so much pain. Everywhere, it seemed, and yet concentrated in her back and in her loins, as if the ache that had been there all day had suddenly exploded.

My baby! she tried to cry out. But no sound came. She couldn't breathe. She couldn't speak. She couldn't even cry.

'We'll get you out, Jenny, don't worry. Hold on!'

His voice was even fainter than before, the roaring in her ears was louder, like the tide roaring into a cave on the shoreline, washing over her in waves, obliterating everything.

To Bryn, it seemed to take for ever. In fact, the emergency services were on the scene within minutes, but then everything was moving in slow motion.

Jenny was trapped underneath a couple of hundred-weight of solid metal. She was unconscious, mercifully perhaps, but that was not all. She had gone into labour. The full force of the situation hit Bryn with the same force

442

as if he too had been hit by the bus. He'd found her – thank God! – but that was small compensation now. He'd found her and he might be about to lose her again. Irretrievably. And the baby that he'd only just found out about. Not that the baby mattered to him at this moment. Only Jenny mattered. And Jenny was in God-alone-knew what condition.

Helpless, able to do nothing whatever to help free her, Bryn turned away, staring up into the deep blue of the sky above the rooftops, and let out a silent howl of agony.

Chapter Twenty-Three

Heather replaced the receiver and turned to Steve and Glad, who stood in the hallway behind her. She was paper white and trembling. From the one-sided conversation they had been able to hear, Steve and Glad had gathered that Jenny had been found, but also that something was dreadfully wrong.

'What is it? What's happened?' Glad asked. Her hand was clutching her heart.

Steve said nothing, simply went to Heather and put his arm around her. He knew how much Jenny meant to Heather and why. She had told him her secret long ago, before they were married.

'She's been in an accident,' Heather said, trying to keep her voice steady and utterly failing. 'She's in hospital now, and they're doing an emergency Caesarean.'

'Oh my Lord!' Glad said.

'I have to go to her,' Heather said. 'Can you take me, Steve? Bryn's there, but I have to be with her too.'

'Of course,' Steve said. 'Vanessa . . .'

'I'll look after Vanessa,' Glad said. 'Don't you worry about her. But you must let your mum know, Heather.'

'Yes . . . yes, of course . . . oh, I can't think straight!' One thought did fight its way to the surface. 'I don't want her coming, though. Not after what she's done.'

'You mustn't talk like that,' Glad said. 'She did wrong, of course, but she loves Jenny just like you do. She's always been a good mother to her. You mustn't let something like this make you forget all the good things.'

Heather closed her eyes briefly. At the moment she could think of nothing beyond the indisputable fact that Jenny would not now be lying in hospital undergoing emergency surgery if it hadn't been for Carrie and her

444

desire to dominate every aspect of their lives.

'Glad's right, Heather,' Steve said gently. 'We all make mistakes.'

'The trouble with Mum is that she won't admit it,' Heather said harshly.

'All the same . . .'

'I know, I know. All right, we'll go up and tell her before we leave. I just hope she won't want to come with us.'

But even as she said it she knew it was a vain hope. Trying to keep Carrie away would be like King Canute trying to hold back the tide.

In fact she was in for a surprise.

'Do you want to come with us, Mum?' she asked, holding out the olive branch in spite of herself. But Carrie shook her head.

'You know I can't abide hospitals.'

'But don't you want to see Jenny – and the baby?'

'If it's all right, you mean.'

Heather swallowed hard. Carrie had voiced her unspoken fear that the baby might not survive.

'Is that what you want, Mum?' she said before she could stop herself. 'It would solve everything, wouldn't it, if the baby died. We could all pretend nothing had ever happened.'

But Carrie denied it vehemently. 'How can you say such a thing? It's my grandchild, isn't it?' Heather's eyes met hers and she amended: 'All right – my *great-grandchild*. It amounts to the same thing.'

If she hadn't been so worried, Heather might have found that funny. As it was, she was in no mood for laughing.

'No, I won't come,' Carrie said again. 'That boy will be there, won't he?'

'Yes, I expect he will,' Heather said, profoundly relieved. The thought of a confrontation between Bryn and Carrie was not a pleasant prospect at the best of times. Carrie had one more surprise for her yet, though.

'You can tell our Jenny from me that if she wants to bring the baby home here, she might as well. Joyce Edgell knows about it anyway, so there's no point trying to hush it up any more.'

Heather stared at her in amazement and saw Carrie exchange a look with Joe. 'We'll manage somehow. Just as long as they're both all right, that's all that really matters.'

'They'll be all right, m'dear,' Joe said comfortingly. The very real bond between them, sometimes obscured by Carrie's bossy ways, was clear to see.

'We'll get going then,' Heather said, feeling suddenly as if she had intruded on a private moment.

Carrie followed them to the front door.

'Heather . . .' she caught at her daughter's sleeve, 'you won't tell her . . . will you . . .'

'About the letters? She'll have to know, Mum.'

'But not now. Don't go upsetting her now. If she's poorly . . .'

'Give me credit for some sense, Mum,' Heather said.

'And you will give her our love?'

'Of course I will.' But she was wondering if that would be possible. The last she had heard, Jenny had been unconscious.

She half ran down the path to the car, nervous energy igniting every nerve and muscle. All she wanted was to be with Jenny, for Jenny to be all right, and for their relationship to return to something like normal.

'She'll be all right, m'dear,' Joe said again as Carrie came back in. 'Things'll turn out, you'll see.'

'Will they?' Carrie felt as though the whole of her world was falling apart and she was floundering in a whirling mill pond of emotions, each clamouring for her attention: the desperate anxiety for Jenny – and for the baby, though until now she had never thought of the baby as anything but an unwanted obstacle to Jenny's future and her own well-ordered life; dread of the now inevitable scandal, the wagging tongues attacking the bastion of her respect-ability and the triumphant glances that would follow her down the street; and guilt. Guilt that even at a time like this she could still feel anxiety over what people would say and most of all guilt at what she had done.

All her life Carrie had forged ahead, taking control of situations, doing what she thought best without questioning what she saw as her God-given right to do so. So sure had she been of her own wisdom and the rightness of her decisions that she had found a way of justifying to herself even the most outrageous actions.

Not this time. Carrie had known, even before Joe had confronted her with it that this time she had overstepped the mark and done the unforgivable, and the knowledge somehow cast doubt on all her other decisions over the years. They had been the stepping stones laying out the path to what was happening now, each one of them inexorably paving the way to disaster. She had sought only to do what she believed was best for her family and this was how it had turned out. For the first time, Carrie acknowledged there was no-one to blame but herself.

'Oh, Joe, I've been such a fool,' she said.

He patted her hand, his old, placating self once more.

'You'm all right, m'dear. And so will they be. You'll see.'

'Joe Simmons – I love you,' she said. And there were tears in her eyes.

Bryn stood looking down at the tiny scrap of life in the incubator. So small, so incredibly vulnerable, and yet so perfect. His baby. His and Jenny's. As yet, no-one would promise him that she would survive. He hoped desperately that was because they were afraid to commit themselves. The thought of that miracle of life, fluttering with each rise and fall of the small chest, being extinguished, was too terrible. Until a few hours ago he hadn't even known he was going to be a father. Now, hope and longing for her filled his world. His daughter. The word itself was a miracle. Bryn bent his head and for the first time since he himself had been a child, he prayed.

Jenny floated up through layer upon layer of cotton wool towards consciousness. Fragments of awareness came to her like haunting dreams and with them, blinded washes of emotion. She tried to grasp at thoughts, force them to

447

take form, and failed. Each time they slipped away from her, elusive as butterflies.

Someone was holding her hand. She could feel the warm pressure of fingers on her own. She forced her heavy eyes to open. A white ceiling, swimming with myriad molecules. The effort was almost too much for her. She closed her eyes again, moving her head restlessly on the pillow.

'Jenny?'

The sound of his voice brought conscious thought within reach once more, though still she could not grasp it, could not believe what seemed more like a dream than reality. She turned her head toward the voice, opened her eyes again, and his face swam into focus. Wonder filled her, and a tide of happiness. Suddenly, for the first time in weeks – months – Jenny felt safe.

'Bryn?' she whispered through dry lips.

His mouth was on her hand where those comforting fingers lay.

'Oh, Jenny – thank God!'

Heather's nervous energy propelled her along the hospital corridor just as it had propelled her down the path of her mother's house. Throughout the hour-long journey it had kept her on edge, so that the bouts of black silence when she was unable to speak were punctuated by repeating the same things over and over again, and her hands fiddled ceaselessly, picking at bits of dry skin around her nails. Now she went all of a rush along the corridor, Steve trailing behind her.

A nurse, all starched linen, intercepted her.

'Can I help?'

'Jenny Simmons?'

'Are you a relative?'

'I'm her mother.' It seemed the most natural thing in the world to say.

'If you'd like to take a seat . . .' The nurse indicated a row of chairs lined up against the wall.

'Can't I see her?'

'She can only have one visitor at a time.'

'Oh, I see.' Obviously Bryn must be with her. 'She's all right though?'

'Just take a seat. I'll get someone to come and talk to you.'

'What about the baby?'

'I'll get someone to come and talk to you,' the nurse repeated.

Steve sat down but Heather couldn't. She paced. Each time the doors to the ward swung open she jumped in anticipation. At last a white-coated doctor approached.

'Mrs Simmons?'

'Mrs Okonski,' she corrected him.

'Jenny's mum, anyway.'

'Yes. How is she, Doctor?'

'Considering what happened to her, she's in pretty good shape. No serious damage as far as we can tell. But she did take a very nasty knock and she had undergone a Caesarean section to deliver her baby. It's all pretty traumatic and what she needs now is plenty of rest. Needless to say, we shall be keeping a close eye on her over the next few hours.'

'And the baby?'

'Holding her own. As yet it's too early to say. Would you like to go in and see Jenny for a few minutes?'

'Can I? The nurse said . . .'

'If it's just yourself, and provided you don't excite her, I think I can allow it.'

'It's all right,' Steve said. 'I'll wait here.'

The curtains were drawn around Jenny's bed. As the doctor pulled them aside for Heather to go in her nerve almost failed her, all that eagerness superseded for a moment by nervous awkwardness and a twist of gut-wrenching terror.

Bryn, sitting beside the bed, holding Jenny's hand, looked up and saw her.

'Jenny?' he said. 'It's your sister.' And that, too, of course, was entirely natural.

Jenny turned her head and Heather saw with a shock that one side of her face was swollen to twice its usual size with a great angry discolouration running its entire length. But there was no sign of the rejection she had been so afraid of. Jenny smiled. And though in the puffed mask it might have appeared almost grotesque, Heather thought that smile was the loveliest thing she had ever seen.

'Oh, Jenny,' she said. 'Oh, darling Jenny. I've been so worried!'

And to her surprise, Jenny whispered: 'I'm sorry, Heather.'

'What do you mean – *you're* sorry?' Heather was fighting back tears. 'We're the ones who should be sorry! Oh, darling – what have we done to you?'

'I'm OK,' Jenny said. Her voice was just a husky little whisper. 'I'm OK – now.' And she managed another smile, tremulous, this time at Bryn. 'Can I talk to Heather? Alone?'

He nodded, bending over to kiss the unbruised part of her face before getting up.

'You won't go away again though, will you?'

'I'll be just outside. Don't worry, I'm not going anywhere.'

Heather took his seat, pulling it close to the edge of the bed.

'Jenny . . .'

'Heather.' Jenny's hand found hers. 'Tell me the truth. The baby . . .?'

'Is doing as well as can be expected.'

'Are you sure? She's not . . . *dead* . . . and they won't tell me?'

'I'm sure. It's touch and go, Jen, but at the moment she's holding her own.'

Jenny's face crumpled. She closed her eyes and a tear rolled out from the corner of the one that was not swollen.

'Thank God!' She was silent for a moment, then she opened her eyes again. 'She will be all right, won't she? She's got to be all right!'

'I think she will be, yes. I expect she's a little fighter – like you. And Jen . . . look . . . there's going to be no more pretence. When she's well enough – when you're both well enough – you can bring her home.'

'But Mum . . .' She still thought of Carrie as Mum and always would.

450

'It's OK. It was Mum said to tell you. And she sends her love.' She hesitated. 'She means well, Jenny. I know some of the things she does are very hard to forgive, but you have to remember she does them because she loves us and wants the best for us. She's never done a single thing out of spite or malice or because of bad feelings. It's just that she's . . . well, a bit like a tigress with her cubs. Stopping at nothing to protect us or ensure our welfare. You must remember that. It's all done out of love.'

'I know that,' Jenny said. 'I've always known that.'

'But there may be some things she's done that are even harder to forgive.'

'Mum is Mum!' Jenny said. 'She's always been the same, and I expect she always will.'

'And me?' Heather said after a moment. 'Can you forgive me?'

'Oh, Heather, I know now how you felt, don't I?'

The nurse was hovering.

'I think that's long enough. Jenny needs to rest.'

'Heather . . .' Jenny caught at Heather's sleeve, 'I just want you to know. When it happened – the accident . . .'

'Yes?'

'I was coming home.'

For the next two weeks, Jenny's baby's life hung in the balance and then one day Jenny got the news she had been waiting for. She was to be discharged and the baby – whom she had named Sarah – was to be transferred to the Special Care Baby Unit in Bath.

Jenny travelled with her in the ambulance and saw her safely installed – that tiny, most precious thing in the whole world – and then David drove her home.

Walking back into the house she had last seen almost three months before was the strangest feeling. Then, she had felt bereft, lonelier than at any time in her life. Now, though she was returning alone, she had so much! Sarah might still be in hospital – oh, how Jenny ached for her, to be able to cuddle her, hold her! – Bryn might have returned to his base, but she knew they were both out there and it was only a matter of time before they would all be together.

They had talked about marriage as he sat beside her bed, holding her hand, but curiously Jenny had felt no sense of urgency for that. She knew now, with a certainty that came from deep within, that married or not he was not going to leave her and Sarah, and the time for hasty propriety was over. Now they had all the time in the world.

'I want to be really better before we get married,' she had said. 'I want to enjoy every minute of our wedding day. And in any case, I wouldn't feel like a proper wife until we can live together, and you can't get married quarters as a National Serviceman, can you?'

Carrie had visited her too in hospital, and restated her pledge that Jenny could come home with the baby.

'We'll just hold our heads up high and show them,' she said, a flash of the old Carrie showing through. 'I'll look after Sarah for you and you can pass your exams and get a good job.'

She was still managing things, Jenny thought wryly, but this time her mother's plans coincided with her own. She might never now be the career journalist she'd dreamed of being, but it could only be an advantage to gain her qualifications whilst she had the chance. After that – who knew? Her brush with death had made Jenny aware of the slimness of the thread upon which life hung and demonstrated how fate could take the most unexpected turns.

When Jenny had unpacked her things, she went back downstairs. Carrie was in the kitchen making a cup of tea for the two of them – David had gone back to work as soon as he had dropped her off. The familiar feel of the kitchen enveloped her, the trappings of home that she had missed so much, and she bent to fondle Sally's silky ears. Sally had been so excited to see her! But Jenny sensed an edginess in Carrie.

'What's wrong, Mum?' she asked, leaning against the corner of the cooker. 'You're not having second thoughts are you.'

'No – no, it's too late for that.'

'You *are* having second thoughts.'

'I'm not. You and Sarah are both going to be all right,

and that's all that matters.' She hesitated. 'I've got to talk to you though, Jenny. There's something I have to tell you, and I only hope you'll forgive me.'

She crossed to the dresser, opened the drawer and took out the pile of letters.

'These are yours, Jenny. I should never have done what I did. I thought I was doing it for your own good. I know now I was wrong.' She looked up, sheepish but defiant. 'I suppose you're shocked.'

Jenny held her gaze steadily. 'No, Mum, I'm not shocked. I knew.'

'Our Heather told you?'

'No, she didn't need to. I guessed.'

'But . . .'

'Not at the time, of course. But as soon as I talked to Bryn. Letters don't usually go astray. And keeping them from me . . . well, I knew it was something you'd do.'

'Oh!' Carrie was totally nonplussed. Not just that Jenny had known for some time and said nothing but that she should consider such behaviour typical of her mother when it was something of which Carrie was deeply ashamed. For one of the few times in her life Carrie wanted to say she was sorry, but words of apology had never come easily to her and they didn't now. Admitting she had been in the wrong was the closest she could come.

'I was only thinking of you,' she said, a touch defiantly.

'I know,' Jenny said. 'I do know that. And what you're doing now . . . well, you're being brilliant. Only please, promise me – no more secrets, and no more trying to run my life for me.' She could hardly believe she was speaking to Carrie like this. The last months had changed her more than she had realised.

Carrie nodded. 'We'll try and make a fresh start.'

The kettle was boiling; she turned to switch it off, wanting only to put this conversation behind her.

'Now, let's have that cup of tea.'

Jenny was not the only one to feel that the time for secrets was over. Heather, too, had realised that keeping them under wraps was no way to deal with problems. So much in their lives had been hidden, one way and another, and it had caused nothing but trouble.

One morning at the beginning of August she queued for Helen's surgery and when she was called in she came straight to the point.

'You remember I talked to you before about Vanessa's nightmares and you said you thought she should have some sort of help to get her over it?'

'Yes, I remember.'

'Well, I'd like you to go ahead and arrange it.'

'I'm glad,' Helen said, 'but you were so much against it. What changed your mind?'

'Oh, I don't know . . .' For a moment Heather sounded a little like Carrie, defensive and impatient. Then she smiled warily. 'Yes, I do know, Doctor. We've been too fond in our family of sweeping things under the carpet. I don't want to do that any more. If you think it would be better for Vanessa to get it all out in the open, then that's what we'll do.'

'I'll make the arrangements,' Helen said. Sometimes, she thought, there were unexpected benefits from the direst of situations.

That evening Reuben Hobbs called a practice meeting. By the time Helen had seen her last patient and gone along to his room, Paul was already there. She was surprised – Paul usually looked in to speak to her as he passed her door. And from the way he was installed in the guest chair, it looked as if he had been there some time.

'Ah, Helen, you're here,' Reuben said rather unnecessarily, looking at her over the top of his spectacles. 'I've called this meeting because I want to discuss your future.'

Helen's nerves jangled. She looked at Paul; he was avoiding her eyes.

Oh God! she thought. *What is he going to tell me?*

'What sort of a job do you think you've done here, Helen?'

And what sort of a question is that? she wondered.

'I suppose I can only say I've done my best. It's not

454

altogether easy, making the jump from hospital to GP but it was – is – what I want, and I've tried to make a success of it.'

'And how do you feel you've been accepted in Hillsbridge?'

'Again, it hasn't always been easy. It takes time to build up trust and in some cases I think my being a woman didn't help. But on the other hand there have been occasions when it's worked in my favour. Ideally, of course, I'll feel I've succeeded when the patients cease to take gender into account and simply see me as their doctor, but human nature being what it is I expect that's a long way off.'

'Hmm. And what would you say if I were to tell you that we'd decided we should let you go?'

Helen's heart dropped like a stone.

'I would be very, very sorry about that,' she said with all the dignity she could muster. 'I think I can be an asset to this practice and I know that I can do as good a job as anyone else – better, because my heart is here. I suppose I would have to accept your decision but I wouldn't accept it lightly. I'd argue my case to the very last and if I still couldn't make you change your mind, well . . .' she took a deep breath, 'actually I think the loss would be as much yours as mine.'

For a moment Reuben returned her gaze, frowning a little.

'Well, Helen, you do feel strongly about it.'

'Yes,' she said, 'I do.'

'In that case . . .' he removed his spectacles, holding them by the stem between finger and thumb, 'I think I've kept you on tenterhooks quite long enough. Paul and I have talked at length about the way we see this practice heading and we are in complete agreement. What we both should like is for you to become a partner.'

'Oh!' Helen said, stunned.

'Is that all you can say?'

'Apart from calling him a complete bastard for putting you through that?' Paul put in.

Helen pulled herself together. 'I must admit you have

taken me completely by surprise, Reuben,' she said, 'but of course, you already know my answer. I've given it to you in answer to your questions, haven't I?'

'You'd like to accept our offer?'

'Nothing would please me more.'

'In that case,' Reuben smiled slyly, 'I think a celebration is called for, don't you? The champagne, Paul – if you would do the honours.'

Paul opened the small refrigerator, where a bottle of Cliquot was on ice, and Reuben retrieved three glasses, hidden in a drawer of his desk.

'To a long and successful partnership.'

'To you, Helen.' Across the rim of his glass, Paul's eyes met hers. They promised their own private celebration later and Helen was suffused with happiness.

The affair with Guy was behind her now. She and Paul had the sort of relationship that would grow and grow. Helen knew that she had found much more than simply the career she had wanted and worked for here in Hillsbridge.

'David, I want to ask you something,' Jenny said. She had followed him outside to where he was washing his car on the Green.

'What's that?'

'Would you be godfather to Sarah? When she's christened?'

'Me?' David looked surprised, but not displeased.

'Yes. You. You are her uncle, after all. But it's not just that . . .' She hesitated, unsure whether it was such a good idea to say the words she wanted to say. But they were there, on the tip of her tongue, so she plunged on. 'I know it won't make up to you for losing Linda and the babies you might have had with her, but it would sort of make her special to you, wouldn't it? More than just a niece? And you'd be special to her.'

A lump rose in David's throat. He polished the car vigorously.

'David?'

'Yeah – all right.' But inwardly he was pleased. He just

wasn't very good at putting his feelings into words.

When Jenny had gone he leaned against the car, squinting in the bright sunlight. It was funny, but he thought he was beginning to come out of the black night of the soul. There were times – not often yet, but getting more frequent – when he could think about Linda without wanting to tear his guts out, days when, to his utter astonishment, he caught himself actually enjoying something, really enjoying it, and not simply pretending. Funnily enough the healing process seemed to have begun the night he'd knocked Billy Edgell down the steps of the Miners' Arms and been helped along by the baby. Somehow, it seemed to him, that having her in the house signified hope and new beginnings. And now Jenny had asked him to be godfather – and a girl had only one of those, he rather thought!

David squeezed out his chamois leather in the bucket of soapy water. He was whistling as he went back to polishing his car.

The pram, coach built, navy, shiny and new, stood in the garden of Number 27 Alder Road. Behind a net to protect her from stray cats, little Sarah was sleeping peacefully in the warm autumn sunshine. In a corner of the lawn Jenny and Bryn sat on the scratchy dry grass, with Sally beside them, talking about the future, whilst Joe pushed the mower over the lawn on the other side of the path. Carrie emerged from the house wearing an apron over her Sunday dress, went to the pram and peeped inside.

Her great-granddaughter. Love and pride filled her. How could she ever have contemplated Jenny giving her up?

Across the road, Joyce Edgell was sitting on her wall, sunning herself and watching the world go by. She looked across and though she was not close enough to see the sneer on her face, Carrie could well imagine it.

'Hmm!' Carrie removed the cat net and the covers, lifted out the small sweet-smelling bundle that was Sarah, and walked out on to the pavement. 'Would you like to see our baby, Joyce?' she called.

457

Joyce averted her head.

'There's nothing like it, you know,' Carrie called. 'Nothing in the world. You'll have the pleasure one day, I expect.'

Jenny and Bryn exchanged a secret smile, and at that very moment Jenny's fingers, picking at the lawn, encountered a four-leaf clover. She looked at it wonderingly, held it up for Bryn to see so that, with Carrie and Sarah in the background, it seemed to make a snapshot for her memory. But to Jenny it was much more than that. It was an omen for the future.